Lin Harper

A Second Chance

harper
house
publishing

harper house publishing
26 Sandringham Court
Streethouse
Pontefract, WF7 6GG
www.harperhousepublishing.co.uk

First published by harper house publishing 06/05/2010

This novel is a work of fiction. Names and characters are the product of
the author's imagination and any resemblance to actual persons, living or dead,
is entirely coincidental.

ISBN 9780956560605

www.harperhousepublishing.co.uk

Printed by
The Good News Press Limited
Hallsford Bridge, Ongar
Esssex

Dedicated to my mum.

With love and blessings
Lindsay Harper
x
21/9/10.

About the Author:

Lindsay Harper (51) is happily married with two grown up children, two young grandchildren and three Springer spaniels. Her philosophy of life is 'If it ain't fun, don't do it.' When she's not writing she is a homeopath, a teacher of T'ai Chi and Pilates, a babysitter and a dog walker! For pleasure she does all of the above. Her aim is to write esoteric and metaphysical fiction for a growing audience. She lives in Wakefield, West Yorkshire. 'A Second Chance' is her first novel.

Acknowledgements:

I should like to thank the following people who helped in my research for 'A Second Chance':

Colin Ruston who helped me to understand what it's like to be a pilot. Pearl Orpin who gave me valuable information about the Second World War. The Anthony Nolan Bone Marrow Trust where I learned all about leukaemia and bone marrow donation. A big thank-you to everyone who read the manuscript for me and gave me great feedback; I learned a lot from your comments. A special thank-you to my daughter Natasha and my friend Keith for being so anal about grammar. I now know everything there is to know about the semi-colon. .

To my wonderful husband Paul and my children who have had to listen to me speak about nothing else but my book for months.

The Spiritualist movement, which gives proof of life after death week in week out, and is a great source of comfort to those in grief. Tricia Edwards, my Life Coach, who has been invaluable in keeping me on track and my spirits high. Finally Dr Wayne Dyer, whom I have never met, but listen to every day. His work is inspirational and his words have helped me find the confidence to fulfil my dream.

Bhagavad Gita

Chapter 2, verse 22

vasamsi jirnani yatha vihaya navani grhnati

naro'parani

tatha sarirani vihaya jirnany anyani samyati

navani dehi

Translation
As a person gives up old and worn out garments and accepts new apparel, similarly the embodied soul giving up old and worn out bodies verily accepts new bodies

From birth comes death and from death comes birth. Just like in the spring new buds grow which blossom into flowers and leaves. In summer and in autumn they change to red, yellow and orange and then blow away. And finally they become dormant in winter, to begin the process all over again the following year. In a similar way the soul enters new bodies for its seasons of infancy, youth, maturity and old age. Then, at the end of its cycle of life, it is born again - accepting a new body for another season. This is an inevitable process in the material existence and is the automatic process that governs birth and death. All beings existing in the material manifestation follow this reality completely.

Chapter 1 – September, present day

Jane sat up in bed with a start, tears streaming down her face, her heart pounding in her chest. She looked at the clock. It was exactly three a.m.

'Not again,' she groaned. Her husband stirred beside her.

'What is it?' Neil asked, still half asleep. Have you had the dream again?'

'I have,' she sobbed.

Neil stretched out and clumsily stroked her back. 'Go back to sleep. You'll be alright.' That was the sum total of his consideration and within a second he was back snoring on his pillow. It was the third time this week she'd been disturbed by the same dream. The first time was a few months ago and it had recurred on a regular basis since. The dream always started the same way. It was incredibly vivid and she could remember every detail. It felt strange to her; it was as if she was participating in the dream but at the same time observing it.

She always found herself in the hallway of a large, grand house, rearranging her hair in the full-length mirror. The face looking back at her wasn't her own, it was the face of a slim, pretty young woman around twenty years of age with long blond hair curled underneath in a hairnet. But they did share the same lavender-grey eyes.

The woman was wearing a black and grey floral print dress which came to just below the knee and was pulled in at the waist with a matching belt. She wore stockings and plain black leather shoes with a low heel. The girl glanced down at her hands and there, on the third finger of her left hand, was a line of exquisite diamonds, set in deep yellow gold.

Just as she'd finished looking in the mirror the door bell rang and the girl hurried toward the door. Jane could recall all the features of the hallway – the lounge leading off to the left, the drawing room to the right. She passed a large hat-stand full of coats and umbrellas. She could remember feeling all sorts of emotions, but mainly anticipation, as she opened the door to see the postman standing there.

Jane looked out of the door to a large lawn with trees and shrubs around the perimeter. In front of her there was a long, sweeping gravel drive leading to two large wrought iron gates at the end. In the distance she could see the church. Tubs of beautiful flowers adorned the front of the house. The postman didn't normally ring the bell but there were quite a few letters he needed to deliver.

'There's lots of post for you today. Is there another one from your young man?' he enquired nosily as he handed her the letters. 'He must write every day.'

'He tries to. Some days he's too busy flying, but he's never gone more than two days without writing. I haven't had one this week yet, so fingers crossed.' She didn't want to appear rude but she wanted the postman to leave, so she could sort through the mail.

'Lovely day for April. It's warmer than yesterday', he said, as though he had all the time in the world.

'Yes, hopefully we'll have a nice summer,' she said, trying to be as polite as she could.

'Well give my regards to your mother. Is she keeping well?'

'She is very well, thank you.' She started to close the door. If he wouldn't take a hint she'd have to be more obvious.

'It was nice talking to you. I Hope you've got a letter, 'bye for now.' Finally he turned and walked down the long drive. The young woman closed the heavy wooden door behind her.

She frantically searched through the letters looking for one in particular. One that would make her heart sing. There was no such letter, but there was an envelope postmarked Cornwall, dated April 8th, 1941. Tentatively she opened it. Fearing the worst, she read,

My dearest Nora

It is with deep regret that we find ourselves writing this letter to you. We received the telegram two days ago to tell us that our beloved son, Daniel, was killed in action over Dunkirk. They said he died a hero's death, helping to bomb a strategic target before he was cruelly gunned down. We are going to have a memorial service for him and we will let you know the date if you can manage to get here.

We're totally devastated, as we know you will be. Daniel was our life, and not only have we lost a son but we have lost the potential of his future family. In the short time that we have known you we've come to think of you as a daughter, as you would have been, should fate not have so cruelly

stepped in. Know deep down in your heart that he loved you, and keep hold of that thought as you go about your life. 'God works in mysterious ways, his wonders to perform'. We pray he called Daniel to him, before his time, for some great purpose. We just can't see it yet.

We do hope you will be able to find it in your heart to keep in touch with us, and if you feel you could handle the memorial service please come, we would love to see you again. You can take some souvenirs of Daniel to remember him by, although, like us, we doubt you will ever forget.

We are so sorry to be the bearer of such bad news and hope your grief lessens over time.

Yours, with love,
Ann and Robert St.Claire.

She dropped the letter and slid down the wall sobbing so much it felt as if her heart was breaking. The sobs turned to loud wailing as she buried her head in her hands. How could she go on without the love of her life? What was the point of her existence without him? She wanted to die right at this minute so she could join him, and hoped that God wouldn't leave it too long before taking her to be with him.

Jane had woken up at this point feeling the same intense pain in her own heart. Who was this girl in the dream? And why did it keep recurring? She felt the emotion as strong as if it'd been happening to her, but how could it have been? It was 1941, almost fifty years ago.

Jane couldn't risk going straight back to sleep in case she returned to the same dream, so she got out of bed and took a few deep breaths to calm herself down. She paid a visit to the bathroom and then went downstairs to make a warm drink. She didn't want to disturb her husband again as he was like a princess sleeping on a pea and particularly fractious if he didn't get enough sleep.

Tonight's dream was the most vivid and explicit she'd had and Jane really wished she could work out what it was trying to show her. She'd looked through dream books but her dream was too specific to be in any of them. There had been one thing that was different about the dream tonight, she'd been shown the names at the end of the letter. She could recall the man's name was Daniel St.Claire and she wondered if just maybe he could be a real person. She needed to find out the truth.

While she was sipping her hot tea she decided she'd go into work early to browse the internet, looking for pilots from Cornwall killed in the Second World War. Surely there must be some sites that'd give her that information. At least it was a starting place because she had to do something to find out what was behind the dream that was disturbing her so badly. She finally went back to bed three-quarters of an hour later, hoping and praying for a few hours undisturbed sleep.

When the alarm went off at six-thirty Jane was still tired. She'd just drifted off into a deep sleep when the wretched alarm had started beeping. Neil was a morning person and always jumped enthusiastically out of bed; sometimes even before the alarm sounded.

'Jane, are you getting up?' Neil asked, far too bouncily for Jane's liking.

'Just a few more minutes,' she groaned and put her head under the covers, hoping that one day this small gesture would actually stop time.

A few minutes passed and Neil appeared with the usual cup of tea placing it on the bedside table next to Jane. 'Come on, if you don't get up now you'll hit all the traffic. Do we have to go through the same routine every morning?' The more time elapsed, the shorter Neil's temper became.

Jane put her hand out from underneath the covers and fumbled for the alarm clock, she pressed the snooze button to gain herself an extra seven minutes.

'This is the last call for Jane Barclay; it's six forty-five and she's going to be late,' Neil hollered from the bottom of the stairs.

After the last call Jane dragged herself out of bed and into the shower. So much for going into work early, she thought to herself. She quickly got dressed; blow-dried her hair and applied the minimum of makeup. Then slowly, without much enthusiasm, she made her way downstairs. Neil had already eaten breakfast by the time she showed her face and he was about to set off.

He gave Jane the routine peck on the cheek and left for work. She made another cup of tea and sat down to enjoy the only bit of peace she got in the day. She often missed breakfast as recently she was too tired to bother and she would eat later at work when she felt a bit more awake. Simon and Lara, her teenage children, were also on their way out.

'Bye mum, Simon is giving me a lift into college today. See you tonight,' Lara shouted and banged the door behind her. That girl never did anything quietly.

'I'm going into town after I've dropped Lara off. There are a few things I need for uni. 'Bye mum,' Simon added as he left.

It was as if the house breathed a sigh of relief and the quiet gave Jane some time to think.

She'd taken to pondering on her life in recent times, and she seemed to be an outside observer to it rather than a willing participant. Each day was a replica of the one before. She'd nothing to look forward to anymore. In fact she couldn't remember a time when she'd actually had a burning desire to do anything. Existing was the word that described her life right now.

Jane had first met Neil, her husband, at university during their first year. They'd been in the same Halls of Residence, on the same corridor, and had met at a party. It hadn't been love at first sight, just a mutual attraction which had developed into a habit. She'd never been out with anyone else after Neil. They'd got used to having each other around and when Jane found out she was pregnant at the beginning of her third year, it seemed natural that they keep the baby and stay together. Jane did her final exams with a huge bump and gave birth to Simon a month later, before she'd received her final results.

Neil's parents were very old fashioned and pressured him into making an honest woman of her. Jane had agreed to get married on the proviso that she could have the baby first. That way she would at least get to wear a figure hugging, long, ivory dress. They had a very low-key wedding. It was a registry office ceremony with only close friends and relatives. Jane remembered the feeling as she said 'I do'. It was as if any spark of hope she had left her that minute, and drudgery was her new way of life.

Her best friend at university, Annabel, was her solitary bridesmaid. She'd volunteered to hold baby Simon throughout the ceremony. The bride, groom and guests were then ferried off to a sit-down meal at a hotel in Horsforth which Madge, Jane's mother, and Neil's parents, had kindly paid for. The speeches were uneventful, just like the rest of the day, and no-one could seem to summon up any enthusiasm at all, least of all Jane and Neil.

Neil's mother was sullen throughout and was still wishing that Jane hadn't got herself pregnant. An uncle of Neil's had taken the photographs which, due to the amount of alcohol he'd consumed, had come out all blurred and cock-eyed. She didn't have one wedding photograph adorning her mantelpiece or walls.

The in-laws shared the care of Simon while the two newlyweds had a week-long honeymoon in Majorca. Then it was on to married life. Jane didn't want to start a career while Simon was still young so she worked in a bar most evenings when Neil got home from work. He'd studied accountancy at university and had secured an internship at Price Waterhouse in Leeds city centre. The money wasn't great to start with, but a promise of a rather large salary in a few years made the first couple of years bearable.

They lived in a small rented house, in a not too salubrious area of Leeds but it was all they could afford. They decided to have the rest of their family while they were still young and Jane gave birth to Lara a year later. Neil passed his accountancy exams and, with a substantial rise in pay, they bought their first house, a small two up-two down terrace house.

When Lara started nursery school at four Jane could start thinking about what career she was going to pursue. She was only twenty-five and she was starting with a blank canvas. She'd always had an interest in property and had an eye for spotting a good bargain. They'd moved up the property ladder quicker than most people of their ages because Jane was good at making deals. A natural progression from this hobby was to go into estate agency. She started as a valuer then took her chartered surveyor exams at night school. Recently she'd been made a partner at the Leeds branch of Brown and Co.

Jane regarded her marriage as a bit of a business deal. They negotiated anything they wanted and had learnt the art of compromise years ago. The problem was that it was Jane who usually did the compromising. But they'd always been a good team and she did love him. Didn't she? But recently she'd noticed a few cracks had started to appear. All their married life he'd taken her very much for granted. They both had demanding jobs but it was Jane that was expected to cook and clean. She also did the laundry, the garden, everything.

They had absolutely no interests in common anymore. Neil was very active; running, squash and weight-training took up most of his time, whereas Jane liked to read and take long walks in the country. She'd always wanted a dog but felt it unfair to take one on when she worked full time and Neil wasn't really an animal lover. She sometimes borrowed her friends' and neighbours' dogs to take on the long summer walks she enjoyed so much. She usually went alone or with Simon, as Neil could never see the point in walking outside when he could take the car to the gym.

They even planned when they made love. It was down to about once a week at the moment, made worse by the dream-interrupted nights. Their sex life could never have been described as exciting or mind blowing. Neil usually initiated it, as she couldn't summon up the enthusiasm of late. He wasn't really into foreplay so he'd climb on board, ride her as fast as he could until he was satisfied, and then roll off. She'd often feel like one of those horses in a rodeo. It was a long time since she'd felt the earth move for her.

They, at least, had the children in common and had both adored bringing up Simon and Lara. But this era would soon be coming to an end. Simon was going off to university in Liverpool in a couple of weeks and Lara was in her final year of college, applying to go to university the following year. Jane had started to worry what would happen to her and Neil then.

They had started going out for a meal once a week to try and reconnect but this had only happened twice, as work meetings had interrupted their plans. They were both thirty-eight but Jane felt like a middle aged woman, with an uncertain future. She'd no excitement in her life and nothing to look forward to in her mundane existence. Life was really passing her by.

The one saving grace was that Jane enjoyed living in the small rural village of Woolley, just outside the city of Wakefield in West Yorkshire. The large detached house in its own grounds was wonderful, with fantastic views of the countryside from all angles. She had five bedrooms, two sitting rooms and a beautiful modern kitchen with a conservatory leading off to the side. She loved her house and looked forward to returning home to it every evening. Even though they'd lived in it for over ten years, she never took it for granted.

She'd often sit for hours in her conservatory with either a cup of tea or a glass of wine admiring the undulating fields and adjacent woods. Foxes often ventured in the garden and she loved to watch the young cubs playing. The only down side, as far as she was concerned, was the commute along the M1 every morning and that's why she was usually on the road by seven-thirty every day, trying to beat the hordes of traffic going into Leeds city centre.

Leaving it so late, she knew she'd get held up but she still took the extra half-hour to drink her tea. The dream was taking a physical and emotional toll on her body. She was very tired but she also felt emotionally drained. She had to get to the bottom of it somehow, for her own sanity.

Actually the commute didn't take any longer than normal and Jane was at her desk just before nine. She usually liked to get into the office before anyone else so she could plan her day, and those of the receptionists, in peace. But she was the last to arrive this morning. Jane looked at her diary. She had a couple of valuations and a viewing starting at twelve, which meant she had all morning to do her investigating.

A couple of hours later she'd found out, to her amazement, that there actually had been a real Daniel St.Claire who had been stationed at Catterick Garrison in North Yorkshire. He'd originated from Cornwall and had been killed in action in 1941. He'd been survived by two parents, who must surely have passed away by now, as they would've been born about the turn of the last century. There was no mention of any other relatives but surely she could hope to find someone still alive.

She logged onto the electoral registers for all the big towns in Cornwall to see if there were any St.Claire's. There were dozens and it would be a daunting, time-consuming task to contact every one.

She then went back into the Royal Air Force Service Records site to see if there was any more information as to where in Cornwall Daniel originated. She clicked back 'records' and '1941-deaths in action'. The site was just about to load when she suddenly glanced at her watch and saw that it was eleven-forty, only twenty minutes to get across town for her viewing. Where had the time gone? She hit the save button and closed down the computer. Daniel St.Claire would have to wait.

The viewing was with a woman called Sally Green. Apparently she was looking for a first house for her and her boyfriend. She wanted modern, as neither of them were DIY enthusiasts. Jane had given her details of a new development in Farnley, just outside Leeds city. The properties were six months old and there was a choice of a two bedroom apartment or a three bedroom mews house. They both had one previous owner and were back on the market, one due to relocation and the other to a break up.

It was just after twelve when she arrived. Sally was already waiting.

'Sorry I'm late. The traffic was bad just outside the office. Sometimes it's dreadful getting out of Leeds.' Jane had to lie because she knew she'd been late setting off.

'No worries. I've just arrived and been getting a feel of the place. I really like it.' Sally looked very enthusiastic.

'Couldn't your boyfriend make it?' Jane asked. She preferred to show a house to a couple so they could make a decision on the spot.

'No, we agreed I would look round first, and if I like it we'll come back for a second viewing.'

'I know the market is a bit slow but properties don't tend to hang around in this development. So if you do like it I'd come back as soon as you can.' Jane was good at her job and knew exactly what to say to keep up the interest.

Sally *did* like the three bedroom mews house. She'd already started planning where she'd put her furniture and how she'd decorate the magnolia coloured walls. Sally had very good taste and would soon have the house looking as though it'd just stepped out of the pages of an *Ideal Homes* magazine. She just hoped Philip would be as enthusiastic as she was. She thought it was highly unlikely, as in their ten years together he'd never shown any sign of wanting to buy a house. He was happy renting. It was only after persistent nagging that Philip had started looking at the details Sally had been bringing home for months.

'I'll have a word with my boyfriend and see if he's available tomorrow dinner time. Is that OK with you?' Sally asked, wanting to strike while the iron was hot.

'I'll check my diary in the office but I'm sure it'll be fine,' Jane said as she locked the front door and got back in her car. The rest of the afternoon she was busy with clients and didn't have any time to think about Daniel. She would carry on with her investigations another day.

September 1940

Nora was feeling both excited and apprehensive as she prepared to get ready for the evening ahead. This would be her first visit to the dance in the local village hall, even though there had been one every Friday night since the outbreak of war. She hadn't been allowed to go before, as her father didn't believe in frivolity at such a young age.

She was actually twenty years old, yet had been treated like a young child by overprotective parents. She'd put it down to two things; her father being a staunch Methodist and the fact that they'd lost their only son at birth. It had made her parents very protective of their one remaining child. Her father had passed away two months ago and, even though she missed him terribly, there was a feeling of lightness in the house that hadn't been there when he'd been alive.

Nora's mother had never been as strict with Nora yet she had been too dominated by her husband to ever contradict his opinions. They hadn't had the happiest of marriages. It had been hard for Nora's mother, being married to a man who had never showed affection to her, or their daughter. He'd lived for the church and had spent any leisure time he'd had preaching or helping with the maintenance of the building. All their social life was centred on the Church. He appeared friendly to the congregation but was very cold and unfeeling at home. Now he'd gone she could start living the life she wanted to live for however many years she had left.

When Barbara, Nora's best friend since school, had asked if Nora could go to the dance she'd expected her mother to say no, upholding her father's values. So she'd been very surprised when she'd said she must go and start enjoying herself, especially in these uncertain times. Barbara was very excited about Friday, even though she was a regular visitor to the dance, as she'd heard that the new recruits from the local RAF base at Catterick were going to be there and she fancied men in uniform.

The two of them had spent ages in Nora's room trying on clothes, seeing if anything in Nora's staid wardrobe was suitable for such an occasion. That was another thing her father had forbidden, colour. Everything in their house was either black or brown, including all her clothes. But with a little imagination and some red ribbon taken from one of Barbara's mother's dresses, they'd made a very reasonable effort at sprucing up a black dress. It even looked quite glamorous.

On Friday night everything was laid out on Nora's bed; the dress, the nylon stockings (the only pair she owned), and her very staid underwear. Her shoes had been polished and she'd borrowed some of Barbara's rouge and lipstick. The only thing left to do was assemble the outfit. Her mother had insisted that she bring the weekly bath forward from Sunday. She'd washed her hair and, to her amazement, her mother had styled it for her. She was starting to see a new side to her mother since her father's death and was only sorry it had been stifled for all those years.

When everything had been put together, and she'd carefully applied the lipstick and rouge, Nora looked at herself in the mirror. Her long blond hair was perfectly styled in a roll behind her head fastened up in a snood with a full fringe curled underneath. Her trim figure was shown off to its best advantage in the black dress she'd adapted. The red ribbon was exactly the same shade as the lipstick. Not bad, she thought admiringly. She didn't look like the plain young girl that usually looked back at her in the mirror.

It was exactly eight o'clock when Nora heard the door bell ring. They were going to be fashionably late. Nora went to kiss her mother.

'Have a lovely time and be careful. Don't be too late,' her mother warned.

'I won't, I promise,' Nora replied.

She was very nervous as they walked into the village hall. She knew she'd led a very sheltered life and hadn't really had an adult conversation with a man, other than her father or one or two elders of the church, since leaving school at fourteen. She'd spent all her time helping her mother look after her father.

She'd just left school and had been about to get a job in an office when he'd had his first stroke. Her father had become even more demanding and his care had proved too much for her mother. So Nora had given up any dreams she may have had for herself and resigned herself to looking after him.

Nora and Barbara deposited their coats in the cloakroom and nipped into the Ladies to make final adjustments to their hair and makeup. Nora followed Barbara into the dance hall. It took a while for Nora's eyes to become accustomed to the dimmed lights. There was a dance band playing on the stage at the front of the hall, it was the first time she'd heard live music and was surprised at how loud it was. Some couples were dancing but most people were standing around drinking and talking.

'Let's find a seat,' Barbara said, 'and wait for someone to buy us a drink.'

'How do you know someone will?' Nora asked naively.

'Because they always do, particularly if you give a man one of your alluring smiles. What man could resist two beautiful women?' Barbara replied.

They headed for the far side of the room where two seats were free at a table. Nora sat down and started to immerse herself in the atmosphere. This is what she'd been missing all those years. She looked around. There were people of all ages; couples, single men and women all looking to have a good time. She saw desperation in the eyes of some, as if they wanted to find the one that could make them happy during this awful war.

'Don't look now, but have you seen those two over there?' Barbara asked.

'Who?' Nora said, looking over to where Barbara was glancing. She noticed two officers in uniform standing at the other side of the room, each holding a pint of beer.

'I said don't look. Oh no! They've seen us talking about them. Hold on, they're coming over. I like the one on the left.' Barbara giggled and smoothed her long flowing locks, which she'd chosen to wear loose.

Nora hadn't even seen the officer on the left, her eyes were focussed on the most beautiful dark brown eyes she'd ever seen. They belonged to a tall, dark-haired, well-groomed man who was making his way over to her, smiling a nervous smile. Nora's mouth went dry and her heart started to race. She just knew she'd be tongue tied if he spoke to her. Luckily the officer on the left spoke first,

'Can I buy you two beautiful ladies a drink?'

Barbara giggled again, 'Yes please I'll have a beer, what do you want Nora?'

'Just lemonade please,' Nora said, blushing as she spoke. She'd never had strong liquor, although she was tempted to try it as it might help her to relax and stop her making a fool of herself.

'Are you going to come up to the bar with me? I get lonely on my own,' one officer asked Barbara and winked. She giggled again and followed in his footsteps, leaving an awkward silence between Nora and the man with dark brown eyes.

'I'm now at an advantage because I know your name. Hello Nora, my name is Daniel.' He held out his hand. She took it and as they touched all her nerves faded. She held onto his hand for as long as was polite.

'Hello Daniel, pleased to meet you,' was all she could find to say. She blushed again.

'I'm very pleased to meet you, Nora. I'm trying very hard to think of something to say that doesn't sound too contrived,' he paused, 'but words fail me. So, do you come here often?' They both laughed.

'No actually, I don't. It's the first time I've ever been. When my father was alive I wasn't allowed to go out in the evening. That probably sounds silly to you, but my father was really strict.' She felt slightly embarrassed admitting that her father had kept her on such a tight rein.

'It was maybe his way of protecting you and showing that he cared,' Daniel suggested.

'I'd never thought of it like that before. Do you always look for the best in people?' she asked.

'I try to. My mother and father are really gentle and loving people. They instilled their values into me from such an early age that I suppose it's rubbed off.' Daniel smiled as he talked about home. He didn't want Nora to see how much he missed his parents. She might think he was weak but he wasn't weak, just sensitive.

'I like the sound of your parents.' Nora felt much more at ease than she'd done at the start of the conversation. She found she wasn't tongue tied at all and was surprised at how natural it all felt.

'Is it just you and your mother left now?' Daniel enquired.

'It is. My dad died a couple of months ago of a stroke. He'd already had a major one five years ago and I'd been helping my mother look after him,' Nora said.

'Does that mean you're an only child?'

'It does.'

'So am I. It looks like we have something in common after all.' He gave her the sweetest smile and Nora felt her whole body melting.

'If you weren't allowed out socialising, what were you allowed to do?' he asked, enjoying their conversation.

'I went to church regularly. My father was a strict Methodist and all our family's social life revolved around the church. It sounds really boring doesn't it?'

Daniel tried to think of something to say that was diplomatic,

'No, it's not boring. I used to be in the church choir myself,' Daniel admitted. Nora couldn't help herself and sniggered.

'Don't laugh. I was also a page boy.' He playfully nudged her arm.

'Sorry I didn't mean to be rude. I bet you looked cute in your cassock.'

'Well enough of that. Let's change the subject.'

'Ok. So Daniel, tell me a bit about yourself.' Nora was relishing the banter and feeling more at ease.

'Er, what would you like to know?' Daniel was stuck for something to say.

'Tell me where you're from. You could start there. And why the RAF?'

'I'm from Falmouth, a town in Cornwall. My father has his own sawmill and my mother volunteers at the local hospital. I went to a good school and passed all my exams. Even though most of my friends joined the navy all I've ever wanted to do was fly, so I enlisted in the RAF as a trainee officer. Sorry, I sound like I'm reading from a script. I'm not used to talking about myself, especially to a pretty young woman.' Daniel winked at her and she blushed.

They were so engrossed in each other they didn't see the other officer and Barbara return with the drinks. Nora looked up and noticed that the two of them seemed to be having a lot of fun. Nora wondered where Barbara found the confidence to be so relaxed in the company of strangers.

There was a lull in the conversation and they both looked around at the room. People had started to take to the floor. 'Do you want to dance?' Daniel asked Nora.

'I don't really know how,' Nora answered. 'I had a few lessons at school but that was a long time ago.' Nora felt embarrassed at not knowing how to do something so fundamental, but dancing was another frivolous act God didn't approve of. Or so her father had told her.

'Don't worry, I'll show you. Just hold on to me tightly and I'll guide you round.' He took her hand and led her onto the dance floor.

Holding on to Daniel was the best feeling in the world. They glided round the room and Nora had never had as much fun. He was an accomplished dancer and the few steps she'd learnt came back to her once she was on the floor. They danced the waltz, the quick step and the foxtrot and even had a go at the jitterbug. They were exhausted as they returned to their seats after dancing for over an hour. Nora never wanted to let him go.

'How come you're so good at dancing?' Nora asked, trying to regain her breath.

'It was compulsory at school. We all hated it at the time but it's stood us in really good stead for impressing the ladies.' He laughed and squeezed Nora's hand.

The rest of the evening went by quickly. They'd found so much to talk about and she'd never laughed as much in her life. Nora glanced at the clock and saw that it was nearly ten-thirty. The band had slowed the music down for the last dance. All the couples congregated on the dance floor so Daniel took hold of Nora's hand and they went to join them.

He put his arms around her, pulling her close and she laid her head on his shoulder feeling his epaulette on her face. He looked so handsome in his uniform. She blushed at the thought of what he'd look like without it on. She'd never seen a man naked. The closest she'd got was at the local swimming pool, but then it was only lanky teenage boys in their swimming attire. Nothing like the broad-shouldered man who was holding her so tightly.

Daniel leant down and whispered in her ear, brushing her face with his lips. 'Can I walk you home? Your friend Barbara seems to be quite happy with Tom and I'm sure he'll see her home. Although I fear for her honour. He's not a gentleman like me,' Daniel laughed.

'Yes I'd like that, but I'll just tell Barbara I'm going.' She went over and whispered in her friend's ear, who gave her a nudge and a knowing wink.

Nora picked up her coat. Daniel put his hand on her back and led her out. Every time he touched her she felt her heart skip a beat. She'd never experienced feelings like this before. He took her hand as they walked through the dark streets, both comfortable with the silence between them. They'd got used to the blackout since the outbreak of war and it wasn't far to Nora's house. She stopped short of her gate as she didn't want to risk her mother looking out of the window and seeing what was about to happen next.

'Is it alright if I kiss you?' Daniel asked.

Her face said it all as they leaned towards each other. There was such tenderness and passion in the kiss. Neither of them wanted it to end. Nora was breathless when they finally pulled away.

'Can I see you again? I've had such a wonderful time. But I won't be free until next weekend. I've a busy schedule all week, but I'm free next Friday if you'd like?' Daniel asked, keeping his fingers crossed.

'I'd love to see you again and I'll count the days until next weekend.' Nora reached up and kissed him again. She was surprised that she was being so forward but it just felt so natural to kiss him. When they did finally part, Daniel walked down the street back to his barracks. Nora was a very different person to the shy young girl that had gone out earlier in the evening. She was in love.

Chapter 2

Neil was intending to go straight to the gym from work; as he did most days. He really enjoyed keeping his body in trim. Usually he looked forward to his workout and pounding the treadmill but recently he couldn't summon up the enthusiasm. He was tired from all the unbroken night's sleep he was getting because of his wife's nightmares. At first he'd shown concern, but when he'd asked her what was wrong she'd never explained their content. She just shrugged and said she didn't want to talk about it.

Come to think of it, she didn't want to talk much at all at the moment. He looked forward to coming to work and talking to his assistant, Sally. They had a great working relationship and she seemed to understand him. They shared the same sense of humour and, as a bonus, she was very attractive to look at.

He'd found himself staring at her lovely figure on more than one occasion. She worked out at the same gym and had a lovely toned body. He used to feel guilty having lecherous thoughts about anybody except Jane, but their relationship wasn't at its best at the moment and his mind had begun to wander lately, especially to Sally. He'd even started finding excuses to work late so he could spend more time with her. He wasn't sure how she felt about him but she certainly didn't discourage his flirting and happily joined in their banter.

It was after six when Sally popped her head round his door and asked if it was OK if she got off home.

'Sorry, of course it is. I hadn't really noticed the time. Are you going to the gym tonight?' Neil asked, hoping she would say yes and make his trip more pleasurable.

'No, not tonight. I'm going to try and persuade Philip to go and look at this house I've seen today,' she said.

Neil tried to hide his disappointment. She'd worked for him for just over a year and he didn't know much about her personal life, apart from the fact that she had a live-in boyfriend called Philip. She and Neil had never socialised outside the office. There was nearly a ten year age gap between them and obviously it wasn't appropriate for her to go out with the boss.

He felt a pang of jealousy when she said where she was going. He might give the gym a miss tonight and just go home to open a bottle of his favourite Shiraz.

'Good luck with that one. Men don't like to commit too soon. I remember it was the same when my wife showed me around our first house,' Neil laughed.

'But I bet you were younger than us. I'm thirty next birthday and Philip is thirty-eight, he's not getting any younger,' Sally said, never thinking about Neil's age.

'Oi, watch it! I'm thirty-eight.' Neil pretended to be offended. 'And yes, we were a lot younger, maybe too young. At least Philip can say he's lived before he settled down.'

'But that's just it. He still says he's too young to buy a house. I'm beginning to think it's just me he doesn't want to settle down with.' She seemed sad as she spoke.

'Well in my opinion he must be insane to not want to settle down with you.'

There was an awkward silence as they both realised the intimacy of their conversation. Their relationship had just moved onto another level and they were now in unchartered territory.

Sally broke the silence first. 'I'd better be off. I'll see you in the morning. Enjoy your evening'. She gave him a coy smile.

All he could add was, 'Good night.' He was never usually short of things to say, especially to Sally, but he was unsure what had just passed between them. Hadn't he just admitted that he and his wife were too young when they'd got married? He'd never spoken it out loud before and it felt a dangerous place to go. What if there were other feelings like that lurking around for him to bring up in other intimate moments? Yes, he would definitely go straight home, probably polish off the whole bottle of Shiraz and hopefully get a good night's sleep.

Sally put on her coat, left the office and walked to her car in the multi storey car park. She hadn't intended to talk to Neil about any of that. It had shocked her how easily it had rolled off her tongue. She hadn't realised how desperate she'd become to have her own house. She was, after all, thirty next birthday and all her friends were married. Most had even started a family. She felt a failure, as she couldn't even get her boyfriend of ten years to buy a house, never mind walk down the aisle. She used to mention marriage and children but Philip would switch off, saying they were OK as they were.

She assumed they were in love. She'd say 'I love you' and he'd say 'me too'. On the face of it their relationship seemed to work and the sex was good. Not as frequent as she would've liked but she put that down to his age. Some weeks she was so frustrated she'd even fantasised about making love to Neil, over the desk in his office.

Was it her imagination, or had Neil been getting more friendly over the past week or so? Nothing concrete had happened, but there were times when she distinctly felt he was flirting with her. Tonight's conversation had been the most intimate they'd ever shared and she felt comfortable with it. In fact more than that, she'd felt a real connection to him. She would've loved to carry it on, but didn't really trust herself to tell him any more intimate secrets. The fantasy could easily have turned into reality back there, as she was sure he was experiencing the same feelings as her.

This train of thought would have to stop as she didn't want to jeopardise her job. It was the one constant in her life, being the personal assistant to a senior partner in a big accountancy firm. She was also studying for her accountancy exams and had mapped out a great career path for herself, despite her background. Her parents had never encouraged either of their daughters to do well at school, in fact quite the opposite. Charlotte, her elder sister, had left school before she'd taken her exams and went to work as a cashier in the local ASDA. Sally had at least finished her GCSE's and had done well, despite the lack of encouragement.

After school she secured a place at the local college, where she'd discovered she had an aptitude for figures and had learned book-keeping. She had started her employment with a junior clerk's position, but had worked hard to get a promotion and was very proud of her current position. Her income wasn't great at the moment, but once she'd passed her exams and was a qualified accountant money would start rolling in. But that was the future. Here in the present she still needed a partner to buy a house with.

Philip had had a long day at work and was looking forward to putting his feet up and watching a film while enjoying a couple of cans of cold lager. What he wasn't looking forward to was being pestered by Sally about the house she'd seen today. He knew she was going to see it at lunchtime and she'd tried ringing him all afternoon to tell him about it, but luckily for him he'd been in meetings.

As soon as she walked through the front door, Sally thrust the details under his nose. He glanced at them politely and listened with half an ear to her description of the perfect modern town house with an en-suite and house bathroom. She seemed smitten with the house and was more or less pleading with him to go and see it with her tomorrow.

There were times when Philip felt guilty about his lack of commitment to Sally, but he'd tried to feel differently. There had never been any one girl in his life that he'd wanted to marry. Usually girls had tired of his attitude and dumped him, but not Sally. She obviously thought she was the one to change him. It was as if he was waiting for that special someone to turn his life upside down.

She was cutting it a bit fine to find him, he thought, as he was already thirty-eight and she hadn't shown her face yet. When he'd been in his twenties, he'd always thought he would be married with children by the time he was thirty, but it had just never happened. He would still like to have children but not with Sally. He was very fond of her, but fond wasn't enough to build a future together.

He really shouldn't have carried the relationship on for so long. Ten years had passed and they'd only started living together two years ago. He was basically a coward and put it down to anything for an easy life. But this attitude was starting to backfire, because life wasn't easy. It was getting increasingly difficult to put her off. Also it wasn't fair on Sally. She was nearly thirty and he knew she could feel her body clock ticking. She'd been a bridesmaid to three of her friends and all she wanted was to be the bride.

He would have to make some sort of decision soon, as she seemed so keen on this house. He hadn't seen her as tenacious as this before. She was determined this time to get what she wanted. Philip used to be like that. In other areas of his life he'd been single-minded and positive. Ever since he was a little boy he'd had a fascination for flying. He'd started by making model aeroplanes and then progressed on to the remote control variety.

Every weekend, when he was young, his dad would take him to Leeds/Bradford airport to see the planes taking off and landing. He'd particularly loved Concorde when it was still flying. As soon as he reached twenty-one he'd started flying lessons and got his pilot's licence two years later. Every birthday and Christmas he would ask for money so he could put it towards his flying hours.

He used to fly every weekend and had started teaching flying lessons to keep him up in the air as long as possible. In the past few years his flying had been put on the back burner as Sally liked them to do things together at the weekend as she didn't share his enthusiasm for the sky.

'Well, will you come and see it with me tomorrow?' Sally's voice woke Philip out of his reverie.

Still feeling a coward he said, 'OK I'll go, but I'm not promising anything.' Sally came over and kissed his cheek.

That seemed to have placated Sally. 'Thank you. I know you'll love it. I'll message the estate agent and say it's all systems go!'

Philip pressed the remote control to start the film, hoping this would curtail the conversation and he could settle down and lose himself in his film and cans of lager.

September 1940

It was a week before they saw each other again and Nora had thought about Daniel constantly. She'd walked about in a trance for the past seven days, daydreaming about seeing him again. She'd replayed their every conversation over and over in her head and she'd kept remembering his touch and how wonderful it had made her feel. She let her mind wander to the kiss... oh the kiss! It had been the very best thing that had ever happened to her and she couldn't wait for a repeat performance.

To help the war effort she'd recently started working at a local farm, collecting eggs. She boxed them, and then delivered them to local shops and wealthy households. It kept her busy and helped to pass the time until Friday.

When they were together they seldom talked about the war or Daniel's imminent departure. He'd nearly finished his officer training and it wouldn't be long before he would be sent into action. There were rumours about a massive raid over Germany and the government was going to need every fighter pilot to be at the ready. She hated to think of him in the thick of things and found it hard to stop herself thinking the worst.

In the following few weeks Daniel and Nora spent as much time together as they could. He'd even started sneaking away during the week to spend a couple of hours with her. They met at the farm where Nora helped out and went upstairs into the hay loft. They kissed and cuddled and Daniel occasionally let his hand move across Nora's breasts. But nothing else happened. They were going to save themselves.

Daniel heard that he would be leaving Catterick in February. He'd been given a week's leave over the New Year so it seemed a perfect time to take Nora to meet his parents. Daniel was a regular visitor to The Old Rectory and Nora's mother was really taken with him. He would make the perfect son-in-law, as she hinted to Nora on more than one occasion.

He shared Christmas dinner with Nora and her mother. It had been a quiet day and Daniel found he was missing his parents as well as the hustle and bustle of a Cornish gathering. It was the first Christmas they'd spent apart. Everyone had used all their rations to put on an elaborate spread and the farmer had given them a duck, as a thank-you for all the help Nora had given him.

Nora's mother had given her permission to travel down to the West Country with Daniel, and had helped her pack a small suitcase with all the essentials that Nora would need.

'You will remember to be polite, won't you?'

'Of course I will mother.'

'I want you to be a credit to the family, show them you're daughter-in-law material.'

'Mother, you're incorrigible. I know how to behave. You've brought me up well.' Nora's mother couldn't help fussing. She would miss her daughter even though she would only be away for a few days.

Nora and Daniel set off by train on the first leg of their journey to Falmouth at nine o'clock on the 29th December. It was the first time Nora had left Yorkshire. She'd been on a Sunday school visit to Scarborough when she was little, but hadn't been on holiday in recent years because of her father's illness.

Daniel had another reason for visiting his parents before he went away. He intended to tell them that he was going to ask Nora to marry him. Daniel's mother had promised the family ring would go to his fiancée. Three generations of women had worn the ring on their engagement to a St.Claire.

He'd already asked Nora's mother for her daughter's hand in marriage while Nora was washing up the Christmas dishes. She'd been delighted and had given him a hug, welcoming him to the family. How she managed to keep it a secret from Nora he would never know. She couldn't help herself and kept winking and grinning at him. Luckily Nora was oblivious to it all.

The train journey seemed endless but Nora had loved every minute. She took in the changing scenery as they passed through one county after another. Her mother had packed Nora's favourite corned beef sandwiches and a flask of tea which they enjoyed in Birmingham station as they waited for the connection to take them on the final part of their journey. Nora marvelled at the countryside as the train rolled into Cornwall. Even the sea looked different. It was deep blue as opposed to the grey, murky version she'd seen in Scarborough, and the cliffs, were the like of which she'd never seen before. She couldn't imagine what it would be like living somewhere so wild and romantic.

Nora had never known such happiness. She'd kept hold of Daniel's arm the whole journey and when they found themselves alone in the carriage they sneaked a long, loving kiss. For the rest of the time she looked out of the window in awe. This was the most exciting journey of her life and she was sharing it with the man of her dreams.

Robert St.Claire collected them from Falmouth station in his new car. He hugged his son and held him for the longest time. She'd never, in her life, seen her father hug anyone and here was Daniel's father showing such a display of affection in public. She felt a little envious. Nora was introduced to Robert and she too was the recipient of a bear hug. She was really taken with this giant of a man. He took the luggage from them both and helped Nora into the back seat.

After only a ten minute drive the car pulled up in front of a large double fronted house set a short way back from the cliffs, overlooking the sea. She could see a lady at the window watching for them to arrive. The front door opened and Ann St.Claire came hurrying to the car.

'Daniel you're home. How wonderful to see you. We've missed you so much.' She held her son close and Nora could see tears in her eyes.

'And this must be Nora. Daniel has written so much about you. It's an honour to meet you at last.' Ann hugged her guest.

'Thank-you for having me, Mrs St.Claire,' Nora said, politely.

'You must call me Ann,' she held on to Nora's hand. Nora had been correct in her assessment of Daniel's parents. She did like them, and for a second wondered what it would be like to call them mum and dad. They were the antithesis of her parents; warm, loving and demonstrative. With all the introductions out of the way they went inside for tea and homemade cakes. Ann had done an exchange with the local farmer. She'd provided him with some pies and he'd given her some mutton. She knew how much Daniel loved shepherd's pie made with lamb, but this was the best she could do.

The few days by the sea passed quickly. The weather was very kind and Nora noticed it was much warmer down here than it was in Catterick.

'Do you want to go for a walk on the beach?' Daniel asked. It was another beautiful sunny day and he knew that Nora loved nothing better than walking along the beach holding hands.

'Yes please. I'll just go and get my coat.' Nora had started to relax in everyone's presence and felt quite at home.

They meandered down the steep cliff path to the beach below. Daniel held onto Nora's hand and as soon as they were out of sight he held her close and kissed her passionately. The nervousness of their first kiss was well and truly gone. They walked for miles, chatting and discussing the future. She couldn't believe she could be so lucky to even contemplate a future with this perfect man.

'You're really blessed living somewhere so wild and desolate,' Nora said, feeling the sea breeze blowing through her hair.

'I know. I do miss the sea when I'm in Yorkshire. It's very beautiful round by where you live though, made even better by your presence.'

'You know how to charm a girl.' Nora had finally stopped blushing whenever Daniel paid her a compliment. As they were walking she kept finding shells or the odd fossil and was creating quite a collection to remind her of this idyllic time.

Daniel went in to work with his father for a couple of hours one day so Nora stayed with Ann. She showed her how to make the delicious fruit cake out of the rations that Nora had sampled on her arrival. Ann and Robert were so hospitable and began to treat her like one of their family.

Without Nora suspecting Daniel had managed to discuss the forthcoming proposal and asked his mother and father about the ring. They were both delighted to see their son so happy. He concealed it amongst his clothes in his suitcase but later that same evening, the night before they were due to return to Yorkshire, he couldn't wait any longer. He went upstairs and popped the ring in his pocket.

'Do you fancy a bit of fresh air?' Daniel asked Nora. 'I'd like to walk round the garden and look at the stars.'

She loved Daniel's romantic nature. He held her hand as they sat on the lovers' seat under the spreading beech tree.

'Could life get any better?' Nora said as she looked up to the vastness of the sky and the myriad of stars that were twinkling, seemingly just for them.

'I think it could yes. Since meeting you my life has finally taken on some meaning. I thought flying would give me that but, although I still love it, it's you that I wake up for in the morning. Nora, I love you with every ounce of my being. Would you do me the very great honour of becoming my wife?' Daniel got down on bended knee and produced the St.Claire ring, pausing before slipping it on her finger, then waited for Nora's response.

She was momentarily speechless. Daniel assured her that he'd received her mother's blessing, and that she'd been delighted with the news. Nora went very shy and quiet. With her head tilted slightly downward said, 'Nothing would give me more pleasure than to be your wife. I'll love you until the day we die and then onward from the grave.' He kissed her and slipped the ring on to the third finger of her left hand. It looked completely at home, as though it had been put on the earth for this very purpose.

He wanted to get married straight away, before he had to leave, but Nora persuaded him to wait and have a grand wedding in more settled times. His mother and father had agreed with her.

Chapter 3

The next day Jane intended to carry on searching for clues as to the whereabouts of Daniel St.Claire. She'd always fancied herself as a bit of a private detective and loved trying to solve the murder mysteries on television before anyone else. It came from being basically nosey. She always knew the business of everyone around her and took great delight in trying to work out what type of people lived in the houses she was showing to others. She'd learnt to tell a lot about a person from their surroundings. She'd also become interested in Feng Shui, the art of moving furniture and belongings around to get the best flow of energy in the house. She suggested it to her clients and they often took her advice. Jane thought it probably contributed to her success at selling houses.

She still felt a little frustrated because the few facts she'd learnt about Daniel St.Claire had given her no apparent reason why she should be dreaming about him. With a little more time and effort she should get some more answers and she was looking forward to searching the internet again to find more clues, and solve the puzzle.

Jane didn't know what to wear today. It was unusually warm for September and the weather forecasters had predicted an Indian summer. She looked in her wardrobe and decided, like every other woman in the world, that she'd nothing to wear. She preferred casual clothes but in her line of work it was usually a suit she chose.

It was too warm for a suit today so she chose a pair of cream, linen trousers and a coffee-coloured sleeveless top. She added gold hoop earrings and a matching necklace. She looked in the mirror and felt suitably dressed for meeting clients. For some reason she felt she had to make a special effort today and styled her dark brown bob a little longer than usual, even using her *'ghd'* straighteners for the perfect chiselled look. She applied blusher to her naturally high cheek bones and an intensely moisturising lipstick; her thin lips needed all the help they could get. Not bad for thirty-eight, Jane thought to herself.

She was still the same dress size as she'd been when she'd got married. She'd never been sylph-like and had a perfect hour-glass figure which fitted easily into a size twelve dress. Her breasts, always on the large side, were still firm and her bottom had stayed pert despite her lack of exercise. Only one or two grey hairs were showing; a few more and she could always dye them.

On the whole Jane was happy in her skin and had never been one for needing lots of compliments to make her feel better. Just as well, as Neil wasn't one for dishing them out readily. His favourite joke was the one about the Yorkshire man whose wife asked him why he never told her he loved her. His reply was, 'I told you on our wedding day and if I change my mind I'll let you know'.

'A man after my own heart,' Neil would say.

Jane had her air conditioning on while driving to work. Usually she would put the soft top down of her Audi TT, but she'd spent so long doing her hair that morning she didn't want to risk disturbing even one strand. The mixture of a beautiful, blue sky and warm sunshine, plus the loud power ballads, gave Jane a real feeling of optimism which she hadn't felt for a very long time.

Today she was the first to arrive in the office and was able to appreciate the silence until the receptionists arrived shortly afterwards. They started talking about the previous night's conquests, and the 'fit man' that one of them had agreed to see on Saturday night. She felt old listening to conversations of such a nature and realised those times had well and truly passed her by.

She didn't know whether it was her new found positive attitude but soon after logging onto the internet she found out that Daniel came from Falmouth. So this narrowed her search down quite considerably. She checked the telephone directory and found there were only ten St.Claire's in and around that part of Cornwall. She would ring them later but now she really must get on with some work.

She looked in her diary and remembered she was doing a second viewing for the couple at the Mews house in Farnley. She really mustn't be late today as she prided herself on her punctuality. Just as she was setting off for the appointment her phone rang.

'Hi Jane, this is Sally Green.'

'Hello. I was just setting off to see you.,' Jane replied, hoping she was going to make a sale today.

'I'm supposed to be viewing 5 Call Mews shortly but I'm afraid my ogre of a boss wants me to work. My partner will still be there though, his name is Philip Sinclair. Please try and sell it to him as I love it and would like to make an offer.'

'No worries. I'll do my best.' At least they hadn't cancelled altogether, thought Jane.

'I'll ring you later this afternoon after I've spoken to him. Sorry about the short notice.'

'Thanks for letting me know. I've persuaded many a man to buy a house against his will,' Jane laughed.

She pulled up outside 5 Call Mews and reversed into one of two parking spaces. Just as she was getting out of her car another one pulled into the next space. A tall, slim man got out. His dark hair was slightly longer than the usual fashion and stylishly messy. He'd either not shaved today or had designer stubble. Either way it made him look rather irresistible. He had the most piercing dark brown eyes that she'd ever seen. He looked almost Mediterranean.

Jane picked her jaw up from the floor and tried to hold together a professional demeanour.

He smiled and said, 'Hello, my name's Philip Sinclair and I'm here to view the house.' He looked toward number 5, giving it a quick appraisal. 'My girlfriend's sent me but I'm afraid she can't make it.' Philip had spoken the words but not for a second did he believe them. He wasn't at all sorry she couldn't make it, as it meant that he would get to spend some time with the beautiful woman who was standing in front of him. He wanted to run his fingers through her hair as it reminded him of dark, melted chocolate.

'Hi, I'm Jane Barclay and I'm the estate agent who's going to show you round.' What a stupid thing to say, she thought, it was obvious that she was the estate agent. 'Your girlfriend has already let me know, thank-you.' She didn't trust herself to say anything else as she opened the door.

He held out his hand for her to shake and she tentatively took it, frightened to touch him in case she couldn't let go. He looked at her and she smiled back. They were both transfixed and stared into each other's eyes. 'Let's start upstairs.'

Jane could feel herself blushing as Philip replied 'yes please' with a touch of innuendo in his voice. Jane tried to concentrate on her sales pitch but was aware of his presence near her at all times. It was as if the room was charged with electricity. She couldn't take her eyes off the most gorgeous man she'd ever seen. They went from room to room, chatting very naturally about anything but the house.

'Well that's it. What do you think? Any questions?' Jane asked as they came back into the living room.

Philip knew she was referring to the house but what he really wanted to reply was 'You're the most beautiful woman I've ever set eyes on.' It was now or never for him. He hadn't been so attracted to any woman before and he was wallowing in the feeling.

'Just the one and it's got nothing to do with the house. I know we've only just met but would you fancy having a coffee with me?' he asked, nervously. 'That's if you've got time.'

Jane glanced at her watch, knowing full well that nothing on earth would stop her having a drink with this man.

'That'd be lovely. I'll follow you. Have you somewhere in mind?' She'd have followed him to the other side of the planet and back.

'There's a nice cafe down the road from here.' He hoped the tone of his voice didn't give away too much. As he was speaking his insides were churning with anticipation and excitement.

Jane's head was in a whirl as she followed Philip to the cafe. She found herself so attracted to this man and was experiencing feelings she'd never even had for her own husband. She'd only known this man for twenty minutes but she couldn't bear the thought of never seeing him again.

Philip ordered two cups of coffee while Jane looked for a vacant table. It was all too reminiscent of the first dates she'd been on when she was a younger girl. The two of them were trying to find interesting things to say to create a good impression. But as the conversation flowed they both began to feel much more at ease with each other.

'Have you time for another one?' Philip said, draining his mug of latte.

Jane quickly glanced at her watch, 'Another one won't harm. I'm hungry, fancy ordering a sandwich?' She looked at the menu.

'I usually have the bacon, brie and cranberry Panini when I'm here.'

'Make that two, it sounds delicious.' Jane reached down toward her bag to get out some money.

'No please, let me. It's not every day someone so attractive let's me buy them lunch.'

'Is that one of your chat up lines?' Jane laughed.

'It's not a chat up line. I'm being genuine.' Philip feigned hurt.

'I'm sorry. I'll take it as a compliment then.' Jane smiled as Philip went to the counter to order. He returned with two more lattes.

'The food won't be long.' He took a sip of his coffee. 'Why did you choose estate agency? You don't seem the type. I imagine you as some sort of designer.'

'Clothes or furniture?'

'Either, was it ever something you considered doing?'

'Funny you should mention that. I studied Art at university and specialised in textiles. I prefer interior design to making clothes.'

'Why didn't you pursue it?'

Jane paused. She contemplated telling him she was single. She felt embarrassed talking about her husband and children, as though they'd no place in her life right now.

'I fell pregnant in my final year and from then on my future plans were scuppered. I kept the baby and got married. That sounds awful; I wouldn't swop Simon for the world, but I often wonder 'what if?'' Jane tried not to dwell on that time in her life.

'It's a similar story to mine, apart from the pregnancy. I'm a mechanical engineer but my first love is flying. I always wanted to be a pilot.'

'Then why aren't you?'

'Good question and I'm afraid I don't have an answer. I just settled for the first job that came my way, not that I actually feel settled. I intensely dislike my job.'

'Then why do it? Surely you could take up flying again.'

'My girlfriend doesn't share my passion.'

'That's a shame. So is this the first house you're buying with your girlfriend?' Jane wanted to know the finer details of his relationship and couldn't fail to see the look of panic on Philip's face when she mentioned his girlfriend.

Luckily for him the waitress arrived with the food and he never got to answer the question. The Panini's were as delicious as Philip had described. They continued to chat over lunch and Jane found she was confessing her innermost thoughts to this near stranger. But he didn't feel like a stranger, she felt like she'd known him her whole life.

Philip felt the same. He usually held something of himself back but here he was, opening up to this beautiful woman. They both talked about their families and younger days and skirted round previous relationships. They shared stories about their past and she even confessed to enjoying wearing shoulder pads in the 1980's.

They both admitted to liking Human League and Duran Duran and they reminisced about all the hideous clothes they had worn. Jane hadn't laughed as much in years. They'd so much in common and had even started finishing each other's sentences.

'I know it's rude to ask a lady but do you mind me asking how old you are?'

'I'm thirty-eight now, thirty-nine soon and then the dreaded big 'four-o' next year,' Jane sighed. 'And I'm not looking forward to it. I can't believe where the time has gone.'

'I'm thirty-eight as well. What a coincidence. I thought we must be similar ages as we like the same music and know the same cheesy television programmes. When's your birthday? We could celebrate together.'

'It's in November.'

'Mine too, what date?'

'The fifteenth.'

'Never! Another coincidence. So is mine. What are the odds of that happening? It must be fate,' Philip had never really believed in fate before, but meeting this woman couldn't be coincidence.

'Yes, I'll admit it is slightly unusual,' Jane said.

'If it's any consolation you don't look it. You look much younger than me.'

'Funny that, I was just thinking the same about you,' she giggled.

Philip loved the way her nose wrinkled when she laughed.

Jane looked at her watch and said with reluctance. 'I really must be going. I've another appointment across town in half an hour. Thank-you for lunch, and the coffee, and the company. I've had a really good time.'

'Thank-*you* Jane.' Philip reached out and put his hand across hers. She felt such overwhelming emotion, tears pricked her eyes.

'I know I shouldn't say this, but I feel I have to. Can I please see you again?' Philip said it with a pleading look in his eyes.

'I don't know, Philip, it could get really complicated. I'm married and you're just looking at buying a house with your girlfriend,' she replied reluctantly.

'Do you think I don't know all that? But I want to see you so much. We could just meet for a coffee in a public place and then I'll not be tempted to do anything that would get me a slap across the face.'

Jane blushed. 'What makes you think I'd let you?' she said coyly.

'Just a hunch.' Philip stared at her with his big brown eyes and she could feel herself succumbing.

Philip passed Jane his phone 'Put your mobile number in there. Let's compromise. We'll not make an arrangement now but I'll ring you tomorrow at work. If it was just a casual cup of coffee we can just leave it at that and no-one gets hurt, but if it's more we can arrange to meet then. Fair? Do we have a deal?'

'That sounds like a plan.' Jane felt comfortable with that and smiled at him. They stood outside the cafe neither of them wanting to make the first move to leave.

Philip took her in his arms and squeezed her tight. She felt so secure and content with his arms round her. He bowed his head and with only the slightest of touches he kissed her. It was just one short kiss but Jane didn't want it to end. She felt herself responding; their tongues touched and it turned into the most passionate kiss she'd ever had.

Philip started to pull away. 'I *will* see you again Jane; I'm sure of it,' and with that he walked away from her, back to his car. Jane operated on auto pilot for the rest of the day and she was very quiet in the evening. But only her son, Simon, noticed.

'What's the matter mum? Are you not feeling well?' he asked. He was very intuitive when it came to his mother's feelings and always knew when something was wrong. In fact he tended to know more about his mother's feelings than she did. He was leaving for university in a couple of weeks and was worried how his mum and dad would cope without his calming influence.

He'd always been the one to keep the family unit together, organising meals out or family trips. Lara was oblivious to anyone's feelings apart from her own and he knew any shred of family cohesiveness would fall apart when he left.

Simon loved both his parents but had always had a lot more in common with his mum. They both had Scorpio birth signs and tended to know what each other was thinking. They were both emotional and very intense and tended to support each other when the people of the more superficial birth signs rode roughshod over their feelings.

He'd felt for some time that his mum and dad weren't happy. He knew only too well the circumstances of their getting together and sometimes felt guilty that they only remained together because of him and Lara.

Despite all this Simon was really excited about leaving home for the first time. He'd chosen Liverpool University for two reasons. Firstly, the course was good, Forensic Science; and secondly it wasn't too far to come home for a decent meal and to get his washing done. He was going into Halls of Residence for his first year, a mixed hall. Simon had never had a serious girlfriend. At the back of his mind he didn't want the same thing to happen to him as had happened to his parents.

'I'm fine darling, I think I'm just a bit tired with all these dreams I keep having.' Jane had told Simon about the dreams but hadn't explained her new theory about Daniel. She knew he would be the first person she'd turn to when she had something to tell. He wouldn't ridicule her the way the rest of her family would. 'I think I'll have an early night and just go and read.' With any luck she would be asleep before Neil went to bed so she wouldn't have to take part in inane conversation when all she wanted to do was replay the kiss in her mind.

She didn't read however because she couldn't concentrate. She kept replaying the moment she'd met Philip, going over every conversation, trying to remember every word that had passed between them. She felt like a love-sick teenager. Any minute now she'd be scribbling in her notebook 'Jane loves Philip' and drawing big love-hearts.

Jane must have fallen asleep as she woke up with a start at three o'clock. Neil was fast asleep beside her. She'd had the dream again, but there was something different this time. She wasn't crying and neither did she have palpitations. Her breathing was calm and she could remember every aspect of the dream.

She still remembered opening the letter and sliding down the wall as she read the contents but she felt detached somehow. It made her even more determined to get to the bottom of this mystery. Tomorrow she would go through the list and ring the St.Claire's. And for the first time after having the dream, Jane went straight back to sleep.

February 1941

The last week before Daniel had to leave was the hardest of their young lives. They held on to each other, trying not to think about what could happen. Nora's mother had made them a nice tea the day before he was due to go and then surprisingly declared she was going out to see a friend on her birthday. This left Daniel and Nora in the house by themselves. They sat on the sofa holding hands and kissing. Nora was fighting back tears, as she had been for over a week. She had a lump in her throat from trying not to cry.

'Daniel, there's something I want to say,' Nora said nervously.

'What is it?'

'I want us to make love before you go. I've thought about it seriously and I'm ready. It'll give me more to remember us by. Every night when I'm alone in bed I can picture you holding me and loving me,' she said tenderly.

This came as a bit of a shock to Daniel. Although he desperately wanted to make love to Nora they'd agreed they would wait until they were married.

Nora got up and led Daniel to her bedroom.

'Are you sure you want to do this?' he asked tentatively.

'I've never been more certain of anything.' She reached up and kissed him. He started to unbutton her dress, all the time looking into her eyes. He slid it from her shoulders and it fell to the floor, leaving Nora in her underwear. She wasn't at all self conscious as she stood before him in her bra and pants. She reached across and undid the buttons of his shirt and then moved onto his trousers.

They kissed again and then he led her to the bed. They finished undressing each other and, very slowly, with the inexperience of youth, he lay on top of her. Nora winced with pain as he entered her, but then they got into their rhythm and, although not the most earth shattering sex, it was loving and tender.

They were both aware they didn't have very long as Nora's mother might return at any minute, but Daniel was a full blooded male and it didn't take him too long to get hard again. The next time they made love neither of them was embarrassed and Nora gave herself to him completely. He knew exactly where to touch her in order to give her the most pleasure. He felt ecstatic as he entered her for the second time. All their inhibitions were gone and at the point of orgasm they both screamed out.

It was with great reluctance that Nora removed herself from Daniel's arms and went to get dressed. They couldn't risk getting caught by her mother. They walked downstairs hand in hand and sat back down on the sofa, trying to act as if nothing had happened. But seeing the after-sex glow they both had about them, you'd have had to be blind not to notice it.

Nora had had an inkling that her mother had left them alone on purpose and she hoped she wouldn't be too disappointed that she hadn't saved herself for her wedding night. Even though Nora knew Daniel was leaving the next day she went to bed with a big smile on her face and a warm glow in her body.

It was with a heavy heart that Nora waved goodbye to Daniel at the train station the next day. The final kiss went on forever.

'I love you with all my heart and soul, my darling, and when I see you again we can be man and wife forever. Keep safe and think of me all the time.' Daniel held onto Nora so tightly that she could barely breathe. He cupped her face between his hands and looked deep into her eyes,

'I'll remember this face every night before I sleep and it'll be the first thing I see when I awake.'

'I love you too and I'll pray for your safe return every night.' Nora couldn't say anything else through the tears. She would miss him with all her heart and now that she'd found him she never wanted to let him go. She kissed her beautiful engagement ring as the train pulled away. She ran along the platform, waving and sobbing, until the train pulled out of sight. She thought the tears would never end.

He promised he would write every day and for two months he kept his promise.

Chapter 4

Rachel, the receptionist who worked in the office with Neil and Sally, was a bubbly, lively person at the best of times, but this morning she was more enthusiastic than ever. She clapped her hands together to get everyone's attention, then addressed the whole office. 'I just wondered what you're all doing on Friday night. Paul proposed to me yesterday evening and he's only gone and organised a surprise engagement party for Friday,' she shouted.

'Way to go Rach,' Annie, her fellow receptionist, called out.

'Although it's not much of a surprise if you know about it,' some Smart Alec shouted.

'He's invited all our family and friends but he wanted to give me a chance to invite all my colleagues at work. Although there can be exceptions!' she said jokingly, directing her comment to the person who was heckling her.

'It's at the Original Oak in Headingley, in the upstairs room. Please see if you can come. We'd love to see you all there.' When Rachel finished her announcement she got a spontaneous round of applause.

Sally joined in the clapping and went over to look at Rachel's ring, along with all the other females in the office. It was a huge square solitaire diamond in, what looked like, platinum. No expense spared there, she thought. She felt a twinge of jealousy as Rachel and Paul had only been going out about a year. They were obviously so much in love it had to be only a matter of time before he'd proposed. Why couldn't Philip be more like that?

'Are you going to go to the party?'

Sally turned round as Neil spoke to her. 'Yes I think I will, if I can drag Philip away from the television for long enough. That's all he wants to do at the moment. How about you? Will you ask your wife?' Sally could never remember his wife's name, maybe because Neil only ever referred to her as his wife.

'Same here. She only ever wants to stay in and read. But I'll suggest it as we haven't done much socialising with the office and Jane hardly knows anyone. It'll give us something to talk about anyway.' He paused. 'I'm sorry to keep moaning about my home life. I'm sure you've got better things to think about than listening to me wittering on.'

'No, it's fine to get things off your chest. I really appreciated our conversation last night. It helps to talk to a friend,' Sally said gently, touching his arm.

Neil's heart jumped in his chest as she referred to him as a friend. He was starting to realise he wanted much more, but friend was a good place to start.

'How did Philip like the house?' Neil asked, remembering her boyfriend's name. That should surely earn him some brownie points.

'He said he liked it, but didn't show much enthusiasm. He didn't talk much at all last night. He said work had been very busy. I need him to make a decision soon. I want to put an offer in.' Sally said.

'Maybe going to the engagement party might just be the catalyst he needs.' Neil added. Although why he was encouraging Sally and Philip to get married he didn't know. He realised he would've been devastated if it had been Sally who'd been making the announcement half an hour ago.

Seven phone calls had drawn a blank and Jane wasn't feeling as positive as she'd been in the beginning. She'd been working on her speech and was going to tell whoever answered that she had an interest in genealogy and was researching her family tree. She'd come across an unknown branch of the family in the Falmouth area and was trying to learn more about them. It sounded much more plausible than saying she'd been dreaming about a strange man and she wanted to see if he'd ever existed.

She dialled number eight on her list. It rang six times. She was just about to put the phone down when it was answered by a lady who was obviously out of breath.

'Sorry, I was in the garden,' a voice with a lovely West Country lilt answered.

'Hello, I'm sorry to disturb you, but do you, or did you ever, know an Ann and Robert St. Claire?' Jane was always nervous at this point.

'I do yes. They were my parents,' the lady replied.

Jane could barely contain her excitement. She took a deep breath and could hardly get the words out fast enough. 'Great. I'm studying my family tree and I've come across this branch of the family. I can't seem to find any details about them. I wondered if you could help. I'm in Cornwall with my mother next week and, if it wouldn't be too much of an imposition, whether I could take up a few minutes of your time?'

'Of course love. I would be more than happy to talk to you, although they've been dead for some time now. But I can try and answer your questions. What day would suit?'

Jane was delighted and surprised at her good luck and wanted to strike while the iron was hot.

'Would Monday be OK?' she asked tentatively. She hadn't even checked in her diary at work. She still had a few days holiday left this year and was sure her mother would enjoy a trip to Cornwall, although she hadn't actually asked her. It had to be next week as she was taking Simon to university the week after. But there was no way she could wait any longer than she had to now she'd made this phenomenal discovery.

'Monday will be fine. If you come about mid morning we can have coffee and cakes. What did you say your name was?' the lady asked.

'I apologise. I didn't introduce myself. My name is Jane Barclay.' Jane felt quite rude. She'd been so carried away with her discovery.

'And I'm Sarah St.Claire.' She gave Jane her address and quick directions and they exchanged goodbyes.

What a wonderful lady, Jane thought. She couldn't believe she'd spoken to the sister of the man she'd been dreaming about for months. It suddenly all felt very surreal. Up to now it had been in Jane's imagination and now it could actually be true. A short shiver went up and down her back.

Jane started to type a memo to her senior partner asking him if it was OK to take a few days leave. September was usually a busy time in estate agency but what with the downturn in the housing market, and the recession, they were having the quietest September for a good few years. She would also text her mum to see if she could spare a few days out of her busy schedule. Since her mother had discovered new technology she loved texting and preferred it to communicating face to face.

Jane hadn't even given Neil or her children a second thought but she was sure they could manage to put a few meals in the microwave for a couple of days. Just then the office phone rang.

'Jane, a Mr Philip Sinclair on line one says it's about 5 Call Mews'. The receptionist put him through.

'Was that a good diversionary tactic?' Philip asked. 'I'd be good at subterfuge.'

Jane laughed. 'Yes, very good. No-one will be at all suspicious now.'

'I said I'd phone. I know it's only eleven o'clock but I wanted to hear your voice. I'm missing you already. You're all I can think about. Have you spared me a thought?' he asked in a plaintive voice.

'Only incessantly.' Jane replied, smiling as she heard his voice. She would have loved to talk to Philip about her new discovery but she was frightened he would think her a bit unhinged. She didn't know how to explain it to herself yet, never mind to someone else. She was so pleased to hear from him and it all added to the increased level of excitement she was feeling at the moment.

'Have you thought about whether you'd like to meet me again?' Philip asked.

'I've thought about nothing else. I'll meet you again but only for coffee, if that's OK?' Jane said, trying to rein in her enthusiasm.

'Are you trying to suggest I have an ulterior motive for our meeting? How could you? I'm as pure as the driven snow.'

'Sorry, only joking.'

'Coffee it is then. Are you free for lunch? Do you want to choose the place this time?'

'My lunchtime is twelve-thirty. How about Barron's, on the Headrow?' Jane suggested. 'If that's OK with you?'

'Wherever you want is perfect. I'm looking forward to seeing you, in one and a half hours and counting. Bye.' Philip sounded elated.

They both hung up. Jane would have to work especially hard for the rest of the day, seeing as it was nearly dinner time and she hadn't done a stroke of work. But concentration still eluded her. Her lunch time couldn't come quick enough and she kept glancing at her watch every five minutes. At twelve-twenty she got up from her desk and went to get her coat. The anticipation of seeing Philip again was nearly killing her.

The place they were meeting was within walking distance. Just as she was walking towards the Headrow she heard a horn. It was Philip. He slowed down. 'Do you want a lift?'

'We're only going over the road. The car park is further than I'll have to walk.'

'Spoilsport. Get in, I'm lonely,' he teased.

Jane opened the door and slid into the passenger seat. She did actually have to slide. Philip had a Lotus and she was nearly horizontal once she sat down. They only went fifty yards to a multi-storey car park. Philip drove to the top floor where there were hardly any other cars. He leant across, gently placed his hand round the nape of her neck and drew her close to him. She felt the passion of his kiss as his tongue darted inside her mouth. He held her so tight and kissed her for the longest time.

Jane felt herself tingle and to her amazement she started to moisten. She'd thought she was going into early menopause as she was usually very dry. She'd even thought about buying shares in KY jelly, she used so much. But one kiss from Philip and all that changed.

'Sorry about that. I couldn't bear to spend an hour without kissing you.' Philip still didn't let Jane go. They looked into each other's eyes and kissed again. Each time was more passionate than the last.

Jane had never really been a lustful person but she wanted to tear his clothes from his body and have him right here in his car. The seats were so flat it was already like being in a bed. When finally they pulled apart Jane couldn't fail to see Philip's erection.

'Yes, I am pleased to see you,' Philip joked. Neither of them was embarrassed. They just laughed, then sat and held hands until it subsided. Jane knew she was being very foolish by taking so many risks. Anyone could have seen them as she was only a ten minute walk from her office. But by this time she was way beyond caring.

'Let's go and get this coffee before we get arrested for lewd behaviour,' Philip joked. 'That would go down well with everyone, seeing our names plastered over the front page of the Yorkshire Evening Post.'

They kept an acceptable distance apart as they walked into Barron's. They could just be two work colleagues having a lunchtime meeting. It was still quiet and there were only one or two tables taken. They chose a booth well away from anyone else. The waiter brought two coffees.

Philip moved closer to Jane, turned and pushed his knee in between her legs. She could feel herself getting more aroused. He started to slide his finger up her thigh. Not too high, but far enough to drive Jane mad with desire. She responded by putting her hand in between his thighs. She could feel his erection now. She slid her fingers along its length, over his trousers. Philip gasped. Short of making love on the bench neither of them could have been more aroused. But to any onlooker they were just sat having coffee. No-one could see what was happening under the table.

Philip looked around to see if anyone was looking and then he kissed her. Not for long but still passionately. Jane was past caring if anyone was watching. Neither of them spoke. They just kept staring at each other.

'I want you,' Philip whispered.

'I want you too, but it can't be here.' Jane responded, her rational side taking over whereas her body yearned for his touch. Reluctantly she withdrew her hand.

They paid for the coffee and walked, a lot closer this time, back to his car. His hand kept brushing hers and he'd occasionally latch on to her fingers. Philip made sure no-one was around and pushed Jane against the car. He kissed her and put his hand inside her blouse feeling her erect nipples. She pulled away and started kissing and biting his neck, not enough to mark him but enough to send him insane with desire. It was his turn to touch her.

Philip opened the door for Jane to get into the car; he quickly went round and got into the driver's seat. Kissing her all the while he worked his fingers up her skirt, pulled her pants to one side and gently inserted his finger. He could feel how wet she was. It didn't take more than a few strokes to bring Jane to orgasm. All the time they were kissing Jane tried to keep an eye out for other drivers returning to their cars.

They knew they would have to pull apart otherwise things would really get out of hand. 'I really must be getting back to work,' Jane said between kisses. 'I'll ring you soon.' She rearranged her clothing;. She was a professional woman after all, she'd better start acting like one.

'Please make it very soon. I think I'm falling in love with you Jane.' Philip was totally surprised by his reaction. He didn't use the L word lightly. In ten years he'd never said it directly to Sally. He'd said 'me too' whenever she told him she loved him, but something had always held him back. He now knew why… he didn't love her. In fact he didn't feel a fraction of the emotion he felt towards Jane after only twenty-four hours.

Jane was feeling very confused as she walked back to work. She took the scenic route to give her time to think. She'd never even thought about being unfaithful to Neil. She knew she didn't have the most exciting of marriages but that was her lot and she tolerated it. She'd just had the best sex ever, with Philip, and they hadn't even made love. Jane had only ever had two partners; Neil and a four-week relationship before him. Neither of them had been, what you'd call, accomplished lovers. But she and Neil had muddled through over the years and she'd just assumed that neither of them had a particularly high sex drive.

She didn't know how she could ever make love to Neil again after today. She thought by now that guilt would have reared its ugly head, but it hadn't. It all felt too perfect. In theory it was only the second time they'd met but it was like they'd known each other forever. He felt so familiar.

Then her thoughts turned to her dream and Daniel St.Claire. Suddenly her life seemed very complicated. She'd started this search for Daniel and she owed it to herself to keep going. She would go to Cornwall next week, which would put a bit of distance between her and Philip. She needed to get the relationship into some kind of perspective. But however she viewed it she was having an affair. Putting some space between them might help her see things more rationally, rather than through pure emotion which it was at the moment.

She hadn't mentioned to Philip that she was going to Cornwall. She would ring him as promised and tell him that she couldn't see him until late next week. It would also give him time to cool off. She found it hard to believe he'd said 'I love you' after knowing her for such a short time and she didn't know if she welcomed his admission or not.

Her confusion was no nearer being resolved as she sat at her desk that afternoon, but drawing up the details of a house she'd just valued helped take her mind off her situation.

Her mother did indeed text her that afternoon and agreed that it was a great idea to go away for a couple of days. Luckily all her University of the Third Age classes didn't start again until October, so now was a perfect time to go. Jane found a hotel on the internet and booked a twin room right in the centre of Falmouth. The weather was still unusually mild and she felt herself looking forward to her seaside trip and getting away from her life, even if only for a couple of days.

Chapter 5

Jane had agreed to go to Rachel's engagement party with Neil. She'd made a real effort over the past couple of days to be pleasant with her family. She didn't want anyone to become suspicious. Her mood felt much more buoyant and she hadn't even had a cross word with Lara, which was a first as they usually rubbed each other up the wrong way. She made the excuse for her bad mood of late by saying she'd been extra stressed at work. Neil had agreed it was a good idea to take a few days away with her mother.

She was even looking forward to the party as she scanned the contents of her wardrobe, deciding what to wear. They didn't usually socialise with people from Neil's work. He'd always maintained that work was work, play was play, and you didn't mix the two. As a result Jane hardly knew anyone he worked with. They'd even missed the Christmas party last year because Neil didn't like to become involved in office politics. She'd never even met his assistant who had been working with him for just over a year.

She chose a long, flowing, brightly coloured chiffon number. The last time she'd worn it was on their most recent holiday abroad. Neil had taken her to St. Kitts for a week to an all-inclusive luxury resort. They'd had a wonderful time. In fact it was probably the last time they'd really enjoyed themselves. That was two years ago.

Jane chose matching jade jewellery, to complement the colour of the dress. She would wear high heels tonight, even though she would probably regret it in the morning, and finished the outfit with a teal pashmina draped over her shoulders. She wore a little make up with just a hint of clear lip gloss.

When she walked downstairs Neil whistled. 'Wow! Look at you.' He looked admiringly at his wife. This was the first compliment he'd paid her in a long time. 'How about we turn up late to this party?' he said as he started kissing her neck. Jane tensed. Neil hadn't touched her since her little indiscretion with Philip.

'Maybe later, we're already behind schedule.' Jane tried to put him off without being too obvious. 'Anyway I'm looking forward to going out with you, it's been a while since we went out and enjoyed ourselves.' She kissed his cheek.

That seemed to go some way to placating him. He went to fetch his jacket. Jane had agreed to drive as it was his work's function and Neil liked to drink. Living where they did, in the back of beyond, meant that someone always had to drive. It took them nearly an hour to get to Headingley and the party was already in full swing when they walked through the door.

'What would you like to drink? I'll go to the bar and then we'll go and find the others.' Neil asked, looking round for Sally.

'I'll have a white wine spritzer with soda please. I'm just nipping to the ladies,' Jane replied.

She returned and had the shock of her life when she saw who Neil was talking to. Then it dawned on her. Neil had talked about his assistant Sally but she'd never made the connection that it could be the same person who she'd shown around 5 Call Mews on Monday. It could only mean one thing, Philip must be Sally's boyfriend. The world had never felt smaller. This was all rather too close for comfort. She now had the advantage over Philip and she took a few minutes to compose herself before Neil saw her.

She hoped Philip's surprised look wouldn't reveal his true feelings. Jane walked over to join the group.

Neil introduced them. 'Ah, there you are. Sally, this is Jane, and Jane this is Sally.' Sally's face lit up when she saw Jane.

'We've already met. You'd mentioned your wife was an estate agent but I never made the connection. That means you've already met my other half, Philip,' Sally said. 'Philip, come over here. Look who I'm talking to. I never realised Jane is Neil's wife.' He turned round from his conversation and spluttered into his lager as he saw Jane.

'Hello. Fancy seeing you here.' Jane tried to make light of the situation hoping to give Philip time to compose himself.

'Well, what a coincidence,' he said. There'd been too many coincidences for his liking recently. Philip prided himself on always being in control but now he felt adrift and he wasn't sure he enjoyed being at the mercy of his emotions. The last two days had been torture for him. Jane hadn't phoned and he'd found himself staring at his mobile for hours, waiting for her to call. He'd been snappy at home and unproductive at work. No woman had ever had such an effect on him and here she was, standing in front of him looking stunningly beautiful, and he had to make small talk when all he wanted to do was take her in his arms and kiss her.

The four of them chatted away for some time. Jane and Philip shared the odd glance but nothing more. Sally grabbed Neil's arm, 'Come and sign the card and look at the present you helped buy. I won't keep him long.' she said.

'No rush, return him when you've had enough,' Jane replied jokingly.

Sally thought that'd be quite a long time. She'd been enjoying flirting with Neil over the past few days. He looked particularly handsome tonight with his short blond hair in an ultra modern style. He always looked slightly tanned and she wondered if he used a sunbed. He'd a great body for his age and working out at the gym was definitely paying dividends. He wore a pair of dark blue tailored trousers, she could tell from the cut they were expensive, with a casual, pale-blue striped shirt. He looked lovely and one of his most appealing characteristics was that he'd absolutely no idea how gorgeous he was.

Neil made such a refreshing change from her moody boyfriend. For the past two days Philip had been like a bear with a sore head. She couldn't say anything without him jumping down her throat. She hadn't dared mention the house again. She hoped after a few lagers tonight he might be a bit more amenable. They were going to have to make a decision soon but she hadn't pushed him as she was beginning to have second thoughts herself. Buying a house together was a lot more permanent than renting. She also wanted to have some fun in her life and fun had been in short supply in her house recently.

Neil took hold of Sally's arm and led her across the room, a gesture which she thoroughly enjoyed. The room was packed with people and they had to squeeze up very close a couple of times. She could feel his breath on her neck as she inhaled his aftershave. She recognised Joop anywhere, it was one of her favourites.

Neil was also enjoying the closeness of Sally. He'd felt very proud when he'd walked into the party with Jane, who was looking particularly stunning tonight, and he thought he might have imagined his feelings for Sally. That is until he saw her. She was the antithesis of Jane. She was sex on legs. Her skirt was so short it resembled a belt and her top was low, both back and front, showing off more of her body than was decent. He didn't mind and neither did any of the other red-blooded males in the room who kept staring at her.

He felt very territorial as he held onto her arm. She had short, spiky red hair this week - last week it had been blond. Her features were elfin-like, which suited her tiny frame. She was either a size 6 or 8, just the way he liked his women. She might have been too thin for some men but he liked feeling her ribs as he brushed up against her. He could feel the stirring in his trousers as they walked across the room.

She led him over to a table. On it was a big card, open and ready to sign. All the people in the office had clubbed together to get the present, Neil's contribution being the most sizeable. They'd bought the happy couple a video camera, a lot more practical than a cut glass vase or decanter which would probably never be taken out of its box.

'Are you glad you came?' Sally asked Neil. She had to get really close to his face due to the loud music in the room; which Neil had no objection to.

'It's been worth it just to see you in that dress,' Neil laughed. 'You do realise that you're no good for an old man's blood pressure.'

'You're not old and you scrub up quite well yourself.' She squeezed his hand. Neil was very glad they were in a room full of people or else he may have done something he would regret. He really fancied Sally and was imagining taking her outside and having her up against the wall. Something he would never dream of thinking about his own wife.

Jane had watched Neil and Sally walk over to the far side of the room and recognised the picture of lust written all over her husband's face. She smiled ruefully and remembered a time when he used to look like that at her. But which man wouldn't fancy Sally? she thought. She had a beautiful body and a lovely cute face.

Jane wondered, 'what does Philip see in me when he has that body to go home to every night?'

'You never phoned me,' Philip said trying to look as though they were having a normal conversation.

'Sweetheart, it's only been two days and I was going to phone, honest, she whispered. 'I've had a lot to think about, it's not every day I'm unfaithful to my husband.'

'These two days have felt like a lifetime to me. I've not been able to concentrate on anything. I haven't been eating and nothing normally hampers my appetite. What are you doing to me?' He looked longingly at Jane and then had an idea, 'Follow me outside in a few minutes. Neil and Sally are talking to their gang from work and should be a while.' Philip headed for the door at the back of the lounge. Luckily for them the toilets were also out that way.

Jane took a quick look round to see if anyone was watching. The coast was clear and she headed off in the same direction. Philip was waiting for her in the beer garden. All her resolve left her as she ran into his arms. Kissing him was the most natural thing to do. How could it be wrong when it felt like this?

'We can't stay out here, we might get caught.' Jane looked worried.

Philip kept kissing her and started to fondle her breasts through the chiffon. She'd gone without a bra tonight and he could see her nipples, dark and inviting, through her dress. He pressed himself up against her and he was hard already. He took her by the hand, round to the outbuildings.

'I wanted our first time to be more romantic but I must have you. I need to feel myself inside you.' Philip was already starting to unzip his trousers. He reached in his pocket for a condom. Jane's head was saying that it was a very dangerous thing to do but her body was crying out for him. Years of frustrating sex and longing was culminating at this point. He lifted her dress up, pulled her thong to one side and entered her. It was so exciting and Jane could feel herself on the verge of coming after only a few thrusts. Philip knew he had to be quick. He wanted the feeling to last forever but they were both so aroused; within a minute it was over.

Neither of them was left wanting as they'd both climaxed together. A double first for Jane. Her first experience of doing it standing up, and her first outside. It felt so dirty and she loved it. She kept kissing him, thrusting her tongue round his mouth. This is what she'd been missing all these years. They'd also been very quiet. She'd felt like crying out when she came, it had been so intense, but she buried her head in Philip's shoulder and stifled the cry. Philip pulled her dress back down and did up his fly.

'I'm sorry our first time was like this but I've had a permanent erection since I saw you tonight it was either this or relieving myself.' Philip looked sheepish.

'Don't be sorry, that was fantastic. I didn't know I could be so turned on.' Jane kissed him.

'Don't talk like that. I can feel myself stirring again. We can't be gone for much longer. People might miss us, although,' he looked at his watch, 'we've only been gone for ten minutes. What a stud,' Philip laughed.

'I'm going to the ladies to sort myself out and to make sure that it doesn't look like I've been shagged senseless.' Jane gave him one last kiss.

What was happening to her? She felt like a brazen hussy, whatever that was, and she wanted more.

Luckily no-one had missed them. Jane made her way to the crowded bar to get herself another drink. One more glass of wine was usually her limit when she was driving, but she downed it in a few gulps before she went to find Neil. He was still talking to his friends from work. She hadn't seen him look so relaxed in a long time. She looked at him fondly and hoped that whatever happened to them in the future he would be happy.

'I'm glad you're back,' Sally said. 'I wanted to ask you something. I'm having a few friends round next Thursday. My friend desperately wants her Tarot cards read and I said I would host a party. If we can get six people together the clairvoyant gives us a discount. Do you fancy it?'

'It's not something I've ever done. Is it spooky?' Jane was apprehensive. She'd had an interest in astrology and always read her stars but communing with the dead was a different matter.

'No. Rosa is great. She's from an old Romany family and she's very accurate. I was sceptical to start with but I've had a few readings with her over the years and she told me things she couldn't possibly have known. It's worth giving it a try. You never know, she might tell you some deep dark secret,' Sally laughed.

'Go on then, I'm all for trying something different. What time do you want me there? You'll have to give me your address.'

'If you can be there for seven she calls people in one at a time. There'll be drinks and nibbles. I get rid of Philip; he goes to play five-a-side. It's a good girly night and it'll give me a chance to get to know you a bit better.' Sally was pleased that Jane had accepted her invitation.

'Thanks for inviting me.' Jane seemed genuinely pleased, only marred by the fact that she was having an affair with Sally's boyfriend.

'I'll give Neil directions to the flat on Monday at work. I can't think straight now. I think I've had one too many vodkas.'

Jane was looking forward to seeing where Philip lived and also what the clairvoyant would tell her. She wondered if she would know about her affair. She might even give her some much needed advice.

Chapter 6

Jane had a headache when she woke up on Saturday morning. She'd opened a bottle of red wine when she'd got back from the party. One bottle had turned into two and she and Neil had stayed up until after one, drinking and listening to music. It was the only way Jane could come to terms with what had happened earlier. She'd had such a wonderful time with Philip, but at the same time she did feel sorry for Neil. She'd heard on *Oprah* that affairs were acceptable as long as you told your spouse. If they also thought it was acceptable, then you could carry on. Ridiculous. How many spouse's would say 'go for it darling, enjoy!'?

She'd tried to feel guilt because she felt she should. Although she was perfectly aware that she was cheating on Neil, she knew she couldn't stop seeing Philip. She also didn't view her relationship with Philip as a casual affair. He'd said he was falling in love with her. She didn't know if what she felt was love but it was a very deep connection. She felt she already knew him intimately, even after such a short space of time.

She would find a time to ring Philip today to tell him she was going to Cornwall. She was going to say it was her mother's idea and she had gone along with the suggestion because it would give her time to think about the future. Hopefully, when she returned, she could find a way to tell him about her dream and her amateur sleuthing.

She was travelling down to Cornwall on Sunday. With a bit of luck the traffic would be quieter than mid-week or Saturday. She used to go to Cornwall every year, as a child, with her parents and remembered the ten-hour journeys. The roads had improved but it was still going to last at least eight hours with all the stops her mother would have to take. She would get her foot down on the motorways to make up some time and when it came to the 'A' roads, hope not to get stuck behind the obligatory tractor.

While Neil was washing his car Jane phoned Philip. They didn't speak for long. Although Philip said he would miss her he understood that she had to go. She promised to send him dirty texts from her bed at night. She'd heard that phone sex was very rewarding and was looking forward to giving it a go. She then threw a few clothes in an overnight bag and sent a text to her mother saying she would pick her up at seven. Madge lived in Horsforth, at the other side of Leeds. It was completely the wrong direction to the M1 going south but that couldn't be helped. After all she was doing her a favour. It'd only add an hour on to the journey. If she'd have planned ahead Madge could have stayed at Jane's overnight but it was too late to arrange that now.

The journey down to Cornwall was very smooth and they pulled into the car park of their hotel at two o'clock. They were supposed to be sharing a twin room but it turned out that they'd been given two singles at no extra cost, much better for Jane and her late night phone calls. She was surprised at how much she was missing Philip. When she got to her room she sent texts to both Neil and Philip telling them she'd arrived safely.

Jane and her mother were very good friends and enjoyed each other's company, in small doses. Madge was a very dominant person, just like her daughter, so they did tend to clash if they spent too much time together. They liked doing the same things and enjoyed a walk along the front before eating in the hotel's restaurant. Jane didn't feel like getting dressed up and going out. Driving long distances always exhausted her, and it was Neil that tended to be the one to drive when they travelled any significant distance.

After a beautiful meal and a couple of drinks in the bar Jane made her excuses and retired to bed for an early night, leaving Madge talking to a couple from Rochdale. Madge had an unerring knack of finding someone to talk to wherever she went. Jane admired her for it and it was one of the reasons why she'd never been lonely, despite being a widow at the tender age of forty.

Madge had never married again. She had always maintained that Jane's dad was her soul mate and that you never came across two of those in one lifetime. Secretly, as Madge would've never admitted to anyone, she'd been disappointed when Jane had married Neil as she knew that they'd never find the true happiness that she and her beloved Bill had known. She'd settled because she was pregnant. At the time Madge had regarded this as a mistake, and still did.

Jane had a quick shower and got into bed to phone Philip.

'What are you doing now?' he asked.

'I'm in bed naked, where are you?' Jane said in as seductive a voice as she could muster.

'Wait a second I'll go and lay down on the bed as well.' She could hear Philip run upstairs.

They spent the next half-hour making lewd suggestions to each other, describing in intimate detail what they were going to do to each other when they next met. Philip asked Jane to fondle herself and despite being a bit embarrassed she did, with much encouragement from him. He also did the same and soon she was a phone-sex virgin no longer. She fell asleep with a satisfied body, and a big smile on her face.

Jane had to tell Madge a lie the following morning. She said she was going to look round estate agencies in the area, for her boss. She would only tell her mother the real reason for the trip if her meeting with Sarah St.Claire was successful. Her mother usually kept an open mind and hopefully she wouldn't judge her or think her insane. Madge was going to have a leisurely breakfast and then look round the nicer shops in town.

Sarah lived just outside Falmouth, in Helford, a beautiful village on the estuary. It took twenty minutes to get there, driving down winding country lanes where it was impossible to get two cars passed each other. She was very impressed when she pulled up outside a lovely, chocolate-box cottage. Jane pulled into the drive and saw it was much larger than it appeared from the road. Sarah was waiting for her.

'Come in, I've just put the kettle on. It's lovely to meet you. I'm Sarah.' She gave Jane a big, beaming smile.

Sarah, Jane figured, was in her late sixties. She was a tall, smart woman and would have been quite a looker in her time. Her hair was nearly white and the short bob really suited her.

'Hello, I'm Jane Barclay.' They shook hands. 'Thank-you for taking the time to meet me. I hope you don't mind me asking, I'm just basically nosey, but you mentioned you were a widow, yet you're still called St.Claire. Why did you keep your maiden name? I was lucky to find you.'

'I was the last in the line of St.Claire's and the name meant a lot to my father. After my brother got killed, my parents asked me if I would keep the family name. My husband was called Brimblecombe so he wasn't worried about holding onto that, and hyphenating was never an option! So that's the reason I'm called St.Claire. A good job really, otherwise you wouldn't have found me. Would you prefer coffee or tea?'

'Coffee please. Milk, but no sugar. Thank-you,' Jane answered.

'Take a seat in the lounge. I'll be through shortly.' Sarah pointed in the direction of a large, bright room at the back of the house. The sun was streaming through the big bay window and Jane got a wonderful view of the garden with its preponderance of flowers and shrubbery.

She glanced round the room and saw a collection of photographs adorning the mantelpiece and every other surface. They were of Sarah, her husband and two children at varying ages. The most recent were only of Sarah and two young boys.

Sarah saw Jane looking admiringly at the photos.

'That's my late husband. He died almost two years ago and there's not a day goes by that I don't miss him. I have two wonderful children, and those are my son's boys'. Sarah pointed to the most recent photograph.

'You have a beautiful family,' Jane said genuinely.

'I know. I'm really lucky. They've both been fantastic since we lost their dad.' Jane could see her pride was tinged with sadness. 'Anyway, enough about me. How can I help you? You mentioned you were researching a family tree. It's always something I fancied doing, maybe I'll get round to it one day. In fact what you've found out will probably get me started.'

'Could you tell me a bit about your mother and father, and Daniel, if that's OK?' Jane asked.

'Obviously I never met my brother; I was born the year after he died. I was a menopause baby and a really nice surprise for my mum and dad after having lost their only child. When I was growing up they talked about Daniel constantly, trying to keep his memory alive. I was a very selfish child and I grew sick of being compared to someone I'd never even met. I tended to switch off, to be honest. I felt I was living his lost life.

'When I was married with my own children my parents stopped talking about him as much and from then on we had a much closer relationship. When my mum was taken ill she started bringing him into the conversation again and this time I was ready to listen. I have some letters and things of his in a box. Would you like me to get them?'

Jane was excited, 'Yes please, that would be great, as long as you don't mind me being privy to such personal information.'

Sarah got up to go and fetch the box. 'No, it's quite alright. It's all in the past anyway and I'm sure my mum would love to know someone has taken an interest in her beloved son.'

Jane sifted through the box, lifting out Daniel's christening book and old birthday cards. It seemed as if Mrs St.Claire had kept everything. She picked up an old brown envelope and gasped as she opened it. She'd found the letter she'd been dreaming about for months! She read it and it was word for word as she'd remembered it. She could have recited it without looking at it, she knew it so well. She slumped into the closest chair.

'Are you alright dear?' Sarah asked. 'You're holding your breath.'

Jane knew she had to come clean and tell Sarah the whole story.

'I'm sorry but I haven't been entirely honest with you.' Jane admitted. She started from the beginning, explaining how it had all begun months earlier with a dream about a young girl and a letter, and how the dream had gradually got longer until she saw the name of Sarah's parents. '...and that's why I'm here. I'm sorry I lied to you but I thought if I told you the story over the phone you'd think I was mad. I know it sounds farfetched, but here I am sitting with the sister of a man I've been dreaming about for months. A man who died in 1941.' Jane still couldn't believe it.

'How interesting and, no, I don't think you're mad. I would've done the same thing. I think it's marvellous. Nothing exciting like that ever happens to me. Funnily enough my mum mentioned this letter. It was written to his fiancée, a girl called Nora who was from up near your neck of the woods. My mother and father had met her the Christmas before he died and they'd given Daniel the family ring for when he proposed. They were to be married when the war was over.

'She returned the ring and this letter just after he'd died and they never heard from her again. They assumed she must have been too overcome with grief to see anyone who reminded her of her fiancé. They wrote to her a few times but the letters were returned saying, 'Gone away'.

'Daniel and my father looked very much alike. Here is a picture of them just before he went to do his officer training.'

Sarah pulled out a picture from the bottom of the box and handed it to Jane. They were two striking men. Daniel being the taller of the two at well over six foot but his father was broader and looked much stronger. They both had the similar mop of dark brown hair and chocolate brown eyes. They were very handsome and, Jane thought, somehow very familiar.

'Don't you think it's funny that they never smiled in old photographs? They both look so serious,' Jane commented.

'Well my father wasn't serious. He loved a laugh and was a bit of a practical joker. This is the ring that I mentioned.' Sarah showed Jane a beautiful line of five huge diamonds in an ornate setting. It was obviously very old and very valuable.

'It's absolutely stunning,' Jane said. It was the same ring that she remembered seeing in the dream, the one the young girl had been wearing.

'I was given it when I got engaged. My son or daughter should've had it next. But my son wanted to buy his own engagement ring and my daughter has never married. I think they call it living in sin don't they?' Sarah asked.

'I think they used to, but it's so commonplace now that lots of couples don't marry. It's a very expensive occasion. Some of my friends have spent nearly twenty thousand pounds on weddings for their daughters.'

'It does seem to have all got a bit out of hand. To me marriage is not about money it's about committing to the one you love. I loved being married and never regretted one day I spent with my husband.' Sarah looked a little sad. 'Have you got a good marriage?'

Jane didn't know how to answer this question. A couple of weeks ago she would have probably said yes, but now she hesitated.

'Sorry, I didn't mean to pry. Tell me to mind my own business, I'm just a nosey old woman with nothing better to do,' Sarah scolded herself.

'Not at all, it's just that I didn't know what to say. I'm afraid I had to get married. We've muddled along OK, but recently I've started to think there is something I'm missing. I don't want to get to the end of my life knowing only mediocrity,' she explained.

Jane found it so easy to talk to this woman she'd only just met. It had also been a relief to finally talk about her dream. She'd kept it to herself for so long.

'I still don't know why I'm having this dream. It's all very interesting finding out about Daniel and the rest of your family, but I don't know if it'll help me understand it.' Jane was still puzzled.

'Maybe you need to keep looking. If it was me I would try and find out about Nora. She must have lived quite near where my brother was stationed for them to meet at all.' Sarah seemed quite excited at the thought of helping to solve the mystery.

'That's a good idea. Where did you say he was stationed?' Jane asked.

'My mum mentioned a place called Catterick, does that ring a bell?' Sarah asked, trying to recall if she'd said the name correctly.

'Yes, Catterick is in North Yorkshire, straight up the A1 from where I live. I could start there and see if I can discover anything else. Nora is probably dead though. Do you know when was she born?' Jane asked.

'Daniel was born in 1920, so he would have been ninety next year. She was probably around the same age so you may be lucky. She may still be alive, people are living a lot longer these days. Also she could have married and had a family. It's definitely worth investigating. Will you keep me informed? I'm really intrigued by this story.' Sarah liked to find things to occupy her thoughts as she often had too much time on her hands.

'I certainly will, seeing as it's your family I'm investigating. I'll let you know what I find out. You've been so helpful and it's been really lovely to meet you. I'm sorry I misled you when I first arrived.'

'Don't mention it. I told you I would've probably done the same. It could turn into a great adventure, and I'm grateful to be a part of it,' Sarah added.

Jane looked at her watch. It was after one o'clock. Where had the time gone? She would have to get back to her mother as she'd told her she wouldn't be very long. She stood up to go. Sarah came over and gave her a hug.

'Take care Jane, and be happy. We all deserve it.' She gave Jane a knowing look, as if she'd already guessed Jane's secret.

Jane would've loved to have confided in Sarah and told her all about Philip but didn't want to risk Sarah thinking badly of her.

They exchanged addresses and phone numbers, Jane promising to keep in touch. She waved goodbye and drove off in search of her mother.

Chapter 7

Neil was quite enjoying his time alone, without anyone nagging him to do anything. Lara was staying at her friends and Simon kept going in and out all Sunday, doing his last minute shopping before leaving for Liverpool the following weekend. Neil caught up on some television that he wasn't allowed to watch when anyone was home. He loved watching sport, particularly motor racing, but he couldn't cope with the incessant comments from the other members of his family, about how it was like watching paint dry. They thought they were being funny but it annoyed him. He didn't make fun of them when they watched the soaps or, that most inane of programmes, *Most Haunted*.

He found his mind wandering to Sally, particularly in that dress she'd worn on Friday night. He still felt aroused thinking about how short it was. He wondered what she did on a Sunday and found himself a little jealous of her boyfriend, Philip, in case they spent a leisurely morning in bed, reading the papers and making love.

He felt as though he should be missing Jane but they hadn't been getting on too well recently. Not since she started having the bad dream. She always seemed touchy these days and, sometimes, very distant. They existed in the same house but with little physical contact.

Their sex life had never been what you'd call prolific, they usually managed it at least once a week. But it had been over a month since they'd made love. He'd been up for it on Friday before they went to the party but Jane had fobbed him off. A man has needs, he thought, and if his wife wouldn't satisfy him he would find someone who would. But would he ever have the nerve to be unfaithful to Jane? Probably not. But a little harmless flirting never hurt anyone, did it?

It was with that thought that he went into work on Monday morning. He was the first to arrive and was just making a pot of coffee when Sally walked in.

'Well fancy seeing you here. This must be a first for mankind, you being here before me. I'll have a coffee if you're making one.' Sally seemed in a particularly playful mood and Neil loved it.

'Coffee coming up. Sit down, I'll bring it over to you.' They went to sit on the comfy sofas in the waiting room.

'Jane's away for a few days so I thought I'd take advantage of the extra time to catch up on some work. What's your excuse?' Neil asked.

Sally didn't want to tell him that she and Philip had had a major row and she'd stormed out, it would spoil the mood. She could see Neil was flirting with her, because of Friday night. They'd spent ages talking at the party and she'd loved it when they'd accidently touched as they walked across the crowded room.

'I've also got some work to catch up on, so I suppose we should go and do it,' Sally said, although she seemed in no hurry to leave.

'Do you want to have lunch today?' Neil asked.

He'd been rehearsing that line for the past three days. 'I could drive us to a lovely pub in Esholt where no-one would know us, if you felt embarrassed being seen with me.'

'I'd love to have lunch and Esholt would be nice, but not for the reason you suggested. It would be an honour to be seen with you. It'll be nice to go somewhere quiet, just the two of us.' She walked past him to her desk, squeezing his hand and looking him straight in the eyes as she went.

Whilst Jane was anxiously pondering her future, Neil was driving another woman out to lunch, reaching across and occasionally touching her knee as he drove.

Jane spent a lovely afternoon with her mother on Monday. She realised that she didn't make enough time in her busy schedule to really talk to anyone. She decided to keep her dream and what she'd found out about Daniel to herself for a bit longer. It felt precious to her and talking about it to all and sundry may sully his memory. But she did want to talk about Neil and, if she was brave enough, about Philip.

She'd been on the phone to Philip for nearly an hour the previous night and they'd been pretty intimate in their conversation. It made her blush thinking back to what Philip had wanted her to do with her phone! But it hadn't been just about sex, they'd also talked about their days. Jane omitted the bit about meeting Sarah but they shared other information, filling in some of the areas they didn't know about each other. How it had come up in conversation she couldn't remember, but she discovered they'd both been born in St Mary's maternity hospital in Leeds. Their mothers would have been giving birth at the same time. Philip was born at three in the afternoon and Jane was born at two-thirty. They were discovering more and more coincidences in their relationship.

Jane drove her and Madge to a lovely country pub for lunch, where they ordered food and drinks and because it was still so warm they went to sit in the beer garden. Madge was very intuitive when it came to her only daughter.

'So what is it you wanted to get off your chest?' Madge asked.

'How do you do that? You always know when I want to talk; do I have a particular look on my face or something?' Jane pretended to be put out.

'Sort of. You look pensive and disappear into a world of your own. You used to do it as a child. What is it, marital problems?' Madge asked.

'You've done it again! Why don't you tell me what the problem is? It'll save me the trouble,' Jane snapped.

'Sorry love, but I've seen it coming for a while. You run around being busy for twenty-four hours a day but you just exist. That's not living. You're so busy making everyone's life easy that you forget to look at your own.' Madge was in full swing.

Jane burst into tears and went quiet for a few minutes. 'Sorry, I don't know where these tears have come from. I haven't cried in years.' She dried her eyes as the barmaid brought over the drinks. 'Neil takes me for granted. I do all the cooking, cleaning, and washing. You name it, I do it, and I work full time, just like him. I'm tired mum, and tired of him.' There, she'd finally said it.

'You poor love. I didn't think things had got so bad. How long have you felt like this?' Madge felt sorry that she'd pushed her daughter.

'I don't know. It's all come to a head recently.' She took a sharp intake of breath, 'and I've met someone.' Jane paused, waiting to see what her mother had to say.

'Is it serious?' Madge asked. Not the response Jane had expected from her.

'It's early days yet. I've known him less than a week but it feels more than a fling. It wasn't planned but I suppose these things never are. I was showing him round a house last Tuesday. We had this instant connection and we went and had a coffee. We've talked for hours,' Jane admitted.

'Have you slept together yet?' Madge asked very matter of factly.

'Mum!' Jane tried to sound indignant. Then, after a pause, 'Yes we have. Again, we didn't mean for it to happen, but we were so attracted to each other. It feels weird talking to you about my sex life.'

'I've had a sex life too. I know children don't like to think of their parents having sex but we do. Me and your dad had a great sex life. I've had other men since, some good, some bad, but you just know when it's right. Is it good with Neil?' Madge was totally at ease with the conversation.

A part of Jane didn't want to carry on down this road but it felt very freeing talking about it. 'It's only ever been good with Neil but with Philip it was wonderful. I experienced feelings I've never known before.' Jane became more animated, as she thought of Philip, and smiled.

Madge too gave a wistful smile. 'I thought one day you'd find out what you'd been missing. It's broken my heart watching you settle for mediocrity. I can't say I condone affairs because someone always gets hurt, but I do think you should explore your feelings for this Philip and see where it takes you. Have you talked to Neil about any of this?'

'Good God, no. Do you think I'm insane? I don't think he'd understand, do you?'

'I don't mean about the affair but have you told him how you feel generally? One thing is certain; people never have affairs if things are rosy in the garden. If you talked about it, maybe you could save your marriage. If that's what you want.'

Jane went quiet and thoughtful. She didn't know if the marriage to Neil was what she did want. It was still early days with Philip but the thought of never kissing him again was too much to contemplate.

Just then the waitress brought the food, and they were soon too busy enjoying scampi and chips to carry on the intimate conversation any longer. They returned to superficial subjects such as what they'd seen on television recently, but Jane had enjoyed the conversation with her mum and felt a little closer to her.

Chapter 8

The short break in Cornwall had been really enjoyable and Jane had to admit she felt better for the rest. Simon had given her a hug when she walked through the door and Lara just waved hello, as she was talking to someone really important on her mobile phone. Jane had got used to not cooking and asked them if they'd like a takeaway. She and Simon wanted Chinese but Lara wanted pizza. They decided to let Neil have the final vote, when he got home from work.

Jane hadn't talked to Neil much while she'd been away. She wanted to put some distance between them, not only physically but emotionally as well. Although she'd had no major revelations about her marriage she didn't feel as anxious and was just going to see how it progressed.

Neil looked genuinely pleased to see her. In fact he was gushing. This took Jane a bit by surprise. He might have missed her more than he'd imagined he would. Neil voted for Chinese and they went to the takeaway together, catching up on what had been happening in each others' lives. Well nearly. Jane omitted her meeting with Sarah and the conversation with her mum while Neil conveniently forgot to mention the quick grope he'd had with his assistant in the back of his car.

Neil and Sally had driven to the pub and the flirting had been ongoing all day. He'd occasionally reach over and touch Sally's leg, she'd conveniently lifted her skirt up to show as much thigh as possible. They'd both booked two-hour lunches on the pretext of going to see a client. Neil parked his car in the 'Seven Bells' car park and looked at Sally. He felt so proud to be seen with such a gorgeous woman. 'What would you like to drink?' he asked as they went to the bar.

'A glass of red wine please. I'll go and find us a seat.' Sally chose a secluded cubicle at the back of the pub and sat down. Neil brought the drinks to the table and sat down next to her.

'Do you want to look at the menu?' he asked, passing it to her.

'What do you fancy?' Sally said.

'You mean other than you?' Neil said and winked. Sally laughed and playfully hit his arm.

'I'll have a warm salmon salad if you're ordering. Let me guess, you're a steak man?' Sally looked him deep in the eyes and smiled.

'I am actually, the rarer the better. I'll just go and order. I'll be straight back.' Neil couldn't wait to get back to the flirting and innuendo. He was only a few minutes ordering the food, he slipped into the seat next to Sally and moved up as close as he could. He placed his arm on the back of the booth; his fingers touching her shoulders. She moved in towards him.

'Great idea of yours, coming out to lunch. It's lovely spending time with you outside the office.' Sally turned to look at him, her face only inches away from his.

'I didn't know if you'd accept my invitation.' Neil said.

'I thought you could tell how I felt about you after Friday night. Hopefully I made it obvious.' She put her hand just above his knee.

Neil was feeling increasingly aroused and desperately wanted to kiss her. All his previous thoughts of faithfulness had gone right out of the window and soon there would be no going back.

'I knew you were flirting with me but I didn't know how far you were prepared to go,' he said, gently stroking her fingers.

'All the way, if you like.' She let her lips brush his cheek.

He turned his head and kissed her. In no time at all their tongues were exploring each others' mouths.

'Er, hum.' The waiter was standing by the table with two plates.

They pulled away and Neil had to adjust his erection, much to the amusement of the young man delivering the food. As soon as they'd finished eating Sally whispered to Neil, 'Let's go somewhere quieter. We passed a lane a bit back that looked secluded.'

They held hands as they walked back to the car.

As he drove Neil had his hand on the inside of Sally's thigh and occasionally his finger would touch the material of her pants. She moaned. She had her hand on the outside of Neil's trousers, fondling his ever-increasing erection. Neil drove on automatic pilot to the lane and went to park at the end. Sally had been correct in her appraisal and theirs was the only car there.

They both got out and climbed into the back. They started kissing and fondling one another. Neil opened Sally's blouse exposing her small, pert breasts. He leant over and took her nipple in his mouth. The excitement was everything he'd dreamed of. Sally had her hand inside his trousers and was rubbing it and up and down. He felt he was going to come there and then, but then suddenly they heard another car. Frantically they pulled away from each other and adjusted their clothing.

The car turned out to belong to an elderly couple who had come to admire the birds on the lake. They'd nearly seen a lot more through their binoculars than they'd bargained for. Sally and Neil burst out laughing. They felt like naughty teenagers who'd nearly been sprung by disapproving parents. The elderly couple gave them a dirty look as they walked past their car, off to find birds of the feathered variety.

The mood had been spoilt, so they tidied themselves up and got back into the front. Sally kissed Neil again.

'If you want a repeat performance you only have to say,' she said, and that was how they left it. Neil was convinced that should they have carried on he wouldn't have been able to resist entering her. He could still visualise her neat, dark-blond pubic hair and pert breasts, and he was still turned on thinking about sucking her nipples.

In fact he felt a stirring in his groin just recalling it. He'd actually been unfaithful to Jane. OK, he hadn't done the deed but he knew they would've done had they not been disturbed. What he had to decide now was whether he was going to carry it on. Sally had made it plain that she was up for it and he did fancy having Sally sitting on top of him while he thrust deep within her. That was what he'd fantasised about since Monday, but he'd also felt guilty. What would Jane say if she knew? She'd be devastated. He would make an extra special effort to be nice to her and they could take it one day at a time.

The Chinese was good and they sat and ate it as a family, which was very rare in their household. Neil and Jane smiled across the table, both feeling a contentment that they hadn't felt for a long time. Maybe there was a chance for them after all.

Thursday was the day of Sally's tarot reading evening. Jane hadn't had a chance to see Philip since she'd come back from Cornwall and was missing him deeply. They'd spoken and sent texts but it wasn't the same. She'd hoped they could get together before the party but Jane's diary was full to the brim, making up for the three days away. She was the only valuer in her office so she was kept busy all day with people who needed to sell their homes urgently.

The party was scheduled to start at seven and Jane hoped Philip would still be there when she arrived. She knew he was going to play five-a-side but surely he would wait to see her? He did, and waved to her from the bedroom window as she got out of the car. Jane wasn't the first to arrive. Sally was rushing around frantically getting drinks for her guests and putting onion bhajis and samosas in the oven.

'Hi Jane, come in.' Sally said, quickly opening the door. 'Make yourself at home. Put your coat upstairs in the second bedroom and then come down and help yourself to a drink when you're ready. The toilet is upstairs at the end of the corridor.' Then she dashed off.

Jane looked around. The flat was very spacious and modern. It had clean lines and was minimally furnished. She smiled and was pleased that she'd guessed Philip's taste correctly. It had a mezzanine floor with two bedrooms and a large lounge leading onto a balcony.

Whenever Jane went into any property she always gave it an appraisal as if she was going to sell it, or rent it out. She annoyed herself sometimes because she did it wherever she went. She walked upstairs to put her coat in the second bedroom. Philip was just coming out of the master bedroom and he pulled her into the room with him.

'I've missed you so much,' he said, leaning in to kiss her.

'I've missed you too,' she replied, returning the kiss.

'When are we going to spend some real time together instead of catching a few moments here and there?' Philip asked.

'I promise we'll sort something out. I've got to go to Catterick fairly soon so you could come with me there and maybe we can stay over.'

'What's at Catterick?' he asked.

'It's just a family thing. I'll explain later.' Jane hadn't intended to mention her forthcoming 'reccie' to anyone, but Philip had seemed so desperate and it was a perfect opportunity for them to spend some quality time together.

They carried on kissing and fondling each other. Philip had exposed Jane's breast and was sucking her nipple, but they were really cutting it fine. They had every chance of being discovered, if someone walked into the wrong bedroom or Sally needed something. Both were reluctant to stop but sanity prevailed. They pulled apart and re-arranged their clothing.

'I've got to go out now, the game starts soon. I'll ring you tomorrow. Can we meet for lunch?'

'That should be fine. I don't know what time but we can discuss it when you ring. Enjoy your football.' Jane squeezed his hand.

'Thanks. I'd rather be staying with you. I love you,' he whispered in her ear and kissed her again.

Jane opened the door quietly and sneaked into the second bedroom, where she deposited her coat. She took a quick look in the mirror and went back downstairs. It seemed as though the clairvoyant had arrived. She was being set up in the small dining room next to the kitchen. Jane looked around and felt awkward because she didn't know anyone. Sally came dashing in.

'Sorry people. I'll introduce you all now. Everyone, this is Jane. She is married to Neil, my boss. Jane this is Zoe, Paula, Sue and Martina. Have you got that?' she laughed.

'I have right now but whether I'll remember in a few hours is anyone's guess.' Jane smiled and went to sit down next to the most welcoming of the faces, the girl called Zoe.

'Have you done anything like this before?' Jane asked with an apprehension in her voice which Zoe immediately picked up on.

'Yes I have. Don't worry, you'll be fine. Rosa is really lovely and she'll explain everything to you. What made you come? Do you want to know anything specific?' Zoe asked.

'I came because Sally asked me to make up the numbers. It's not something I would normally do, so I thought what the hell, try something new.' She didn't add that she wanted to see where her lover lived and that she thought she might get to see him.

A petite, slightly-built woman walked into the room. She had short black hair and emerald green eyes and was very striking to look at. She was wearing a smart suit in a deep red which complemented her hair. Jane guessed she was the clairvoyant, though she didn't look at all as she'd imagined. She'd pictured more of a hippy type in a long flowing skirt with permed hair.

'Hello, my name is Rosa. I've already met some of you before.' She glanced around and saw some familiar faces. 'The way I like to work is to begin with people who haven't been to me previously so they're not sitting here feeling anxious.' Rosa looked directly at Jane. 'If it's OK I'd like to start with you'

'I suppose so. I might as well get it over with,' Jane said, with an embarrassed laugh. She followed

Rosa into the dining room. She'd created a lovely, relaxing atmosphere with candles, lamps and soothing music. The curtains were drawn and the lights were dimmed. Jane felt immediately at ease. Rosa signalled to her to sit down on the chair opposite her. She'd laid the table with a deep red-velvet cloth and there was a pack of cards in the middle of it. She handed Jane a card. It said 'Rosa: the Happy Medium.' Jane sniggered and any nerves that she'd been feeling left her immediately.

Rosa looked directly at Jane. 'You've come here at exactly the right time because your life is going to change beyond your wildest dreams and what I tell you tonight will most definitely help you.' She gave Jane the deck of Tarot Cards.

'Please shuffle them and then lay them face down on the table.' Jane did as she was instructed. 'Now, if you'd like to chose eleven cards and hand them to me. Don't think too much about it, just let your hand go to where it feels drawn.' Jane tried to stop herself thinking about which cards to choose and let herself be guided.

'I'm going to lay the cards out in the shape of a Celtic cross. It'll tell you about your past and your future and how you have to act to achieve what you want. There are twenty-one Major Arcana cards in a tarot deck. When they come up they have important messages for you. Are you ready?' Rosa looked at Jane.

Jane felt excited and was looking forward to what this lovely woman had to say. Rosa turned the first card over; it was the six of swords.

'This card tells me that you're in the process of a big change. It's as if you've left one shore and are floating at sea, not quite sure where you'll land. It's a time of indecision for you. You'll be given great challenges and if you can change your mind about things you will change your world.'

The second card that turned over was from the Major Arcana, The Lovers. Jane smiled to herself.

'This card usually signifies a love affair taking place and, for you, I feel it is with someone you've known before.' Rosa studied the card.

Jane's heart sank. This couldn't be true as she'd never met Philip before. Rosa must have got it wrong.

'There is a very deep connection between the two of you but it's not the right time yet as too many people will get hurt. You've some more work to do, to discover your true self, before all the pieces fall into place.' Rosa continued.

Jane felt it was all too cryptic and wished she would just give her some plain and simple advice. The atmosphere in the room suddenly changed and Jane gave a little shiver.

'I have a man here with me,' Rosa said. 'Don't be scared. He is a loving man who wants to know how Madge is doing.'

This stopped Jane in her tracks. Rosa could see with the look on Jane's face that she'd told her something important.

'He's saying he's sorry he left you so young but it was his time. He has been watching you ever since and was very pleased that you finished your exams with everything that was going on.'

Jane knew Rosa was talking about her father. She'd been only fifteen when he'd died suddenly of a heart attack. She'd wanted to leave school, without doing her 'O' levels, because she was grieving so much. Her mother had persuaded Jane to stay on because she'd said it was what her dad would've wanted. He'd always been so proud of her academic achievements and had felt it was really important to make something of herself. She'd listened to the advice and had done very well, considering the circumstances.

'He has a message for your mother. He says to tell her to remarry. She was such a wonderful wife it seems a shame to deprive another man of such love.'

Jane tried to hold back the tears. She'd tried to encourage her mother to remarry over the years but she said she would never find another man who could hold a candle to her father.

Rosa continued. 'He says to tell her not to feel guilty for falling in love and that he's happy for her. He will see her again and then they can be together, but for now she deserves to be happy.' Rosa went quiet for a short time. 'He's gone. Does what he said make any sense to you?' Rosa asked.

'It was my dad,' Jane said, trying to compose herself. This Rosa is good after all, she thought. But she still didn't understand the previous message.

'Don't worry, everything will become clear to you in time. Just go with it and don't try to be in too much of a hurry to sort it all out,' Rosa said, as if she were reading Jane's mind.

Rosa had taped the reading, for which Jane was grateful as the rest of it was a bit of a blur. She told her that her son was worried about what would happen to her when he left and that he was nervous about leaving home. He was also a very troubled soul. Her daughter was a very strong character and Jane had not to be surprised if she went to do something such as voluntary work in Africa for at least a year. Jane laughed at that, as she couldn't imagine Lara in the heart of Tanzania without her hair straighteners and mobile phone. Rosa saw the amusement in Jane's eyes and told her not to underestimate her daughter. 'She isn't as shallow as everyone seems to think.'

The reading seemed to last for hours but when Jane looked at her watch, only half-an-hour had gone by. Rosa picked up the cards and turned off the tape. She handed it to Jane. She held onto her hand.

'You've been blessed with something that not many get an opportunity to experience, and that's a second chance. Use it wisely,' Rosa said, with a knowing expression on her face.

Jane looked baffled but it was obvious that Rosa wasn't going to elaborate.

'Will you ask the next person to come in please?'

Jane had been dismissed. She went to sit back down next to Zoe. 'Was it good?' she asked.

'Yes thanks, I really enjoyed it. I don't understand a lot of it but she told me it would eventually make sense, given time,' Jane said.

'It's quite frustrating when she gives you clues and you've to work the rest out,' Zoe agreed. 'Why can't she just come out and say it?'

'Exactly what I was thinking.' They both laughed.

Jane had enjoyed her evening and realised that she didn't make enough time to socialise with friends. She'd only known Sally when she arrived, but left having found a new friend in Zoe. They exchanged mobile numbers and agreed they would meet for lunch soon.

Chapter 9 - November 1971

Nora had had a good life. Not great or wonderful, but a good one, and now she was coming to the end of it she felt like reflecting over its entirety.

Her biggest achievement had been raising her daughter, Daisy. That would be the saddest part of dying, leaving her beloved daughter without a mother at such a young age. She hoped Daisy would be strong and make a great life for herself. With her mother gone she could concentrate on finding a good man and maybe have some children to share her abundant love with. She'd sacrificed enough of her life and when the cancer had returned two years ago Daisy had wholeheartedly devoted herself to her mother's care.

Nora had known great love but it had been taken from her at the tender age of twenty. She and Daniel had only had a short time together but with him she'd found true love and the union had produced Daisy, for which she'd been eternally grateful. She'd never forgotten Daniel. He'd been in her prayers every night and she'd read the letters he'd written to her at least once a year.

It had been a very sad occasion when Nora had chosen to return her engagement ring and sever all contact with the St.Claire's. She did so to save their family name because, soon after hearing the news of Daniel's death, she found out she was pregnant with his child. She didn't have many regrets in her life but that was one of them.

In hindsight she should have kept in touch but, as time went on, it became too difficult, particularly after she'd met and married Derek. She felt sad that she'd deprived them of ever knowing their granddaughter.

The man she did actually marry was named Derek Ledbury. She'd met him during her voluntary work at the farm in Catterick. He was a friend of the owner and he'd sent out on the grapevine that he was looking for a wife. She married him because he was prepared to take Daisy on and raise her as his own. They'd never had any more children, it just didn't happen. Nora felt he resented her for that fact though it was never proved whose fault it was. But she was never interested in having any tests to find out why she'd never conceived, she was happy with just having Daisy.

The marriage really was one of convenience. Derek wanted a housekeeper and so Nora obliged. She did the cooking, cleaning and all domestic chores whilst Derek earned the money. He was a manager at the local foundry and they had a house in Richmond, which came with his job. He provided well for her and Daisy and she was never short of new clothes or a new gadget for the house, the only thing she was short of was love. Derek saved that for his female factory workers. He'd always had a roving eye and Nora got used to looking the other way when it came to his indiscretions.

She knew she was the talk of the small town of Richmond and she could see the pity in other women's eyes when they saw her shopping. She liked to pretend she was unaffected by his behaviour but deep down it hurt, and when his latest lover found out she was pregnant with Derek's child Nora decided enough was enough. She packed a couple of cases and summoned up the courage to leave him, taking her daughter with her. She rented a small room, sued him for a divorce and with the generous settlement bought a small terraced house in town.

She then had to get work but with her very limited skills and lack of experience it was difficult to find anything that paid a decent wage. She used what little money she had left from the divorce settlement to put herself through secretarial college. She was a natural at shorthand and typing, and finished top of her class. This meant she had the pick of the best jobs and after a few interviews she chose a position as personal assistant to the Managing Director of a glass factory, where she was to remain for the next twenty-two years.

She never married again and devoted her life to bringing up Daisy. Because of the divorce Nora had to be both mother and father, and try to provide all the luxuries Daisy's friends with two parents had. Sometimes this meant working two jobs so for some years she worked part-time at the local Conservative club, behind the bar.

Daisy was a wonderful child, very well behaved and respectful of all people. Luckily Nora still had her mother alive and, even though she was getting on in years, she always looked after Daisy while Nora was at work. When Daisy was old enough she took a paper round to help her mother out but it didn't detract from her studies. She was a very studious girl, passed her eleven plus easily and won a place at the local grammar school.

Nora had been so proud when she had sent Daisy off to school in her brand new uniform, which had cost the earth, and equipped with her writing materials, PE kit, slide rule, dictionaries etc. Her boss, Mr Pullen, had been very understanding at the time and had offered her overtime for extra money. She'd always been convinced that he didn't need the extra hours work and that he was just doing it to help her out. That was the kind of man he was.

Nora was forty-four when she first found the lump in her left breast. She ignored it for a long time but as it increased in size she decided she must go to the doctor's. He rushed her straight into hospital and she had a total mastectomy. She had other tests to see if it had spread but the surgeon seemed to have removed it all. She had radiotherapy, a relatively new treatment, which was supposed to help prevent it recurring.

She had taken six weeks off work, which Mr Pullen had paid her for, and Daisy had taken two weeks leave to help look after her mother immediately after the operation. Daisy had secured a very good job in the local bank. She'd done exceptionally well in her school exams and was destined for a good career in banking. She'd been promoted twice and she already earned more money than her mother.

Eventually Nora recovered and went back to work. Things returned to normal. Then, sadly, Nora's mother died at the ripe old age of eighty-five.

Attending her mother's funeral was one of the hardest things Nora had ever had to do, as she'd been there for her every step of the way, supporting and loving both her and Daisy.

Nora had to go back to the hospital every year for a check up and for the first four years everything was fine. But then she started to feel tired and her back ached. She tried to put it down to getting old and working too hard but deep down she knew the cancer had returned. The breast cancer had moved to her lymph nodes and then spread to her bones. There was little hope of recovery. The doctors gave her about six months to live.

That was two years ago. She'd taken redundancy from work on the grounds of ill health and Mr Pullen made sure she had a good pension. Daisy continued to work at the bank and was now in charge of a department, Loans and Mortgages. Nora kept herself busy trying not to dwell on the prognosis and was as cheerful as she could be considering the increasing pain she was in. She used to go into the local hospice for respite care, and to give Daisy a rest. This was where she found herself now.

Nora knew this time she wouldn't be going home and she was glad. She'd fought the cancer for two long years, trying one experimental drug after another, and she was tired. She knew she couldn't be strong any longer as the pain was just too great to bear. She was constantly on a morphine drip and even that only took the edge off it.

She didn't know whether it was the drugs or her mind hallucinating but she'd started to see figures at the bottom of her bed. She could have sworn she saw her father yesterday. He appeared in the same austere clothing he'd always worn, but he had a smile on his face. She laughed as she thought, obviously it was a hallucination as he'd never had a smile on his face when he was alive!

Nora spent most of her time asleep. She didn't have many visitors. Daisy was at her bedside constantly and Mr and Mrs Pullen went every other day. They'd become her surrogate parents and on their last visit she'd asked them to look after Daisy for her. Mrs Pullen had held her hand and they'd cried together, both aware that this was probably the last time they would see each other. Mr Pullen had leant over, given her a kiss on the forehead and said goodbye.

Nora had lots of acquaintances but very few friends and she preferred it that way. Her family had been her life and she was content with that. She didn't want anyone else to see her like this and would rather they remember her as the vibrant young woman she'd been most of her life.

She couldn't eat solid food anymore and was on a glucose drip. Daisy had reluctantly nipped out to get herself a sandwich. It was important for her to be there when her mother drew her last breath. Nora had joked that she would hold on until after lunch. She opened her eyes to see if Daisy had returned and got the fright of her life when she saw a dozen or more figures hovering at the far side of the room. She blinked to see if they would go away but they didn't. Just at that moment Daisy returned.

'Can you see them darling?' she asked in a faint whisper.

'Ssh mum, don't try to talk.' Daisy went to hold her mother's hand.

'They're all standing by the bed. Tell me you can see them,' Nora pleaded.

Daisy turned to where her mother was looking and all she saw was a thin mist she assumed was smoke coming in through the open window.

'They've come for me. There's mum and dad, and I can see Daniel. He's here, Daniel has come. He must have been waiting for me all these years.' Nora seemed the most lucid she'd been for a few days and had an excited edge to her voice. Her speech was clear and her morphine drugged eyes now seemed fully aware. She looked deep into her daughter's eyes and said, 'I'm going now my darling. Don't cry too much for me. I'm not going far and will only ever be a thought away.' And with that Nora drew her last breath.

Daisy sat and sobbed. It felt as though her life had come to an end with the loss of her mother. She held onto her hand for a while, before going to call the nurses. She'd been the best mother any girl could wish for and she would miss her desperately. She'd hated to see her suffer at the end, but now she could always remember that peaceful face. Daisy felt a draught on the back of her neck and could have sworn something touched her on the shoulder. She got up to close the window.

Her mother looked as if she was sleeping. All the pain had left her face. She was at peace. Hopefully it wasn't the ranting of a dying woman, and it had been the love of her life who had actually come for her. What a wonderful thought! Nora had told Daisy that Daniel, not Derek, was her father as soon as they'd got divorced. She'd felt obligated to keep up the deception while she was married but felt no such loyalty to him afterwards.

Daisy remembered feeling glad that Derek wasn't her father as she felt he'd never really liked her. In fact, he used to make her feel really uncomfortable with the way he used to stare at her, and she was pleased when they'd left him to go and live on their own. She never missed not having a father, her mother had been more than enough parent for anyone. She'd got to know Daniel through her mother talking about him and reading his letters. They'd kept his memory alive through all those years. It seemed a fitting end to the love story that he'd come to get her, to take her to wherever you went to when you died. She promised herself that she would investigate this further, as knowing where her mother had gone might help ease her grief and give her some hope.

She really should go and tell the nurses about her mother, but surely a few more minutes wouldn't do any harm?

Chapter 10

The day Jane had been dreading had finally arrived. She was taking her little boy to university. He wasn't going to be there to chat with when she came home from work or to watch silly television programmes with. She realised that she'd more in common with her son than she had with her own husband. They talked a lot more than her and Neil ever did and spent more time together. What it would be like in the house with him gone was anyone's guess.

This past week she'd seen Philip every day, even if only for a few minutes. He would drive to where she'd parked her car just to give her a kiss before she set off for home. They'd had lunch twice in the week, once in an Italian bistro and then just a quick sandwich in Subway, but they hadn't been able to make love. They were both feeling very frustrated about that and would have to find an opportunity to rectify it soon.

She hadn't really noticed that Neil had been working late, she was too preoccupied with thoughts of Philip. Neil had taken to sleeping in the guest room most nights, as Jane's dream was happening more frequently. Luckily for her it didn't hold the same emotional tie as it had done previously. Each day when she woke up she promised herself that she would try to sort some time out to go and search for Nora. But what with preparing for Simon's imminent departure, and fitting in seeing Philip, she hadn't made it a priority.

She'd had another revelation that week, Lara had come home from college more animated than she'd seen her in a long time. Apparently year thirteen had had a talk in General Studies from a man who worked for VSO, Voluntary Service Overseas. She'd come home with all the application forms, all this from someone who wouldn't even buy a Big Issue because she thought they were sold by homeless scroungers. Jane had never understood where Lara had got her right-wing views from, but she did seem genuinely interested. She had shown Jane and Neil the brochures at the dinner table. Simon had taken the proverbial, so she'd told him to, 'bollocks!' Jane would miss the banter between the siblings. What amazed Jane the most was that in the space of a week one of Rosa's predictions had come true.

There was a meeting coming up at college for the parents of anyone who wished to be considered for VSO and Lara had made Jane put it in her diary. It seemed that she was serious. If this most unlikely of predictions could come true, what else would?

Since the tarot reading Jane had been trying to think of anyone she'd met in her past who could come back into her life and that she would be tempted to have an affair with. It seemed highly unlikely and no-one sprung to mind. She tried to make Philip fit the description by imagining she'd met him at a roller disco or at the local swimming pool when they were children, but she was clutching at straws. They'd been born in the same hospital, if that counted, but she couldn't really say she'd known him at a day old.

She managed to put it out of her mind for most of the time and tried to get on living in the present rather than waiting for the future to happen. The present was getting Simon to Liverpool by early afternoon. Neil's Range Rover was loaded up with boxes, cases, a stereo and a television. He was nearly ready to go. Jane kept wiping tears from her eyes as she watched him empty his room. It was just her and Neil that were taking him. Lara said that she'd other things to do, but deep down inside Jane knew she wouldn't be able to contain the tears saying goodbye to her big brother. They may constantly bicker but they did love each other and because the age difference was so small they were the best of friends.

Simon knocked on the door of Lara's room and walked in. They gave each other a hug. He promised he would text all the time. He looked as though he had a tear in his eye when he finally emerged from the room. He was such a sensitive soul and Jane knew he would miss his family.

Jane gave Simon a hug in the kitchen and shed her tears there, rather than embarrass him in the Halls of Residence in front of his potential friends.

Neil had suggested that once they dropped Simon off and got him settled they should find a room in a hotel and acquaint themselves with Liverpool. Jane wasn't sure this was such a good idea but agreed anyway. They hadn't had much time to talk recently and she'd never followed up on her mother's advice of seeing if their marriage would work.

Simon joined the queue to register and collect his keys. With Neil's driving the journey had only taken just over an hour and it was one-thirty as they pulled up outside the Halls, on the outskirts of the city. It was a large campus comprising of individual blocks circling a large grassed area. While Simon was at reception Jane and Neil sat in the car. She was unusually quiet. Neil took hold of her hand. He still loved her despite everything that had been going on.

Neil had been determined not to carry on seeing Sally, but working so close to her made that almost impossible, particularly when she had made it so blatant that she wanted the affair to continue.

He'd avoided any social contact with Sally for nearly a week, choosing to bring sandwiches from home for lunch. He ate them while he was still working, rather than risk bumping into Sally in the staff room. He also knew the company policy, which he'd helped set up, which stated that any relationship between staff had to be declared. Then each case would be assessed on its merits to see if it would be allowed to continue without one of the parties having to leave. He knew that if anyone found out about him and Sally it would be her that would lose her job.

That aside, when Sally had come into his office at six o'clock Friday evening all his good intentions had gone out of the window. She was wearing a figure-hugging, pale pink cashmere jumper with a tight-fitting, black, pencil skirt and high, black stilettos. She looked stunning and very sexy. He had a thing about stiletto heels and wished Jane would wear them, but she said they gave her backache. She was always so practical and no fun.

He recalled their conversation. 'I thought everyone had gone,' Neil had said, surprised to see her.

'There's only me left; I thought you couldn't ignore me if there were just the two of us. You've hardly spoken two words to me since Monday. If you felt guilty about our time together you should have just said. I can take a hint. But I've missed our little chats I wanted to tell you about my tarot evening.' Sally looked hurt.

'Sorry. I've been trying to come to terms with cheating on my wife. We've been married for more than eighteen years and I owe her some loyalty surely?' Neil was looking for approval from Sally, who felt suitably admonished.

'I'm sorry too. I've only been thinking about myself. I wasn't looking at it from your perspective. I realise you've a lot more to lose than I have. I've just got a boyfriend of ten years who refuses to commit,' she said, shamefaced.

'You'd lose your job if we were found out,' Neil added.

'I think you're worth taking the risk for.'

He looked at her longingly and beckoned her to come closer. She walked toward him and sat on his desk. She bent down to kiss him, very tentatively at first but then with a passion that reminded him how it had felt on Monday, in the back of the car. He slid his hand between her legs and felt how moist she already was. His fingers slid inside her and she moaned for him to continue. She undid his trousers, released him from his pants, and sat astride him. He slowly entered her. It was heaven. He could feel her tightly round him as he held her buttocks and thrust up and down.

They both came together and Sally shrieked as she had her most intense orgasm ever. Neil was spent and all previous thoughts of Jane vanished as he was exactly where he wanted to be. They carried on kissing. Neil walked over to lock his door and pull his blinds down. He then slowly undressed them both and they made love again, much slower and more carefully this time. Each making sure the other got the maximum amount of pleasure. It was seven-thirty when he looked at his watch. They'd made love three times in an hour-and-a -half. Neil joked that it wasn't bad for a man of his age. Sally asked him if he wanted to go again.

Reluctantly they got dressed and Neil realised he would have some explaining to do when he got home. Sally would be fine as Philip was playing football.

That had all happened over a week ago and there had been numerous fondling sessions and sneaky kisses since. It was the fact that they could be caught that turned them both on so much. They would send each other texts asking what they were thinking. Neil once told her that he'd got his erection out under the desk and was playing with himself and would she like to finish him off. She went into his office, the blinds had still remained drawn from the other night, and brought him to a climax while he was sitting in his chair.

Luckily for him, Jane hadn't seemed suspicious and had seemed distracted herself. They'd just kept out of each other's way as much as possible. This weekend had been his idea and thought he would give it one last attempt at saving his marriage. He was besotted with Sally and got hard every time he thought of her but he needed more than lust. He and Jane had never had the passionate sex that he had with Sally but they did have friendship. Sex was great but you had to have more. The last time he'd had sex with Sally was yesterday. It was up against the wall in the mens' toilet. They were taking more risks and it was only a matter of time before they were discovered. He wanted to give his marriage one last shot before he was forced into making a choice.

Sitting, holding onto his wife's hand, Neil knew he'd made a good decision spending some time with her. She was deeply affected by Simon's departure. In fact he'd always been jealous of the relationship Jane had with their son. A relationship he would've loved to have emulated with Simon. He'd dreamed of going to football matches together or going running but sadly Simon hadn't shared his love of sport and would rather sit and talk to his mother for hours on end. He was envious of their closeness.

Simon was sharing a room with another student and as he was the first to arrive he chose the side of the room which had the best views over the grassy courtyard. He started unpacking the boxes with his mother's help. In no time at all he had everything exactly as he wanted it; books on shelves, clothes in drawers and shirts in the wardrobe. He positioned his television and stereo and sat down on the bed Jane had just made for him, surveying the room that would be his home for the next academic year.

Neil slipped Simon a few twenty pound notes, gave him a man hug and walked down the corridor back to his car. Jane followed, trying to fight the tears. He promised he would ring and they could text and she was not to worry, he would be fine. As he saw his parents get into their car he smiled to himself, his new life had begun.

Neil parked outside the tourist information and went in to try and find them a hotel. Amazingly enough there was a vacant double room at the Adelphi, the famous four-star hotel that had been the subject of a television documentary. It had been totally refurbished in recent years and their room was luxurious. They both felt awkward as they looked around. It was as though they were strangers staying together for the first time, and not a married couple who'd been together every night for the past eighteen years.

It had been advertised as a double room but it more resembled a suite. The bed looked as though it was super king-sized and there were two large sofas at the other end of the room. Jane appreciated the sheer decadence of the accommodation and however it panned out with Neil she was going to make the most of her night of absolute luxury.

Sally had been upset when Neil had told her of his plans to go away with Jane and had tried to persuade him not to stay overnight. She was worried he would make a go of it with his wife, leaving her out in the cold. She'd given up trying to persuade Philip to buy a house and was trying to find a way of splitting up with him without hurting his feelings. Her main problem was that she didn't want to be on her own. She'd been a part of a couple ever since she was seventeen. She was frightened of giving Philip up if Neil didn't want her and couldn't risk Neil falling back in love with his wife during a romantic weekend away. She'd sulked but it had made no difference, Neil had already made up his mind.

Neil had suggested going out for a meal to an expensive restaurant but the menu at the Adelphi looked so delicious they decided to eat in the hotel restaurant. He ordered a bottle of Bollinger on ice, which was delivered to their room. Jane was taking advantage of the spacious whirlpool bath so Neil poured her a drink and took it to her. She smiled. 'What have I done to deserve this?' taking the champagne from him. She sipped the cold bubbly and slid down further into the luxury of her hot bath.

'I know it's been a traumatic day for you and if a man can't treat his own wife what is the world coming to? Mind if I join you?' Neil asked, already starting to undress. Jane found that she didn't mind and realised that it had been a long time since she'd seen him naked. When they'd been sharing a room she'd usually been asleep when he came to bed, and recently he'd slept in the guest room.

She still admired his body with his broad athletic build and long muscular legs. He had a thin covering of blond hair on his chest and his pubic hair had a faint ginger tinge to it. She found herself comparing him to Philip, who in stark contrast was thin and dark haired with a lot more hair evenly dispersed over his chest, legs and arms.

Neil stepped into the large tub. He sat down behind Jane and started to fondle her breasts while nuzzling her neck. He'd never been one for long foreplay but she did find herself being turned on even though her mind kept wandering back to Philip and how aroused she'd been when he'd taken her in the beer garden.

Concentrate, she told herself, and turned to kiss him. Neil was very aroused by now and asked her to turn round and sit on him. It was his favourite position and water splashed everywhere as he speeded up to his climax. When he had finished he lay back in the bath taking up most of the room.

Neil reflected on what love-making was like with Sally and realised that there was absolutely no comparison with what had just happened with Jane. He loved his wife but he didn't fancy her anymore. Whilst he'd been thrusting in and out it was Sally's face he'd imagined, not his wife's.

Jane climbed out of the bath, leaving Neil to it, and put on the complementary fluffy bathrobe. She too was feeling a little deflated and had hoped that after so long without making love it would be far more satisfying than it had been. Philip had made her knees go weak after only kissing her but sadly Neil hadn't had the same effect.

She tried to recall if he'd ever had that effect on her and couldn't really remember a time when he had. She switched on the flat screen television for some distraction and poured herself another glass of champagne. If she was going to get through tonight she could at least be a little tipsy; champagne always went to her head.

Jane had packed the most expensive little black dress she had ever owned and was glad she had. Prada wouldn't look out of place in the Adelphi. She had teamed it with her Jimmy Choo stilettos and Louis Vuitton clutch bag. She was in designer heaven as she joined Neil in the bar. He hadn't taken as long to get ready as he usually did and had gone ahead to order drinks. Also he wanted to ring Sally, away from Jane's beady eyes.

The hotel dining room was beautifully decorated with immense chandeliers dangling just above their heads. They were shown to a table in the middle of the large room. A pianist was playing love songs in the background creating a most romantic ambience. Jane wished that it was Philip she was sitting down with. The atmosphere wouldn't be wasted on the lovers.

They both chose deep fried prawns with a sweet chilli dip to start. The soup course was pumpkin and sweet potato. Jane opted for sea bass on a bed of teriyaki noodles and Neil had his usual choice, a rib eye steak, rare. He didn't have a sweet tooth so ordered cheese and biscuits for dessert, but Jane had her favourite, white chocolate crème brulee. They shared a bottle of red wine after they'd polished off the rest of the champagne. Neil ordered a brandy to finish and Jane ordered a Baileys on the rocks. The conversation flowed freely, mainly due to the large quantity of alcohol consumed. They reminisced about old times with the children and shared memories. It was the only thing they seemed to have in common.

Jane kept letting her mind wander to Philip, what he would be doing and the conversations they could be having. She realised they were never short of things to talk or laugh about. Neil suggested another drink in the bar but Jane started to yawn and hinted that she'd like to go back to the room. They retired to bed at just before midnight; shared a quick good night kiss and rolled over and went to sleep.

Breakfast was a quiet affair. Neil read the Daily Telegraph and Jane pinched the supplement to flick through. They set off for home at ten o'clock. Neil had the radio on the whole time and Jane heaved a sigh of relief when she let herself in through the front door of her house, just over an hour later. The next overnight trip, she promised herself, would be with Philip and hopefully would be more successful than this one had been.

Chapter 11

It was now November and fast approaching Jane and Philip's birthday. Since the fateful trip to Liverpool Jane and Neil hadn't attempted to go out together again. She'd seen Philip regularly over the past months and they'd managed a couple of quickies in the car but it wasn't fulfilling for either of them. They wanted to share long love-making sessions in the comfort of a bed, rather than a quick grope in her uncomfortable back seat.

November was a quiet month in estate agency as people were thinking about buying Christmas presents rather than houses. She booked Monday 16th November off work and had decided that she and Philip would go up to Catterick and spend a long weekend together.

Jane was trying to work out what to tell Neil about her imminent weekend away and how to explain to Philip about her being in Catterick. She could really do with enlisting her mother's help in the deception but she wasn't sure she would go along with it. Her mother prided herself on her honesty and integrity. She planned to tell Neil that she was going on a trip with her mother to see an aunt who they'd lost touch with years ago. She wanted to tell Philip a similar story, the only difference was that she was working on behalf of her mother to try and find an aunt that Madge hadn't seen for years. Both excuses were plausible, they just needed Madge to collude. Jane was getting tired of lying and hopefully sometime during the trip she could tell Philip the truth.

Jane hadn't seen her mother more than once since the Cornwall trip as all Madge's courses had started again. She could hardly fit Jane in between water colour painting, yoga for the over sixties and Spanish for beginners. She'd also started a new course which would fit in nicely with Jane's excuse, Genealogy. She decided she would call on her mother on her way home from work. Madge was usually in around tea time.

She could always come clean and tell her mother the truth about the dream but she was so reluctant to talk about it. She also wanted to explain in more detail about what the clairvoyant had said. The tape that Rosa had made for her had been in her bag since the reading and she wanted to play it for her mother. Jane phoned her just as she was leaving work to see if she was in and, as luck would have it, she was. Jane even secured an invitation to tea.

She knocked on the door of the 1960's chalet - style detached house and walked straight in. It was the house her parents had lived in since they'd got married. It was too big for Madge, but she was reluctant to move and leave the memories of her wonderful marriage behind. Madge was in the kitchen preparing tea. It would be meat and two veg, or a pie, as she'd never got into all this 'new fangled food' as she called it. She would never eat pasta or rice. The house was in desperate need of updating and the kitchen units were the original pine wood. Jane cringed every time she went in as though she were letting her profession down by allowing her mother to live in a house that was so old fashioned.

'Hello love. You look a bit off colour, is everything alright?' Madge was never one to beat about the bush and always said exactly what she was thinking, often catching her unsuspecting audience by surprise and rendering them speechless.

'Yes mum, everything's fine,' Jane lied.

'I don't believe you but you can tell me over tea. I've got some beer or some wine if you'd like.'

Jane looked a little suspicious as her mother never usually kept any alcohol in the house, except sherry at Christmas.

'Which is it to be?' Madge asked, going to the fridge.

'I'll have a beer with a drop of lemonade if you have it,' Jane answered.

'Good choice, seeing as you're driving.' Madge happily poured out the beer into a tall glass Jane had never seen before.

She thought her mother's behaviour was a little odd and she hoped she wasn't starting with dementia or anything as Madge would be sixty-five next birthday.

'I'm glad you've popped round, there's something I've been meaning to discuss with you.' Madge looked a bit sheepish.

'There's something I want to talk to you about. Who's going to go first?' Jane asked.

'Let's eat first, news always sounds better on a full stomach.' Madge poured herself a large glass of white wine. Jane looked a little worried now and hoped her mother wasn't going to confess to having some incurable disease.

'While we're waiting for tea to be ready I can play the tape for you that the clairvoyant made.' Jane had briefly mentioned the tarot reading and her mother had been fascinated to hear what Rosa had said about her beloved husband.

'That's a good idea.' Madge visibly let out a sigh of relief as she realised she wouldn't have to tell Jane her news just yet.

Jane started the tape and realised she'd forgotten a lot of what Rosa had said to her. Madge was obviously moved as Rosa talked about her husband and how he wanted her to be happy. She was also intrigued by the Lovers card that Jane had turned over. Jane was hoping that it would make it easier to ask Madge her big question.

The oven pinged, signalling that the casserole Madge had cooked was ready. She served the food out and called Jane into the dining room.

'What *is* going on mum? You never eat in here and you never drink.' Jane was definitely worried by now.

'Sit down and I'll tell you.' Jane looked anxious. 'Don't look like that, it's nothing to worry about. I've met someone. He's in my water-colour class and we have joined the genealogy class together. His name is George, he's a widower and he's sixty-two.' Madge spat the words out, without drawing breath.

'Whoa, slow down mum.' Jane looked shocked. In all these years her mum had never sat her down and told her that she was seeing someone. If Madge had a date it just used to pop into the conversation. This must be serious.

'Tell me more.' Jane was intrigued.

'He joined the class in October and because I knew the ropes the teacher asked him to sit next to me. We just hit it off. He has the same interests as me and when he told me that he wanted to research his family tree I offered to go with him. We've seen quite a lot of each other and I met his daughter last week. I realised I hadn't told you yet, so here I am confessing all. You're not cross are you?' Madge looked at Jane for reassurance.

'Of course I'm not cross. A little surprised but that's all. Don't you think it's a coincidence that Rosa mentions you being happy and finding someone else at the very same time that you do?' Jane was starting to believe there was something to this clairvoyance.

'Apparently those on the other side know everything we do and try to communicate with us in any way they can. It just so happened that you were having a reading and your dad must have thought he would come and take the opportunity to talk to you,' Madge said knowingly.

'How come you know so much about the other side?'

'I do read you know and when I lost your father I found comfort in all sorts of books, some about spirituality and reincarnation. I wanted to know he'd gone somewhere and wasn't just lying in the ground. I frequently visit his grave to stand and talk to him. I've often felt his presence around me, both at his grave and in this house.'

Madge was full of surprises tonight. 'Why didn't you tell me any of this before?'

'Because I believe everyone should come to it when they're ready, and not be forced to listen to someone else try and convince them.'

'You never fail to surprise me, mum. When can I meet George then? I need to check to see if he is suitable material for my mother,' Jane said jokingly.

'Soon, just let me get used to having him in my life. It's been a bit of a culture shock having to take another person into account when I've been able to please myself for so many years. He's already turned me to drink,' Madge said, taking a long swig of white wine. 'Anyway that's my news, what's yours?' Madge was relieved to be out of the spotlight and felt happier, taking the more comfortable role of listener and advisor.

'Two things,' Jane started. 'I've been meaning to tell you something for ages but I thought you might think I was going mad. However after your little revelation I shouldn't have bothered.' Jane proceeded to tell Madge all about her dream, from when it had started to the present. 'I'm sorry I lied to you in Cornwall. I went to see Sarah St.Claire. She's Daniel's sister. I wanted so much to tell you then, but I didn't know your beliefs and it's such an unbelievable story.' Jane looked very apologetic.

'I'm only sorry that you felt you couldn't tell me. I thought I'd always given the impression that I was open-minded. I think it's a fascinating story and I'd like to help. I can study the family tree in my genealogy class, if you don't mind that is?' Madge looked really fired up by the idea.

'That would be great, and it leads me on to the second thing.' Jane paused. 'I want to go to Catterick and see if I can find anything out about Nora, but there's just one thing; I want to take Philip. I know you don't condone affairs and I wouldn't ask if I wasn't desperate. I'm still seeing him but we never spend any time together. I've really tried with Neil but I don't think it's going to work. I want to spend some time with Philip and see if it still feels right.' Jane knew she was pleading.

'How does that concern me?' Madge asked, dreading the reply.

'I want to tell Neil I'm going away with you for the weekend to see an old aunt we've lost touch with. He shows so little interest in me now he won't even question it. Please mum,' Jane begged.

'You know I don't like deceit and if Neil asks me outright where you are, I'll not lie. But I suppose you can tell him you're with me. I never see the man anyway. I think the last time I set eyes on him was Christmas.' Madge still looked disapproving, but inside she was smiling. She didn't want Jane to think she openly approved but, if it would give her daughter some much deserved happiness, then she would play along with it.

'I also want you to meet Philip. I know you'll like him.' Jane was beaming.

'Let's take it one step at a time. You always want to rush into things. Everything has its place and time,' Madge said wisely.

'Since when did you get so profound?'

'I've always been like it, you've just never noticed.'

Jane went over to kiss her mother. They finished their meal in relative quiet, each pondering the others' news.

'Well it's been an evening for disclosure hasn't it?' Madge said. 'And now I'm going to ask you to leave. I've got to get ready and George is picking me up in half-an-hour,' Madge glanced at her watch, 'and the thought of you two bumping into each other without me being prepared makes my blood pressure soar sky high.' She laughed.

Jane took the not so subtle hint, collected her things, and went outside still reeling from her mother's revelations.

Chapter 12

Philip had told Sally that he was going away on a project from work. Not that she seemed to care anymore. She'd gone from a woman possessed, whose only aim in life was to own a house and get married, to a carefree, independent workaholic. He didn't know which one he preferred. She didn't get home until after seven every night and hardly spoke to him then, choosing to spend her evenings on the computer. It definitely made a pleasant change from all the nagging. If he had a suspicious nature he would have sworn she was having an affair.

Neil bought the story about tracing the old aunt and even wished her luck in finding her. As she went to pick Philip up from their designated meeting place she breathed a sigh of relief, a whole weekend without the awful atmosphere at home. Neil had become very bolshie recently, picking fault in everything she or Lara did. He'd never been a strict parent and it was usually Jane who had disciplined the children, but she now found herself defending Lara and telling Neil to cut her some slack. He blamed work but Jane believed there was more to it than that. When she came back from this weekend she would have it out with him.

She smiled to herself, a whole forty-eight hours of Philip to herself. This would be the longest time they'd spent together. She was looking forward to leisurely walks and loads of sex. Philip had surprised her by booking his colleague's holiday lodge just outside Richmond for the weekend. It was apparently a romantic hideaway in the woods, miles from any other signs of life. Just perfect for what she had in mind.

Philip was leaving his car at home as she was picking him up outside the front entrance to the park, near his house. She had thought it a strange rendezvous point but as she spotted Philip she saw the reason why. He was standing there with his holdall by his side and a lead in his other hand. Attached to the lead was the cutest Springer spaniel puppy she'd ever seen. She parked the car and went to cuddle the liver-and-white ball of fun, not even stopping to say hello to Philip.

'Hello to you too,' Philip said laughing. 'Let me introduce Toby. I hope you don't mind it was a condition of our renting the lodge. Steve had arranged to go there himself this weekend. But I begged and pleaded and he said the only way we could have it was to take Toby with us, so he could take his wife to Paris instead.'

'Mind? No way. I love dogs and it'll be a pleasure to have him.' Toby had already jumped onto Jane's knees and was happily licking her face.

'I've always wanted a dog and I love borrowing other peoples'. How old is he?' Jane asked, stroking his soft fur.

'Steve said he's seven months and we've to take really good care of him. It's the first time they've ever left him. He's the baby they never had.'

'Who's a lovely little baby then? Are you coming on holiday with Uncle Philip and Auntie Jane?' She spoke to him in a voice that she usually reserved for babies or small children. He gave her an extra special lick.

'Where will he sit? My car isn't exactly designed for dogs,' Jane asked, looking at her beloved Audi TT and visualising muddy paws all over her back seat.

'Steve sent his blanket and his seat belt so we can fasten him in the back. We can always buy one of those waterproof seat covers if we need to.'

'Let's get him buckled up then.' Jane opened the door, pulled the seat forward and Toby jumped in. He looked very comfortable lounging on the back seat, sitting on his blanket. The journey was scheduled to take about an hour-and a-half. They stopped after an hour at a service station for Toby to relieve himself and for them to have a coffee. Steve had given Philip good directions and they pulled up outside the lodge exactly at the time they'd planned.

It was a Norwegian pine chalet with a balcony across the front of the property. It could have been transported from the fjords and looked so cosy and inviting. Philip had the key and opened the door. There was an open fire with logs all ready to be lit and someone had deposited a hamper of food on the dining table. There was a note inside the hamper, 'Thanks for having Toby for us, I hope he's not too much trouble. Steve and Paula x x.'

'How sweet of them, and look at all this lovely food!'

Jane's mouth was watering as she saw the French Cheese and bread, a bottle of wine, bacon, eggs, mushrooms and two sirloin steaks. They would only need to go a local shop and they would be sorted for meals. Toby was chomping at the bit to be let off his lead.

'What if he doesn't come back?' Philip said, worried that he would have to go home without Steve's beloved pet.

'He will come back if we go for a walk with him. Let's just get changed and take him,' Jane said enthusiastically.

'I can see this dog is going to get more attention than me this weekend.' Philip tried his sulky face.

'Come here you,' Jane said and both Toby and Philip walked toward her. She looked down at Toby. 'You've had yours. It's Uncle Philip's turn.' She wrapped her arms round him and gave him a long passionate kiss.

'That's OK for starters I suppose.' Philip was still pretending to sulk. Jane playfully hit him and Toby joined in the play fight, jumping up and down and barking.

'I've got a rival for your affection,' Philip said as he bent to stroke Toby.

'And he's so much better looking.'

It was a beautiful autumnal day. There were still a few burnished orange leaves on the trees. The temperature felt quite crisp and there was a clear, deep blue sky. They hadn't seen any rain so far in November and the ground underfoot was dry and springy. After putting on their walking boots and fleeces the two of them, plus Toby, ventured into the woods to explore.

Philip took Jane's hand as they walked. They'd let Toby off the lead and he scampered about in the crunchy leaves in front of them. He was really enjoying playing, finding the slightest thing fun. Jane thought that humans could really learn a lot from the canine world, discovering pleasure in the most simplest of things. It was so lovely being together without having to look over their shoulders all the time. They walked and talked and laughed, thoroughly enjoying each others' company. Sometimes they didn't speak and wallowed in the silence of their surroundings. It was comfortable and neither of them felt inclined to fill the gap. It was twilight when they got back to the lodge. Toby just flopped down in a heap on the rug and was snoring within thirty seconds.

'How about we take advantage of the peace and quiet and go to bed ourselves?' Philip asked, kissing Jane's neck.

'Only if you promise not to snore.'

'Sleep wasn't what I had in mind.' He took hold of her hand and led her to the bedroom. They both took one look at the four-poster bed, which was so inviting, and went to lie down. Philip leaned across to kiss Jane. It was a very tender kiss, not like the frantic ones of late that had been hurried in case they were caught. They both took their time and undressed each other. Philip admired Jane's curves. 'You're so beautiful,' he said as he bent down to kiss her breasts.

Jane ran her fingers tenderly across his naked skin. Philip moaned with pleasure. 'A bit harder,' he said.

She gently applied more pressure with her nails down his back,

'That's perfect; you can do that all day.'

He groaned. She was having the desired effect of arousing him and she could see him harden. She loved turning him on. He traced the outline of her body with his finger and she shivered with delight at his touch. He kept teasing her by running it up the inside of her thigh, lightly touching her pubic hair, parting her lips and then moving away again. When she could stand it no longer he knew she was ready for him. He gently guided himself inside her. It felt very different to their last, hurried session. He wanted to make it last as long as he could, enjoying the incredible feeling of her around him.

The intensity of Jane's orgasms when she made love with Philip amazed her. She felt the trembling from her head to her feet and it lasted for what seemed like minutes. She never wanted the feeling to end.

'I love you Jane.' He had waited to tell her until after their love making so she knew he really meant it. He'd said it many times to her but she'd never felt like she could reply until today.

'I love you too.' She started to cry.

'Whatever is the matter? That was the last reaction I'd hoped for.' He wiped away a tear.

'I'm sorry. It's just that I'm so happy. I've been waiting to feel like this all my life and now that I do I feel a bit overwhelmed,' Jane sobbed.

Just then Jane felt a little wet nose on her toe. Toby had woken up and wondered why he was being left out. Against her better judgement she let him jump up onto the bed and he snuggled down between them. Jane stroked his soft fur and he fell back to sleep with a contended sigh.

It was seven o'clock when Jane woke up. She must have drifted off to sleep after making love. She looked at the other side of the bed and it was empty, Philip and Toby were gone. The bedroom was dark but she could see a light in the living room. She threw on her clothes and went to find Philip. The room was glowing with candle light. He'd laid the table and was just pouring the wine.

'Hello sleepyhead. I was just coming to wake you, dinner is ready.' Philip handed her a glass of wine.

'You do spoil me,' Jane said, sipping the wine. 'What's for dinner? I'm starving.'

'For starters I've heated the brie and camembert cheese with the warm French bread. For main course there is steak with a mushroom omelette. I found some ingredients in the cupboard, and there's fruit for dessert. How does that sound?'

'Like I've died and gone to heaven. Not only does it sound delicious, I didn't make any of it, which is even better.' Jane went to sit at the table. Everything looked so perfect. He'd also taken the trouble to light the fire and it was crackling away in the hearth. The meal was every bit as delicious as it sounded.

'You kept your culinary skills a secret didn't you? Where did you learn to cook like that?' Jane asked, finishing her last mouthful of tender sirloin.

'My mum showed me a lot of it as I was growing up. My dad was so useless she didn't want to inflict any son of hers on a woman if he wasn't adequately house trained,' Philip replied.

'Well she certainly did a good job. You can inflict yourself on me any day,' Jane teased.

'I intend to later, I'll just let my dinner settle. By the way, Toby also enjoyed my cooking. I found a couple of frozen sausages in the freezer. I heated them and he ate them with his dog biscuits.' He bent down to stroke Toby who was sitting as his feet.

'No wonder he's ignoring me if he gets spoilt like that,' Jane laughed.

Philip topped up the wine and they adjourned to the large, comfortable sofa. It was so deep Jane's feet didn't touch the floor, so she tucked them underneath herself and cuddled up to Philip. Toby went to lie in front of the fire. There was no television, which suited them both. Jane thought back to her last weekend away with Neil. The contrast was striking. There was no lull in conversation tonight and they found so much to laugh about.

Jane drained the bottle of wine into their glasses. 'Well that's gone. What are we going to drink now?'

'Hold that thought.' Philip sneaked into the bedroom and went to fetch the bottle of brandy he'd hidden in his overnight bag.

'Good thinking, I'll get the glasses.' Jane looked in the cupboard to see if she could locate something other than the wine glasses they'd been using. Steve was obviously a brandy drinker as she found two brandy glasses at the back. Philip poured them each a generous measure.

'I've got some CDs in the car, I'll just go and get them,' Jane offered. She came back in with a black case full to the brim of every type of music you could think of.

'Any requests?' she asked, opening the case.

'Surprise me,' Philip said.

Jane looked through her case and laughed. Philip joined in as he heard 'Don't You Want me Baby?' coming through the speakers.

'That takes me back. Who is it now? Don't tell me.' After a few seconds, 'The Human League,' Philip said triumphantly.

'Well remembered.' They continued to play 'guess the 80's songs' for a while longer. Jane would choose a song and give Philip thirty seconds to guess it. He was very good.

'Just shows what a sad loser I am,' he said as they finished the last of her 80's CDs.

'I don't think you're a sad loser. I think you're gorgeous.' She leant over and gave him a loving kiss.

They only intended to have the one brandy but they were enjoying each others' company so much that before long half the bottle had gone. It was after one when Jane started to yawn. Philip took Jane by the hand and led her to the bedroom; a perfect end to a perfect day.

Chapter 13

Jane slept soundly and woke naturally, without the alarm, at eight. They'd made love again into the early hours and Philip was still sound asleep. She sneaked quietly out of bed and went to let Toby out, who was sitting patiently by the door. The air was still cool and she went to fetch her coat before going to sit on the balcony with a mug of steaming hot tea. She intended to go into Catterick village and wander round to get a feel for the place. She would look in the churchyard to see if Nora was buried there and then look around to find any houses that resembled the one in her dream.

She hadn't had a clear view of the outside of the house, but she could remember seeing the long, pebbled drive when the woman in her dream had opened the door to take the letters from the postman. Maybe she would recognise it as she walked past. Also village shops were always a good place to hear about gossip so maybe she could ask there.

Jane returned the favour from last night and made Philip bacon and eggs. As they were cooking she went to wake him. He looked really sexy as he hadn't shaved and still had stubble on his chin. She bent over and kissed him.

'Leave the designer stubble. I love it.' Jane stroked his face.

'Stop it, otherwise we'll never get anywhere. It's today I'm being Sherlock Holmes isn't it? Have we a plan?' He playfully pushed her away.

'Yes, we're starting in Catterick village and looking for a lady called Nora. I don't know her surname, so it should be really easy!' she joked

'Needle in a haystack seems to spring to mind.'

Toby was excited to be going out again, although it wouldn't be nearly as much fun for him as he'd have to be on his lead when they walked through the village.

They slowly negotiated the pot holes of the lane, Jane wishing she'd got Neil's Range Rover rather than her low sports car. She could see why everyone drove 4x4's in the country. She passed through the streets of Richmond on her way back to the A1 and Catterick. Little did she know she'd actually driven past the very house where Nora had lived most of her adult life, knowing that would have saved her so much time.

They parked outside the small churchyard and went to examine the headstones. Toby stayed in the car as Jane didn't want to risk the wrath of the villagers by having him cock his leg up on a grave or two. They went through the graves systematically but found no mention of any Nora. Jane realised a Christian name wasn't much to go on.

Next they wandered along the streets to see if she recognised the house. But she was looking for it from a completely different perspective. No luck there either. The village had a post office and she was just about to go in when she saw an old man across the road. He looked at least seventy so he may have heard of Nora. It was worth a try. She walked over to him.

'I'm really sorry to bother you but I'm trying to track down a lady by the name of Nora, she would be well into her eighties by now. Does that name ring a bell with you?'

'Nora? Let me see, my memory isn't as good as it was.' The old man pondered. 'I think a Nora used to help out on my old man's farm when I was little. It's a long time ago mind, my dad's been dead these twenty years.' Jane could almost see the cogs whirring.

'Do you remember anything about her?' Jane crossed everything there was to cross.

'She lived over there,' he pointed to a big old house next to the village green, 'but there's no-one from around here living in it now.' He paused to think. Jane looked to see if it rang any bells with her.

'I seem to remember her crying one day and she didn't come into work for a few days. I think her sweetheart got killed in the war.' He was obviously trawling his memory banks.

This is what Jane had been waiting to hear. Philip stood patiently, not understanding any of it. But as he looked across to the house that the old man had pointed at he got a strong feeling of déjà vu.

'Do you remember what happened to her then?' Jane asked, hoping the old man could recall some more details.

'I'm sorry love, I didn't pay much gorm. I was only a bairn at the time and not interested in all that adult talk. I know who might remember. Nora had a friend called Barbara who's never left the village. She must be ninety by now, but you might catch her on one of her good days. She lives with her daughter down Mill Lane. Turn left there,' he pointed to the street on the left, 'then go right to the end, it's the last house on the right. Sorry I couldn't be more help. I hope you find what you're looking for.'

'No, you've been fabulous and really helpful. Thank you so much for taking the time to talk to me.' Jane shook his hand. The old man shuffled off.

'Where are we going next?' Philip asked.

'I want to go and see if Barbara will talk to me. Are you coming?'

'No, I won't if you don't mind. I'll take Toby for a bit of a walk. Ring me when you've finished.' He gave her a kiss and watched her walk off in the direction of Mill Lane. Philip actually wanted to go and look at the house that had given him his déjà vu. He'd never been to Catterick before so it must remind him of a house elsewhere.

Jane found Barbara's house easily. That's the beauty of a small village, she thought, everywhere was easy to get to and everyone knew everybody else. It was very much the same where she lived in Woolley. She knocked on the door and waited. She was just about to walk away disappointed because she thought no-one was in, when a petite, grey haired lady opened the door.

'Sorry about that, I was just giving mother her elevenses. How can I help?' she asked.

'I was told that I might find a Barbara living here, is that your mother?' Jane asked.

'It is. Can I ask why you're looking for her? You do know she is over ninety?' the lady asked suspiciously.

'So I understand. I came to the village looking for a lady called Nora and I met this old man, who said that Nora and your mother used to be friends.' Jane explained.

With that piece of information the lady signalled Jane to come inside.

'Sorry about that but you can't be too careful nowadays,' the lady said, leading the way.

Jane followed her into the room and saw a frail old woman sitting propped up in a high back arm chair.

'This is my mother, Barbara, and my name is Sylvia.'

'My name is Jane, pleased to meet you.' She held out her hand and Sylvia shook it.

'Mother, you've got a visitor.' Sylvia bent down and shouted in her mother's ear. Jane thought if she wasn't deaf before she would be now.

'Me, a visitor? I don't know anyone. They're all dead,' Barbara said grumpily.

'She's come to ask you about Nora,' Sylvia shouted.

'She's been dead years,' she added. Obviously subtlety wasn't Barbara's strong point, thought Jane.

'Sorry about my mother,' Sylvia apologised. 'As you heard she doesn't get many visitors. I can probably help. I knew Nora. What do you want to know?' she asked, hoping to share the gossip.

Jane didn't know where to start with Nora's life. 'Everything really. She lived in the big house on the green I understand?'

'She lived with her parents and when she was nineteen her dad died of a stroke. There was just her and her mother living there until Nora got married and moved away.'

Jane interrupted 'Who did she marry? I thought she lost her fiancé in the war.'

'That's right she did, but between you and me she had to get married. I think her fiancé left her in the family way.' Sylvia whispered the last sentence as though telling some deep, dark secret.

'Don't you be whispering about my friend.' Barbara seemed to come alive as she spoke and sat upright in her chair. She didn't look like the frail old lady of before. 'I'll tell you what happened. She was in love with that lad. They thought the world of each other, not like the fly-by-night I got saddled with. They were going to get married. She had the ring and all. But then he went and died.

'She was devastated but she had to pull herself together for the sake of the baby. She told everyone it was her new husband's but I knew better. She only married him to give the baby a name. They moved to Richmond, where he worked, and I didn't see much of her after that. We wrote for a while and sent cards for birthdays and Christmas but that was that.' Barbara looked sad as she recalled the events. 'I heard she died of cancer. She was only fifty-one. She only had one daughter, a girl called Daisy.'

'Do you know where I might find Daisy?' Jane realised that without her there would be no more story. She had got much more information, but still nothing that explained the dream.

'I don't love, I'm sorry. I lost touch after Nora died. It is after all, thirty- eight years ago.' Jane was amazed at how different Barbara was to the woman of earlier. She seemed totally with it and had an incredible memory for her age.

'She might still be in Richmond but it's a much bigger place than here. I can give you the address that I used to send cards to if you like. Fetch my diary Sylvia.'

Sylvia got up and went to the desk. The tables had indeed turned and Barbara was very much in the driving seat in their relationship now.

'That would be great, thank-you.' Jane still had a tiny ray of hope of continuing the search.

Just then the door bell rang.

'We are popular today mother.' Sylvia went to the door.

'It's your young man Jane, he thought you'd been a long time and he was making sure you're alright.' She showed Philip into the room.

Barbara was finishing copying the address down for Jane when she looked up.

'Well I'll be blowed! Here we are just talking about Nora and in walks someone who looks the spitting image of her Daniel. Can you credit it?' Barbara said in amazement.

'What are you talking about mother? Put your glasses on.' Sylvia looked embarrassed at her mother's outburst.

'I don't need my glasses on. I'm telling you if my memory serves me right he looks just like him.' Barbara was adamant.

Philip was starting to feel uncomfortable with all eyes on him. 'Sorry to interrupt but I'd better go back outside, I've left Toby tied up in the garden. I'll wait for you Jane.'

'I'd better be going as well. I've taken up so much of your time. Thank-you for all the information. It's been lovely to meet you both.' Jane got up to leave.

'What relation did you say you were?' Barbara asked.

Before Jane could think about it she said, 'Oh I'm no relation,' and then she could have kicked herself, because how else was she going to explain her interest in Nora.

'Are you sure? You've such a look of the family. The eyes are a dead giveaway, not many people have lavender-grey eyes.' Barbara stared intently at Jane.

'Leave the girl alone mother, she has to go.' Sylvia started to take control again and once more Barbara slumped into the chair.

Jane, Philip and Toby started walking back up Mill Lane to the car.

'That was weird,' Philip said, 'thinking I look just like someone who's been dead for years.'

'She's just an old woman seeing things. We'd just been talking about him and he was probably in the forefront of her mind.' Jane said, trying to excuse the old woman.

She tried to recall the picture of Daniel that Sarah had showed her. Come to think of it there was some resemblance. They were both tall, had brown hair and brown eyes, but that could also describe a million and one other men on the planet.

Talking of weird, how come Barbara had thought she looked like Nora's side of the family, when she was no relation at all? This story was getting more complicated by the minute. Just as one question was answered at least another two were waiting in the wings.

Chapter 14

Lara was missing her mother. She never thought she'd admit to that but being alone with her dad was torture. She'd previously got on better with him, as he always took her side in an argument, but recently he was always in a bad mood. In the two days since her mother had been away he'd hardly been in the house and when he did bother to come home it was usually to shower and then go back out again.

She was also missing her brother, Simon. Now everything was changing she was amazed at what she had taken for granted. She would've given anything to go back a few months to when she'd come home from college and had seen Simon and their mum sitting in the kitchen talking and laughing, sharing their day. She'd been envious at the time; the two of them seemed to get on so well and she'd felt like an outsider. It had been her own fault as they'd always invited her to come and sit with them. The stroppy teenager in her had declined and she usually went straight up to her room. She could still hear them chatting while she was in her bedroom but pride stopped her from going back downstairs.

Now there was none of that laughter, even when mum was home everything had gotten too serious. She spoke to Simon regularly on the phone and he seemed to be having such a great time. She was so bored with her life. She'd even looked into joining VSO to get her away as soon as possible. She could cope with somewhere a bit basic as long as they had running water and electricity.

The parents of her best friend, Rebecca, had just got divorced and when she talked to her about it all the signs were there in Lara's family. Dad had taken to sleeping in the guest room, he said it was because mum kept him awake. They never went out together anymore. Mum did her own thing and so did dad. They'd always used to eat together as a family, mum had insisted on it, but even that had gone. Dad was never at home at mealtimes any more.

If they were going to split up she was glad she was a bit older and was leaving to go to university soon. It wouldn't affect her as much as it had Rebecca. Her friend's mum and dad had started having problems when she was only thirteen and she'd gone to school crying on many occasions. The worst thing about divorce was whose side to be on. She assumed she'd live with her mother but she hated the thought of only seeing her dad once a week, when they went to the pictures and McDonalds. Maybe she ought to discuss it with Simon, he'd know what to do. He'd always been the level headed one whereas she was the volatile, shout now - discuss later, type.

It was Saturday night and she'd nowhere to go. What a loser! If she'd known her dad was going out she would've invited some friends over. In fact she still could. She would text her mum to ask if it was OK. It was maybe too short notice for some of them but surely Rebecca would come. Should she ask some lads over? It would definitely be more fun, but they might drink too much and things could get broken.

What the hell! You're only young once, she thought. She sent the polite text to her mum asking if a couple of girlfriends could come round and then she texted all her college friends. Before long she'd invited twenty of them. In fact some were only acquaintances but they would make up the numbers.

She'd told them to come round at about seven and that they couldn't stay long because she didn't know what time her dad was coming home. But it wouldn't be before eleven surely? She wondered where he'd gone on a Saturday night without mum.

Rebecca had got a new boyfriend she'd met doing her weekend job at Pizza Hut. As luck would have it her day shift finished at six, so she told Lara that she'd go home, quickly shower and then set off. She asked if Ben could come and bring a few of his friends from work. 'The more the merrier,' Lara had said.

At seven o'clock people started arriving. Her girlfriends from college hadn't been able to buy alcohol but the boys had got hold of it somehow. Lara had invited Dylan, a boy she really fancied, and he'd turned up with two massive bottles of cider. When she asked him where he'd got it from he said he had an older brother who owed him a favour.

Rebecca arrived at seven-thirty with Ben. His friends, six in all, came a while later carrying two boxes of lager. They were over eighteen and all had ID. Lara put on some music and the party got under way. More alcohol appeared and Lara was getting nervous about her mother's lovely house. Maybe a few friends would have been OK, but on her last count the number was up to twenty-five.

Luckily the house was in its own grounds, so at least there were no neighbours to disturb. The weather was too cold for anyone to go outside so everyone was inside and every room had people in. Lara wasn't enjoying herself, as she was spending all her time going from one room to the next making sure nothing got broken or spilt on her mum's cream carpets. If only she'd been content with watching *X-Factor*, she thought.

With each can of lager consumed the decibels increased and Lara could see it all getting out of hand. She went to find Rebecca and caught her just going into Simon's old bedroom with Ben.

'What do you think you are doing?' Lara said quietly through gritted teeth.

'Chill, will you? We're only having a bit of fun. Have a drink. It was your idea this party.' Rebecca was already the worse for wear. She giggled as she continued into the bedroom. She turned back to Lara and said, 'You're only jealous 'cause you're not getting any,' and then she kissed Ben. Lara couldn't believe her best friend had just said that to her but she put it down to the drink talking. She hoped that's what it was anyway.

Just then she heard a tremendous crash from downstairs and then a scream. She ran downstairs as fast as she could, then into the kitchen and saw one of Ben's workmates with his head though the plate glass window in the kitchen door. There was blood everywhere and the boy was very still. 'Someone call 999,' Lara shouted as she ran over to him.

Almost everyone close by had had far too much to drink and were completely useless. But at the other end of the kitchen a relatively sober girl was speaking to emergency services explaining what had happened.

'What's the address here?' she shouted to Lara.

'Brackenridge, The High Street, Woolley. Tell them to hurry.' Lara started to panic. She could see blood oozing out of his neck. Luckily it wasn't spurting because that would've meant he'd severed an artery. She knew all those years of watching Casualty with her mum hadn't been in vain.

The boy was moaning with the pain, which was also good. Wasn't it? She tried to keep him still. Rebecca and Ben had come downstairs after hearing all the commotion. Ben ran over to his friend.

'Greg, can you hear me? I'm here mate.' He turned to Lara 'Is an ambulance on its way?'

'Of course it is stupid, what did you think we're going to do, put a plaster on it?' Lara was losing it. She wanted her mum and dad, they'd know what to do. She got her phone out of her pocket and speed-dialled Neil's number.

'I'm sorry this mobile is switched off. Please try later,' greeted her on the first ring. She could phone her mum but she was somewhere in the wilds of Yorkshire with her grandma, looking for a decrepit old aunt.

The siren was getting louder and soon the ambulance pulled up outside the house. Two paramedics dashed over to the limp body of Greg.

'What happened?' one of them asked to anyone who was listening.

'He was messing about with me and he just tripped and went head first through the window,' said the guilty voice of one of Ben's other friends.

The paramedics hooked him up with a saline drip, gave him some pain relief and slowly transferred him onto the stretcher. A piece of glass was still jutting out of his neck. Greg had lost a lot of blood and was barely conscious. A few of the girls had started to cry and the boys were comforting them. Everyone seemed to have sobered up.

'Has anyone notified his next of kin?' one of the paramedics asked.

'No, but I'll ring his parents. Which hospital are you going to?' Ben asked.

'Barnsley Hospital is the closest. I've already radioed in. Is there an adult in the house?' He addressed Lara, but he'd already guessed the answer to that question. He'd been a paramedic too long and seen too many teenage parties end in tragedy.

'No, sorry. I've tried calling my dad and my mum is away.' Lara looked sheepish.

'Well I think you need someone here with you. Shock is a very insidious thing and can creep up on you unawares. I'd recommend everyone go home, apart from a close friend who can stay with you.' The paramedic spoke the last sentence loudly so everyone downstairs could hear. Coats were fetched and the large gathering was soon reduced to a handful of people.

'I'll stay with her,' Rebecca volunteered; the catty comments of earlier were forgotten.

'I'll try my mum,' Lara said. Jane picked up on the second ring.

'Hello darling what can I do for you?' Jane asked, happy to hear from her.

'I've done something really silly,' Lara said. 'You know I asked you whether I could have a couple of girlfriends round? Well I didn't. Oh mum.' She started to cry.

'Tell me what's happened.' Jane was worried.

'I invited a lot more people to come around for a party and this boy had an accident. He fell through the glass door in the kitchen and they've taken him to hospital,' she said between sobs. 'I'm so sorry, can you come home?' Lara sounded desperate.

'Have you rung your dad?'

'Yes but his phone is switched off. I wasn't going to bother you but the paramedic said I shouldn't be on my own, because of shock or something,' Lara sobbed.

Bloody typical, thought Jane. The one weekend she was away Neil also had to go AWOL. But then she thought of her poor daughter alone in the house.

'Of course I'll come home, but it'll take me a while to get there.' Luckily she hadn't opened the bottle of wine yet. They'd both fallen asleep again and had a late dinner.

'I'll see you as soon as I can. Keep trying to contact your dad.' Jane attempted to hide the disappointment in her voice. Karma, she thought. She was being punished for being a married woman and having such a good time. It was her's and Philip's birthday tomorrow and they'd planned to stay another night. She'd also intended to look around Richmond for any clues as to the whereabouts of Nora's daughter, Daisy, although she was waiting for some Divine inspiration on that one.

Jane came off the phone and sighed. Philip looked concerned, 'Is everything OK?'

'No it's not. My foolish daughter thought she'd have a party. When the cat's away and all that. Apparently some boy fell through the glass door in the kitchen, although how on earth he's done that is anyone's guess, it's reinforced glass. I've got to go home. I'm really sorry.' Sorry couldn't begin to describe how Jane felt at leaving Philip.

'These things can't be helped. Are we taking our things home now or will we be able to come back?' Philip was obviously disappointed.

'You can stay here and I'll return some time tomorrow, once we've located Neil. Lara only needs one parent around. That's if you want to.'

'I've brought my laptop with me. So I could do some work if you'd pop round to my house and phone me with the e-mail addresses that are on a sheet of paper on my desk. I might as well make myself useful. At least I have Toby to keep me warm in bed.' He pulled Jane toward him and gave her a lingering kiss. 'I'll miss you. I've got used to having you around.'

'It'll be late when I get home. Isn't Sally around for you to ask?'

'No. She's gone to see her mum in Scarborough.'

'I'll call on my way home. You'd better give me your key.' Philip took it off his key ring and handed it to her.

Jane left everything just as it was for Philip to tidy up. They shared one last passionate kiss. 'That's to remember me by. See you some time tomorrow. Love you,' Jane said, as she made her way to the car.

'Love you too. Hurry back'. Philip stood at the door and waved her off.

It was nine-thirty on Saturday night so the A1 was quiet. She kept checking for speed cameras and the police. When it was all clear she put her foot down and she reached the outskirts of Leeds in just under an hour. She'd rung Lara again on her hands-free. Rebecca was still there, although Ben had gone to see Greg in hospital. They'd not heard how he was.

Philip and Sally lived in Morley, a small town outside Leeds, just off the motorway. Convenient, as Jane wanted to check that Lara was alright. She'd tried Neil's phone again but just got, 'there is no-one available to take your call. Please try later'. That was an improvement. He'd at least switched it on. Hopefully Lara had got through to him and he was on his way home. If that was the case Jane would still call at the house to check on Lara. Then she could drive back to Richmond to continue her birthday celebrations.

She pulled up by the apartment block that Philip lived in. She couldn't get near the entrance because everyone seemed to have two cars nowadays and all the visitor spaces were taken. He lived on the first floor so she ran up the steps, got out Philip's key and opened the door.

Strange, all the lights were on. Sally must have forgotten to turn them off when she left. She heard what sounded like laughter, coming from upstairs. The walls were so thin, it must be from next door. She walked across to Philip's study/dining room. It was the same room where she'd had her tarot reading. It looked very different now, with Philip's paper strewn all over the desk. Much more businesslike, but she preferred the calm, soothing environment that Rosa had created.

She soon located the addresses he wanted. She tore the page off the pad and was just about to ring Philip with them when she thought she'd give Neil one last try. His phone started to ring. But she could hear the familiar ring tones of his phone coming from upstairs.

She kept it ringing and followed the tone. She could definitely hear laughing, not from next door but from the main bedroom. The answer phone clicked in at the same time the ring tones stopped. Jane stood outside the bedroom door dreading what she was going to find. She remembered the lascivious look on Neil's face as he'd watched Sally at the engagement party. She wondered just how long it had been going on. She then thought about her own infidelity. How had things got into such a mess?

She stood there for a few minutes wondering how to play this. She could either be very mature about it or she could act like a spoilt child. She opted for the latter and barged in. She'd never seen anyone move as fast. Neil leapt off Sally in a split second. He took one look at Jane and groaned.

'It's not what you think…' Neil started to say.

Jane interrupted, laughed and said, 'You have no idea what I think.'

Sally tried to hide under the covers muttering, 'Sorry,' over and over again. Funnily enough neither of them had stopped to ask Jane where she had got a key from. They were far too busy feeling guilty.

'You're wanted at home. There's been an accident and Lara needs us. Seeing as we were both out, she thought she'd have a party and a boy has been injured. So if you could spare the time Lara would like both her parents with her.' She used her most sarcastic voice. Her speech over with, Jane turned and went back to her car.

She sat trembling in the front seat. She wanted to cry but tears wouldn't come. How could something so sweet turn so sour in such a short space of time? A few hours ago she'd been dozing after a mammoth love-making session. Now her marriage had fallen apart and her life would never be the same again.

Neil came running down the stairs and banged on her window.

'We need to talk,' he mouthed through the glass.

'I know we do, but hadn't we better wait until we've calmed down? This is not the time, Lara needs us. I'll see you at the house.' She purposely didn't call it home because right now it was anything but.

Jane beat Neil to the house and ran in to see how Lara was doing. Apparently Rebecca had just gone. Her father had collected her as it was getting late. Lara went to hug Jane.

'I'm sorry mum. I've made such a mess of things haven't I?' Lara cried.

Jane couldn't very well criticise after what had happened in her own life over the past few hours. So she held Lara and stroked her hair. Just then Neil dashed in and went over to his daughter. She fell into his arms and they hugged. Neil signalled 'thank-you' to Jane - for not saying anything to Lara about what she'd just witnessed.

Jane went into the kitchen to assess the damage. The floor was covered in bits of glass and blood. She thought cleaning up would help distract her so she found the dustpan and brush and swept up the glass. Then she mopped up the blood. In no time at all, the entire kitchen was back to normal, which was more than she could say about their lives.

Chapter 15

'Do you mind if I go to bed, I'm really tired?' Lara asked, yawning.

'Go ahead sweetheart, there's nothing more we can do tonight.' Jane went to kiss her goodnight.

'Wake me if you hear anything. He won't die will he?'

'I certainly hope not,' Jane replied. Lara looked frightened as she went upstairs.

Jane had rung the hospital to ask about Greg. At first they wouldn't tell her anything because she wasn't a relative, but when she'd explained that the accident had happened in her house they were more forthcoming. She'd been told that he'd undergone emergency surgery to repair the vessels in his neck. The operation had been a success, but he was still critical. The next few hours would be the key. She wished she could speak to Greg's parents but, until last night, Lara had never met him so that was out of the question.

In between all the drama Jane had found time to text Philip. She told him things hadn't gone to plan and she would explain more tomorrow. Although it was nearly midnight she knew her and Neil would have to talk. She also knew she would have to come clean about her affair. It was unfair for Neil to take all the blame.

He looked dreadful, sitting in his arm chair, draining a large tumbler of whisky.

She went to sit on the sofa facing him. For a while there was silence.

'Do you want a drink?' Neil asked, getting up to go and refill his glass.

'Yes please, a large gin and tonic would be great. And would you put some nice music on while you're there?' Jane hoped some soothing music would warm the chilly atmosphere.

Neil was surprised at how rational Jane was being. He was waiting for the almighty row. He didn't know what he was going to say and thought the large whisky would give him clarity. He didn't know at what point he'd fallen out of love with Jane. They'd taken each other for granted for so long that he couldn't remember a time when it had been anything other than mediocre. What he felt for Sally was real, not just a fling. He would have to tell that to Jane. He knew it would destroy the family but, being honest, it had been destroyed years ago.

They had turned into one of those couples who had stayed together for the children, and now the children were leaving the cracks in the relationship were beginning to show. He poured Jane a rather large gin and tonic. She would need it, he thought. Then he put a Classic FM CD on. Nice, relaxing music was just what they needed.

He handed Jane the drink and went to sit down.

'Who's going first?' Jane asked, wanting to get it over with.

'I suppose I'd better since I'm the one caught with my trousers down so to speak,' Neil said, attempting to lighten the conversation

Jane felt guilty watching him squirm as he'd never been one for confrontations. This must be really difficult for him.

'Do you want a divorce?' Jane asked.

'I haven't given it much thought. Shouldn't it be me asking you as I'm the one in the wrong?' Neil replied.

'Technically yes, and technically no.' Jane was speaking in riddles. 'Didn't you stop to think how I had the key to Sally's flat?' she asked, drawing it out for as long as possible.

'No. I assumed the door was open and that you'd somehow found out about us and had come for a confrontation.' Neil looked baffled.

Jane felt like laughing with the absurdity of it all. In fact, she did and couldn't stop until tears were rolling down her cheeks. Neil just stood and looked on in amazement. He put it down to delayed shock. What else could it be?

Jane pulled herself together and wiped her eyes.

'While you've been having your sordid little affair with Sally I've been seeing her boyfriend, Philip. That's why I'm laughing. We're both as bad as each other.' She felt the weight just lift from her shoulders as she confessed her guilty secret.

Neil just continued to look at her, open-mouthed.

'Stuck for words are you?' she laughed.

Neil was speechless. He wanted to be angry, indignant, livid... but he couldn't summon the energy. Instead he just smiled. 'What a pair of idiots.'

'So, what next?' Jane asked, glad it was all out into the open.

'I don't know what to say. In all the ways I had envisaged having to tell you about this I can honestly say I never imagined this situation.' Neil looked shell-shocked. 'How long has it been going on?' he asked, not really wanting to know the answer.

'For about two months, ever since I showed him round 5 Call Mews. Sally viewed the house first and he came to see it the day after. I seem to remember you had her work through her lunch hour that day so she couldn't make it. So, actually, it could be deemed to be your fault.' Jane laughed.

'Snap. We started around the same time. Sally confided in me that Philip wasn't really into buying a house,' Neil said.

Jane couldn't believe she was talking so rationally about the possible break up of her marriage.

'It's not been right for some time has it?' She admitted.

'No, sadly it hasn't,' Neil replied, shaking his head.

'Are you serious about her or is she just a fling?'

'She's not just a fling but, as I say, I haven't thought about the future.' He seemed confused.

'I was up in Richmond with Philip, not my mum, and if it's alright with you I'll go back tomorrow and talk to him.' Jane hoped that Philip wasn't too confused by her text.

'You devious minx,' Neil joked. There was no point in recriminations or pointing the finger of blame. The situation was how it was and had to be dealt with as amicably as possible, for the sake of Simon and Lara.

'Let's have another drink to celebrate,' Jane said draining the last of her gin and tonic.

'Celebrate? What are we celebrating?' Neil asked, incredulously.

'The fact that we've talked rationally and exchanged more conversation tonight than we have over the last two months. Cheers!' Jane raised her glass.

'Cheers! Here's to adult conversation,' Neil said, clinking Jane's glass.

They carried on talking a while longer and seemed to be back to their old selves. Ironic really, they agreed, seeing as they'd been through such turmoil.

'What are we going to tell the children?' Neil asked.

'Nothing for now. The atmosphere in the house has been so bad recently Lara won't know the difference. Anyway, we can milk the fact that she is feeling guilty for a few more weeks. And there's no point in worrying Simon.' Jane said, trying to be practical.

'True. Can you imagine how much trouble Lara would be in if all this about us hadn't come out. She should be grateful.'

'I'm going to have an early start tomorrow. I'll go in and see Lara to tell her I'm going back to Richmond, but I'll be back tomorrow night. What a way to celebrate your birthday! Will you be around for her?' Jane asked, worried that Lara could still be suffering from shock.

'I will. I'll ring Sally tonight. She'll be worried because she genuinely likes you. This'll be killing her.' Neil thought of poor Sally in the flat on her own.

'I like her as well, so please tell her there are no hard feelings. But don't tell her about Philip. He should be the one to break the news,' Jane said.

'Fine, I don't want to make things any more complicated than they already are. Thank-you Jane.' He'd had a glimpse tonight as to why he'd fallen in love with her in the first place.

She went to kiss him on his cheek; turned and walked away to bed.

Chapter 16

After Neil had made his abrupt getaway Sally had sat on the bed they'd just shared, crying. She stayed there, in the same position, for over an hour, thinking about what a mess she'd made of her life.

She would probably lose her job and, watching the way Neil ran after his wife, the man she loved. She hadn't meant to fall in love with him. It had started as a fling to get back at Philip for not wanting her, but they'd had such a wonderful time together. She had finally found someone who could satisfy her sexual desires.

She wished it had been someone else and not her boss. Nor the husband of a woman who, in other circumstances, would've been a good friend. As the phrase went, 'you can't help who you fall in love with'. But she wished it wasn't true.

Neil had rung her later that night. She'd been reassured when he told her he still felt the same way about her. He'd said they would have a long discussion later, but right now he had to put his family first. She understood this and started to pull herself together. She was a successful woman with a bright future ahead of her and she mustn't forget that.

She thought back to her own tarot reading. She'd been so busy on the night, listening to what other people had to say and being a perfect hostess, that she'd put her reading out of her mind until she'd recently found time to listen to her tape in peace.

She thought back to what Rosa had said and realised it was already starting to come true.

Rosa had seen an incompatibility in a relationship, though you didn't need to be a mind reader to know that she and Philip weren't a match made in heaven. She'd drawn the Tower card which usually signified a huge upheaval. Rosa thought it was in every aspect of her life. She was going to move home and, at the time, Sally thought it was into the Mews house Jane had shown them. There would be changes at work; but she hadn't expected it to be the loss of her job. The next few months would be very traumatic but, after that, peace and tranquillity would reign and she would be the happiest she'd ever been.

Sally held on to that thought as she went to sleep, hoping tomorrow would bring more clarity. Seeing as neither Neil nor Philip was going to be around she actually would visit her mother and step-father in Scarborough, instead of pretending to go as she'd told Philip.

Jane rang the hospital on Sunday morning to find out how Greg was. He'd had a comfortable night and there was a slight improvement. She asked if he was receiving visitors. The sister had said she would check with his family and ring her back. Then Jane sneaked into Lara's room.

'Lara, I need you to wake up for a minute,' Jane said, gently nudging her daughter's shoulder.

Lara stirred. 'What did you say?' She was still half asleep.

'I'm going back up to Richmond to collect grandma. I'll see you later. I've rung the hospital and there has been a slight improvement in Greg's condition.' Before she'd finished speaking Lara had fallen back to sleep. Jane quickly scribbled a note and left it on Lara's desk explaining the conversation they'd just had, in case Lara had no recollection of it.

There was even less traffic on the road than the previous night so Jane pulled up outside the chalet at just before nine. Philip was walking round the garden with Toby. Once the dog saw Jane he scampered over to her, his tail going fifty to the dozen. He jumped up and gave her a big wet kiss.

'Someone's obviously missed me,' Jane said.

'Not as much as I did.' Philip went to kiss her. 'What's been going on? I didn't sleep a wink last night wondering what had happened. You and your cryptic message.' Philip said.

'Let's go inside, it's a long story.' Jane went to put the kettle on for a drink of tea as she'd been so eager to get back to Richmond she'd left without having breakfast. 'I think you need to sit down. There's no easy way to tell you this.'

'This sounds ominous.'

'No I'm being serious, listen. When I arrived at your flat last night all the lights were on. I just assumed Sally must have left them on by mistake. I'd found the e-mail addresses you wanted and I was just going to leave when I thought I'd ring Neil one last time. You'll never guess what? I heard his mobile phone ring upstairs and, to cut a long story short, I found Neil and Sally upstairs in bed together.

I'm really sorry to be the one to tell you.' She looked at Philip closely to gauge his response.

She didn't exactly know what Philip's reaction would be to the news of his girlfriend's infidelity, but she didn't expect him to jump up punching the air with his fist as if his favourite football team had scored the winning goal at Wembley.

'Yes! I'm free!' He declared. 'I've wanted to finish with her for so long, even before I met you, but I just didn't know how. And now she's done it for me.'

'Aren't you the slightest bit upset? You were together for ten years.' Jane was shocked by his reaction.

'Honestly, no. I don't know what that says about me as a person but I'm relieved. Now it's all out in the open I can get on with my life and spend more time with you. By the way, happy birthday.' Philip had a big smile on his face.

'Happy birthday to you, too.' But Jane didn't feel like smiling. She felt more like crying and thought Philip should be comforting her, sharing their sorrow in a mutual closeness. For her it was a big deal. She and Neil had been married for over eighteen years and, yes, she was having an affair. But she couldn't just forget about their life together.

'I'm sorry it's not the reaction you wanted but I'm not pretending to be upset just to make you feel better.' Philip saw the look of disappointment on Jane's face.

'I don't expect you to lie but a bit of compassion would have been nice. I was the one to find them and I've been up most of the night talking to Neil. I've a family to think of. I can't just selfishly put myself first like you seem to have done.' Jane had real animosity in her voice.

'You think I'm selfish for wanting what's best for me? Well I'm sorry, I don't see that as selfish. Just sensible.' Philip was starting to rise to the bait.

'I nearly feel sorry for Sally. I can't believe you can be so heartless.' Jane's acerbic tongue was getting some practice as she laid into Philip.

Little Toby had taken himself under the table. He didn't like arguments and had started to whimper.

'Now look what you've done.' Jane went to comfort the dog.

'Me? It's you that's shouting and picking an argument. If you remember I was the one who was pleased.' It took a lot to rile happy-go-lucky Philip, but Jane had managed it this morning with her irrational behaviour. Maybe he had been a bit insensitive, but his was an honest reaction. How could he be blamed for that?

'I see I've wasted my time coming back,' Jane snapped.

'If you're going to be like this all day you probably have.' Philip walked away. The joint birthday they'd both been looking forward to was slowly going from bad to worse. Neither of them was going to back down, so Philip wanted to remove himself from the situation before either of them said anything they would regret later. He picked up Toby's lead, which made the puppy come out from under the table.

'I'm going for a walk. Do you want to come?'

'Don't you walk away from me, I haven't finished.' Jane wasn't to be pacified.

'Oh yes you have. No-one speaks to me like that. We're not married yet,' Philip said, incredulous at her last statement.

'Yet? Try never. If and when I marry again it'll be to someone with feelings. I went to hell and back last night. A boy nearly died in my house and all you can do is jump up and down for joy. You haven't even had the decency to ask how he is.' She was on a roll.

'You didn't give me a chance to ask anything before you jumped on your high horse. I hope it's a good view from up there because from down here you look pretty silly.' Philip walked out of the room beckoning Toby to follow.

Jane shouted after him, 'If you go now don't expect me to be here when you get back.'

He didn't even look over his shoulder. Jane slumped into the nearest chair and wondered how it had all got so out of hand. All she'd wanted was a lovely birthday with Philip. They could have had a pub lunch and a nice walk before coming back later in the day. Yet here she was, on her own, after a really stupid argument that was all her own doing.

She'd always had a volatile temper. Her family had got used to it over the years, but this was the first time that Philip had seen this side of her and she wasn't proud of it. She didn't seem able to stop once she started, as though she was trying to push away anyone who cared for her. She seemed to want to test their resilience, which was fine when you'd been married as long as her and Neil, but was not a very good idea in the first throes of romance when you were trying to impress one another.

Jane was reluctant to go home with this awful atmosphere between them so she decided to sit and wait for Philip and Toby to return.

They weren't very long because Philip's heart wasn't in the walk. He still couldn't understand how the argument had started. Women! He would never understand them. That was one of the main reasons he'd stayed single for all these years. But he'd thought Jane was different. This was their first row and he didn't like it. Maybe it was for the best though, as he'd set Jane high on a pedestal and was beginning to realise she was only human.

As he approached the Lodge he saw her car and he breathed a sigh of relief. She hadn't gone home after all. Hopefully she'd calmed down and they could pick up where they'd left off, before the stupid argument.

Jane had been watching for him to return and ran outside to meet him. He held out his arms and she ran into them.

'I'm so sorry,' she said. 'I don't know what came over me. It must have been delayed shock or something. I'm not usually a mad woman.'

'I'm glad about that and I'm sorry too. I was very insensitive. Shall we start again, from when you first got out of the car?' he asked.

'That's fine by me.' She gave him a long, lingering kiss

'That's more like it.' He held onto her hand as they went into the lodge. Toby was much happier too, he went to sit in front of the fire and was asleep in no time at all. Jane would miss her little friend when Philip took him back. She'd got used to having him around. If she and Neil did split up one of the first things she'd buy would be a Toby replica.

Jane and Philip didn't go out for lunch. He made some sandwiches with food he found in the cupboard. Then they talked. It wasn't quite the birthday celebration they'd had in mind, but they were together and the argument of the morning was put behind them.

'Are your sandwiches OK?' Philip asked. 'I could only find a tin of corned beef in the cupboard.'

'Now I know I've never mentioned my penchant for corned beef. People laugh at me when I own up to liking it.' Jane laughed. The jovial atmosphere had returned.

Philip had decided he was going to go home, talk to Sally and then move out. He didn't need a flat as big as the one they lived in. A studio flat would suit him until he'd decided on his future plans. Jane was going to stay put for the sake of the children. She didn't want to disrupt Lara just before her mock 'A' level exams. But she didn't know, yet, whether Neil would stay or move in with Sally. She and Philip had also decided they would carry on with their relationship, but continue to keep it quiet. She would introduce him to Simon and Lara eventually. There was no rush and she wanted to do it right this time.

When they had to leave they packed the car, fastened Toby in his seat and were on the road by three o'clock. It was getting dark when they arrived home. Philip had phoned Sally, who told him she was in Scarborough and wouldn't be coming home until Monday. That would give Philip chance to pack up all his belongings in preparation for when he found a new flat.

Jane had given Toby a big cuddle when they handed him back. Steve and Paula had rung Philip's mobile as soon as they'd landed back in Manchester to find out what time Toby was being dropped off. Even Philip would miss him and both of them asked if they could borrow Toby again, one day soon, to take him for a long walk.

Jane dropped Philip off at home. She didn't go in as the events of yesterday were still too raw. They hadn't made love today. Somehow it hadn't seemed appropriate.

'I'll ring you tomorrow. Good luck with talking to Sally.' Jane leant over and kissed him.

'I'm really sorry about earlier, have you forgiven me?' Philip was suddenly feeling insecure.

'Of course I have. I was more to blame than you. One little argument isn't going to change the way I feel about you, silly.' Jane hugged him tight.

'You do know I love you, don't you?' Philip nuzzled into Jane's neck.

'I do, and I love you too. We'll see each other soon.' Jane tried to prise him off her. She wanted to get home and check up on Lara.

'Sorry, I'm being pathetic. I'm going to be a man now and pull myself together. See ya,' Philip said, putting on his deep masculine voice. They both laughed. Philip reluctantly got out of the car. He wasn't looking forward to the next few days, made all the harder by knowing he wouldn't see Jane. He leant over and sneaked one last kiss.

'Get on with you. I'm going home to see my wayward daughter.' Jane started to pull away. Philip waved as he watched her drive away in case she looked in her rear view mirror.

Jane walked into her house and found Lara and Neil sitting together on the settee, watching *The Simpsons Movie*. They both looked up when she walked in. Then Lara jumped up. 'Happy Birthday mum.' She gave Jane a big hug, then went to fetch her card and present. Neil looked up and asked if she was alright. He looked as if he hadn't had a wink of sleep. Lara came in with a big bunch of flowers. 'These are from me and dad,' she said, 'and this is just from me.' She gave Jane a small gift wrapped box. In it were some beautiful amethyst earrings.

'Oh Lara they're beautiful! But you shouldn't spend all your money on me.' She carefully removed them from the box and put them on.

'I thought they'd match your eyes,' Lara said thoughtfully.

Jane looked in the mirror. They did. 'They're perfect, thank-you so much.' She kissed her daughter.

Thirty-nine, Jane thought, as she turned toward the mirror. She examined her face to see if another line had appeared, but luckily none had, although she was very surprised after the tumultuous events of the past twenty four hours.

Her potential birthday disaster seemed to have been salvaged. Simon had texted earlier to wish her happy birthday and told her that her card was in the post. He'd forgotten to post it until yesterday, so she should get it the next day.

'Do you want to go out for tea?' Neil asked, apprehensively, not knowing how Jane would react to his suggestion.

Jane was tired and all she wanted to do was to go and lie in a hot bath, but she said, 'Yes, that would be lovely. Have you anywhere in mind?'

'You get to choose, it's your birthday.' Lara said. If her normally stroppy, sullen teenage daughter was as pleasant as this all the time, she would let her have an illicit party more often.

'There's not much open on a Sunday, so why don't we go to 'The Old Bakery' and then visit Greg in Hospital,' Jane suggested. 'The Old Bakery' was a lovely country pub in Haigh, a small village five minutes up the road, on the way to Barnsley Hospital.

'What a great idea. I'd like to see how he's getting on,' Lara said, brightening up at the suggestion. I'll just go and get changed.' She darted upstairs. Jane carefully arranged the bouquet of flowers in a large pottery vase that one of the locals had made her and tried to summon up the energy to play happy families. She had a quick shower to refresh herself and then changed into a totally new outfit.

Next Jane rang the hospital and spoke to the sister in charge. Greg was continuing to improve and his parents said he could receive visitors, though not for very long. He was in ward eleven and visiting was between six-thirty and eight-thirty.

Conversation at the pub wasn't forced between Jane and Neil; in fact it was like old times. They acted as normally as possible for Lara's sake, and it wasn't an effort. They both seemed relaxed in each others' company. The meal was lovely and Jane was hungrier than she thought. The corned beef sandwiches she'd had at lunchtime hadn't filled her. She had two courses and two large glasses of wine, purely for medicinal purposes. Because it was her birthday Neil was driving.

When they got to the hospital Greg's parents were by his bed. Greg had his head and neck bandaged up and was still intubated, but he was conscious and Lara thought he looked more alive than he had the day before.

Jane and Neil introduced themselves and apologised on behalf of their daughter for the impromptu party that had been the cause of their son's accident. Mr and Mrs Holliday were very understanding and even apologised to Lara for scaring her. They said that Greg had always been an accident waiting to happen, being so boisterous and never knowing where to draw the line. Greg couldn't speak but he rolled his eyes at his mother's last statement. The family didn't stay long but Lara said she would visit again if it was OK with Greg. He smiled. He thought, why wouldn't it be OK for a gorgeous, voluptuous brunette to visit him and look into his eyes?

Chapter 17

Madge and George were spending more and more of their time together. He stayed at her house during the week and she stayed at his at the weekend. They attended the same adult education classes and were enjoying learning everything there was to know about genealogy. Jane had told Madge about meeting Nora's friend Barbara and the other information she'd discovered, but they too had drawn a blank with Daisy. Without her married name it was almost impossible to locate her as she could be anywhere in the country, or even outside it. The address that Barbara had given Jane was a dead end. The current residents had been there for over twenty years and couldn't recall anyone of that name.

Despite being happy in the new relationship Madge still liked some time to herself, so she made George go home two nights a week. On those nights she would put on her old tracksuit and lay on the settee with chocolates and a romantic novel. She was blissfully happy. She hadn't felt like this about anyone since her late husband. George was also besotted. He hadn't been a widower as long as Madge. He'd lost his wife to cancer three years ago and hadn't felt ready to date until he'd met Madge. His wife had only been fifty-eight when she died and he was angry for a long time afterwards.

One of the women where George worked had recently lost her husband and she'd got solace from attending the local Spiritualist church. She'd not had a message directly from her husband but she knew a lot of people who had received them from their loved ones and it had helped them come to terms with their loss. She'd asked George if he would like to go with her one Sunday night. She explained that it was more religious on Sunday with prayers and readings as well as a demonstration of mediumship from the platform. George was game to try anything, and he particularly hated Sundays since his wife had died, so he'd said yes.

He met her outside Dewsbury Spiritualist church for the seven o'clock service. He used to go to church as a young man but, as a lot of people do, he'd let his religion lapse as the pressure of adulthood and family life had taken over. He was surprised that it actually looked like a church. He'd expected more of a church hall feel. There were chairs set out like pews and a platform at the front with flowers and the Spiritualist creed on display.

He liked the fact that the service was taken by lay preachers and that anyone could address the group. The church was packed with people of all ages; there were teenagers, young married couples and the old set who'd probably been attending since before the war. It was an upbeat and positive service with lots of laughter. He found he really enjoyed himself. That had been the beginning of his love affair with the Spiritualist movement and it had also become his social life. Everyone always stayed for a cup of tea and a chat after the events so he got to know a wide circle of people in a short space of time.

When he'd first met Madge he didn't tell her about this part of his life. He intended to bring it into the conversation gradually to see what her reaction would be. She turned out to be very open-minded and had similar beliefs to him, although she'd never attended a church. It took him a while to convince her, but eventually she did agree to go with him, although he took her to a Saturday meeting. These weren't as religious and featured a demonstration of mediumship by a couple of visiting speakers.

She'd found it fascinating and had been amazed when the medium looked in her direction and said, 'Can I come to the lady in the blue jacket?' All eyes were on Madge as she turned round to see who everyone was looking at before realising it was her.

'Er, yes. I suppose so,' Madge said nervously. Everyone laughed.

'Nothing to worry about love,' said the friendly man on the platform in a strong Yorkshire accent. 'I have a man with me now who says he's recently been in touch with you. He's laughing, saying you don't hear from him in over twenty years and now he contacts you twice within a month. Does that mean anything to you?'

'It does actually.' Madge thought back to the message Jane had received from Rosa, the lady who had read the tarot cards.

'He says he's glad you've found happiness. He's wanted that for you and he's joking that it didn't take you long. He also has a message for someone with a name beginning with J. I've a feeling it's a lady. Can you tell her that it'll all become clear soon and not to give up hope.' The medium paused for a second and laughed. 'He is giving you a bit of a telling off as this lady is going through a very rough patch at the moment and she needs to talk to you, but you've been so busy you haven't spared much time for her. He's telling you to, 'Please make more of an effort.' He's saying, 'Goodbye for now,' and he will see you again, though not for a long time. 'Thank-you love and God bless!' The man turned away and gave his attention to a gentleman on the back row.

Madge felt suitably admonished. She sat and pondered the message the medium had just given her. It had obviously been for Jane, and she assumed he was talking about the situation with Daisy. It was her turn to give Jane a message and it would come as a bit of a shock because she hadn't told Jane she was going to the meeting that night.

She didn't know why she kept things a secret from Jane because when they'd had the long talk in Cornwall, and again when Jane had come round to the house, she'd felt really close to her. But since that time she had closed up again and Jane hadn't even met George yet. It was really unfair of her to exclude Jane from her life, particularly at this difficult time. Madge felt guilty that she hadn't known how hard a time Jane was having, but she'd been so wrapped up in her own life she hadn't taken the time to enquire how Jane was coping. But now she'd had a bit of a reminder from her late husband, so she promised herself that she would make more an effort to be there for her daughter.

On the face of it Jane was coping with the situation at home. Life looked pretty much the same as before, apart from Neil sleeping in the spare room every night and still seeing Sally. He'd told Jane that he loved Sally, and when she felt ready to tell the children he would move in to Sally's flat.

Jane was still trying to be grown-up about the situation but she couldn't help feeling rejected. She'd been replaced. Jane had usually managed to remain positive throughout her life so far, but now she was depressed. It wasn't something she'd felt before and she wasn't sure how to deal with it. It was making her feel isolated and withdrawn.

She'd let her relationship with Philip cool a bit. They still saw each other and had made love once since Richmond, but her heart wasn't in it. She felt she couldn't give the relationship a proper chance while her home life was still in such turmoil.

The dream was back with a vengeance. It was occurring every night and she was getting very little sleep. She'd put the search for Daisy on hold. She'd drawn a blank and didn't know what to do next. She'd had a couple of phone calls with Sarah in Falmouth and told about the visit to Catterick, but now she had Christmas to get through and other things to think about. It seemed as if, when she was actively searching for Daniel and Nora, the dream subsided. But when she put it all on the back burner the dream returned. Something wanted her to continue trying to solve the puzzle.

Simon was due to return any day soon for the Christmas holidays. He hadn't been home this term and she hadn't been to see him. University life was great and he loved it. They'd texted and spoken on the phone regularly but she was looking forward to seeing him again. Lara was spending more time at the hospital with Greg. They seemed to be enjoying each others' company and he was well on the way to recovery. He had fewer bandages on and was now eating solid food.

Life went on as usual for everyone around her. Even her mother's love life seemed sorted, but Jane felt adrift, as though she'd no direction in her life. Work was the same, a bit quieter at this time of year with nothing particularly challenging. She felt lonely and misunderstood. When she'd started the affair with Philip she'd felt wonderful, as though her life finally had meaning. But because of all that had transpired recently this feeling hadn't lasted and she was as confused as ever.

She thought she might visit Rosa again to see if she could shed any light on the situation. Even though it had only been a few weeks since she'd seen her it felt like a lifetime ago. Philip still wanted her as much as ever and was always telling her that he loved her, but she felt that she couldn't commit to him. It was as though she needed to find herself before deciding to having a meaningful relationship with anyone.

Jane really needed someone to talk to who would listen without judgement. She'd enjoyed talking to her mother in Cornwall but since that time she hadn't seen her for long enough to continue their discussion. She would ring her in a while to see if they could meet. Maybe Madge would be able to give her some much needed advice.

Chapter 18

Sally was enjoying her new life and had stopped feeling guilty about her new relationship, now that it was out in the open. It had been a bit nerve-wracking at work when Neil had told the Managing Partner about them. He'd offered to resign and find a new position but it hadn't been deemed necessary because he'd told them that he was serious about Sally and that he and his wife were getting a divorce.

The only concession was that Sally now worked with one of the other partners on a different floor. During their working days they only occasionally saw each other at lunchtime, but he usually went home with her for tea.

After the affair had been made public Philip had moved out of the shared flat. He'd found a studio apartment near work. After the initial break-up he and Sally hadn't spoken. When she had returned from Scarborough on the Monday afternoon Philip was already in the flat. He'd taken the day off work to pack. She looked around and his belongings were conspicuous by their absence.

'Does this mean you're leaving?' Sally asked.

'I think it's for the best under the circumstances, don't you? I know I haven't been happy for ages, I just didn't have the balls to tell you,' Philip admitted.

'But you went to look at that house. What was that all about?'

'I don't know. I kept hoping you'd realise we weren't compatible. But you never did.' Philip felt ashamed.

'To be honest, I agree. I was only thinking about owning a house. I hadn't given our relationship that much thought. Sorry,' Sally said.

'I've already found a flat and I'm going today. I was just waiting until you got back.'

'No hard feelings?' Sally asked.

'No. Would you be hurt if I said I just feel relief?' Philip sighed. He realised he didn't care enough to have any hard feelings.

'How about a friendly hug, for old time's sake?' Sally went to embrace him for the last time. It felt awkward and they both pulled away quickly.

'We haven't even discussed what happened,' Sally added.

'Is there any point? It's all water under the bridge.' Philip had already picked up the first box he was taking to the car he'd borrowed from a friend.

Conversation closed.

And that was it. Ten years of being together and what had they to show for it? Some happy memories but nothing else.

On the other hand Sally's life with Neil was wonderful. He'd come round to her flat for tea most days but hadn't stayed the night yet. They made love at least once a day, still keeping the passion alive by doing it in places where there was a chance they could get caught.

She smiled to herself as she thought about the cinema trip last week. They'd sat on the back row like young teenagers and participated in some heavy petting. Neil promised he would leave Jane after the Christmas holidays and move into Sally's flat. She believed him, even though some of her friends were sceptical, arguing that all married men say they are going to leave their wives but few actually go through with it.

They'd even looked through holiday brochures together because once he'd moved in they were going to treat themselves to a really nice holiday. The future looked rosy, just as Rosa had predicted. Although she did say it wouldn't be plain sailing, as it had been so far.

Neil was getting impatient to leave the family home and move in with Sally. The *detente* was still in force between him and Jane, but it was obvious that neither of them was happy. He still preferred to work late and eat his evening meal by himself in front of the television. Luckily for them the house was big enough that they could live totally independent lives while being under the same roof. After making the decision to split up he just wanted to get it over with.

He'd started going back the gym three times a week. Now he was going out with a younger woman he had to make sure he kept in good shape. Simon was due home from university any day and Jane had promised that at the earliest opportunity they would sit down as a family and discuss the future.

They'd decided to put their house up for sale. Neil didn't want it and Jane couldn't afford to buy him out. He would move in with Sally, and Jane would rent a house until she decided where she wanted to be. Both had seen a solicitor, setting the wheels in motion for the divorce. It was going to be on the grounds of irretrievable breakdown of marriage, rather than adultery. He knew he shouldn't move out the week before Christmas but he didn't want to stay and play happy families. He wanted to spend all his time with Sally, having lots of sex.

Simon came home on the 17th December. Neil was chomping at the bit to tell both his children the truth. Greg had been discharged from hospital and he and Lara were now officially an item. He spent nearly all his time around at their house and had become like a member of the family. Hopefully Lara would cope with the news of her parents break up better now she had a significant other in her life.

The day after Simon came home Jane made a lovely roast dinner and the whole family sat down to eat together. Maybe for the last time, Jane thought. After everyone had eaten Jane started the conversation. 'Me and your dad have something to tell you both.'

'About time,' Lara interjected. 'You're splitting up and want to discuss the future.'

Both Jane and Neil looked shocked. They thought they'd done their best to hide it from her and here she was pre-empting the conversation they'd been planning for weeks.

'How did you guess?' Jane asked.

'Guess? It's been written over both your faces for ages. Just get it over with and then we can all get on with our lives.' Lara looked relieved that it was finally out in the open. She'd hated walking on eggshells in case she said anything to upset the delicate balance in the household.

'How do you feel Simon?' Jane asked her son. Neil hadn't said a word yet. So much for sharing the burden.

'I've been speaking to Lara on a regular basis so I know the gist of things. We're not the children you seem to think. I've left home and Lara will be going next year. We both want you to be happy, and it's obvious that neither of you have been for a long time.' Simon looked lovingly at his mother, who started to cry.

'Since when did you two become so wise? It seems to me that you're behaving like the grownups while me and your dad are the children,' she said between sobs.

Neil spoke at last. 'Thank-you for being so understanding. It's taken a huge weight off my shoulders and I hope it has off your mother's.'

'Just one question,' asked Lara. 'Why now, after all these years?'

Jane looked at Neil, wondering whether to go for it and tell the whole truth.

Neil answered for both of them. 'Let's just say that it's become apparent we've nothing in common any more. I've met someone else and I want to be with her.'

The calm look on Lara's face turned to anger. 'So you've been cheating on mum. How could you do something so cowardly?'

'I know,' said Neil 'I should have waited until we split up, but these things happen. No-one plans for it.'

'Rubbish. You mean you didn't plan to screw another woman, it just happened?' Lara said, in full flow. 'Yeah, right. And I was born yesterday.'

'Lara, don't speak to your father like that. He's explaining what happened. Where has this grown up attitude gone all of a sudden?' Jane wondered if she were to confess all whether she would get the same reaction, but it was obvious that Neil was taking the blame and she was grateful for that.

'It's OK Jane, I asked for that. I'm sorry if the truth hurts, but you asked me and I told you. I'm not proud of what I did, but if it's any consolation your mother and I have talked about it and she's fine with the situation.' Neil was trying to be as diplomatic as possible.

Lara wanted to do her usual routine of storming off to her bedroom but since she'd had been going out with Greg, who, at twenty, was much older than her, she was trying to be more mature.

Before she could say anything else Simon spoke. 'Who is this woman dad? We might as well know if she is going to be in our lives. If that's OK with you, mum?'

'Of course it is darling. I know the woman myself and she's actually very nice,' Jane said, thinking back to the day Sally had rung her to apologise.

She'd been sitting at her desk at work, the week after BC day. Neil and her had started referring to it as 'being caught day', shortened to BC. The phone had rung and the receptionist had said there was a Sally Mills on line one. Jane thought nothing of it as *the* Sally was called Green.

'Hello, Jane Barclay speaking. How can I help?'

'Hi Jane, it's me Sally. Please don't put the phone down,' she begged.

'Hello Sally. Why did you give a false name? Jane asked.

'I thought if you knew who it was you wouldn't speak to me, but I forgot to change my first name. I'd make a rubbish private detective.' Sally gave a nervous laugh.

'I wouldn't have put the phone down on you. I think you're very brave for ringing.'

The conversation had continued, with Sally apologising for her affair with Neil. She said it should never have started, although she wanted Jane to know she did love him and it wasn't a fling. Jane then apologised for the affair with Philip and after half-an-hour's conversation the two women were like old friends, which they could have been in differing circumstances, thought Jane sadly.

Neil hoped Lara would listen to what he had to say without flying off the handle again. 'She was my assistant. I've been working with her for over a year but I swear nothing happened until September. I really like her; she's eight years younger than me, never been married and has no children. Her name is Sally. I say was my assistant, she has now been moved to work for another partner.' Neil looked like a different person when he talked about Sally, Jane noticed.

'Are you going to live with her?' Lara asked in a petulant voice.

'Yes, we were just waiting to tell you two and then I'm moving in.' Neil said.

'What will happen to the house?' Lara asked.

'We're putting it up for sale,' Jane said. 'You'll come and live with me, we can discuss where later. I thought we'd rent to start with. There'll be a bedroom for you Simon as well.' Jane had pulled herself together and was much more in control.

'While we're bearing our souls there's something I want to tell you.' Jane had finally plucked up enough courage to tell them about her dream. She might as well as they were all together. 'Now or never!' she thought.

Neil signalled Jane to be quiet as he thought she was going to spill the beans about Philip and he didn't think it was necessary. But she smiled and gently nodded her head.

'If I'd have been honest about this in the first place all this mess might never have happened. Are you sitting comfortably? Then I'll begin. It all began a few months ago. I don't know when exactly but I started having a dream. I can't say it was a nightmare but I'd suddenly wake up crying. I always disturbed your dad. It started with the odd night but then it became more frequent.

'I didn't tell you or your dad,' she addressed Lara, 'because I assumed you'd think I was mad. In hindsight that was the wrong decision as I could've really done with some support. In the dream I saw a woman from the Second World War era living in a large house. She'd just received a letter saying her fiancé had been killed in action. The woman started to cry and then I woke up and it was just as if I was the woman. I was also crying, my heart was beating fast and I felt such strong emotion I couldn't go back to sleep for fear of returning to the dream.

'Eventually I saw the end of the letter and there was a name, Daniel St. Claire. I've been researching the name for weeks. I've found out that he was a real person who was killed in 1941.'

'Wow! Mum, that's awesome,' said an incredulous Lara.

'Wait, there's more. You know when I went to Cornwall with your gran? It was to meet his sister. She's still living in Falmouth.'

'How did you find all this out?' Neil asked. He was amazed at his wife's revelation and he felt quite ashamed of himself. How could he have been so oblivious to what his wife had been going through?

'I researched it on the internet. I logged onto the Royal Air Force Service Records site and followed the links. I clicked on to back records and looked for '1941 Deaths in Action'Plus there are other sights with information about certain squadrons. He was in the 219 squadron stationed at Catterick.' Jane felt quite proud of discovery. 'His sister actually had the very same letter I'd dreamt about. Can you believe it? It turns out the woman in the dream was called Nora and she was also a real person. When I went up to Catterick it was to look for her. She died in the 1970's but had a daughter, and that brings me up to date. I'm trying to locate the daughter, Daisy, but not having much luck. There you have it! My little secret is out in the open. What do you think?' Jane heaved a sigh of relief.

For a while all three were speechless. Simon spoke first 'Why do you think you had this dream, mum?'

'That I don't know, but what I've come to realise is, while I'm actively looking to solve the mystery, I don't have the dream. But when I put it on the back burner, like now, the dream becomes more frequent. I still haven't worked out why me. If something needs to be put right or needs to come out into the open, why should I have been chosen? I'm not influential and have no experience in situations like these plus I live in the back of beyond. What can I do?' Jane had never managed to find an answer to these questions.

'I don't know, but if there's anything we can do to help, just ask.' Lara offered.

'I wish you'd have confided in us sooner.' Simon said, looking slightly disappointed with his mother.

'So do I sweetheart, but as I said I thought your dad would have me committed.' She laughed and Neil joined in.

'Your mother has a point. I know I'm not the most open minded of people but it's hard not to believe you when you have so much evidence.' Neil felt bad that Jane had so little faith in him, because she was probably right about his reaction.

Whenever she'd talked to him about subjects such as her interest in Feng Shui or Astrology he'd been very dismissive. He was only interested in factual subjects and things that could be proved. That was why he had such an affinity with numbers, they were safe. But he admired Jane for her tenacity and determination to get to the bottom of the mystery and, hopefully, he could be more open-minded in the future.

At the very least this conversation had changed the subject and let him off the hook for the moment. Everyone had seemed to have forgotten his confession about Sally.

Jane felt a weight had been lifted off her shoulders and, hopefully, with a little more perseverance, she could make a bit more progress in the search for Daisy. This revelation had brought a natural end to the previous discussion. That would save for another day. She wouldn't have to lie to her family again, she only had to tell them about Philip and then she would be absolved.

Chapter 19

Since moving to his studio flat in the middle of November Philip hadn't been feeling at all well. He'd been experiencing dreadful pains in his legs. It had started as a sharp ache and then it had felt like his legs were burning, leaving him with a constant nagging in both thighs. At first he put it down to stress because of the break up with Sally. Maybe it had affected him more than he cared to admit. He was also anxious about Jane. He really loved her and was scared she was going to break up with him because she couldn't cope with all the stress their relationship brought.

The pain had got so bad last week he'd called in sick at work and taken himself off to the doctor's. The doctor couldn't shed any light on it but agreed to send him for tests in case it was vascular and he had a blockage in his veins or arteries. He couldn't put it down to exercise because he'd recently turned into a bit of a slob and he hadn't done any walking since he'd been in Richmond.

He'd suggested to the doctor it could be from lack of sleep. He was usually an eight hour a night man but recently he'd been waking at four every morning with the excruciating pains in his legs. The GP had prescribed sleeping tablets which Philip wasn't keen on taking. He would rather have an extra can of lager or glass of wine, but he couldn't keep doing that or the pains in his legs would be the least of his problems.

What the last week had taught him was that he had to re-examine his life. He'd been drifting for the whole of his adult life. There wasn't one area of it he was satisfied with. He didn't like his job as a mechanical engineer. His interest in it had started when he had wanted to learn how to mend aeroplane engines, so he'd studied the subject at university. However aeronautics were such a small part of the course that he'd chosen to take the most popular subjects, ones that would give him the best career prospects.

He'd always been quite lazy, although he preferred the word unmotivated. His first love was, and always had been, flying. He could never understand why he'd given up his dream of becoming a pilot. He knew his eyesight had prevented him becoming a commercial pilot with the major airlines but smaller, private companies wouldn't rule him out. He could have also joined the RAF. He remembered his father trying to persuade him that the forces were a good career choice, but Philip had been adamant that hell would freeze over before he would enlist.

He'd actually got his commercial pilot's licence. It had cost him a small fortune over the years but he never used it. He had also been a flying instructor many years earlier.

He promised himself that he really must get back into flying, although with the pains in his legs as bad as they were at the moment he would find it difficult to concentrate. But it was a thought that recurred on a regular basis. There had been talk at work about voluntary redundancy and the bosses were asking for volunteers. It had been swimming around in his consciousness since they suggested it and the more he thought about it the more appealing it became.

Apart from Jane nothing was keeping him in this area and with the money he would receive he could relocate to the coast and teach flying lessons, or pilot a small biplane giving pleasure flights to tourists. He'd always had an affinity with Cornwall and knew that there were plenty of flights from the mainland to the Scilly Isles.

He would love Jane to go with him but he'd suggested it once in passing and she had said she wasn't ready to leave while her children were young. Philip didn't think seventeen and eighteen was too young, but he hadn't argued.

Although he loved Jane he didn't know if he was prepared to give up his dream again, to stay in a place that he didn't like, doing a job that wasn't fulfilling. He'd always felt that Sally had been a burden on his freedom. He'd no other family round here. His mum and dad had taken early retirement and lived in a small villa in Murcia, on the Costa Brava. He had an elder brother, but they weren't close, as Pete was fifteen years older than him. Philip had been a mistake, a gorgeous mistake his mother called him, but she'd been going into the change when she'd fallen pregnant. It had been a standing joke that she never knew how she conceived as she and his dad had so little contact in that department. It was akin to the Immaculate Conception.

They'd willingly raised Philip but as soon as he'd left for university they took early retirement and were off. He never blamed them and visited at least once a year. In fact, come to think of it, he could do with a holiday. He hadn't seen them since the beginning of the year but he spoke to them regularly on the phone. His dad had just invested in a web-cam so they could nag him face to face about not getting married and having children.

Pete had only produced one grandchild for them, a sullen boy like his father. They hardly knew him because he wouldn't drag himself away from his mother's apron strings long enough to pay them a visit. It had been a constant disappointment to them that Pete had married his childhood sweetheart Janet, whom they'd never seen eye to eye with. They still held onto the hope that Philip would marry a nice girl and provide them with a granddaughter they could spoil.

Philip thought just before Christmas was a perfect time to visit his parents, for a couple of reasons. The weather would be warmer in Spain and Jane was having a cooling off period while she sorted things out with Neil.

He hoped the warm weather would also help his legs. That thought sealed it for him. He dialled their home phone in Spain.

'Hi mum, it's me.'

'Philip, what a nice surprise.' His mother always sounded so delighted to hear from him.

'Do you fancy a visitor?' Philip asked, already knowing the answer.

'Michael, Philip's coming over, isn't that great?' his mum shouted to his dad, who was probably out in the garden. Philip heard a muffled reply, but couldn't make out what his dad had said.

'So is it alright if I come for Christmas?'

'Of course it is, it'll be lovely to have you. When are you going to come?'

'I'll book my flight when I've finished on the phone. Maybe tomorrow or the day after, depending on the flights.'

'Let us know exactly and we'll meet you off the plane.'

'Look forward to seeing you soon, mum.' Philip said goodbye and hung up. All he needed to do now was book a ticket and then ring work to add another couple of days onto his holiday. He got straight onto Jet2.com and secured one of the last seats on the plane going to Murcia on the 21st December.

Hopefully Jane would understand why he was going. Then, when he came back in the New Year, they could make a fresh start. He thought back to the first argument they'd had in Richmond and hated to admit that things had never been the same since then. In fact it was just after that weekend that his legs had started hurting. They'd been having such a lovely time until Jane had to rush home. Then, when she returned, all hell had broken loose. She'd turned into a mad woman and he'd found her hard to cope with.

Despite that he'd never had such strong feelings for a woman. He could honestly say that she was the love of his life and if it didn't work out with her he would resign himself to being a bachelor. Never mind what his mum and dad wanted for him.

Thinking back to his legs, the only time they didn't hurt was when he was making love with Jane. It must be something to do with his mind being elsewhere. He desperately wanted to speak to her, to tell her about new plans to go to Spain. He took out his phone and rang her number. 'Hi love, I just thought I'd give you a ring. What are you doing?'

'Nothing much, do you want some company?' Jane was at a loose end and Sundays weren't her favourite day.

'Yes please.' His eyes lit up at the thought.

'I'll get ready and come straight round,' Jane said, excited at the prospect of seeing Philip. He still had the power to give her butterflies. Neil was at Sally's and Lara was watching TV with Greg in her bedroom. Jane hoped that's what they were doing anyway! Simon had gone to see his old college mates at the pub, so none of them would miss her. Since Lara's outburst Jane hadn't plucked up enough courage to tell them about Philip, but they'd never said anything else to Neil and seemed to accept him seeing Sally.

Neil had finally settled on December 28th for moving out. It had been decided that it was just too much hassle to move before Christmas. Madge was bringing George for dinner. Neil's mum would join them as well. Probably the last Barclay Christmas she would be involved in.

Jane had finished her Christmas shopping and had only the last-minute fresh produce to buy. She hadn't seen very much of Philip recently, although she'd spoken to him daily on the phone. They hadn't made love much either, and since her sex life had really picked up because of him, she was getting withdrawal symptoms.

Philip's flat was just outside Leeds City Centre in the new development by the river. It was in a prime location, overlooking the Royal Armouries. It was a tiny flat but big enough for him. It was on the fifth floor and she was feeling lazy, so she took the lift. Philip was waiting for her. He took her in his arms and kissed her.

'I've missed this,' he said, squeezing her tight.

'And I've missed this,' she said, undoing his trousers. Jane had felt horny all the way in the car and couldn't wait to rip his clothes off.

'That's my girl.' He led her to the bedroom. If he wasn't mistaken Jane seemed like her old self, the woman he'd fallen in love with. He wondered what had happened to bring about the change.

There was urgency to their love making, as there had been in the beginning. Lust fuelled their desires and he entered her without any tender foreplay. Both wanted it hard and fast and they came within a few minutes. He pulled out breathless and lay next to her. Despite the urgency, she was satisfied.

'That was wonderful,' she gasped.

'It's certainly brightened my Sunday up,' Philip said. She playfully hit his arm.

He thought about his legs for a second and, yes, the pain had gone. He made a mental note to tell the doctor the embarrassing truth. He'd mentioned the pains to Jane and told her he'd been to the doctor's.

She lay in his arms, occasionally reaching up to kiss him. She knew it wouldn't be long before he was hard again and they could make love, more slowly and tenderly this time.

'I hope you don't mind but I've booked to go to Spain to see my parents in a couple of days. I know you're having a final family Christmas and I haven't seen them for ages.' Philip was a bit wary about telling Jane in case she lost her temper as she had before.

'What a great idea. It'll do you good. The temperature might even help your legs,' she said.

'That's what I thought.' He was pleased she'd reacted that way and gave her an extra-long, passionate kiss.

'What was that for?'

'For being you, just like your old self.'

'I'm sorry if I've been a bit distant recently. I'd been worried about telling Simon and Lara, but we both explained things and they were fine.' She omitted to tell him about the dream and her confession to her family because she still hadn't found the courage to tell him yet. The longer she left it, the harder it became to broach the subject. She hoped when she did finally tell him he wouldn't be angry with her for keeping it from him for so long.

'I'll be back just after New Year's Day. Has Neil decided when he's moving out?'

'Between Christmas and New Year he thinks and, to be honest, I can't wait. A new start and all that. I'm putting the house up for sale in January, when people start looking for property again. It shouldn't take long to sell. We've always had a lot of interest in the house even when we weren't selling it. But I'm in a bit of a quandary. I don't know where to move to. Lara still wants to stay near college, and her new boyfriend, but it would be more convenient for me to move to Leeds.'

'I've got a decision to make myself.' Philip hadn't mentioned to Jane about the chance of voluntary redundancy before. He explained all about it and she thought it was a great idea.

'You haven't been happy in your job for a long time. What will you do instead?' she asked.

'I don't know,' he lied. He wasn't going to let her know about his plans to take up flying again until there was something more concrete to tell her.

'Something will come up. Talking of things coming up, are you ready to go again you insatiable woman?' Philip said.

'Yes please.' Jane rolled over and sat on top of him. He loved this position and relished having his wonderful girlfriend back.

Chapter 20

Before Philip set off to Spain he sent off a speculative e-mail to a company in Cornwall which ran pleasure flights to the Isles of Scilly, attaching his curriculum vitae and asking if they'd any openings for an experienced, albeit little rusty, pilot. He would leave it in the lap of the gods.

He felt much better about leaving Jane after their love-making on Sunday, and after their long chat he felt a lot more secure in their relationship. She'd looked positively radiant when she'd left, ready to take on her potentially stressful Christmas.

The taxi was due any minute to take him to Leeds/Bradford airport. He looked at his watch and worked out that in four hours time he would be sitting on his parents' balcony enjoying one of the many glasses of red wine he intended to drink over the festive season. He'd decided he was going to tell them all about his relationship with Jane. He needed someone to talk to, and run his plans past, and they never judged him. They'd supported him even when he'd made stupid decisions. Hopefully they wouldn't see the split with Sally as foolish, or judge him because he was having an affair with a married woman. It did sound sordid when he put it like that but hopefully he could convey his depth of feeling and prove to them that Jane really was the love of his life.

The flight was on schedule and, amazingly enough, his case was the first to be loaded onto the carousel. He spotted his dad in the terminal and went over to give him a hug. He loved his parents, though sometimes he forgot how much until he saw them again. His mum was waiting for them back at the villa. Although she didn't like to admit it her health wasn't as good as it used to be. She'd aged since he last saw her and her back was giving her a lot of pain.

But despite this she still spoiled him rotten, getting up to fetch his drinks and food, in order that he could have a much deserved rest. He always felt relaxed in their company. As he sat on the balcony drinking the red wine he'd promised himself his dad came and sat with him.

'We've got you a special Christmas present, but you have to have it early,' his dad said. 'I got talking to a man at the golf club who has a friend that runs a flying school a little further up the coast. He offered to let you fly one of his planes, if we pay for the fuel. So that's your present, fuel for a plane,' he joked.

'Thanks dad, you must be psychic.' Philip sounded as excited as a small child who had been bought his favourite toy. 'I've been thinking a lot about flying recently and I intend to take it up again.'

'I know it's short notice but I've arranged for you to go tomorrow, because they're closed over Christmas. I'll drop you off, go for a round of golf, and pick you up later in the afternoon.' He loved seeing his son so excited.

This holiday was going to be even better than Philip had expected. As he lay in bed later that night, excited about tomorrow, the pain in his legs hit an all time high and no amount of pain killers would take the edge off it. It was so intense it brought him to tears and he was frightened it would stop him flying. But something happened that had never happened before. The pain suddenly stopped. One minute he was rolling around in agony and the next minute nothing, the pain had completely gone. He was so relieved, but baffled as to what was causing it. He drifted off to sleep and didn't wake until early the next morning.

He had a breakfast of fruit while sitting on the terrace waiting for his father to get ready. He hadn't realised how much he'd missed flying and couldn't wait to be back up in the air.

The airfield was only twenty miles up the coast. Philip spotted the planes from the road. He started to identify all the ones he could see. A habit he'd had from his youth and never grown out of. He would be borrowing a flying suit because he hadn't known about the surprise, but he did keep his pilot's licence in his wallet.

His dad introduced him to Ted, whose school it was. Philip followed him into the office to have a chat. Ted asked Philip about his experience and was satisfied that he could go up on his own. Forms were filled in for insurance and then Philip was ready to go.

He couldn't wait to get into the cockpit. Ted came with him to make sure he was familiar with this particular Cessna Skycat, a two-seater, trainer plane. Philip had learned in one, so he was familiar with the controls. He put his headset on so he would be connected to the tower at all times. They agreed that he would fly for thirty minutes and then land. Both felt it was long enough for a first flight in a long time.

Philip was cleared for takeoff and started the engine. He pulled back on the control column and headed down the runway. When he was at sufficient speed he pulled up and the nose of the plane lifted. He was up in the air for the first time in over two years. It was exhilarating. There was no other feeling like it on earth apart from, maybe, sex, and then it would be a close call.

The sky was a cobalt blue and there wasn't a cloud in sight.

'Tower to Delta, come in please,' a voice came over the headset.

'Delta to tower, receiving. Everything hunky-dory up here. I can't believe I've left it so long. See you soon, over and out,' Philip replied. He continued to climb, surveying the surrounding countryside until he was at his desired height and speed. He then relaxed and enjoyed the flight.

Just at that moment Philip got an excruciating pain in his legs. It nearly took his breath away. Please, not up here, he thought. Then his eyesight blurred, he blinked a few times and instinctively, for safety, he put the plane on auto pilot. He rubbed his eyes and when he opened them it was dark. The sky was now black with heavy cloud. The only lights were from his cockpit. The plane was no longer a Cessna and he was looking at the controls of an old Spitfire which had been decommissioned after the Second World War.

He looked around and noticed smoke coming from his wing. 'Shit.' It was on fire. The flames were spreading up the wing and would be in the engine any second. The plane started to nose spin.

'Mayday, Mayday, Mayday! Sp3,Sp3,Sp3. I'm going down!' he screamed into the radio microphone in his oxygen mask. Before he had chance to eject another explosion hit the cockpit and all he could feel was a searing pain ripping through his legs. Then he blacked out.

The next second Philip found himself back behind the control column of the Cessna surrounded by brilliant blue sky and with a scorching sun. He was aware of a voice in his headphones,

'Tower to Delta, Tower to Delta. Is everything OK? Come in please,' the concerned voice said.

Philip managed to get his thoughts together sufficiently to speak. 'Delta, receiving. I'm coming in. I'll explain when I get down, over and out.' The pain in his legs had gone and his eyesight was fine. What had just happened to him? He managed to focus his concentration and prepared to slowly descend to the runway. His way was clear and he decelerated until his wheels smoothly touched the ground, then he applied the brakes. He taxied back to the small terminal and switched off the engine. That was the last thing he remembered.

Ted ran over to the plane and found Philip unconscious in the front seat. He radioed control and told them to call an ambulance. It arrived within minutes and Philip was taken off to the hospital in Murcia.

It was four hours later when he opened his eyes and found a doctor examining his chest with a stethoscope.

'Ola senor Sinclair, como esta?' Philip looked confused. 'Sorry, how are you? You gave us quite a fright.' The doctor now spoke perfect English.

'I think I'm OK I've just got a pounding headache.' Philip was groggy. He looked around and saw his mum and dad sitting by his bed and Ted standing by their side. His mother looked deathly pale.

'What happened up there, mate?' Ted asked.

Philip couldn't tell them about his hallucination. He just said his eyesight went a bit blurred and he didn't remember anything after landing.

'We'd like you to stay in so we can run some tests. We need to get to the bottom of what happened,' the doctor said. 'Have you had anything like this happen to you before?'

'No. I've been seeing my GP for pains in my legs but we put it down to stress. I've had a lot on my plate recently,' Philip confessed.

'We'll take some bloods, then give you an MRI and a CT scan to rule out things like epilepsy or a stroke,' the doctor said.

It was a very efficient hospital and before he went to bed that night all the tests had been performed. He telephoned Jane to let her know that he was in hospital. She was very worried and wanted to fly over. He told her there was absolutely no need and he would keep her informed. What a time to be taken ill, two days before Christmas!

All the tests came back negative. He didn't have epilepsy, a brain tumour or anything else equally as sinister. The doctor put it down to a panic attack and discharged him on the proviso that as soon as he returned home he would make an appointment with his own doctor.

If he'd thought his mother had spoiled him before, it was nothing to what she did now. He wasn't allowed to move from the sun lounger unless he needed to go to the toilet. He was surprised she hadn't suggested a bedpan, although he would've drawn the line at that. She brought him drinks, food, a book, magazines and even set up the portable television in case he wanted to watch it.

Jane rang every few hours to see how he was getting on. She and his mother had become quite close through all the conversations they'd had and they loved gossiping about Philip, sharing stories about him, much to his disgust.

He hadn't had a recurrence of any of his symptoms and felt pretty much back to normal by Christmas day. It was unusual to spend the day outside in the warm sunshine eating a turkey dinner on the terrace but it was something he could become accustomed to.

The day after Boxing Day Philip returned to the airfield with his dad. He'd arranged to go up in the plane with Ted. The first time they went up Ted flew the plane and Philip was an observer. The second time Philip took the controls. He performed perfectly, doing everything by the book. He felt calm all the time he was in the air. The odd thing was, just before the strange episode he'd been perfectly calm, loving the sensation of flying. He'd felt confident and, he knew it sounded corny, he felt he'd come home.

Philip hadn't mentioned the episode to anyone. He didn't know who he could tell who wouldn't think him mad or seriously ill. Maybe Jane would understand so he would think about confiding in her. He stayed an extra couple of days with his mum and dad until they finally stopped fussing over him, accepting his word that he was back to his old self.

They had a long discussion about Jane. He told them of his strong feelings for her and they were pleased. It wasn't that they didn't like Sally, it was just that they hadn't thought she was right for Philip. They said they would love to meet Jane, as she sounded so nice on the phone, and Philip promised that if it worked out he would bring her to meet them soon.

When he finally returned home he felt rested and ready to start the New Year. He was excited at all the new opportunities that could possibly come his way. He turned on his computer to check his mail and saw that he had an e-mail from the flying school in Cornwall. They thanked him for his interest and coincidently a pilot was due to retire on the grounds of ill health in March so, would he like to come down for a test flight?

He felt that the New Year was going to be good for him as he pressed 'send', informing them that he would love to come down and have a test flight at their earliest convenience.

Chapter 21

The Barclay Christmas couldn't be described as either peaceful or calm. Jane could barely concentrate on anything other than Philip lying in hospital in Spain and it was apparent that Neil didn't want to be there. He was texting Sally every five minutes.

Mrs Barclay, she didn't like informality, arrived on Christmas Eve from Cheltenham. Neil picked her up from the train station as she'd never learnt to drive. In fact she hadn't learnt to do much of anything, apart from criticise and she had a degree in that. Having said that, she practiced enough. For starters the train was delayed and it was full of riff-raff. Then she complained that Neil had parked too far away and she'd had to walk, the traffic was busy in town, etcetera. Jane had learnt to switch off for most of the time but when it was constant, it got very tiring.

The other thing Mrs Barclay was good at was praising her son. Everyone paled into insignificance compared to her precious Neil. He'd told his mother of the impending split and she'd immediately started to criticise Jane for not being a good enough wife and driving her son away.

Over the years Jane had learnt not to argue. Mrs Barclay was totally irrational when it came to Neil and no amount of arguing would convince her otherwise. It had been a sad day when Dennis, he liked informality, had died. When Jane was feeling cruel she thought he died young so he didn't have to listen to his wife a moment longer, but she would never have said that to Neil. She'd adored his dad and he'd always defended her position. He could see the flaws in his son and saw that he took Jane for granted. Neil was like he was because of his mother. He'd never lifted a finger when he lived at home and had expected life to continue in that vein when he'd got married.

It had been a great disappointment to Mrs Barclay when Jane had fallen pregnant. Jane still thought his mother believed he would marry into royalty. She'd never really forgiven Jane for deliberately getting pregnant to snare her son. Then a thought hit her, one big bonus of getting a divorce was that she would never have to spend another Christmas with the perfect Mrs Barclay. Whoopee! What a thought. Poor Sally, it was her turn now.

Needless to say Mrs Barclay and Madge didn't see eye to eye. They hadn't seen each other for years as the last time Mrs Barclay had come up to stay Madge had arranged to spend Christmas in Scotland. Something that Jane had been sorely tempted to do as well. This year Madge had agreed to come because she wanted George and Jane to get to know each other. It was hoped that George would be a calming influence on the two women, because Madge wouldn't take a leaf out of her daughter's book and ignore Neil's mother. She rose to the bait every time.

Both Simon and Lara were having dinner at home, although Lara would only be there in body, her spirit would be with Greg somewhere in

Wakefield. They all managed to get through the Christmas Eve dinner without too much fuss. Simon acted as peacemaker, distracting his grandma from making snide comments. Neil spent a lot of the time out of the way, making phone calls while Jane washed everything up by hand instead of using the dishwasher, so she could stay longer in the kitchen.

Simon was his grandma's favourite, Lara was too outspoken for her taste. She believed that women should have few opinions and keep quiet, particularly when talking to men. She also didn't like the way Lara spoke to her father and blamed Jane for not disciplining her at an early age.

Jane went to bed early on Christmas Eve. She took a bottle of red wine upstairs and watched television while texting Philip. Mrs Barclay was Neil's mother after all, so he could entertain her.

Christmas Day got off to a flying start as Mrs Barclay believed presents should be opened after dinner and Lara wanted to open hers straight away. She'd got a new, top of the range, hairdryer and she wanted to try it out. One argument down at least another ten to go, thought Jane.

Madge and George arrived just after twelve and Jane had never been more pleased to see her mother. At least now she had an ally. It was time to start on the sherry and Neil gave his mother a large glass as she said, 'just a small one for me.'

A small one my arse, thought Jane, she'll have polished the bottle off before we've started on the main course.

'How lovely to see you Madge,' Mrs Barclay said, through gritted teeth.

'Likewise Joyce.' Madge knew how to rile her. Ding! Round one.

Dinner was served at two because, guess what? Mrs Barclay liked watching the Queen at three. Jane really warmed to George. He was a kind, gentle soul. Even Mrs Barclay didn't moan when talking to him. He put everyone at ease and kept the conversation going.

'We've had an idea,' Madge said, looking at Jane. ' Both of us would like you to come to one of the meetings we go to, to see if someone can shed any light on the Daisy situation. You never know, you might get a message.' Deliberately bringing the subject up to goad Mrs Barclay.

Mrs Barclay couldn't bear to be left out of the conversation. 'What's that?' she asked.

'We go to the Spiritualist Church and wondered if Jane would like to come one day,' George said.

Jane cringed, waiting for the reaction.

'How fascinating! When my dear Dennis died I went to a meeting myself. I found the whole experience very comforting,' she said.

Well, you could have knocked Jane down with a feather. No criticism or negative comments. Even Neil looked shocked.

'That's how a lot of people start, when they lose a loved one. I went after I lost my wife and I've been involved ever since. Did you carry on going?' George asked.

'No. I went to a special service with a friend. She didn't go again and I didn't want to go by myself.' For a second Mrs Barclay seemed vulnerable and Jane started to feel sorry for her, but only for a second.

George kept Mrs Barclay, 'call me Joyce', talking all over lunch, letting everyone else breathe a sigh of relief. The food was beautifully cooked and as usual everyone was completely stuffed before the dessert. Three bottles of wine were empty on the table and a good time was had by all.

Madge went into the kitchen with Jane.

'What do you think?' She turned back to look at George.

'I think he's lovely, I think you've got a real gem there mum. Anyone who can charm Mrs Barclay, 'call me Joyce', deserves to be canonised.' They both laughed. 'Seriously, keep hold of that one. He obviously idolises you and I've never seen you look so happy'. Jane was really pleased for her mother.

'How's Philip?' Madge asked.

Jane had told her mother about Philip being in hospital. 'He seems a lot better and his mum isn't as worried, so that must be a good sign. I just wish I could be with him.'

Madge put on her stern voice. 'He'll be back soon and I think you've enough on your plate without running off to foreign climes.'

'I know. I just miss him,' Jane said wistfully.

'Is Neil still moving on the 28th?' Madge asked.

'I think so, the van's booked and he's started to pack.'

'Are you OK about him going?' Madge touched Jane's arm tenderly.

'To be honest, I can't wait to get on with the rest of my life. We've been getting on each others' nerves again recently and we had been getting on so well.'

'Let me know when you want to go to the Spiritualist Church, won't you? Now Christmas is nearly over you can resume your search. Let's hope the New Year can bring some answers,' Madge said, philosophically.

Chapter 22

Neil dropped Mrs Barclay back at the station the day after Boxing Day. She thanked Jane for a wonderful time. She seemed as if she'd meant it. As she left she gave Jane an awkward hug and told her she hoped they wouldn't lose touch, even when her 'misguided son had left'. Had Jane heard correctly? Had she criticised her beloved Neil?

'I know you think I'm a silly old woman for sticking up for my son but I can't help it. I do love him, though I see his flaws like anyone else. I know you've done your best to make him happy. He's just thrown away a good relationship. I hope his new floozy is worth it.' Jane was very grateful for the acknowledgement and returned the hug, which was the only physical contact that had passed between them in all these years.

The house returned to normal after the Christmas festivities. Presents had been put away and the alcohol returned to a cupboard until next year. Although there wouldn't be a next year in this house Jane thought, wistfully. She would have to think about where she was going to live if the house sold quickly.

The previous few days had been so hectic that Jane hadn't had much time to sit down and relax, so tonight she was going to treat herself to an evening watching a romantic comedy she'd taped on her Sky Planner. Everyone else was out. She had her bottle of red wine and a box of chocolates ready but just as she sat down with her remote control the telephone rang.

'Hello, is that Jane? It's Steve here, from Steve and Paula and Toby.' He sounded slightly nervous.

'Hello, how is the little man? Sorry, I should ask, how are you?' Jane realised her slip of the tongue and laughed.

'Don't worry, everyone asks about Toby first.' He laughed as well. 'We're all fine. I hope you don't mind me ringing but Philip gave me your number. I'd like to run something by you if that's OK?' Steve said nervously.

'You want me to have Toby again?' she asked hopefully.

'Well, sort of. I've been offered a great job in Dubai starting in February but Paula won't even consider it because of Toby. I thought that if I could find a home for him she might reconsider. So I wondered if you'd think about having him.'

'February, you say? I might be living somewhere else by then. I assume Philip has filled you in on my domestic situation. I'm just about to start looking for a place to rent. I've always wanted a dog and I did fall in love with Toby. I'll think about it for a few days, but I'm certainly not saying no.' Jane was trying to be rational, instead of just following her heart and saying, 'yes please!'

'I don't know if it would be of any use to you but, if we go, we'll be renting out our house. The job is for two years but you could take it for a shorter time if it would help?'

'Where do you live?' Jane asked.

'We live in Garforth. It's a semi-detached cottage with lots of land and no other houses nearby. We love it.' Steve went on to describe the house.

'That would be fine for me to travel to Leeds and not too far for Lara to get to college. She starts driving lessons next week and I intend to buy her a car. Could we come and see it?' Jane asked, excited that she would get to see Toby. Lara might also fall in love with the spaniel, which would make her decision easier.

'I'll run it past Paula and ring you back if that's OK. I haven't told her I'm ringing you,' Steve said, slightly more confidently than he'd been at the beginning of the conversation.

'Thanks for thinking of me and I'll speak to you soon. Bye.' Jane put the phone down. She might finally get a dog after all. Life without Neil was already looking good.

Neil did move out on the 28th December. There were no tears from anyone. Simon and Lara had volunteered to help and carried some of Neil's boxes to the car. Simon hugged his dad then prised Lara off him so their parents could speak in peace.

'Well this is it,' Neil said. 'Did you ever think we'd get to this stage? I don't think I did.'

'I'd never really given it much thought until all this happened. There have been times when I've not been happy, but isn't that the case with all relationships?' Funnily enough, Jane didn't feel like crying. Maybe it would hit her later.

Neil just stood there. He was reluctant to get in the car and leave. He was going to miss his house nearly as much as he was going to miss his family. He couldn't help wondering if he was rushing into things.

''Bye then.' Neil held out his arms for Jane to hug him. He looked sad.

Jane saw the look on his face. 'We'll keep in touch, but this is for the best. At least this way we can stay friends. I really hope it works out for you and Sally.' Neil climbed into the Range Rover. Jane would miss the vehicle because, although she loved her car, it wasn't as practical as Neil's. She felt very mercenary, thinking about cars as her husband was leaving the marital home.

Sally was waiting for Neil to arrive. She'd moved a lot of her things so he could have half the wardrobe, and she'd made space for him in the bathroom. She was very nervous because she desperately wanted it to work. Her friends had warned her that it was too soon to move in together, that he was still on the rebound, but she wouldn't have it.

In fact she didn't have much support from anyone. Her mother had flown off the handle when she'd confided in her, she didn't approve of affairs and breaking up marriages. She'd said Sally should be ashamed of herself, carrying on with a married man and, 'that's not how she'd been brought up'. When it was put like that, she didn't feel very proud of herself. She'd set out to ensnare Neil with her looks and body and it had worked. They still couldn't keep their hands off each other. She just hoped that there was more to this relationship than sex.

Neil was wondering the same thing as he pulled up outside the flat. He'd been looking forward to his freedom so much and now it was finally here it was a bit of an anti-climax. The phrase jumping from the frying pan into the fire sprang to mind. Well, no point in looking back. He'd made his decision and he was determined to make it work. He waved to Sally as she came out to greet him.

'Hello. I finally made it,' Neil said, enthusiastically.

'Do you want a hand with the boxes?' Sally offered.

'Please, those two are the lightest.' It only took three journeys to empty his car. Sally stood and watched him unpack, grinning like a Cheshire cat. She'd finally got her man.

'Come here and give me a welcoming hug.' Sally knew it wouldn't stop at a hug and her new sex life was well and truly beginning.

That evening Jane rang Philip in Spain.

'Hi, it's me,' Jane said. 'Steve rang me today, but I suppose you knew that, seeing as it was you that gave him my number. Did he tell you what he wanted?'

'He briefly mentioned it, but you tell me.' Philip did know but he didn't want to spoil Jane's surprise.

'He wanted to ask if I would consider adopting Toby. What do you think?'

'Do you really need my opinion? I'd have thought you'd have already made up your mind. You love that little dog.' Philip smiled, imagining Jane's excited face.

'I know, but I'm trying to be practical. I think I'm going to say yes though.'

'You've always wanted a dog and now, with Neil gone, there's nothing stopping you. I can't wait to see you, it's only a few more days now.'

'Are you feeling better?' Jane asked.

'I'm completely back to normal. Are you OK without Neil?'

'I am actually. The house is lovely and peaceful.' She didn't tell him about her feelings of loneliness and abandonment. Hopefully they would soon pass and she'd be back to her optimistic self in no time at all.

Chapter 23

The holiday had revitalised Philip and it had helped put his life back into perspective. He'd decided that he would apply for voluntary redundancy as he definitely didn't want to continue working as a Mechanical Engineer, even if he didn't get this flying job. A test flight had been arranged for the third weekend in January and he was looking forward to it immensely. He'd contacted the local flying club and had booked some flying hours because he didn't want to appear out of practice when he went to Cornwall. From now on he was going to make things happen. He'd wasted too much of his life drifting and he would start to make positive decisions rather than relying on the *laissez faire* attitude he'd had most of his adult life.

He also needed to reassess his personal life. He would really like to settle down and get married. He sincerely hoped it would be with Jane. He was unsure about having children, particularly if he stayed with her. They hadn't discussed having a family but he doubted she would want to start again when her two offspring were nearly grown up. But it was still early days to discuss the future and make any firm decisions. He was just looking forward to seeing her again. She was coming round after work today and it would be the first time he'd seen her since he'd come back.

They'd had plenty of conversations over the phone and, as neither of them had a party to go to, they'd spent most of New Year's eve talking to each other. He'd have to take out a mortgage just to pay his phone bill. He was going to tell her about his redundancy decision and his test flight but wasn't sure he wanted to talk about his 'episode'. He liked to pretend it had never happened and sometimes could almost believe it himself, as it hadn't happened again.

He still hadn't made an appointment to go to his GP even though he'd promised the Spanish doctor he would. The pain in his legs had definitely subsided and it could only be described now as a dull ache. His sick note was due to expire tomorrow and he was returning to work. He'd been off for over two weeks and he really didn't want to go back.

He'd spent a lot of time reading and he'd caught up on most of the books he'd been given as presents for his last two birthdays and Christmas. He felt reading was a lot more productive than sitting in front of the television watching mindless, depressing programmes. Just another step in the improve Philip Sinclair for 2010.

It had been weeks since Jane had agreed to go to lunch with Zoe, the girl she'd met at Sally's house the night of the Tarot reading. She felt a bit awkward as Zoe was Sally's friend and Jane didn't want her to have to take sides. So instead of ringing, Jane sent a text to see if she was still interested in meeting up. Zoe texted back that she was really glad Jane had made contact and she'd love to have lunch. Would today be too soon?

They arranged to meet in Starbucks on the Headrow at one o'clock. Jane walked in to find Zoe already sitting at a table, drinking coffee and eating a big piece of carrot cake. They both looked pleased to see each other.

'Sorry, I've already ordered and I didn't know what you'd want,' Zoe said through a mouthful of cake.

'It's OK, I'm a few minutes late. I'll just get myself a coffee and join you.' Jane went to the counter to order, returning minutes later with a latte and a lemon muffin.

'I'm sorry to hear about you and Neil. If it's any consolation Sally isn't the flavour of the month with us at the moment. We think what she did was despicable,' Zoe said angrily.

'It was inevitable really. If it hadn't been Sally, one day it would have been someone else. Anyway I'm not that squeaky clean. I've been seeing someone.' Jane found it easier to confess all to someone she didn't know too well.

'Tell me more,' Zoe lent forward, interested to hear the latest gossip.

'I'm seeing Sally's ex, Philip.' She waited to see Zoe 's reaction.

'You lucky cow!' Zoe joked. 'He's a real hunk. We all fancy him. It's his aloof attitude and smouldering good looks that send women mad.'

'Honestly! He's no idea. He's really modest but I think he's gorgeous. No-one's ever had the effect that he has on me. When I saw Rosa I thought she was going to foresee my relationship with Philip but she told me I would fall in love with someone I'd known before. To be honest, I can't get this out of my mind. Other things she predicted have already come true, so I sometimes think I'm wasting my time with Philip as there might be some other man waiting for me round the corner.' That was the first time Jane had admitted that and was wondering whether it was the real reason for playing it cool with Philip.

'I know Rosa is good but don't spoil a perfectly good relationship on the grounds of what she predicted. She can't possibly be right one hundred percent of the time. If you like Philip, and he likes you, go for it.'

'I do like him, but to be honest I'm enjoying being on my own. I got together with Neil when I was only nineteen. We had to get married. We had two children straight away and that's been it. I don't know if I'm ready for another serious relationship so soon, though I am getting a dog!'

'What kind? I love dogs,' Zoe said.

'A Springer spaniel. A friend of Philip's is taking a job in Dubai and they have this dog they need to rehome. Neil never wanted a pet so that's something else I've done now that I'm on my own.' Jane got really excited when she talked about Toby.

Steve had phoned Jane back the next evening. He'd spoken to Paula, who'd reluctantly decided that she was prepared to let Toby go to Jane. But she'd also decided that she wanted to sell the house, which meant Jane wouldn't be able to rent it from them. This actually suited Jane fine as she was settled where she was, at least for the time being until the house sold. She'd worked out her finances and with Neil's contribution to the mortgage she could afford to stay there. Neil was quite happy for her to do this. Since Neil had moved out the atmosphere in the house was back to the peace and calm of old.

'I've never had a dog myself but my parents have always kept border collies,' Zoe said.

'Dogs are much more reliable than men. They don't expect anything apart from food, walks and affection. I can't wait to adopt him. Are you happily married?'

'I am yes, but I didn't settle down until I was twenty-eight. I sowed plenty of wild oats before that and I feel I got it all out of my system. I married Martin when I was thirty. I think it's a good age. I haven't told many people this but I've just found out I'm pregnant.' Zoe looked radiant.

'Congratulations! That's fantastic. How many weeks are you?'

'About nine I think. It's still too early to make it public but it's also the reason I'm stuffing my face with Carrot cake and everything that moves.' Zoe laughed.

'How exciting. Is your husband thrilled?' Jane asked.

'He is, but he won't let me do anything. I keep telling him it's not an illness and that I'm only pregnant.'

'I'd make the most of it if I were you. Neil never lifted a finger once I'd had the children. I don't know why I put up with it so long. Hindsight is a wonderful thing,' Jane said wistfully. They talked about the pregnancy for a while longer.

Eventually Zoe glanced at her watch. 'I'm afraid I've got to get back to work. I can't walk as fast as I used to. I'm also exhausted from standing up all day. I don't know how long I'll be able to carry on doing my job.' Zoe was a retail manager at Marks and Spencer's.

Jane offered her some consolation. 'It does get easier once the first three months are up. You should start feeling better. Well, I'm really glad we got together. I thought it was going to be awkward, what with Sally being your friend, but it was lovely to talk to you. We'll have to do it again sometime.' Jane had really enjoyed her girly chat.

'Absolutely, and don't forget to give Philip one from me!' Zoe joked.

Jane felt better about the Philip situation as she walked back to work. Talking about it had helped and she couldn't wait to see him later that day.

Philip held onto Jane as though they'd been apart for years. He couldn't stop kissing her and it was obvious from his erection that he wanted her. She could feel herself getting aroused from the first kiss and it was only a matter of minutes before they were ripping each other's clothcs off and making mad, passionate love on the settee.

'Happy New Year and welcome back.' Philip said. 'My New Year's resolution is to do that as much as possible.'

'Mine was to give up eating so much cheese, but I prefer yours.' She rolled on top of him again ready for round two.

'Being ill has certainly not affected you in that department.' Jane waited to get her breath back. 'That was fantastic.' They decided that twice was enough for now and went searching for the clothes they'd strewn around the room.

Philip suddenly became less frivolous, 'There's something I want to discuss with you.'

'That sounds ominous. I hope it's nothing serious.' Jane was hoping it wasn't anything to do with his legs.

'I've been offered voluntary redundancy at work and I think I'm going to take it,' Philip said.

'Is that all? I thought from the look on your face it was really serious.' Jane was relieved.

'There's more. You know my passion for flying? Well I'm taking it up again. Before I went to Spain I e-mailed a company to see if they'd any openings for a pilot. And guess what? They replied and they've invited me for a test flight in two weeks.'

'Again, well done you. Why didn't you mention it to me before?' Jane wondered.

'Because I honestly thought nothing would come of it.' Philip cringed as he said, 'It's at Lands End.'

'Lands End, Cornwall? That's not very local, is it?' Jane was shocked.

'No, it's not. What do you think?' he asked.

'If it's your dream I think you should go for it. But if it involves me moving to Cornwall, forget it. My children and my job are up here and I'm finally starting to make a new life for myself. I don't want to up-sticks and move to the other end of the country.' The pitch in Jane's voice was getting higher as she was feeling more exasperated. If he got this job all the new-found happiness she'd started to feel would disappear with Philip to the other end of the country. Just when things were starting to come together; how could life be so unfair?

'I'd a feeling you'd say that. I was dreading telling you. Anyway I might not even get the job.'

'If you don't get that job there'll be others. I really want you to follow your dream. If you don't go because of me you'd always regret it, and then you'd start to resent me. I wouldn't want to be responsible for your unhappiness anymore than you'd want to be responsible for mine.' Jane couldn't believe she was being so rational because inside all she wanted to do was yell, 'don't go!' But she knew in her heart what she'd said was the right thing. 'Let's take it one step at a time and not worry about the future until it arrives. What we've got now is great, let's not spoil it.' Jane kissed him

'Since when did you become so wise?' Philip hugged her to him.

'I've no idea. It just seemed like the right thing to say.' Despite the bad news Jane was already starting to feel an inner peace. She was going to let fate take its course for a change, instead of trying to force things to happen.

Chapter 24

With Philip in Cornwall, Simon back in Liverpool and Lara away on a field trip it seemed the perfect opportunity for Jane to return to Richmond to see if she could shed any light on the whereabouts of Daisy. She would pound the streets asking people if they knew of her and she'd go into the local library to look at back issues of papers. Everything she thought a private detective would do.

It was a pity she couldn't take Toby as he would've loved to explore the fields around Richmond; it was such a beautiful town. But she wasn't collecting him for another three weeks and she was counting the days.

She'd put a few things in a holdall in case she decided to stay the night. She could do that now, seeing as she was young (well youngish!), free and single. She threw it all in the boot of the car and set off. It was only ten o'clock when she arrived in Richmond. She parked in the most central car park and put enough money in the meter to last all day.

The task ahead was quite daunting, so what harm would a quick coffee and bacon sandwich do? She found a greasy spoon and sat down with the local paper. She was going to ask everyone she came into contact with if they'd heard of anyone called Daisy. The only information she had was that the lady would be in her sixties by now. The cafe owner hadn't heard of anyone by that name and neither had the other customers he asked on her behalf.

Feeling warmer and replete after her breakfast she went to find a local map in the tourist information office. They hadn't heard of anyone called Daisy either. She found the local library and asked how she could look at back issues of papers. It was all on microfiche so she found a space on a table and started scrawling through. After only an hour she was bored and decided that she wasn't patient enough to make a good private detective after all.

She'd felt more productive out on the streets so she left the library and walked to the Town Hall. There was a board outside it advertising up and coming events and concerts. She stopped to look and, to her astonishment, in prime position, was a poster advertising 'For one night only International Mediums, Steven Holford and Daisy Ledbury. Plus personal book signing of Daisy's new book, *From Darkness to Light*'. Jane couldn't believe her luck. The event was tonight and on a handwritten note it said that there were only a few tickets remaining. It might not be the correct Daisy but it was the only lead she had. She rang her mother.

'You'll never guess what I've found,' Jane said when Madge answered. 'There's a local medium called Daisy who's performing at Richmond Town Hall tonight. Do you want me to get tickets for you and George?' Jane couldn't get the words out fast enough.

'Yes, that would be nice. We were going to go to Dewsbury Church tonight but a few extra miles won't make much difference. It's a bit of a coincidence don't you think, that the Daisy you're looking for could be a medium? Until I met George we would never have considered going to see one, but George always says things happen for a reason and I'm starting to believe him,' Madge said.

'I'm going to go now mum, to make sure I get the tickets. It starts at seven and it's at the Town Hall in the middle of Richmond. Come early so you can find somewhere to park.' Jane hurried off to buy the tickets.

The poster was correct, there were only five tickets remaining, on the second to the back row. She purchased three and went outside to decide what to do until seven o'clock that evening.

Daisy was always slightly nervous when it came to performing in front of large audiences and this one was going to be big. Richmond Town Hall was always a sell-out, probably because it was her home town. She toured all over the British Isles and had even demonstrated abroad. Hence she could use the term, 'International Spiritualist Medium' on her advertising. For this current tour she'd teamed up with an up-and-coming new medium called Steven Holford and the two of them were going down a storm. He had the charisma and the looks and she had the experience and the accuracy. It made for a winning combination.

But today nerves were getting the better of her and she had a gnawing feeling deep down in her stomach, which she tended to get when something unusual was going to happen. That was the down side of being a medium, she thought. When it concerned her own life she didn't get to know anything specific she just got one of her feelings, and she was having one now.

Daisy discovered she had the gift not long after her mother died. On her deathbed Nora had asked her if she could see anyone else in the room. She couldn't make out definite figures but could see a mist of some description at the end of the bed. She'd gone to close a window, in case it was smoke from outside, but it had made no difference.

Soon after that Daisy had started to hear whispers. It was either schizophrenia or she was hearing Spirit. She preferred the latter explanation. She became interested in finding out what other people believed happened to you when you died, because her mother had died so young. She read lots of books on the Spiritualist movement. The famous medium Doris Stokes was still alive at the time. She was a lovely, down to earth woman who was not 'away with the fairies'.

Daisy went to a couple of Spiritualist Church services and was immediately given a message that being a medium was what she should be doing with her life. The rest was history. Without hesitation she'd given up a lucrative career in the bank. She'd now been earning her living as a medium for over thirty years. She did private readings and, like tonight, demonstrations to a large audience. But she'd never forgotten her roots and still did services for expenses at the local Spiritualist churches. She was always on the lookout for new mediums to take over when she retired and that's how she'd come across Steven. He'd been the medium in a church she'd visited down in the Midlands when she'd been on tour the previous year. She'd been very impressed with him and had invited him to work with her.

The one sadness in all these years was that her mother had never come back to her with a message. Everyone else in her family, her father and grandparents, had visited her. But she'd never understood to this day why her mother had never contacted her.

Daisy always liked to arrive early at a venue and, even though she knew the Town Hall like the back of her hand, she was in her dressing room by six. She liked to sit quietly and contemplate, getting rid of any outside stresses that modern living brought with it. She'd still not managed to throw off the gnawing feeling, deep down in her stomach, that she'd had all day. Now she assumed it had something to do with tonight.

The show would commence with both the mediums walking onto the stage. Since working with Steven they used more special effects to create an eerie atmosphere which ran up enormous bills for dry ice. Daisy would explain the format of the` evening and explain how mediumship worked, that they were only acting as vessels for Spirit to come through and they just passed on what they were given, which was sometimes why messages were cryptic. They never tried to interpret the messages as each one was intended for a specific recipient. Steven would warm up the audience for the first hour and then Daisy would come on stage for the remainder of the evening. As long as Spirit were coming through thick and fast she would keep on going, and one evening she was still giving messages at midnight. You certainly got value for money watching one of their shows.

Jane met Madge and George outside the Town Hall at six-thirty.

'That's good timing. I've just arrived.' Jane said.

'We set off in plenty of time in case we couldn't find anywhere to park. I assume you got the tickets?' Madge enquired.

'I managed to get three of the last five. We're right at the back of the hall. Not the best seats but at least we got some.' They joined the queue, waiting to be let in.

The Hall was already over half full. Jane was so excited, realising that months of searching could finally be over and she would have one more piece of the jigsaw puzzle. At least she hoped she would

Even though they didn't have the best seats in the house they still had a clear view of the stage. When the curtain went up, there wasn't a free seat in the auditorium. At exactly seven o'clock everything went black and deep red lights illuminated the stage, followed by billowing dry ice. It looked impressive, she would give them that. The music reached a crescendo and on walked Daisy Ledbury and Steven Holford.

Jane wondered if Daisy Ledbury had ever appeared on television because she did look very familiar. Lara liked to watch *Most Haunted Live* and other, similar programmes. Jane wondered if she could've seen her on one of those. She was a tall, slim woman who looked to be in her early sixties. She would have had very dark brown hair, if not black, at one time, but now it was salt and pepper with a predominance of white at the front. She exuded confidence and was a strikingly beautiful woman for her age.

Daisy was just about to speak and introduce the evening when a strange feeling came over her, so strange it rendered her speechless. Steven looked across to check everything was OK. If she didn't speak within the next five seconds he would take over.

But Daisy did speak, 'I'm sorry. You'll have to forgive me but something has just happened to me that's never occurred in all my time as a medium. My mother is with me. I've longed for a message from her for all these years and now, here today, I feel her presence. I know this is your evening but I felt I had to share this with you all. I don't know what she wants to say at the moment. If it becomes clear I'll let you know.' The audience gasped and gave her a spontaneous round of applause. Daisy thanked them.

'But enough of me, let me introduce to you an up and coming talented young medium who's going to begin proceedings tonight. Please put your hands together for Mr Steven Holford.' Daisy had managed to reconnect with her professional demeanour and signalled for Steven to do the explanation while she went backstage to see if she could shed some light on what she'd just experienced.

Daisy had felt her mother's presence as clearly as if she had been sitting in front of her. What was strange though was that it seemed her mother didn't know she was there. She'd no message for her and she wasn't showing Daisy anything. After thirty-eight years you'd think she'd make some effort, Daisy thought ungraciously. It was so frustrating for her. So near, yet so far.

Steven was drawing the first part of the show to a close and it was nearly time for Daisy to go on. The audience were given a fifteen minute comfort break and then the demonstration continued.

'They're a good audience out there tonight, very receptive,' Steven said as he came off stage. 'Are you alright now? You had me worried earlier.' Daisy had become like a second mother to him and he cared about her deeply.

'Yes, I'm fine love. My mother's spirit is still here, but I'm not getting anything else. Are you?' Daisy asked on the off chance.

'Sorry, nothing, but the Spirits are very strong tonight. You may get something out there. Good luck, not that you ever need it.' He kissed her cheek and she walked out onto the stage.

From the platform most of the audience was in semi-darkness. She quickly surveyed the room to see where she would be going first. She looked at the back row and saw a glimmer of light above the head of who she thought was a youngish woman, but then the light darted over to the left side. She said, 'Can I come to the gentleman in the khaki jacket?' and so it went on. Steven had been right in his assessment of the audience and the strength of Spirit, but at the end of her performance Daisy was none the wiser about her mother's appearance.

The proceedings came to a natural conclusion just after ten-thirty. Daisy had recently written a book and her publicist wanted her to sign copies of it in the foyer, after each performance. The table was laid out with the books and there was already a queue waiting to meet her. Steven had started selling the merchandise and was responsible for keeping the queue in an orderly fashion.

Jane had been really impressed with Daisy and had purchased a book from Steven.

'What did you think of them?' Jane asked George as they joined the queue to meet Daisy.

'I can honestly say she was one of the best, most accurate, mediums I've ever seen. He was good as well, but she was excellent. She seems such a lovely person.'

Jane was starting to get nervous as she approached the front. 'What have I to say to her?'

'I'm sure you'll think of something, although you can't say much here, you'll hold up the queue.' Madge said. 'Maybe suggest having a chat later.'

Jane handed Daisy the book 'Who would you like it dedicated to?' Daisy asked without looking up.

'Nora. I mean Jane, sorry.' Jane realised her slip of the tongue. She didn't know what had possessed her to say Nora.

Daisy looked up and made eye contact with Jane. It was like looking at a reflection in the mirror; they both had the most unusual lavender-grey eyes.

'What made you say Nora?'Daisy asked. It was as though a light bulb had just switched on in her head and she was starting to understand.

'I'm sorry, she's related to someone I'm looking for,' Jane replied.

'Well you may have just found her.' said Daisy smiling. 'Have you time for a chat after I've finished here?'

'Yes, that would be great, thank-you.' Jane looked at the woman fondly. She was starting to believe she'd found the correct Daisy.

'I'll get Steven to show you to my dressing room and I'll meet you there as soon as I've finished.' Jane knew it was all starting to fall in place for her.

It was after eleven-thirty when Daisy finally arrived at the dressing room,

'I'm sorry I've kept you waiting. People wanted to talk.'

'Don't worry about it, we're in no hurry,' Jane said, just thankful for any time Daisy could spare.

'Please tell me why you're here.' Daisy was waiting for the answer to her prayers.

'It's a long story though I bet you already knew that,' continued Jane. 'Let me start at the beginning. Months ago I began having a dream about a young girl who lost her fiancée in the Second World War. I had no idea what it was about. But I started doing research and found out that the man in my dreams was a real person called Daniel St.Claire and the girl was called Nora. I found Daniel's sister, a lady called Sarah St.Claire, who still lives in Cornwall, but I've been searching for months to find out who Nora was. I went to Catterick before Christmas and found a friend of hers who told me that Nora had moved to Richmond when she got married. She'd died young leaving a daughter called Daisy. I came up here today to see if I could find evidence of Daisy and I saw your poster. That's why I'm here, to find out if you are *the* Daisy. I need to know why I keep having this dream and you are my last hope.' Jane waited with baited breath.

Daisy just smiled. 'I knew today was going to be unusual, my gut never gets it wrong, and yes, I am *the* Daisy. My mother Nora died in 1971 and my father was a man called Daniel St.Claire. You're correct with your information. He was killed in the Second World War in 1941, but as to why you're dreaming about them, we'll have to work it out.'

Jane was so relieved she could have cried. Madge and George stood there open-mouthed.

'It's been a very strange day,' said Daisy. 'Let me tell you my story. My mother Nora died of cancer at 51. She was my life. I was so distraught I needed to find out where people went when they died and that got me into mediumship. I've been a very successful medium for over thirty years but in that entire time my mother has never come back to me to give me a message, until tonight.

'This morning I woke up with a gnawing feeling in my stomach, which I know from experience is a sign. When I went onto the stage tonight I could feel my mother's presence. What is more unusual is that she didn't know she was here. What date were you born?' Daisy asked.

'The fifteenth of November, 1971.' Jane didn't know where this was going. Daisy grinned.

'My mother died the fifteenth of November 1971. Do you know anything about re-incarnation and past lives?' Daisy asked, knowing such a question would stretch the imaginations of most open-minded people.

'Not really,' Jane replied.

'If this is what I think it is you're going to be in for a very big shock. I've heard it happen to other people but never anyone close to me. Look at me, what do you see?' Daisy looked at Jane.

Jane was confused. 'I don't know what you mean.'

'Really look at me. Tell me what you see,' Daisy reiterated

'I see a lady with very dark hair that has gone white at the front, who has unusual grey eyes. She is tall and slim with a larger than average chest. She has high cheek bones and thin lips, too thin some may say.' Jane started to see what Daisy was getting at.

'Look in the mirror over there and tell me what you see.'

Jane didn't need to do it as, apart from the white hair at the front, she might as well have been describing herself.

'What does it mean?' Jane was a bit apprehensive as to what Daisy was referring to.

'I think there's a possibility that you've lived before, as my mother.' Daisy paused. 'But this is all new to me and I'll have to do some more research.' This even stretched the boundaries of Daisy's belief system and she couldn't believe what she'd just said out loud.

'This would explain why she came to you in your dreams and why I've never had a message from her. For whatever reason, as soon as she died, she came back to earth for another life. What time were you born?' Daisy enquired.

Madge knew the answer to that one. 'Twenty past two in the afternoon.'

'That was the time my mother died, thereabouts. I remember I had just been out to get a sandwich and she'd held on until I got back.' Daisy recalled.

'But why?' Jane asked. She had so many questions.

'I don't know. From what I've learnt from my guides we go back to the Spirit World to take stock, and then we come back if we want another experience of the earthly plane or there's some unfinished business. But usually not until years later.' Daisy was at a loss for a more rational explanation.

'Suppose it's true, why now? Why come to me in a dream?' Jane asked, still finding it hard to believe.

'Maybe it was the only way Nora could communicate with you. It sounds as if it's more than a dream. Maybe a memory?'

'That actually makes sense, in a weird sort of a way. When I woke up I felt like I *was* the woman and that I was experiencing all the emotions she was feeling. But I wonder why it's all happened so recently. I've never had anything like it happen to me before. I can't say I would ever have described myself as psychic and I've never had any interest in the spirit world.'

'I can only go on what I've read. It's not in my experience. I've heard when all's not well in someone's life circumstances and events show up to facilitate change. Is that the case for you?' Daisy asked.

'Yes, my husband and I have recently separated. I went to see a clairvoyant at the end of last year and I picked the Lovers card. She told me it represented a love affair with someone I'd met before. It didn't make any sense at the time.' Jane recounted the story.

'If Nora has come back, maybe Daniel has too. They may have come to finish what they started.' She was saying the words but even Daisy was finding it hard to digest.

Madge and George couldn't believe what they were hearing and no amount of Spiritualist Church services could have prepared them for this leap of faith.

'Does this mean I'm your mother?' Jane asked, laughing nervously.

'A part of you could be, yes. But you're still your own person. Her soul will have merged with yours at birth, or so I understand. You must realise I don't understand much more than you do. You've answered one question tonight but it's brought up a dozen more. I'm still trying to process all the information.'

It was now well after twelve and they were all mentally and physically exhausted.

'Let's leave it for tonight and talk again tomorrow. Are you staying here in Richmond?' Daisy asked them all.

'We're going home to Leeds tonight,' Madge said, as she took hold of George's hand. She needed to feel grounded after the surreal conversation that they'd just experienced.

'I booked into a bed and breakfast when I knew I was coming here tonight,' Jane said.

'Here's my card. Give me a ring in the morning and we'll meet for breakfast.'

Jane had been looking for Daisy for so long she'd thought when she eventually found her everything would fall into place. This wasn't going to be the case as she was more confused than ever.

Chapter 25

Jane hardly slept a wink all night. She'd so much going on in her mind. She kept replaying the conversation with Daisy and was finding it all hard to believe. She'd heard of reincarnation. Wasn't that what Buddhists and Hindu's believed? But she'd never examined the concept in any depth, she'd had no need to. Her mother and father had brought her up in the Church of England and although she never went to church she still held on to the beliefs they'd taught her. Reincarnation of this type wasn't part of the Christian faith.

She'd finally given up on sleep at six-thirty and decided to have a long soak in the bath. It was eight o'clock when she rang Daisy.

'Hello, its Jane from last night.' Jane didn't know what else to say.

The devilment in Daisy wanted to say, 'Hello mum,' but she refrained as she didn't think Jane was ready yet for her sense of humour and probably wouldn't see the funny side of it. 'Would you like to come round for breakfast so we can talk?'

'That would be lovely. Where do you live?' Jane asked, getting a pen to write down the directions.

'You need to go back along the road as though you're going to Catterick and after about two hundred yards you'll come to a sharp right-hand bend. Signal left by the bend and you'll see a narrow lane. Turn down there and I'm in the house at the end. How long will you be? And do you eat full English breakfast? I don't normally, but some Sunday's I treat myself.' Daisy said.

'I certainly do. I'll look forward to it. See you at nine.' Jane went to finish getting ready. Even though she'd only just met Daisy she did feel very much at ease with her, as though they were old friends. Though, if what Daisy was telling her was the truth, they were so much more.

Jane thought it very strange to think that another person's soul was inside her. How much of her was Nora and how much of her was Jane? Were there other people walking around with someone else's soul inside them? And how could you tell? She'd so many questions and the more she thought about it, the more mindboggling it became.

She followed the directions Daisy had given her and turned into the narrow lane ten minutes early. The house at the end was large and impressive with a castellated front. It must have been a folly at one time, she thought. The gardens were beautifully landscaped and it obviously had acres of land. It was certainly much bigger than her own, seemingly modest, abode. Being an International Spiritualist Medium must be very lucrative, Jane thought, as she drove up to the house.

Daisy opened the door as she heard the car.

'Welcome Jane, lovely to see you again.' Daisy greeted her with a hug.

'Hello. It's nice to see you too. You've a beautiful house.' Jane looked on admiringly.

'Come in. I'll show you around. Do you have an interest in houses?'

'I do. I'm afraid I'm an estate agent, for my sins.' Jane laughed.

They walked into a large hallway with a sweeping staircase through the middle. All the rooms branched off this hall. Daisy led her into the kitchen, which had an Aga as its focal point. The room had a warm, cottage feel and was the hub of the house.

'I spend most of my time in here. The lounge is through there,' Daisy said. They walked into another large room which still had the original features of the old fashioned sash windows and shutters. Everything looked antique, even the curtains, they were made of heavy burgundy brocade. The decoration was modern and fresh, a stark contrast to the furniture. It worked beautifully.

'As much as I love looking at houses I feel very rude because I've come to see you. So let's finish the tour later,' Jane said as she walked back into the kitchen, where she immediately felt comfortable.

'I've just got to cook the eggs, everything else is ready. How do you like them?' Daisy asked.

'However they come. I'm not fussy.'

'We'll have scrambled. Let's choose one healthy option in the midst of all that fat,' Daisy joked.

'This is a very big house. Do you live here on your own?' Jane was being her usual, nosey self.

'I do now, yes. I never married but I did live with someone, a man much older than me. When he died he left me this house. We never had any children, so there's just me left rattling around in this big old space. I often think about selling it but we loved it here and I still feel Edwin's spirit around. Though when I get a bit older I'll have to move. I can't keep it clean now. I already have a cleaner who comes in twice a week.'

Breakfast was delicious and Jane devoured it all as though she hadn't eaten for a week. But as soon as they'd finished she was eager to talk about last night.

'Can you tell me what you know about reincarnation?' she asked.

'Lots of religions such as Hinduism and Buddhism believe that when you die you come back to earth in another body, to experience life again. Your memory is erased so you don't remember your past lives, but there have been occurrences when people have started to remember. I recall a lady called Bridie Murphy, an American woman, who could remember a past life in Ireland. She came across to the place where she thought she could remember living and found gravestones of herself and her family. They made a film about it. Your story is very similar. No-one really knows why some people find out they have lived before and other people don't. Maybe if you made a pact with someone to meet in this life, you're both slowly remembering. Your memories are coming to you in your dreams? '

'Yes. I can understand that. Tell me again what makes you think I'm a reincarnation of your mother.'

'In all my years as a medium my mother has never come back to me, which would make sense if she'd come straight back down to earth. She and

Daniel could have made a pact to see if they could live their lives again. But this time together. In the spirit world anything is possible. You must admit we look alike.'

Jane had to agree. 'Yes I can definitely see the resemblance, with our high cheekbones and eyes of the same colour.'

'The same as my mother's, a most unusual shade. Plus, I knew my mother's spirit was around last night, though she was totally unaware of it. You were just watching my show as a member of the audience. When you said the name Nora by mistake it all started to make sense. It feels like the correct explanation. I'm waiting for confirmation from the Spirit world but haven't been shown anything as yet.' Daisy still seemed convinced.

'Why do you think she's come back?' This was the burning question for Jane.

'Probably because she has something to tell you and needed to get your attention. The only way to attract your attention was through your dreams because until recently you'd never been to a medium or even knew what they did. Nora must have a message for you. Maybe it's telling you to meet up with Daniel again or some other reason we don't know about yet.'

'I've been thinking about it and, as I mentioned last night, I did actually go and have my Tarot cards read before Christmas. She told me that I would fall in love with someone I'd known before. I wonder if she meant that I would meet Daniel again. Also my mum was given a message in a Spiritualist church for me. She was told that it would all become clear in time. Maybe it will.' Jane mentioned the forays she'd made into Daisy's world.

'Did you say Daniel had a sister who's still alive?' Daisy asked.

'Yes, a lady called Sarah. She must be about your age. She lives in a little village just outside Falmouth. I'll be ringing her when I get back. Do you want me to pass on your number? She is, after all, your aunt!' Jane laughed.

'Yes please. I would love to speak to her. Yesterday I thought I'd no family. Today I've found out my mother and possibly, father have reincarnated, and I've an aunt. I've learned more in the past couple of days than I've learned in all my thirty years as a medium. I feel a bit overwhelmed.' Daisy had tears in her eyes. 'I was in Falmouth last summer, on tour at the Town Hall. She may have come to see me.' Daisy was looking forward to, hopefully, meeting the lost side of her family. 'Has Sarah got family?'

'She has a son and a daughter. The son has two little boys, or so I understand. I've only met Sarah though, and just seen photographs of the others. She's a widow.'

'Are you going to carry on your search for Daniel?' Daisy asked hopefully.

'I might do, but not yet. I've had a lot of stress in my life recently and this has taken up so much time and energy. I wanted to find out about Nora and Daniel, and I've accomplished that, so I feel satisfied for now. If what you say is correct fate will guide me to where I need to be in the future. But I'm going to have a bit of a rest now, if that's OK?' Jane suddenly felt depleted.

'Of course, whatever's best for you. It's still your life and you're in charge. Nora's spirit has only merged with yours. You can only ever feel her essence, so don't feel she's taking over you.' Daisy could sense that Jane was a little apprehensive about her new situation. 'I'd like to find whoever is carrying around Daniel's spirit, if it's all the same to you, and I would like to meet Sarah if she's willing.' Daisy looked for Jane's approval.

'Absolutely, and I want to know too, though not just yet. It's a lot to process for a complete novice like me.'

'Changing the subject, would you like to see the rest of the house?' Daisy looked enthusiastic and it was obvious she was very proud of her home.

'Yes please. You'll have me selling it for you soon!'

Jane left Richmond just before lunchtime. She and Daisy hugged each other and said they would keep in touch. Whatever happened in the future she'd certainly met some wonderful people and made friends for life.

Chapter 26

Neil knew he was in trouble when he started to become aroused by his new assistant Lauren. Things weren't all as they should be in the Sally and Neil household. He knew in the first week he'd made a mistake and now, two months on, the mistake was being compounded daily. He'd thought they had more in common than just great sex, but he'd been wrong. They both liked to exercise, but it turned out there was only enough room for one beautiful body in the house and now their egos were competing constantly.

Sally desperately wanted it to work and had become clingy, even mentioning marriage. Neil now understood why, if she'd done the same with him, Philip had felt pressured.

He still enjoyed shagging her, but that's all there was now. They didn't make love. They did it in every place they found exciting. They'd even done it in the mixed sauna at the gym. He still fancied her, but it was only his dick talking. He realised that when his affections had turned to Lauren. He'd turned into a sex-crazed maniac. But it was only to make up for what he wasn't getting elsewhere, a good relationship.

He missed Jane so much. He missed the long talks they used to have and the lovely meals round his expensive dining table. Sally thought a lovely meal was putting a Chicken Tikka Masala in the microwave. She was a career woman and didn't have time for cooking, or so she'd told him. Jane had a much more successful career yet she'd always managed to produce beautiful meals every day.

Eight years hadn't seemed like a big age gap at the beginning but now it was starting to become an obstacle. Sally wanted to go out all the time, finishing off the evening in a club. All he wanted to do was go to bed. He didn't really have anyone to talk to about his situation as a lot of his friends at the gym were really envious of him. They all fancied Sally and couldn't possibly understand there was more to life than sex. The old adage that the grass is always greener on the other side was completely wrong in his opinion. Sod the grass, he joked, he wanted to go home.

Tonight was the talk at Lara's college about VSO. The man from the organisation who had spoken to the students now wanted to talk to the parents, to tell them what it entailed. Neil would never have believed that he could look forward to a boring talk so much. He'd spoken to Jane earlier in the day and they both wanted to attend.

He also missed his house and everything in it. He'd loved living in Woolley and felt that he was the king of his own castle as he used to pull into the long driveway. He'd thrown all that away for a silly fling which he could now admit that was all it had been.

Jane hadn't put the house on the market yet. She'd said she'd been too busy. Secretly he hoped that she was holding on to it on the off chance that they could once again live in it as a family. She'd told him of her plan to adopt Toby and Neil would welcome the puppy with open arms if it would mean she would give him another chance.

He was going to suggest a chat with Jane after the meeting. No doubt Lara would be off with Greg somewhere so he would just drop the idea of a casual drink into the conversation. They hadn't spoken more than a few words to each other for weeks and this would be a good chance to catch up and show what civilised human beings they were.

Jane had been surprised that Neil had wanted to go to the meeting at Lara's college. He'd had to be forced to even go to a parents' evening when he was at home, and now he was volunteering to go to a meeting that would be about as interesting as watching paint dry. Zoe had given her the heads up on the Neil and Sally front and had warned her that all wasn't rosy in the garden. She had taken great delight in passing on that snippet of information. Jane wondered if he had an ulterior motive for going to the meeting tonight. He'd offered to collect her from home but she'd declined, saying she would drive herself. She didn't want to be beholden to him.

The meeting was in the large hall at the college. Jane had already found a seat when Neil walked in. He did look good, she had to admit. His blond hair was short and spiked with whichever hair product he was using at the time. He was wearing a pair of new denim jeans and a matching top with the sleeves rolled up. Sally's influence, she thought. He'd also lost a bit of weight and the weight training had increased the size of his chest. He was still a good-looking man.

He smiled when he saw her and went to sit next to her. He kissed her cheek.

'Being a cradle snatcher obviously suits you,' Jane teased, 'you look good.'

'Thank-you. And so do you.' Recently Neil had taken for granted Jane's hour-glass figure and her ample chest. She was showing a bit of cleavage in the deep blue silk blouse she was wearing. He'd always thought he preferred stick thin, but she looked incredibly voluptuous tonight and he could feel a stirring in his jeans. Luckily they were loose fitting so it wouldn't be too obvious. Lara was sitting with Greg and other friends at the front of the room. She waved when she saw them.

Lara had been pleased that both her parents were coming to the meeting because, although she was putting on a brave face, she really missed her dad and hated only seeing him once a week. She had been getting on a lot better with her mum recently and had been so excited when Jane had told her they were getting a puppy. She was also glad they hadn't moved. It would have been even more difficult to cope if they'd had to move to Garforth, but luckily that was out of the equation now.

The driving lessons were going well. She'd had eight already and the instructor said she was a very fast learner. Greg joked that he was only saying that because she wore a short skirt for the lessons. She was undecided about VSO now she'd met Greg. She really liked him and didn't think she could be away from him for so long. She'd originally planned to go for a year. Partly to get away from the awful atmosphere at home but now that wasn't an issue. The shortest time she could volunteer for was six months, but she knew he wouldn't wait that long for her, not when he was only twenty.

She'd recently gone on the pill as Greg was always suggesting that they sleep together. She'd gone to see the doctor on the pretext that she was suffering from excruciating period pains every month. She'd kept meaning to tell her mother but had never found the right time. She did want to have sex with Greg but was afraid that, once she did, he would finish with her. She liked to think he was better than that but that's what her friend Rebecca had thought. As soon as she'd lost her virginity to Ben he'd ended their relationship. The bastard! Lara told him she would give it some serious thought and, maybe, they would try it this weekend.

The talk lasted just over an hour and was as stimulating as they'd thought. Lara didn't seem to be as enamoured with the idea since Greg had come on the scene, so they might be wasting their time.

'Do you have to rush off? I thought we might call for a drink,' Neil suggested.

'OK. I'm not doing anything else. Sorry, that sounded ungracious.'

'Where do you fancy?' Neil asked.

Jane hadn't had time for tea and was hungry. 'Have you eaten?'

This was more than he could have hoped for. 'No. I called at the flat to get changed and came straight out.'

Jane noticed that he hadn't said home. She would see if what Zoe had told her had some substance. 'Will Sally not have made you any tea?' she asked.

Neil laughed. 'Sally doesn't do cooking. I've seen the inside of a freezer more in the last few months than in the rest of my adult life.' She could see he didn't really think it was funny.

'Let's go to Ronaldo's,' suggested Jane. 'I'll see you there.'

Neil couldn't believe he was actually going out for a meal with his ex-wife. He referred to her as his ex, but they'd never got round to signing the divorce papers. They'd seen a solicitor when it all blew up but neither had felt it to be all that urgent since.

They met outside the restaurant and he held the door as she walked through. Just like old times, he thought. They used to come here regularly which is why the owner came straight up to greet them and shake their hands.

'Long time, no see, my friends. A table by the window, as usual?' Giovanni welcomed them as though they'd never been away.

The food was still beautiful and Jane had a surprisingly good time. When Neil was on top form he was excellent company. She could tell by the way he talked he wasn't happy in his relationship and that he thought he'd made a huge mistake.

'Are you happy?' he asked, suddenly becoming serious.

'I am actually, yes. I'm enjoying my freedom. I'm sorry if that's not what you wanted to hear.'

Neil looked deflated. 'I'm genuinely pleased for you because I realise now I didn't treat you very well and I took you for granted. I didn't appreciate what I had and I'm so sorry.' He ran his fingers over her hand. 'It might make you feel better to know that my mother gave me a right earful on the way back to the station and told me I was a prize idiot.' Neil looked ashamed.

'Good for her,' Jane laughed.

'Are you still seeing Philip?' Neil enquired, hoping she would say no.

'Yes I am, and before you ask I still like him as much as I did.'

Neil was disappointed. He quickly changed the subject. 'Anyway enough of my self pity, tell me about your adventure. Any news?'

He seemed genuinely interested so Jane recounted her time with Daisy and what she'd found out. She thought Neil would laugh when she mentioned reincarnation but he was fascinated and listened attentively. She told him that she'd given her sleuthing a rest for the moment. It had all got a bit much.

Then she told him Philip had applied for a pilot's job in Cornwall. She didn't know why she mentioned it but she couldn't fail to see the look of utter delight on Neil's face when she told him. Funnily enough she hadn't told Philip that Neil was going to the meeting. She'd given the impression that it was only her and Lara. She felt like she was playing a dangerous game.

Neil insisted on paying the bill, even though Jane had offered to go halves. He thanked her for a wonderful evening, took her in his arms and gave her a lingering kiss on the lips. She didn't pull away and kissed him back. His heart skipped a beat. There's still hope he thought, as he drove back to the last place on earth he wanted to be.

Back at the flat Sally knew she was losing Neil and felt powerless to prevent it. He'd told her he was going to a meeting at his daughter's college but no meeting went on until nearly midnight. It was two months since he'd moved in and not once had he brought his son or daughter to meet her. He kept saying it was too soon and that they were still upset.

Her friends had been right when they'd said he was on the rebound, although she couldn't really call them friends any longer. Some of them, particularly Zoe, had made it clear they didn't approve of affairs with married men, and she knew that Zoe had recently become friends with Jane.

In September, when Neil was interested in her, she'd thought that she'd died and gone to heaven. But it had turned to hell in such a short space of time.

Sally was in bed pretending to be asleep when Neil climbed in beside her, turning his back toward her. It wasn't her imagination; she really could smell Chanel No 5.

Chapter 27

Simon had heard from Lara that their mother and father were getting on well and had started to spend a bit more time together. He hoped it was what they both wanted. Lara was very happy with the situation as she'd really missed her dad. Apparently she'd even asked mum if there was any chance of letting him come home. She'd kept Simon informed by text and his mother rang him once a week. He was going home this weekend, primarily to see Toby, but also because he wanted to talk to his parents. It was now the end of February and he was over halfway through his first year. His exams would be at the beginning of May and then that would be it, home for the holidays.

He loved his course. It had definitely been a good choice. He also loved university life in general and he and a few of his friends were already looking for a flat to share for their second year. What he was finding difficult was his love life. He'd only been in the Halls for a few weeks before he started to find one of his friends, very attractive. They all went out in a group and it seemed that the feeling was mutual. There had been a lot of flirting and a few surreptitious touches after they'd had a few drinks.

He hadn't talked about his feelings to anyone and it was starting to weigh heavily on him. Perhaps it wouldn't lead anywhere and he didn't even know if he wanted it to. But he knew that something had to change soon. He would have to make a decision one way or another, or move on. He hadn't spoken to Michael about their mutual attraction, he'd been avoiding it. However Michael had recently suggested they go out for a drink tonight, just the two of them.

Simon had never admitted he was gay. In fact he wasn't so sure that he could be described as such. He'd never been attracted to a man before but neither had he been attracted to many girls. It was Michael in particular that he liked. He loved his smile and his designer stubble as well as the way he wore his hair, slightly longer than was fashionable.

They'd met on the first day of term in the queue to register for accommodation. They were both on the same corridor in Halls of Residence and Michael was on the same course as Simon's roommate. He would often pop around to borrow books or notes. In fact he popped around more when he knew Simon's roommate would be out. They would sit on the bed, chatting and listening to music.

Simon knew Michael was gay as he'd had a couple of dates with a guy on Simon's course, but he thought he hadn't officially come out because he was trying to keep it a secret. They'd started to discuss it a couple of times but had been too embarrassed.

Michael was coming around at eight and they were going to walk into town rather than go to the union bar. He'd had a shower and was just deciding what to wear when Michael knocked on the door. He quickly pulled on his jeans and opened the door with his tee shirt in his hand.

'Hi you're a bit early, come in.' Simon beckoned as he pulled his tee shirt over his head.

Michael stood and admired Simon's slightly hairy chest and the beginnings of a six pack. Since going to university Simon had taken a leaf out of his dad's book and had joined the gym. He could tell the difference. Because he was so slender it hadn't taken him long to build up good muscle definition. Michael looked as though he approved.

'Hurry up and get dressed before I do something I'd regret'. Michael said, pretending to avert his eyes.

Simon laughed, but felt a nervous jitter in his stomach. He'd liked the admiring glances.

'Have a seat. I'm nearly ready, just got my hair to do.' He put some gel on, then grabbed his jacket. He reached across Michael to grab his keys and leant on his shoulder. The touch sent a frisson of electricity between them. Simon had never experienced anything like it before and wanted more.

'I'm ready.' Simon opened the door.

'It's a good job otherwise we might be staying in.' Michael winked and teasingly nudged Simon's arm.

Michael took Simon to a gay bar. It was a real eye-opener for him. Men were openly kissing and fondling each other. No-one was embarrassed and neither were they looking over their shoulders to see if anyone was watching. Everyone seemed completely relaxed. Even Simon didn't feel out of place. They had a few drinks; pints of lager to start with, and then moved on to tequila shots. Simon drank more than usual to give him some Dutch courage.

'Are you having a good time?' Michael enquired. His face was so close to Simon's he could feel his breath on his cheek.

'Yeah, great. Good idea of yours to come here.' Simon looked directly into Michael's big, blue eyes. With that Michael couldn't help himself. He leaned forward to kiss him. Just a quick one to gauge Simon's reaction, but when he didn't object Michael kissed him again.

Simon saw this kiss as a turning point in his life. It was no longer harmless flirting, it had moved on to the next stage. He felt very nervous and was unsure whether he was ready for what was coming next. Michael didn't put any pressure on him to go any further but, as they talked on the way back, Simon knew that he would. He really did have something to talk to his mum and dad about now. He knew his mum would be fine with it but he was unsure about his dad's reaction. His father had always been a man's man and Simon didn't know how he would cope with a gay son. He would find out in two days.

Because Simon was coming home Jane had invited Neil to spend Sunday with them. They'd been seeing each other more regularly and Neil often popped in on his way home, using the excuse of seeing Lara. But they both knew the real reason why he called. Jane had started to feel that she was cheating on Philip. She still saw him about twice a week and they usually made love. It was still good between them. She felt happy with the relationship as it was and wasn't looking for anything more. Neil was still living with Sally and he'd also found that more tolerable of late, solely because he was seeing a lot more of Jane. It felt like they'd just started dating and they were getting to know each other all over again.

They'd taken to flirting and sharing innuendos. He loved it. This sort of thing had been missing from their relationship in the past couple of years. He desperately wanted to go back home but he didn't want to rush Jane and suggest it in case she rejected him. This way he could still hope. Jane had mentioned that Philip hadn't heard about the job he'd applied for yet. Everyday Neil hoped Jane would tell him that he'd been successful and was moving to Cornwall. Neil imagined himself comforting her, saying he was there in case she needed him. Then he would make his move. He had it all planned out.

Simon arrived home early Saturday morning, Jane collecting him from the station. She noticed he wasn't his usual cheery, optimistic self.

'Is everything OK love? You're not working too hard are you?' Jane tried not to probe too deeply because she knew from experience that he would clam up.

'Yes, I'm fine, and no, I'm not working too hard. I think I've just got a little over tired,' he lied.

Jane decided to leave it at that because she knew he would tell her when he was ready. She'd always had an intuition about her son and knew something more than tiredness was bothering him.

Simon did want to talk to his mum first, but felt that might be disloyal to his dad. They should both get the chance to react together. He would have to keep it to himself for a whole day as his dad wasn't coming until the Sunday. Michael had wanted to come home with him, for moral support. He remembered the day he'd told his parents and, even though they'd come to terms with it eventually, it had been one hell of a shock for them. Simon had thanked him for the offer but said it was something he had to do on his own.

Since they'd spent the night together on Thursday they hadn't been apart for a second. They'd both missed lectures and seminars, just staying in Michael's room, getting to know one another. They both felt the relationship could be serious. Michael confessed to being in love with Simon from the first time he'd set eyes on him. He hadn't made a move because he wasn't sure it was Simon's thing. As the weeks progressed Michael had started to believe that Simon did fancy him, so finally he'd plucked up enough courage to ask him out for a drink.

Saturday was interminably slow and Simon found it hard not to tell his mum and Lara. It was just like old times, sitting in the kitchen chatting while Jane cooked the meal. The only difference now was that Lara joined in. Simon thought she'd really grown up. Greg was obviously having a positive influence on her.

Simon and Greg met for the first time that Saturday evening and they seemed to hit it off straight away. Lara signalled to him to come into the kitchen and asked Simon what he thought of Greg. Her big brother's approval was very important to her. Simon agreed with his mother's assessment, that he was a genuinely nice guy and a good stabilising influence on Lara. She left the room with a cheesy grin on her face and went to give Greg a big kiss. They went out leaving Jane and Simon alone for the evening.

Just as they were sitting down to Simon's favourite meal, Jane's homemade lasagne, the phone rang. It was Neil.

'I don't suppose I could come round tonight could I? Sally's out on a hen night and I'd really like to see Simon,' he asked in a pleading voice.

Jane looked at Simon. 'Your dad wants to come and see you, is that OK?'

One day less of this torture, he thought. 'Yeah, that would be great.'

'You can come straight around. Have you eaten? I can save you some lasagne if you like'

'I had a sandwich earlier but I can always eat your lasagne. I'll bring the wine. See you soon and, Jane, thanks.' Neil went to his wine rack and grabbed the most expensive bottle of wine there. It certainly was a celebration, spending Saturday night with his wife and son, something he'd never thought he would do again.

It only took him twenty-five minutes to drive to the house. He knocked on the door out of politeness. Jane shouted, 'Come in'. She and Simon were just finishing off the cheesecake and the first bottle of wine. Jane smiled when Neil walked in and looked lovingly at her family. She'd taken them so much for granted before and really hadn't appreciated all the good things she'd had.

She went to get Neil's lasagne out of the oven and they all sat round the dining room table, chatting and catching up on each other's lives.

'Shall we go and sit in the lounge? It's a bit more comfortable,' Jane asked, fitting straight back into her role as carer.

It was now or never Simon thought. 'In a bit mum. I like it in here and I want to talk to you both, if that's OK?'

'Of course darling. I knew something had been bothering you since you came home.'

Neil, of course, knew nothing about it. He missed out on so much by not living in the house.

'I don't know where to start. I've met someone and I think it's serious,' Simon said.

'Way to go son,' Neil interrupted. Jane could have kicked Neil, as she could see how difficult it was for Simon. She already had a feeling what was coming next.

'You may not be saying that when you know who it is.' Simon continued. 'I've liked this person since the first week of term and we only got together on Thursday.'

'Why the suspense?' Neil asked. Bless him, thought Jane. He'd never been good at judging situations.

'Because this person is called Michael.'

Simon paused. There was a deathly silence.

Jane was the first to speak. 'As long as you're happy darling, that's enough for me.'

'Absolutely.' Neil added. He was trying his best, but both Jane and Simon could see he was floored.

'I'm sorry if it's a bit of a shock. It was a shock to me. I know I've never really had a girlfriend but I assumed it would happen in its own time. But I've never met a girl I liked any more than as a friend. Until Michael, I hadn't really liked a man either,' Simon confessed.

'Tell me about him,' Jane said. Neil just sat there, drinking too much wine.

'He's twenty-one, he lives in London and he studies Physics. He came out when he was eighteen and I'll be the first serious boyfriend he's had. He's taller than me, with blond hair, and he has the same build. He has the most piercing blue eyes and I think he's very good-looking. We like the same music and stuff, and he doesn't like sport either. He wanted to come with me this weekend but I wanted to tell you first. I would like you to meet him though.' Simon's face shone when he talked about him.

'We'd like that, wouldn't we Neil?' She kicked him under the table.

'Absolutely,' was all Neil could find to say.

'Tell me how you met,' Jane said. She hated watching the two men struggling for things to say and it was down to her to keep the conversation flowing.

'We actually met on the first day of term, the day that you took me to uni. He was standing next to me in the queue. I noticed him staring at me and when I smiled back, he blushed. We became friends from then on and it just developed over time.' Simon finally started to relax. He knew he could rely on his mother to make him feel better. It was just his dad he had to work on. Maybe his mum would have more luck convincing him things were going to be OK.

'I'm going to leave you to digest both your food and my revelation. I'll go ring Michael. I told him I would be telling you tomorrow but I'll go put him out of his misery.' Simon left the room.

Jane could see Neil was shocked but she didn't expect the reaction he had. He burst into tears. She'd only seen him cry once before and that was when his father had died. He had a tear in his eye when the children were born, but this was all-out sobbing.

'Whatever is the matter?' Jane went around the table and held him, pulling him close.

'I don't know,' sobbed Neil. 'It's all got a bit much for me. I had no idea our son was gay and I should have known. Is it something I've done?' he asked bewildered.

'I think it's more what nature's done. How do you think you've made our son gay?' Jane was quite amused.

'I don't know, maybe I wasn't a good enough father to him.' Neil was clutching at straws.

'You've been a perfectly good father to him and you can continue to be so by telling him everything is OK. He always looks for your approval and you'll be a great man if you can give it now,' Jane said, sounding totally sincere. 'Go to him. It's you he needs to be fine with. He knows I'll love him whatever. I'll load the dishwasher and I'll have a big glass of wine waiting for you.' She went to kiss Neil on the cheek but, at the last moment, kissed him full on the lips.

Jane went to sit in the lounge to watch television. When Neil and Simon came downstairs they were both smiling.

'Thanks mum, for being so understanding and thanks dad.' Simon gave Neil a big grin. 'My mates are also home this weekend. I forgot it's Rob's birthday so if you don't mind I'm going down the pub. I'll probably crash at a mate's.' All the worry had left Simon's face.

Once Simon had left Jane said, 'Whatever you said to him obviously worked, thank-you.'

'All I said was...'

Jane interrupted Neil. 'I don't want to know, it's between father and son. Come and have a glass of wine.' She was too relieved to rehash the conversation.

Neil went to sit next to her on the sofa. God, he did love her.

Jane was becoming increasingly confused. Her heart wanted Philip, but right at this minute her head and body wanted Neil. They had shared so much over the years and tonight's little revelation proved how much her family still needed her.

She turned the television off and they talked. They reconnected with what had attracted them to each other all those years ago. They drank wine and continued talking. When Jane looked at her watch it was nearly midnight.

'You've had far too much wine to drive home, you'll have to stay.'

'Is the spare room made up?'

'There's no need.' Jane took him by the hand and led him upstairs.

Chapter 28

The test flight had gone very well and the instructors had been pleased with Philip's flying ability. The plane, a Beachcraft Superking Air 200, was slightly larger than he was used to and carried up to ten passengers, but he handled it well and the instructor had only picked him up on a couple of minor mistakes. He'd felt like he was taking his test all over again.

The owner of the company, a Mr Terry Trevellan, conducted the formal interview after the test flight had finished. Philip was well prepared and answered all the questions with clear and succinct answers.

The job wasn't due to start until the beginning of March. They said they would let him know in due course whether he'd been successful. If the standard of the other applicants was very good they would be holding second interviews in a couple of weeks.

Philip returned home feeling optimistic. Even if he didn't get that particular position there'd be others. He'd taken the first positive step in changing his career. His application for voluntary redundancy had been accepted and he was due to finish at the end of February, two weeks later. They'd offered him a very lucrative package so he could be financially independent for at least a year without needing to earn a penny. He could really get his flying hours up then.

The job in Cornwall was a double-edged sword for him. It would be a wonderful opportunity but it meant leaving behind the woman he loved. Jane had been correct in her assessment of the situation. If he turned it down he would eventually become resentful and would always wonder 'what if'. He was trying to be philosophical and leave it all up to fate. What will be, will be, he thought. Long distance relationships had been known to work. Who knows? She may change her mind and join him once Lara went off to university.

Philip never did return to the doctor's because the pains in his legs stopped as suddenly as they started, and he hadn't had a recurrence of his hallucination. He decided it had all been caused by stress and tried to put it behind him.

The previous day he'd had a very strange request from his brother, who lived down in Kent. The phone had rung just as Philip had got home from work.

'Hello Philip, it's Pete. How are you?'

'I'm fine. This is a surprise. To what do I owe the pleasure?' Pete and Philip maybe spoke a couple of times a year, at birthdays, so this phone call was completely out of the blue. They were always polite to each other, but not much emotion passed between them as they'd never been that close. Pete had been a stroppy teenager when Philip was born and hadn't shown much interest in the new baby at all.

'I'm ringing to ask a favour. Our James is studying the Second World War for his History GCSE and he's found out there's a museum dedicated to the war near you in York. It's called Eden Camp. Have you heard of it?' Pete asked.

'I have, yes. I think it was a concentration camp for Italian and German soldiers during the war, but that's all I know.'

'It was, yes. It was turned into a military museum a few years ago. I was wondering if James could come and stay with you for a couple of days, maybe next weekend, and you could take him. I know it's short notice but mum told me you're thinking of taking voluntary redundancy and might be leaving anyway.' Pete knew he was being a bit cheeky.

'That's right I am. I suppose he could come next Friday and we could go to the museum on Saturday.' Philip felt that Pete had put him on the spot but he couldn't think of a valid reason to say no.

Philip didn't really know his nephew and hadn't seen him all that often. Even when they had they hadn't exchanged more than a few words, as James had always been playing on his computer games. Philip hoped in the past year he'd turned from morose teenager to something bordering on human.

'That's great Phil, I owe you one.' Pete only ever called him Phil when he wanted something. 'I'll put him on the train Friday afternoon. Could you pick him up from the station after work?'

'That should be fine. Let me know what time the train get's in.' Philip couldn't help but feel he'd been railroaded. After he'd asked his favour Pete didn't want to chat and soon curtailed the conversation. Philip's next weekend had been planned out for him but, hey, it'd be something different.

Philip was counting down the days to leaving work and spent most of his time doing crossword puzzles. He saw no point in starting any new projects. He'd usually leave around four and then often call in the office to see Jane and pester her. She didn't mind, it gave them chance to see more of each other. She didn't seem to be as free as much in the evenings. She was either doing things with her family or going to meetings at work.

Philip waited at the station for James. The last time he'd seen his nephew he'd been short for his age, worn thick-rimmed glasses and had hair in no obvious style. He could hardly believe it was the same person that he saw coming through the turnstiles. In fact if James hadn't waved Philip would have let him go straight past. James was now taller than him, had long hair dyed black and sported a piercing in his eyebrow and his nose. Philip wondered what his poor overprotective mother thought of his look. Good for him, Philip thought, he'd finally grown a pair!

James still couldn't be described as chatty but he did, at least, make some effort. He thanked his uncle for having him and said that Eden Camp was going to be 'wicked'. Philip though most of the soldiers who'd fought in the war would turn in their graves at the sight of James, but his enthusiasm was to be encouraged.

As they were driving back he said to Philip, 'Will you please call me Jimi? I spell it J-I-M-I. I hate it when my mum and dad call me James, but they won't shorten it.'

'Certainly, if you'd prefer it.' It made no difference to Philip.

'And can I dispense with uncle and just call you by your first name? Do you prefer Philip or Phil?' Jimi asked.

'I actually prefer Philip. No-one's really shortened my name before, apart from your dad, funnily enough'

'How ironic!' Jimi was nothing like Philip had imagined a sixteen year old to be.

Philip was making burgers for tea. He didn't know what sixteen year olds ate but he didn't think he could go far wrong with cheeseburgers and wedges.

'Have you got any cans of lager?' Jimi asked.

'Does your dad let you have them?' It was then that Philip realised that Jimi had grown up.

'Yeah, I have some Friday and Saturday. I wash glasses at the local pub and dad buys them for me with the money I earn.' Philip really should have checked with his brother, but decided to give Jimi the benefit of the doubt.

They watched a couple of films as they ate dinner and drank the lager. Jimi offered to wash up but Philip said he'd do it, so Jimi went to bed to listen to grunge music on his i-pod. Philip knew he was getting old when he couldn't actually describe it as music. One night down, one to go, he thought, though he had to admit it hadn't been half as bad as he'd feared.

Jimi was up early the following morning, an amazing feat in itself Philip thought, and had eaten breakfast by the time Philip had showered. He was raring to go to Eden Camp and was looking through the brochure he'd downloaded from the internet. Philip didn't remember ever being so enthusiastic about any school work, particularly History which he'd found incredibly dull. But he'd been passionate about flying at Jimi's age. There was something for everyone, he thought.

It took less than an hour to get to Eden Camp. They arrived just as the gates were opening. Jimi asked if it was OK if he went around by himself because he knew what he was looking for. Philip said yes then studied his brochure to see what he wanted to look at. The camp was a series of Nissan Huts built around a central courtyard with each hut having different theme. As he wandered from one display to the next he felt very nostalgic about the war and wondered what it would've been like to be in the thick of things. The whole place had an unusual atmosphere, not surprising he thought, considering what it used to be. After a while it began to get very blustery. The air had been completely still when they arrived. He looked to the horizon and saw the trees were bolt upright. This gave the whole place an eerie feel.

After about an hour of wandering from one hut to the next he'd had enough of the damp, dark spaces showing death and destruction from actual film footage. He decided to go and explore outside. It was freezing cold and the biting wind made him raise his collar and put his hands in his pockets. He wandered over to the display of Second World War bombers and fighter planes.

Then it happened again, when he was standing looking at the Spitfire. His world went dark and he was in the cockpit of the very plane he had been looking at a second earlier. It played out just the same as before. He looked over at the wing and saw that it was on fire. He radioed, 'Mayday! Mayday! Mayday!' Then he felt a direct hit. He looked to his left and just before it all went black he spotted a Messerschmitt flying away. He remembered thinking, this was it! He was going to die. His final thought was of Nora and her sweet face.

He came round on the cold, hard floor with one of the guides leaning over him. 'Are you alright sir? I think you must have fainted or something. Is there anyone I can call for you?' he asked, looking very concerned.

'My nephew is around somewhere, but I feel fine now. Thank-you all the same.' Philip felt very embarrassed as a crowd gathered around him. He tried to recall what had happened. At first it had seemed like a dream but then, bizarrely as it sounded, he felt as though he'd actually been transported back in time. It seemed as if he was remembering what had happened to him in the past. Who was this Nora that had come into his mind? None of it made sense but this had happened twice now. Why him?

The most worrying thing was whether or not it would stop him from flying. His intuition told him that there was absolutely nothing physically wrong with him and that it was just an overactive imagination. But on the other hand it had all been so real. He felt as if he could have been that fighter pilot. He knew he couldn't ignore it this time. He would have to make an appointment with some sort of a doctor to discuss the matter further. He just hoped he didn't need a psychiatrist.

He rose slowly to his feet and then paused for a second to see how he felt. The guide was still very worried about him but Philip assured him he would be fine. He located his mobile phone and rang Jimi's number to find out where he was. They arranged to meet by the cafe. The rest of the visit went off without a hitch and they left Eden Camp at about four, after a very fruitful day for Jimi. Philip enjoyed watching him being so animated. He had a real interest in the war and enjoyed sharing it with his uncle. Philip had had a good time despite his little incident and realised he knew a lot more about the war than he'd previously thought.

Philip put Jimi on the train back home after lunch on Sunday. They'd really enjoyed each other's company and Philip said he could visit whenever he wanted. When he arrived back at his flat there was a message on his answer phone from Mr Trevellan asking him to ring him back.

Philip rang the number and a woman answered. 'Hello could I speak to Mr Trevellan please, it's Philip Sinclair. I'm returning his call.' He felt quite nervous as he held the phone.

'Hi, it's Terry here. Sorry to ring you on a Sunday but I thought you'd like to know as soon as possible. We'd like to offer you the position, if you're still interested.'

Philip was momentarily speechless.

'Er, thank-you and, yes, I'm still interested,' Philip said finally.

'We'd like you to start next week if you can, but I realise it might be too short notice.' Terry said.

'I don't finish work until the end of next week so I could start the week after, if that's of any use to you?' He hoped that delaying an extra week wouldn't make any difference to the offer.

'Great, that's perfect. Geoff, who's retiring, has let us down. He's leaving two weeks earlier than planned so we're in the proverbial. I'll get my secretary to ring you tomorrow to finalise the details. Welcome to the company and I wish you many happy hours flying with us. Speak to you soon, bye.' With that Terry put the phone down. Short but sweet, he thought.

So that was it. Philip's new life was about to start. He was very excited but now he would have to do one of the hardest things he'd ever had to. Tell Jane he was moving to Cornwall.

He phoned her straight away and asked her if she would come around that evening, to talk. There was something in Philip's voice that was a dead giveaway.

'You've got the job, haven't you?' Jane asked.

'Is it that obvious? Yes I have, and I've accepted it. But I want to talk to you, please come.' Philip almost begged.

'I want to talk to you too. I'll set off soon. See you shortly.'

Jane sighed. She would have to look Philip in the eyes and she was sure he would be able to tell she'd slept with her husband last night. Could her life get any more complicated? Neil had stayed in her bed. They'd just lain next to each other at first. He hadn't wanted to make a move until he knew she was ready. Jane hadn't known whether it was the effect of the wine, but she had wanted to make love to Neil. She still saw him as her husband and because she'd entertained the idea of him coming back home she wanted to see if the love-making could be any better than it had been in Liverpool.

It was. He'd been gentler than he'd ever been before and his new-found experience had really improved his technique. She was also less inhibited than she'd been before, with him. They'd tried new and different positions and they'd made love for hours, Neil making sure that Jane was satisfied before he climaxed.

She'd finally gone to sleep in his arms and they woke in almost the same position in the morning.

'I love you so much,' Neil had said to her on waking. 'I don't expect you to feel the same way yet, but would you consider having me back, sometime in the future?'

'I don't think I ever stopped loving you. I just needed to be with someone else for a while. I don't want to make a decision yet, until I've spoken to Philip. Let's just enjoy the moment.' Jane said.

Chapter 29

Jane was dreading talking to Philip. She'd thought he was the one and would have sacrificed anything for him at the beginning. But since September their relationship had changed. It was the nature of all affairs. The most exciting part was the illicit sex, in all sorts of places, and the risk of being caught. Once they'd begun having sex anywhere and anytime some of the thrill had disappeared. She did love spending time with him and their love-making was still wonderful, but she had a separate life which she couldn't ignore. Her work and motherhood still took up most of her time.

Life had been so complicated recently. There had been the accident with Greg, Simon's revelation about his personal life, Lara's possible year abroad, the list was endless. And they were all making demands on her time and emotions. Of course one of the biggest things in her life was something she'd chosen not to share with Philip. There had been times when she'd wanted to tell him about Daniel, Nora and Daisy, but the longer she left it, the harder it had become. In hindsight she should have told him the story a long time ago, but it had never seemed the right moment. If she told him now he would be well within his rights to be annoyed and feel betrayed. They'd shared so much in other ways but she'd continued to lie to him about that. After the incident at Catterick, when Barbara had said he'd a look of Daniel, they hadn't mentioned it again.

She'd never had to tell Philip about her dreams because she'd never had one when she'd slept with him.

Jane knocked on the door to Philip's flat and walked straight in. Philip went over to kiss her. She returned the kiss but felt awkward. He noticed straight away.

'Things are changing between us already, aren't they? He looked sad.

'It's inevitable. You're starting a new life and I'm happy for you, I really am. But, yes, things have changed. When do you go?'

'I finish work next week and they want me to start the week after. I've got to go and find somewhere to live next weekend. It's all been a bit of a rush as the pilot who's retiring has left two weeks early and they've a lot of flights booked.'

'I have an idea,' Jane said. 'I know it's not in the right area of Cornwall but when I went away to spend some time with my mum there, last year, I met a lovely woman called Sarah. She lives in a big house with a small annexe at the side. She might let you stay there for a couple of nights while you get sorted. Do you want me to ring her?'

Jane realised she had offered before she'd really thought it through. She would have to warn Sarah not to mention Daniel and also keep quiet about the real reason for their meeting. The lies just kept getting bigger, she thought. She also felt guilty about not having spoken to Sarah since her meeting with Daisy. She'd been so wrapped up in her own personal life she hadn't made time to keep the promise she'd made to her.

'That'd be great, if you don't mind. It'll be so much easier to find somewhere to live if I'm down there.' Jane could see that Philip was really excited about his new life, even though he was doing his best to contain his emotions.

'I'll ring her later tonight, when I get back, and let you know what she says,' Jane said.

'So this is it. Are you sure you won't change your mind and come with me?' Philip already knew the answer.

'No, love, but we won't lose touch. You're far too important to me for that to happen. I do love you and we've had a fantastic six months.' Jane felt like crying; but she wanted to be strong for Philip, because he looked as if his heart was going to break.

'Why couldn't I just be happy in my job? Why have I got to mess it all up?' he asked in frustration.

'Because you have to follow your bliss and be true to yourself. You know that really. I envy you, in a way, because you're doing something you've wanted to do your whole life. Most people just talk about such things, but you're going to do it. To be honest it's made me doubt myself. I thought estate agency was my life but now I've realised it's just a job. It was a safe option after I'd had the children but, as much as I enjoy it, I don't get up every morning and look forward to going to work, the way I know you will. I thought making partner would be the icing on the cake but it's given me a lot more stress and taken up a lot more of my time.' Jane was shocked at herself. She didn't know where that little diatribe had suddenly come from. It was something she'd considered before but had never voiced out loud.

'Does that mean you might consider moving in the future?' he said hopefully.

'Let's leave the future where it should be, in the future.'

'What did you want to talk to me about?' Philip asked, remembering what she'd said on the phone.

Jane was regretting saying anything to Philip. Since arriving she'd decided not to talk about her night with Neil. It would only cause an argument and she wanted them to part on good terms.

'Nothing really. I just wanted to tell you about Sarah and see if you wanted to stay with her,' she lied.

Philip wasn't convinced but let it go. He'd learnt to read Jane and he knew there was something she wasn't telling him. He guessed it was to do with Neil and, even though he hated to admit it, he thought they would get back together when he was out of the picture. There had been a few things Jane had been unintentionally dropping into the conversation recently.

Before Jane arrived he'd decided that he was going to ask his boss if he could leave a few days earlier than planned. He was only filling time and he needed to get down to Cornwall. He'd a feeling that this would be the last time he saw Jane for a long time.

He leant over and kissed her. 'You've been the best thing that has ever happened to me and I'll miss you so very much,' he whispered.

Jane couldn't hold back the tears any longer. She held on to Philip tightly and kissed him again. The passion came flooding back and within minutes he was undressing her. They made love with the urgency of their first time. He took her there and then on the settee, thrusting deep within her. He wanted to possess her and needed something to remember her by when he was alone in Cornwall. He came within minutes and was totally exhausted when he finally withdrew. Jane looked at him lovingly and wondered why everything had to be so complicated, and why she had to be in love with two men.

She'd read about others in such a situation and had always believed they just wanted the best of both worlds. But now she found herself in the same dilemma and it was hell. Right at this minute there was nowhere else on earth that she would rather be than here with Philip, but earlier the same morning she'd been in bed making love to her husband. What am I turning into? she asked herself.

With Philip gone she could hopefully decide once and for all who she wanted to be with. She would have to risk Philip finding another love in the short term, but she was going to give it another go with Neil. She owed it to her family to see if it could work. Neil had realised his mistake and he did seem to have changed. He had become a lot more attentive recently. He was even looking forward to having Toby, who was arriving tomorrow.

Philip and Jane got dressed. The mood was sombre because they both knew it was the end, for now. Philip hoped it would be a temporary parting, but he would have to give her space and wait for her to come back to him. If she ever decided to.

He said, 'I know you came here to talk to me about something. Let's not part without being honest.' Philip knew he'd live to regret this.

'I think I'm going to let Neil come home,' she confessed. 'He's been coming round the house more frequently, to see Lara. They miss each other so much. I know it's the best for them.'

'Is it best for you?' Philip asked, already, in his heart, knowing the answer.

'I don't know. I've lived with him for years and we did have some good times. He does seem to have become more thoughtful. I'll just have to see how it goes.' She hoped she wasn't hurting Philip too much.

Philip wanted to rant and rave and tell her she was being stupid, but instead he just said, 'I suppose you owe it to yourself to try. Keep me informed and let me know if I still have a chance with you.' He couldn't believe that he was being so understanding.

Neither could Jane. 'Seeing as we're being honest, there's something else I've kept secret from you. It's to do with our visit to Catterick, but I don't feel ready to tell you yet. I'm going to put it all down in a letter and send it to you when you're settled.' A coward's way out, she knew, but at least it would leave no secrets between them.

There was a pause in the conversation and they took it as a sign for Jane to leave. They both wanted it over as quickly as possible because it was too painful. They kissed for one last time; a tender, loving kiss.

'Bye Philip. I'll ring you later, when I've spoken to Sarah. Let me have your address when you find somewhere to live. And take care. I love you.' She couldn't speak anymore through the tears.

Philip felt the tears rolling down his own cheeks. 'Do you remember when you showed me round the house? I kissed you and said 'I will see you again Jane'. I'm going to say it for a second time because I know I will see you again. We have too much together to let it all go. My world has been a much better place with you in it. I love you. Be happy'. Philip turned away and, with that, Jane walked out of his flat and out of his life.

Chapter 30

How Jane drove home without crashing the car she would never know. She sobbed throughout the whole journey and kept asking herself over and over if she was doing the right thing. Only time would tell. She didn't feel like letting Neil know what had happened just yet. She wanted time on her own. She would keep her promise to Philip and ring Sarah. She would also ring Daisy to catch up.

The house was in darkness when she returned home. She took a quick shower to see if she could salvage her tear-stained face. She dressed in her casual clothes and went into the kitchen to make a cup of tea. She carried it in to the lounge and sat down to make her phone calls. Sarah picked up the phone on the fifth ring and said, 'Hello.'

'Hello Sarah. It's Jane here. Sorry I've not been in touch but it's been a bit hectic here. How are you?' Jane could hear Sarah sniff and, from the tone in her voice, she sensed she'd been crying.

'Ah Jane, it's nice to hear from you. You must excuse me. I'm a bit upset,' Sarah said, trying to pull herself together.

'I'm sorry to hear that. Anything I can help you with?' Jane asked, concerned.

'You don't know how much I wish you could help,' Sarah continued. 'You know I have two grandchildren, my son's boys. Well the youngest, Oliver, who's five, has been poorly for ages. He's had a cold since Christmas and has been sleeping for over sixteen hours a night. His mum took him to the doctors to see if he was a bit run-down, what with starting school and everything. The doctor did some tests and two weeks ago he was diagnosed with leukaemia. Oh Jane, it's an aggressive form and without a bone marrow transplant he'll die.' She started sobbing again.

'Oh my God,' was all Jane could say, thinking immediately to her own children and how she'd feel if it was one of them.

'My son, his wife and his brother have all had blood tests to see if they were a match, but they all came back negative. I had my blood test last week, along with my daughter, and we're waiting for the results. Oliver is in hospital, isolated from everyone in case he picks up another virus. It breaks my heart to see the little fellow. He's so pale and weak. I have to find a way to help him.' She paused. 'Anyway, enough of my troubles, how are you?'

'I can discuss it with you another time; you've obviously got a lot on your plate.' Jane felt guilty for thinking of her minor troubles at a time like this.

'Please tell me,' Sarah pleaded. 'I could do with a distraction.'

'If you're sure, there were two things actually. One, a friend of mine is moving down to Lands End and has to find a place to live. I thought if you didn't mind he could stay with you in the annexe for a couple of nights. He'd pay you. It's a bit short notice; I know. Next week actually, but he'll understand if you're too busy,' Jane said.

'No, it's fine, I'd love to help. What's he coming to do?' Sarah asked.

'He's landed a job as a pilot, no pun intended, flying tourists to the Isles of Scilly.'

'How wonderful, what a fantastic job. The Isles of Scilly are spectacular. Is he a special friend?' Sarah enquired, with a knowing tone in her voice. In the few conversations they'd had since Christmas Jane had alluded to someone special in her life.

It was Jane's turn to sound sad. 'He was, but whatever happened between us is water under the bridge. My husband is going to be moving back in.' Jane tried to sound positive.

'Are you sure that's what you want?' Sarah was concerned. 'You don't sound too convinced.'

'I think so. It's all a bit raw. It only happened today but I'm sure it'll be fine. There's one more thing on that subject. I haven't told him anything about Daniel and why I came to see you. Do you think you could just say we met in the village and happened to strike up a conversation? I'm sorry if it puts you on the spot.' She felt guilty asking Sarah to be deceitful.

'That's fine by me love. I'm sure you have your reasons.'

That was what Jane loved about Sarah, she never judged or pried into other peoples' affairs.

'Secondly, on a much happier note, I've found Daisy.' She'd been filling Sarah in on her progress with Nora but hadn't told her anything about Daisy.

'Have you? How fantastic! You must tell me all about it.' Sarah sounded so excited.

It took over half-an-hour to tell the story, from going to Richmond and seeing the sign for the medium, to the end when Daisy thought Jane was her mother, Nora, reincarnated. '... and there you have it. I know it sounds difficult to believe but that's where we're at. What do you think?'

'I don't know what to think. It's all new to me. But it's a wonderful idea. Are you happy with the explanation?'

'I don't know. It was a major shock and I suppose I'm just coming to terms with it. But what's really good is that I've found your niece. I said I'd contact you on her behalf, so if you want to get in touch you can.' Jane paused to draw breath.

'Oh, how thoughtful,' Sarah said. 'Well I never, I have a niece. Isn't the universe fantastic at rearranging itself for us like that?'

'I suppose so. I never thought of it like that. It just seemed like a series of coincidences but, when you tell the complete story, it is wonderful.'

'Carl Jung called a series of happy coincidences synchronicity and wrote a whole book about it. You should read it,' Sarah suggested.

'I will, just let me write that down,' replied Jane. Anything would be useful in learning more about her unusual situation. She wrote 'Synchronicity' in her notebook. They'd been on the phone for over an hour and Jane wanted to ring Daisy. 'Well Sarah, I'm going to go now. I'll keep Oliver and all of you in my prayers and hope you get some good news this week. I'll also pass your number on to Philip, so he can ring you and arrange to come and stay. I'd like to see you again, soon. Maybe I could come down in summer. But we can always discuss that later. I'll speak to you soon, take care. Bye.' Jane loved talking to Sarah, but the phone call had been tinged with sadness about poor Oliver. She wished there was something she could do.

She couldn't face talking to Philip again so she sent a long text telling him of her conversation with Sarah and giving him her phone number.

He was grateful she'd texted because he couldn't face talking to her either. Mobile phones were such a wonderful invention, he thought.

Jane felt emotionally drained and thought the only way she would feel better was to have a large glass of wine. It seemed to be the panacea of all her ills! She hadn't eaten since breakfast, as her rumbling tummy was reminding her. She couldn't be bothered to cook, so she thought she'd just make herself a sandwich. As she was buttering the bread, a thought came to her. It was a long shot but, if Daisy was Sarah's niece, she was actually a blood relative and could also be tested to see if her bone marrow was a match for Oliver. What a genius, she thought to herself!

She knew it was a tall order, to go to all this trouble for a family she'd never met, but Daisy was a compassionate soul and spent all her time helping people. She would ring her now. Armed with her large glass of wine and ham sandwich, she went to sit in the same place by the phone. She'd soon be moulded to the seat, she'd spent so long sitting there.

Daisy didn't pick up the phone. Jane realised it was Sunday night and she'd probably be at a Spiritualist Church service. She left a message, telling her not to bother ringing back tonight, as it would probably be late when she got in and Jane fancied an early night.

She could do with speaking to her mother but, likewise, she'd be with George at a Church service.

Toby was arriving tomorrow and she realised she'd completely forgotten that she'd booked the next couple of days off work. What a nice surprise, she thought. She would go and prepare his bedding and food bowls, so he would immediately feel at home. She'd bought him a lovely new, luxury faux suede sofa bed. Only the best for her new doggie friend.

Jane decided to treat herself to a long, luxurious bath. One way or another it had been a hell of a day. She didn't get to have sex with two different men every day. What a tart, she laughed to herself as she went upstairs.

Daisy was indeed at a Church service but wasn't the medium on the platform. She'd gone as a member of the congregation to see if she would receive a message about her mother, or Jane. She also wanted to find out who Daniel's soul had been born into. She'd spent a lot of time thinking about Jane when she'd left and had pulled out all the old photographs of her mother, to see if there was more than a passing resemblance. A lot of Jane's mannerisms were just like her mother's; the way she flicked her hair and how her nose wrinkled when she laughed. They both had an optimistic view of life and were strong women who knew their own minds.

Some of the photographs of her mother could have been of Jane. She hadn't realised how similar they were until she'd started looking through them. There were still so many questions that needed answering. The main one being, why had Nora come straight back to earth and not waited a few years? She'd been doing a lot of reading about reincarnation and learned it was generally accepted that souls went back to the spirit world to recap on their lives. They needed to see what lessons they had learnt, and then decide what they could learn in the next life.

It seemed Nora had come back the instance she died, presumably with Daniel. Daisy didn't know if they would've been born in the same place or even in the same country. Apparently, when a soul is born, it has no memory of any past lives, so the chances of Nora and Daniel finding one another were already pretty slim. Sadly Daisy didn't get a message from the platform so she would have to keep looking for answers elsewhere.

Chapter 31

Sally was preparing herself for the end of her relationship with Neil. She knew he wanted to go back to Jane, as he'd already threatened her with it in an argument the previous week. She'd resigned herself to the fact and, wisely, knew she didn't want to be with anyone who didn't want her. She'd assumed they loved each other but it turned out they didn't have enough in common to sustain a lasting relationship. Neil didn't enjoy the things she liked doing. He said he was too old to go clubbing, preferring to stay in with a bottle of red wine.

Luckily she didn't work alongside him at the office anymore. Since moving upstairs she didn't have to see him, unless she went out of her way to. Hopefully when he did leave to go back to Jane (that is, if she'd have him) they could be civilized about it, because Sally didn't want to jeopardise her job.

If she was to stay in her current flat she would have to advertise for a lodger to help pay the bills. That idea appealed to her and she thought it could be quite fun, particularly if she found a woman with whom she could also become friends. She decided she was going to lay off men for a while. Well, not altogether. But she didn't want a serious relationship for a long time. Sally hadn't been on her own, without a boyfriend, since she was eighteen. But now she was getting accustomed to it, relishing the idea of pleasing herself for a while. She'd made a serious error in judgement when it came to Neil, so she needed both the time and space to get back on track.

She'd returned from the hen night at nine o'clock that morning, only to find the flat empty. She could guess where Neil was. When he'd returned just before dinner they'd had another row. She was tired of arguing and had asked him to leave. He'd stormed off, but not having taken anything with him she knew he'd be back. She wanted to clear the air and tell him that she didn't bear a grudge.

The love she thought she'd felt for him had soon disappeared because of the arguments. She'd rung up some of her friends to tell them they'd been right. After they'd gloated for a while they started to feel sorry for her and arranged a girlie night out, so she could drown her sorrows. She would have to start going out with the girls at work because, apart from Rachel, most of them were single. As she would be, once Neil deigned to show his face and she could ask him to leave for good.

Neil had packed a few things in a case and booked into a hotel. He'd said he would pick the rest of his things up when he knew where he was going to live. He'd thought better of ringing Jane and asking if he could go there. He didn't want her to think he was just using her because he'd nowhere to stay. If and when he did return, he wanted it to be perfect.

Neil was genuinely sorry for leading Sally on. If he and Jane hadn't have been caught maybe their relationship would have come to a natural end without all the upset. But that was water under the bridge.

He hadn't told Jane about staying in the hotel. He wanted to wait until she contacted him. He went to work on Monday and kept his head down. Hopefully Sally would keep her own counsel and he'd get the chance to tell the board in his own time. He would have to eat a bit of humble pie, admitting he'd made a mistake but, hopefully, all would be well when Jane said he could go back home.

Lara had texted him to tell him Toby had arrived. She'd seemed thrilled and Neil wished he'd been there to share in the excitement of him arriving. He'd never been a dog lover before, but he knew Jane was and at the moment he would do anything to make her happy.

It was after lunch before Neil heard from Jane. She was out walking Toby and rang him on her mobile.

'Hi, it's me. Can you talk?' Jane often asked this. There was nothing more annoying that someone setting off in full flow when it was an inconvenient time.

'Hello love, yes it's fine,' Neil said, happy to hear from her. 'What can I do for you?'

'I was wondering, if you'd nothing better to do, would you like to call in for a chat on your way home from work?'

'That'd be great. I'll leave early and I'll be there about five-thirty. See you soon.' He was in a much better mood all afternoon. He'd smiled at everyone and was so much more productive than he'd been all morning. Five o'clock couldn't come soon enough for him. He kept his fingers crossed that she was going to tell him he could move back in to their home.

Daisy had returned Jane's phone call early Monday morning. Jane told her about the previous night's conversation with Sarah. Daisy was overjoyed that she wanted contact. Jane then had to tell her about poor Oliver. Daisy was devastated. Of course she would do anything she could to help. Jane told her of the plan for Daisy to be tested, to see if she could be a bone marrow donor. She then suggested that if Sarah was in agreement Daisy could drive to Woolley, and then they could travel down to Cornwall together. It would be a shame that they had to meet under such difficult circumstances, but time was of the essence.

Jane was glad that she'd booked the day off work as she'd spent most of it on the phone or walking Toby. She'd very quickly realised that he was going to be a handful but, he was such a loving little dog, it would all be worth it. All the walking would certainly get her fit.

It had been an emotional time when Steve and Paula had dropped Toby off. Paula couldn't stop crying and Jane had joined in when she saw how distraught Paula was. She promised she would take regular photographs of him and would even set up a webcam so they could see and talk to him at the same time. The job in Dubai was initially for two years but Paula knew that after that amount of time it wouldn't be fair to ask for him back. He was going to a new home and she would just have to get used to it. Steve acted like the big tough man but Jane could see he loved his dog. She promised to take good care of him and love him as much as they had done.

When they'd finally driven away, Toby had come to sit at Jane's feet and given her his paw. That signified that he wanted his tummy tickling. He was starting as he meant to go on! He seemed at home straight away. Giving him three Bonio's helped the proceedings. She showed him to his new bed and he quickly settled down and went fast asleep. She really envied him, and wished she could be more like that, just cuddle up and sleep through all the turmoil of her life.

Whilst Toby was sleeping, she rang Sarah back and put the suggestion to her about Daisy being tested to see if she could be a bone marrow donor. She offered to bring Daisy down as soon as it could all be arranged.

'You'd both do that for me?' Sarah started to cry.

'I told you I wanted to help and Daisy does too. We'll both come down later this week, as long as you don't mind me bringing my little dog,' Jane said.

'You're all more than welcome to stay here. Philip will have already gone. He's coming down early, arrives tomorrow and is staying until Thursday. I assume you don't want to see him,' Sarah said diplomatically.

'I think that's for the best. So, shall we come Friday, or do you want to leave it until next Monday?' Jane wanted to be as accommodating as possible. She felt the pain in her heart as Sarah talked about Philip. The feeling was still so raw. She hoped that it wouldn't always be like this.

'Let me ring my son and tell him the good news. Then I'll get back to you. Thank-you both so much. Now you have the answer to your question.' Sarah said.

'What do you mean?' Jane asked, puzzled.

'You wanted to know why you were dreaming about Nora and Daniel. I think you've just answered your own question,' Sarah said with a knowing tone in her voice.

Sarah rang Jane back later after she'd spoken to her son, and it was agreed that they would go down to Cornwall the following Monday.

Jane hadn't had time to prepare a meal for her and Neil as she'd just come back from the final walk of the day. She was debating what to do when Madge popped around for a chat. Her mother had an unerring knack of knowing exactly when Jane needed her and could have been a medium herself.

Madge could spot the sorrow in Jane's eyes 'Have you let him go?' she asked.

'I have. He was offered that job in Cornwall and, without hesitation, he accepted it. He wanted me to go with him.' Jane nearly cried again as she talked about it.

'Weren't you tempted?' Madge was disappointed and had hoped that it would work out for them both.

'No, I wasn't actually. I'm settled here and what would I have done down there without my family around me?' Jane had a determination in her voice.

'But you'll never know if it would've worked.' Madge was a romantic at heart and liked an ending that was against all the odds, not the safest option.

'He's leaving this week to go to Cornwall. We said goodbye yesterday.' Jane tried not to show how much she was still hurting.

'Do you think you've made the right decision?' Madge asked.

'I'm going to strangle the next person who asks me that! I don't know. How can anybody know? I just felt it was right and, before you say anything else, I've asked Neil if he wants to come home.' She waited for her mother's reaction.

'You know what's best for you, I'm sure,' was all Madge said. At one time she would have made a sarcastic comment and criticised Jane's decision but instead she stayed calm and kept her own counsel. George really was having a positive influence on her.

'Are you not going to say anything?'

'No. It's not up to me. You'll do what you think is best,' Madge said.

'But you think I've made the wrong decision, don't you?' Jane seemed to be goading her mother and wanted to be told that she'd made a huge mistake but Madge didn't take the bait. Instead she changed the subject.

'Have you spoken to Daisy recently?' Madge asked.

Jane knew when she was beaten and so went on to tell her mother all about her conversations with

Sarah and Daisy about poor Oliver and what had been arranged.

'It's a good thing you've done there love. I'm very proud of you and, seriously, if you think it's right to have Neil back, I'll support you one hundred percent.' Madge squeezed her daughter's arm.

Just as Madge was about to go, Neil pulled up in his car. They hadn't set eyes on one another since Christmas. Madge kissed Jane and went out to her car, walking past Neil as she went.

'If you hurt my daughter again you'll have me to answer to. Take that as a warning.' She gave Neil a sickly sweet smile and turned away.

Chapter 32

Philip had hired a van to move all his belongings. Not a large one because he didn't possess very much. He'd always lived to a minimum so consequently moving was relatively easy.

Work had agreed to him leaving a week early. They'd thanked him for all his hard work and wished him well in his new career. His colleagues had made a collection and had bought him a watch. How original, he thought. But he mustn't be ungrateful, after all it was a flying watch, although he failed to see what the difference was between it and a normal one.

Philip thought he must have missed out when God was giving out emotions because he felt nothing when he walked out of the door for the last time. He'd given them fifteen years of his life and he felt nothing. It seemed the only emotion he could feel was for Jane. It still felt as if his heart had been ripped out whenever he thought of her.

He was going to stay with Sarah for a couple of days, on Jane's recommendation. She'd been really lovely on the phone and had told him he was more than welcome to come and stay. She'd told him he'd be no trouble and she would welcome the company. He was going down today, Tuesday, and he would spend Wednesday and Thursday looking for somewhere to live. He'd told *Island Flights* he would go in on Friday to start his training, which would carry on over the weekend, so he could start properly the following Monday.

He finished packing by eight and he was on the road by eight-thirty. He wasn't sorry to leave Leeds, as without Jane he'd no ties to the place. He'd phoned his mum and dad to tell them about his new job in Cornwall. They were very pleased for him, though not so pleased about him and Jane going their separate ways. They'd had high hopes for the two of them.

The journey down took eight hours, with a couple of stops, and he pulled into Sarah's drive at six o'clock. The security light came on as it was already starting to get dark. He looked toward the house and saw a tall, slim woman coming to the door. He pressed the doorbell. Sarah opened the door and did a double take at the sight of Philip.

Standing tall at a little over six foot, with long brown hair and piercing brown eyes, Philip was always a sight to behold but the strangest thing for Sarah was he reminded her of the picture she kept of her father and dead brother. It was going to be very frustrating because she'd given her word to Jane she wouldn't mention anything about Daniel or the reason for their meeting.

'You must be Sarah. I'm Philip, Philip Sinclair.' He held out his hand in greeting.

Sarah tried to clear her throat, 'Did you say Sinclair? My name is St.Claire.'

'What a coincidence,' Philip said. 'It's quite an unusual surname, although probably not down here.'

'There's still not that many of us. That's why my father wanted me to keep the name when I married.' Jane hadn't mentioned his surname to her. Surely she'd made the connection although, she thought, you often couldn't see what was right in front of your eyes.

Jane had spent all this time searching for Daniel, and her lover was the double of him. Sarah couldn't explain it but she'd heard of such things happening. When Jane had first told her about her dream, and the search for Daniel and Nora, she'd done some research of her own and learnt about the possibility of reincarnation. If this was the case she was standing in the same room with the reincarnation of her brother... and she couldn't even tell him.

Although, in all honesty, what could she say? He'd think she was insane and go and check into a hotel. She would discuss it with Jane, who was coming down the next week. But surely if she'd had her suspicions she would've mentioned it?

'I'll just go and get my case, if that's OK?' Philip said, looking awkward.

Sarah realised she'd been standing, staring at him. Poor man, he must feel really uncomfortable.

'Sorry for staring, you look like someone I once knew. Have you been down here before?' she asked, trying to reassure him that she wasn't mad.

'No I haven't, but an awful lot of it does look familiar. As I was driving down I seemed to recognise places. It must be similar to somewhere I've been before,' he said, trying to come up with an explanation.

She couldn't very well tell him that he'd lived here in a past life. How could that ever come up in conversation?

'I've made a meal for you. I hope you're hungry.'

'You shouldn't have gone to so much trouble but, yes, I am hungry. Motorway service station food leaves a lot to be desired,' Philip said, thinking back to the Cornish pasty and cold chips he'd had for his lunch.

'It's shepherd's pie, made properly, with lamb. Do you like that?'

'Have you been talking to Jane? It's my favourite. My mum makes it for me when I stay with her. Most people make it with beef but it's much better with lamb.' Philip was amazed at yet another coincidence and was convinced Sarah had been talking to Jane.

'No, I've never talked to Jane about what you eat. She only mentioned you a few times. I got the impression she thought I wouldn't approve, what with her being married and all.'

Whether he was a reincarnation of her brother or not she felt very comfortable around him. They had a lovely meal together and chatted like old friends. By the end of the evening she felt like a second mother to him. It was nearly midnight when they said goodnight and went to their beds. It had also been a long time since Philip had had as much to talk about. He knew that he'd made a good decision, coming down here. It already felt like home.

Philip was up bright and early the next morning as he was going to drive down to Lands End. He'd searched the internet and had found a converted pigsty to rent in the tiny hamlet of Chenyl. It was only about a fifteen minute drive from *Island Flights* so would be convenient for work. He didn't care that it was isolated. He hadn't come down to Cornwall for a social life, he'd come here to fly and to find himself, whatever that entailed.

He'd arranged to meet the owner of the pigsty at eleven. The property was on their land but had its own drive and garden. It was all on one level and consisted of a lounge, one bedroom, a shower room and a kitchenette. It was small, but fine for one person, with more space than the studio flat he'd just left.

It was three hundred and fifty pounds a month, which he thought was very reasonable and, as the tenant, he got one free ticket a month to the Minack Outdoor Theatre because the owner was the director of the company. Philip couldn't believe it had been so easy to find somewhere to live. By midday the contracts were signed and he was going back to Sarah's for his belongings which he'd placed in her garage.

By early afternoon he'd transported all his belongings to his new house and had plenty of time to go to *Island Flights* to tell them he'd arrived. It was a real bonus for him as one of the pilots was testing a plane and invited Philip to go up with him. Could the day get anymore perfect?

Chapter 33

As Philip was moving his belongings into his new house, Neil was moving his back into his old one. Jane couldn't help thinking as she watched him that she'd rushed into her decision. She'd really enjoyed having her own space, being able to please herself as to when she ate and what to watch on television.

Lara was spending more and more of her time with Greg. He'd moved into a shared house with a couple of friends from work and they were both enjoying their new found freedom. While cleaning Lara's room Jane had seen the packet of contraceptive pills on her chest of drawers. At least she was being sensible but Jane found it hard to reconcile the fact that her little girl had grown up so quickly. All this meant that she hardly ever saw her. She'd even taken a case of clothes so she didn't need to come back every day. Jane thought she was rushing into things a bit but, after all, she would be eighteen in a couple of months. The same age as she and Neil had been when they first got together.

Within a matter of hours Neil was firmly ensconced back in the house. He'd taken the day off work to move his stuff but it hadn't taken long because it was mainly clothes, CDs and books. He hadn't taken any furniture. As he was starting to rearrange the book shelves he shouted to Jane, 'Put the kettle on love, I'm gagging for a drink. I thought we might go out for some lunch later, to celebrate.'

Neil flopped down on the settee and flicked the television on with the remote control.

Jane's heart sank. What had she done?

'Lunch would be lovely but you'll have to make your own tea, I'm taking Toby out. See you in a bit,' Jane replied, as she quickly made her retreat.

Toby was going to be her lifeline to the outside world. She could lose herself on the long walks and it would give her much needed time to herself. She'd invited Neil back because she'd thought it best for the family and for Neil. She'd felt sorry for him and, after all, he had been making a concerted effort. She just wondered how long he would be able to keep it up now he'd got his own way.

Jane felt exhausted, not just physically, but mentally and emotionally. She was getting increasingly frustrated at always feeling this way. She'd given so much of herself to everyone around her recently that she didn't seem to have any reserves left to draw on. She was finding work hard. Since making partner she seemed to have been given the total responsibility of selling all the houses. She knew that's what she was paid to do but the senior partners didn't seem to take into account the falling market. They were always finding fault and criticising her about the figures, asking how she was going to improve.

Sadly, she didn't have an answer, and who cared anyway? In the great scheme of things, did it matter if someone bought a house? There was a little five year old in Falmouth with leukaemia, who would lose his life if a bone marrow donor couldn't be found. The whole situation had put her life into perspective and Jane was starting to get very disillusioned with the rat race she was involved in.

She walked for longer than planned and poor Toby looked asleep on his feet when they got back. She gave him a Bonio and he took it to his bed. Neil was having a shower.

'Hi, you were ages. Fancy a shower before we go out?' he said with an evil glint in his eye.

What Jane actually wanted to do was crawl into bed and sleep for a week but she thought she'd better make an effort. She didn't want him wandering again because she didn't keep him satisfied.

She started to undress and crept into the shower cubicle with him. He got aroused so much quicker than before and within seconds he had her up against the glass door entering her and thrusting as deep as he could. He lifted up one of her legs so he could get in deeper. Jane groaned. She'd forgotten how well endowed he was. Another thing that had changed about his love-making was that he was very vocal. He was always asking her to talk to him about what she wanted to do, and if he told her he wanted to screw her once he must have told her a dozen times.

One positive for Jane was that he never just pulled out and got on with his day, he always made sure she got the same amount of pleasure as he did. Neil seemed insatiable and was ready for another session in a very short space of time.

'You should be flattered I want you so much,' Neil said, as he nuzzled her neck.

'I am, but I do need to be able to walk tomorrow,' she joked. 'Anyway, I thought you were treating me to lunch.'

'OK, it'll wait,' he said, looking down at his expanding erection.

Jane got out of the shower and quickly grabbed some clothes. Neil took even longer than usual to get dressed and do his hair. She went downstairs to catch up on some work while she was waiting. She never used to have to bring work home but nowadays she got so behind during the day she had to work nearly every evening. It was getting her down. The partners weren't happy that she was taking three days off next week, but when she'd explained the reason why they could hardly object.

She hadn't told Neil about her visit to Cornwall with Daisy the following Monday, knowing her luck he would suggest tagging along. And, when she explained to him on the way to lunch the reason she was going, that's exactly what he did. He thought she'd need some moral support and, as he was owed quite a lot of holiday, he'd said it would be a good opportunity to spend some quality time together. Jane agreed, but still tried to talk him out of it. However he was adamant. She would have to ring Sarah and Daisy to make sure they didn't mind him coming along.

They decided to go to the Sancere hotel in Newmillerdam for lunch. It was a quiet little village built round a man-made lake, close to where they lived. They both had a two-course meal with a couple of glasses of wine. Jane wasn't her usual, exuberant self.

'What's on your mind love?' Neil asked. 'You're not regretting having me back already, are you?' He tried making light of the situation, but she could see that he was worried.

'No, it's nothing like that. I'm thinking about work, which I seem to do a lot recently. I feel guilty for having time off. It's that bad at the moment.'

'Why don't you give it up? Neil suggested out of the blue.

'And do what?' Jane was shocked, as Neil had always liked the fact that they were an equal partnership bringing in two good incomes.

'Whatever you want. I earn enough money for both of us and you deserve a rest. I was too selfish before to suggest it, but I want to show you I've changed. At least think about it.' Neil squeezed her hand.

She leaned over and kissed him. 'Thank-you for the thought, and I will think about it.'

One kiss wasn't enough for Neil so he put his lips to hers and thrust his tongue in her mouth. It was much too erotic for a hotel dining room, albeit that they were tucked out of the way. Jane thought back to when she and Philip had had sex, more or less, in Barrons and so felt she couldn't criticise Neil. She should be flattered she turned him on so much.

After lunch Neil suggested a stroll round the lake. He must have been taken over by an alien, Jane thought. He'd never seen the point in walking for walking's sake. He held her hand as they strolled into the woods. She wasn't really dressed for the occasion. She did have boots on but she'd put on a short skirt and a cashmere jumper. Luckily it was a mild winter's day, though it seemed more like spring.

She soon found out the reason for Neil's sudden enthusiasm with nature. He leant against a tree and pulled her towards him. He started kissing her, getting more passionate as the kiss went on. She could feel his erection through his trousers. She'd made love outside with Philip on a number of occasions and she'd liked the excitement of it all, but this time they were so exposed. There was a real risk of them being discovered. Jane thought, what had Sally done to him?

'Neil, are you sure about this? Someone could come past at any minute.'

'That's half the fun, surely,' he said, then carried on kissing her.

He put his hand up her skirt and pulled her tights and pants down so that he could slide his finger inside. Despite herself she groaned and wanted more. She could feel how wet she was becoming. It only took her a few seconds to orgasm and before she knew it Neil was undoing his trousers and was slipping himself inside her.

'Hurry up,' Jane said, looking around to make sure they were alone.

Neil was oblivious to everything apart from thrusting in and out, groaning all the time.

'Ssh! Don't be too loud.' Jane put her hand over his mouth.

They were just off the main path and any unsuspecting dog walker could have caught them at any minute, but in less than five minutes it was all over. They both adjusted their clothing and carried walking round the lake as if nothing had happened.

So this was the new Neil, she thought. She just hoped she could keep up with him.

Chapter 34

When she returned home Jane rang Sarah to see if it was OK for Neil to stay as well. She'd offered to book them both into a hotel but Sarah wouldn't hear of it. Sarah didn't seem to want to talk.

'Is everything OK?' Jane asked, suspecting she already knew the answer.

'No it's not. I heard today that I'm not a match for Oliver, and neither is my daughter. We can't donate our bone marrow and we're running out of options. He's been put on the national donor list and we just have to hope and pray that a match is found while he's still strong enough to receive it.' Sarah was desperate and Jane felt helpless.

'Let's keep our fingers crossed that Daisy can help.' Jane tried to sound positive for Sarah's sake. She couldn't bear to think of her new friend suffering so much.

Monday couldn't come quick enough for all concerned. Daisy was to travel down to Woolley on Sunday afternoon. They would then get up at the crack of dawn on Monday to avoid the traffic. The appointment at the hospital was on Tuesday.

Jane had gone back to work after her two days off and had to fit a full week's work into three days. It meant she didn't get back into the house until after seven every night. Neil had had to prepare tea. At one time he would have sat there waiting for her to come home but his culinary skills had definitely improved while he'd been away. She was treated to a couple of complicated pasta dishes, and a risotto which was particularly delicious.

Neil asked her again if she'd considered his suggestion of stopping work. She could take time to reassess her career. He wasn't suggesting retirement, just a change of direction. Neil had never needed to reassess his career because he'd always wanted to be an accountant, and after sixteen years he still loved it. There was something very satisfying about making sense out of a bunch of figures. His career was going from strength to strength and he was always being headhunted by larger offices. But it would necessitate a move to London or Manchester which he wasn't prepared to do.

Jane had thought about his kind offer to be the sole earner for a while and as each day went by she was more than tempted, but what would she do instead? She hadn't had a lifelong ambition, such as Philip's of being a pilot, or Neil's of being an accountant.

She'd toyed with the idea of taking up Feng Shui and being a consultant, helping people to either sell their homes or feel more comfortable in them. She didn't know if there would be enough demand for her to make a living out of it but it was something she could investigate when she returned from Cornwall.

The journey was much quicker because of setting off at five in the morning. Even better, for Jane, was that Neil was driving and the Range Rover was a comfortable ride. Both Daisy and Jane slept part of the way down. Neil either had the radio on or was talking. He'd never been one for silence and both women would've welcomed a bit of peace and quiet.

Jane often forgot she was the common denominator in the Daisy-Sarah relationship and without her they would've never known of each other's existence. She could put out of her mind the idea that she might have been someone else in a past life when she was alone, or with her family. But when she was with Daisy she was reminded of the possibility every minute. She was very nervous as they pulled up outside Sarah's house.

Neil offered to stay in the car while they met as he didn't feel he belonged in their little gathering. Jane thought that was very sweet of him and she kissed his cheek as they got out. She went to ring the bell, Daisy standing behind her. An obviously nervous Sarah opened the door. They all just stood and stared at one another.

'Sarah, this is Daisy and Daisy, this is Sarah. You both know me, as either Jane or Nora.' She thought humour might break the ice and she was correct. Hugs were exchanged all round and they went into the lounge to sit down. Neil was invited in and ordered to make tea, for which he was grateful, as tears had started to flow.

It was a very emotional time for the three women. Daisy was meeting an aunt she hadn't even known existed. Since losing her mother she'd had no family. Both her parents were only children, or so she'd thought, so there hadn't even been any cousins to keep in contact with, until now.

Sarah wanted to know everything there was to know about Daisy. 'Please start at the beginning and tell me all about yourself.'

Daisy took a deep breath and started to tell her story. 'I was brought up in Richmond where my mum lived with her new husband. I take it Jane told you she married after she'd lost Daniel?'

'She did yes.'

'My childhood was pretty ordinary until my mum and dad split up. It was then I discovered that Derek wasn't my dad, and mum started to talk about Daniel. She told me wonderful stories of how they'd first met in the dance hall and how he'd literally swept her off her feet, dancing the night away. You could tell from her tone that they really loved each other.

'It was the 50's, when I was growing up, and mum was so brave bringing me up by herself. Every other woman at the time seemed to tolerate a bad relationship, but not her. We still did alright though. I didn't want for much and she always made sure we had a holiday every year. I actually remember one year coming here to Cornwall for a week. We booked into a hotel in Bude. We travelled by coach and had a lovely break. I assume she didn't want to come down this far in case she bumped into your mum and dad or something. I never asked about Daniel's parents. It just never came up in conversation.'

Sarah interrupted, 'It would've been lovely for mum and dad to know you, but I understand your mother had her reasons for keeping you quiet. But it's such a shame as neither of them would've judged her. They were such kind people. They'd have helped in any way they could have. Sorry, do go on.'

'My mum developed breast cancer when she was only forty-four. She never told me at the time how serious it was, but I guessed. She struggled with her health after that but she did her best. I helped as much as I could. It was the main reason I didn't go to university. I was clever enough to go but I couldn't bear the thought of leaving her when she'd done so much for me.' Even after all this time Daisy could feel her eyes filling up as she thought how much her beloved mother had suffered.

'Did you marry?' Sarah asked.

'No. While mum was alive I devoted myself to her care. I had the occasional boyfriend but nothing serious. I really wasn't bothered. I knew she would die young and I wanted to be with her until that time. Treatments for cancer weren't as effective back then. I finally lost her when she was only fifty-one. It was the saddest day of my life.' Daisy went quiet and tears filled her eyes.

'How did you become a medium?' Sarah asked when Daisy had regained her composure. She felt quite guilty asking all these questions but she had a lifetime to catch up on.

'It took me ages to get over the death of my mother and I found comfort in the Spiritualist Church. I was given a message nearly straight away telling me I had the gift and that's what I should be doing. Every one of my friends thought I was mad, giving up a very lucrative career in banking, but I trusted what I'd been told and I've never looked back. I feel like I'm helping people doing what I'm doing. I know banking is helpful but it would've destroyed my soul.

'I would've liked children but by the time I met Edwin, who was fifteen years older than me, I was approaching the change and it just never happened. Edwin made me blissfully happy and we shared twenty glorious years together before he was taken from me. I was telling Jane when she came to see me that the house I live in is far too big for me, but I feel close to Edwin there. I feel his spirit still inhabits the house.'

'I feel the same about this house,' Sarah said. 'I've often felt Gerald, my late husband, around me. I've even smelt the after-shave he used to use when I'm sitting in his chair.'

Jane sat and smiled as she listened to the two long-lost relations catching up on one another's lives. Nora's intention had been to bring the two women together, and Jane had the feeling that Nora was making it up to both of them for the fact that she'd deprived Sarah's parents of their first granddaughter.

After all the reminiscing their thoughts turned to the present.

'I can't thank you enough for coming down and doing this for us. My son Ben and his wife Anna are coming round tonight, so you can meet them before tomorrow. Even though you have your mother's eyes,' Sarah was addressing Daisy, but she looked at Jane as she spoke, 'you have a look of my brother. Here's a photograph of Daniel and his father taken just before he enlisted.' Sarah handed the photograph to Daisy.

As soon as she held it, in her mind's eye, she was shown a young man in jeans and a sweatshirt with longish brown hair and stubble. He was smiling at a young woman who had her back to the camera, so she couldn't see the face. The image quickly faded and she realised she'd just been shown Daniel in this life because he bore a striking resemblance to the photograph she held in her hand.

Just at that moment Neil brought in the tea. 'Here you are ladies, the solution to the world's problems. Sorry it's taken so long but I got carried away watching the golf. Shall I be mother, no pun intended?' They all started to laugh. Daisy and Sarah had a lot more catching up to do. As soon as tea was finished Jane signalled to Neil to leave them to it and together they went up to their room.

'Come here you. I haven't had a kiss since we left home and I'm getting withdrawal symptoms.' He took her in his arms and started to kiss her. Neil had been back in the family home six days and on every one they'd made love at least twice. Neil's libido was off the scale and Jane was starting to feel quite sore, as if she'd got honeymoon cystitis.

She was praying for her period which was due any day now. In fact, wasn't it due last week? Panic gripped her as she tried to recall when she was last on.

She pulled away from Neil, he looked hurt.

'Don't look like that, we've just arrived and it's someone else's house. Just let's wait for a while.' Neil was sulking.

She looked around for the bag with her diary in and realised she'd left it in the lounge.

'I'm just going to get my bag from downstairs. Have a cold shower if you need one!' They both laughed.

She was just about to go into the living room when she overheard Sarah and Daisy's conversation. She paused and listened to what they were talking about.

'She's such a lovely girl and I hope she's done the right thing going back to Neil. He seems a nice enough man but I just can't see them together. She's such a calm soul and he's always so busy, he'll tire her out.' It was Daisy's voice Jane could hear.

'I agree, I do like him and he seems to love her, but I know what you mean. Can I let you into a secret while she's not here? It involves you too.' Sarah whispered.

Jane had to put her head closer to the door to hear the next part of the conversation.

'Have you heard her talk about her young man, Philip?' Sarah asked.

'She has alluded to him but I think she was embarrassed about admitting to having an affair,' Daisy said. 'I got the impression he meant a great deal to her as she always had such a faraway expression on her face whenever she talked about him.'

'Well he came to stay with me last week and I couldn't believe my eyes when he knocked on the door. He's the spitting image of Daniel. You know Jane was interested in finding him. Well I think she did, without even knowing it.' Sarah waited for Daisy's reaction.

Daisy chuckled a little. 'That would make sense as when you handed me the photograph I got a flash of a young man, who looked like my father, with a girl. She had dark hair, like Jane, but I couldn't see her face.'

'For a second I forgot you're a medium and see things. Do you ever get used to it?' Sarah asked.

'Not when it involves my life. So, not only do I have a reincarnated mother alive but also a father. Does Philip know anything about all this?' she asked.

'No. Jane made me promise not to mention where we'd met so I don't think she's told him the story. It's very hard to talk to someone about such a sensitive subject, particularly if it's all new,' said Sarah.

'Are you going to tell Jane about your suspicions?' Daisy asked.

'If I can get her on her own. That's if Neil ever leaves her side,' Sarah said in frustration.

Jane didn't need to be told. She'd heard everything and was dumbfounded. Could Philip really be Daniel reincarnated? And how had she not guessed, particularly after Barbara had seen him in Richmond? But at the time she hadn't known anything about reincarnation. It all started to make sense to her now; when she thought back to when she'd first seen him and how he seemed so familiar after such a short space of time. The intensity of their relationship and how they'd fallen in love so quickly should have given her a clue.

Beforehand she'd had trouble deciding how she was going to tell Philip her story, but now it would be impossible. He would never believe her and it would probably destroy what little friendship they had left.

Then she remembered that she'd come downstairs for her diary. If she was pregnant it would be a nightmare because there was no way of knowing who the father was without a paternity test. She was being punished for her promiscuity and other people would suffer into the bargain.

She knocked on the door and went in.

'Sorry, I've just come for my bag.' Jane went to get it from the side of the settee.

Both Daisy and Sarah looked sheepish and wondered if she'd overheard them. Jane didn't feel like telling them what she'd heard, so she got her bag and went back upstairs to Neil. He'd taken her advice and was in the shower, though probably not a cold one. She looked in her diary and saw her last period was at the end of January which meant she was a week late already. She'd been under a lot of stress recently and that could explain her lateness. No need to panic just yet. It's not as if she'd been negligent, she still had a coil in.

Jane and Neil were going out for a meal, leaving the new found relations to get to know each other. Ben and Anna were expected any minute and after meeting them they would drive into Falmouth and find an Indian restaurant, because a nice, hot, chicken madras would make everything alright.

Chapter 35

Jane was going to go the hospital with Sarah and Daisy. She felt as if she was intruding because she wasn't a blood relation, but they'd insisted. Without Jane they wouldn't have found themselves going to the hospital at all because it had been her idea in the first place. Neil had left bright and early as he was going to try his hand at sea fishing. He felt he had no place in the day's events.

Oliver was on the children's ward in Falmouth Infirmary, in a separate isolation room, and all precautions had been taken to prevent infection. No newcomers could go in and Jane had to look at the poor, defenceless little boy through the glass.

She waved and he gave her a beautiful smile. It broke her heart to see such a young life holding on by the skin of his teeth. He had tubes coming from his nose and a drip in his arm. Ben and Anna were already with him and mouthed, 'Hello,' through the plate glass. Sarah had to be scrubbed in and had slipped into a gown and mask before she could go and see her grandson.

Daisy and Jane followed the consultant into his office.

'Please sit down,' he said. 'Thank you for taking the time to come. Do you know what we expect of you today?' The doctor addressed Daisy.

'Ben told me a bit but I'd like you to explain it to me again,' she said nervously.

'Oliver has leukaemia and his only hope of survival is having a bone marrow transplant. Tissue type is inherited and classified by a group of protein markers known as Human Leucocyte Antigens or HLA for short. Thirty percent of patients needing a transplant identify a donor with matching tissue type within their own family, but we have tested all Oliver's immediate family and they don't match, so that's why we're testing you.

'In a minute we'll take a saliva swab from you, and if it shows you appear to be a potential match you'll be asked to submit several more fresh blood samples. A blood stem cell transplant can be given by a donor who shares the same tissue type. Are you with me so far?' Daisy nodded. 'Healthy donor bone marrow is introduced into the patient's blood stream much in the same way as a blood transfusion. If the new bone marrow takes, or engrafts well, it begins producing normal healthy blood cells and the patient can begin to hope for recovery. Does that make it any clearer?' he asked.

'Absolutely, thank-you. So what do I do now?' Daisy asked.

'My nurse will just take a swab from the inside of your mouth. Then you can sit in the waiting room or go for a coffee until the result comes back from the lab. If you're a potential match you'll be asked to give blood.'

With the swab at the lab being analysed, there was nothing to do but sit, wait and pray. Jane paced up and down hoping that the reason she'd had her dream in the first place was to help Oliver.

The nurse called them back into his office after about half-an-hour.

'Good news, you passed the first stage. Now I have to take some blood samples. This will take longer to analyse so if you come back at twelve I should have the results by then. We're rushing it through because time is of the essence. I should warn you that if you are a positive match you'll be having the procedure today, but let's cross that bridge if, and when, we come to it.' The doctor, who was taking the blood samples himself, signalled for Daisy to lie down on the couch.

With the blood on its way to the lab they went to find Sarah to see if she wanted to join them for lunch. She'd been crying again and Jane felt so helpless. None of them ate more than a few mouthfuls of dinner. Ben popped out to see how they were holding up and he kept repeating how grateful they all were to Daisy and to Jane for suggesting it.

At twelve on the dot all three women went back to get the results. Ben left to be with Anna. They could hardly bear the anticipation. Was it Jane's imagination or was the doctor smiling? She tentatively knocked on the open door.

'Come in ladies. Mrs St.Claire, how nice to see you again.' Jane wasn't imagining it, he was in a good mood.

'Well Daisy, are you prepared for this?' He paused for effect 'You're a positive tissue match.' He grinned. Sarah burst into tears and hugged Jane. Daisy felt a little overwhelmed.

'What's next?' she asked, looking terrified.

'We'll admit you into hospital today and give you a general anaesthetic to do the procedure. Bone marrow is taken from your pelvic bone with a needle and syringe. You'll be required to stay in hospital for two nights because you'll feel tired and have a little soreness in the lower back. The bone marrow will then be transfused into Oliver and, once we're sure the procedure has worked, you can then be discharged.' The doctor paused to make sure Daisy understood it all. 'The next step is for me to take your full medical history and give you a thorough medical examination to confirm your fitness. Then, all being well, we can proceed later this afternoon. Do you want to tell Ben and Anna the good news?' the doctor asked Sarah.

'Yes please.' She nearly ran out of the door.

'It's a really good thing you're doing,' said the doctor. 'You'll never actually know what this'll mean to the family. We'll take good care of you. There really is nothing to worry about.' He was a very good doctor, thought Jane. He'd seen the worried look on Daisy's face and had tried to put her mind at rest.

'Are you OK?' Jane asked, holding onto Daisy's hand.

'I will be. It's all been a bit of a rush and I can't believe, of all people, I am a match. Don't get me wrong, I'm absolutely thrilled, but I've not been in a hospital since I lost my mum thirty-eight years ago. I've been really lucky with my health.'

'Do you want me to go and get you some things from Sarah's, seeing as they won't let you home?'

Jane asked, feeling sorry for Daisy, who looked a little out of her depth.

'Please, and don't forget to get me some books and magazines. If I'm going to be stuck in here for a few days I'll need something to do. Could you also do me a favour and ring Steven? He'll only worry if he can't get hold of me.'

Jane and Daisy went to find Sarah and her family, who were hugging each other and weeping. When they saw Daisy they cried even more. Words could never express their gratitude. They looked over to Oliver who was holding up a sign in his best handwriting that read, 'Thank-you Auntie Daisy'.

Fishing was something that Neil had never tried. It all seemed a bit too static for him, sitting on a river bank contemplating his navel. But hopefully sea fishing should be slightly more exciting. He had to think of something to do for the day while they were all at the hospital. He parked his car and walked up to Falmouth harbour where he was to join the trip. The weather wasn't very good and the sea looked rather choppy. He was in two minds whether to cancel and do something else.

He'd been back with Jane a week today and he was really glad it was all working out. He'd seen Sally at work last week and they'd been perfectly pleasant to each other. He could see why he'd been enticed by her in the first instance as she was still absolutely gorgeous. He was so confused. When he had her he didn't want her, but now he'd given her up, his desire for her was even stronger.

The main reason he'd insisted on coming to Cornwall was so he wouldn't be tempted to get in touch with Sally while Jane was away. Jane hadn't particularly wanted him to come and he was going to tell her he'd changed his mind, but when he saw Sally in the tea room bending down to put milk in the fridge, he'd thought better of it. He knew it wasn't good for his marriage but every time he made love to Jane he remembered Sally and what they'd done together.

Neil knew Jane hadn't really been up for outdoor sex at Newmillerdam, but Sally would've been, and he'd found himself thinking of her all the time he was screwing his wife.

He could tell Sally still had feelings for him, even though she was doing a good job of convincing herself otherwise. He'd been the one for Sally and emotions didn't get turned off that easily. She'd really wanted it to work. Sitting on the boat, going out to sea, he tried to imagine what she'd be doing now. He was so tempted to text her to make sure she was alright and that there were no hard feelings.

Sea fishing wasn't much better than he'd imagined, particularly on a cold wet day like today and he was glad that he'd only signed up for a four-hour slot. He got back to the cottage mid afternoon and he thought he'd relax with a newspaper until everyone got back. He might even treat himself to a nap.

Chapter 36

It was now a month since Daisy's procedure and Oliver was doing well. It appeared that the bone marrow had taken and he'd started to produce healthy blood cells. It appeared that the bone marrow had taken and he'd started to produce healthy blood cells instead of those riddled with cancer like before. He was getting stronger by the day and didn't have to be in complete isolation anymore.

Either Ben or Sarah kept Jane and Daisy updated every couple of days.

Daisy had indeed stayed in hospital for two nights. She'd had her own room with a television and had appreciated the rest. Sarah had remained at her bedside the whole time. She thought that Daisy was a lot braver than she'd given herself credit for. The pain she experienced was only minor and by the following weekend she was back at work giving demonstrations and a few private readings.

Jane and Neil had left Daisy in Cornwall because they both had to return to work. Lara had stayed at home to look after Toby because Jane had decided that it wouldn't have been fair to leave him all day in a strange house, but Lara was chomping at the bit to return to Greg.

Because Jane hadn't had a period by the time she got home she went to buy a pregnancy testing kit. She was very nervous as she peed on the stick. She'd bought one of the foolproof kits that actually said 'you are pregnant' or 'you are not pregnant'. What next? A voice shouting out the news in a toilet cubicle?

She realised she was hyperventilating by the time it came up, 'You are not pregnant'. She breathed a sigh of relief, but then found herself thinking, had she done it incorrectly? And would she have to do it all over again later?

Two weeks later Jane was moaning with period pains at the very same time as Sally was throwing up in the toilet cubicle at work.

Sally suspected she was pregnant when she found one of her contraceptive pills in the packet at the end of the month. It should have been empty. She worked out that she'd missed it on the day Neil left. It'd been such a traumatic day for her, taking it had never entered her head.

She'd started feeling sick straight away and her breasts were already two sizes bigger, yet she was only six weeks along. She'd done a test at home and taken a sample to the doctors. There was no doubt. There was also no doubt in Sally's mind about whether she would keep the baby. She'd never believed in abortion, and adoption was out of the question. She was, after all, thirty now and she might not get another chance at motherhood.

Luckily she was coming to the end of her accountancy course. It would finish in July, she would qualify in September, and she would give birth in December. That meant that she would be eligible for promotion and a salary increase which would be useful, as she would need every penny to pay for a nursery or a childminder.

Because she had such a naturally slim figure the bump was already starting to show so she started wearing baggy clothes to work. Gone were the days of pencil skirts and skinny jeans, she was happiest in tracksuit bottoms and sweatshirts. What she hadn't done was tell Neil. She knew she would have to sooner or later but the rate at which she was growing it would be earlier than she'd first anticipated.

Neil was still at home with Jane, who was getting snippets of information about the couple from Lauren, his new assistant. Lauren told Jane that Neil still asked after Sally, who tried where possible to avoid him at work. She took her lunch hour at eleven, or three, when she knew he would be working.

Sally didn't expect anything from Neil and was prepared to bring the baby up by herself. She didn't even expect any money. If he wanted to contribute, all well and good, but she was too proud to beg. She'd only told one other person. When it had been confirmed she'd driven to Scarborough to tell her mother, face to face. She'd got exactly the reaction she was expecting. Her mother called her stupid and irresponsible and hoped Sally was going to screw the father for every penny he had.

Listening at her mother ranting and raving Sally was amazed she'd turned out to be a relatively balanced person. Her mother was so angry and critical of everything; she was glad it hadn't rubbed off on her. Charlotte, her sister, was a carbon copy of their mother. She knew how to work the system and the more she could screw out of the government, the better. Sally had done well for herself and even this mistake didn't put her in the same league as her mother or sister.

Since splitting up with Neil she'd become friends with Zoe again and she was thinking of telling her about the pregnancy. Zoe was over seven months into hers and it would be useful to talk to someone who'd already been through everything she was experiencing. She felt lonely and needed someone else to talk to. Jane would have been an ideal candidate but she thought approaching her would really be pushing her luck.

Life had returned to the mundane existence of before in the Barclay household. Jane had started to hate her job, was threatening to resign and taking Neil up on his suggestion of letting him be the breadwinner for a while. She'd been meaning to do it for weeks but something had held her back. She liked the fact that she earned her own money and didn't want to be reliant on anyone. Neil had changed and hadn't returned to his selfish ways. He was still very attentive and still very horny but something about their situation told her to be wary and not to trust him absolutely.

Every day when she woke up she intended to write to Philip. There had been no contact at all since the text message she'd sent telling him Sarah's number. She still missed him but had expected her feelings to lessen over time. But that wasn't happening. She was missing him even more. She'd lost count of the number of times she'd picked up the phone to ring or text him, then had lost her nerve at the last minute.

She missed their daily conversations about nothing in particular. His lovely smile, the way he kissed her and especially the way he'd made her feel during their lovemaking. Even though it had improved between her and Neil there was absolutely no comparison with how she felt with Philip. In every way Philip was better for her and she'd thrown it all away for the sake of her family's feelings and the fact that she was so stuck in her ways. She wouldn't even contemplate making a fresh start. She'd gone for the easy option. Her mother had warned her but she hadn't listened.

Jane knew how Philip was fairing because Sarah told her. He loved his job, had fallen in love with Cornwall and, no, he wasn't seeing anyone else. Sarah and Philip had forged quite a friendship and visited each other on a fairly regular basis.

Jane was a tad jealous of their relationship. It felt as if she was being excluded, but it was, after all, her own doing. In the beginning Philip had started asking after her, but not lately. She assumed he no longer saw the point because he knew she'd made up her mind she was never going back to him.

One of the main reasons Jane had returned to Neil was she thought that was what her family wanted, but it had made no difference one way or the other to Simon and Lara, who were getting on with their lives regardless of who she was with. Lara and Neil didn't see much more of each other than they'd done when he was living with Sally. Jane tried not to dwell on her decision but often wondered whether she'd made the correct one. She'd lost much of the new found excitement she'd experienced in her time with Philip and had soon settled back into the mediocre rut she'd been in most of her married life.

Lara was coming home for tea tonight and Jane had learnt by now that meant she either wanted something or needed to talk. It was probably about her eighteenth birthday, which was on the seventh of May. She'd talked about having a party and was probably looking for funding because after the last escapade she wouldn't be having it at their house.

Jane had asked Neil not to be too late home from work so she was finishing at five come hell or high water. At four forty-five Cyril Brown, the managing partner, walked into her office, without knocking of course. He threw a sheet of paper on her desk.

'You think an A4 sheet is sufficient explanation as to why your figures were down last week, for the fourth week running?' he bawled.

For a second Jane was lost for words and just looked at him.

It was the straw that broke the camel's back. 'Hang on a minute Mr Brown. What right have you to come into my office shouting your mouth off, treating me like an office junior when I am in fact a partner in this firm? The reason the figures are down is because, if you hadn't noticed, we're in a recession which, contrary to popular belief, is not my fault. Wake up and face reality. Three estate agents in Leeds closed down last month. We're not doing too badly thanks to all my hard work which, I might add, I don't get any thanks for.' She paused for breath.

It was his turn to be speechless. Jane had never retaliated like that before. He'd never seen her so angry and he rapidly started to back pedal.

'Well there is...'

'Stop right there. I haven't finished.' She was on a roll. She picked up her pen and reached for a piece of paper. On it she wrote 'I resign with immediate effect,' then dated and signed it. She threw it at Cyril Brown. 'And if you don't like it, sue me!' And with that she picked up her coat and bag. 'I'll be back for the rest of my things tomorrow,' she shouted at him.

'Look Jane, I'm sorry if I was a bit hasty...' but he was saying it to himself. She'd already walked out of the door.

Jane's anger turned to elation when she realised what she'd done. She was a free woman at last. She wanted to tell someone and suddenly felt an overwhelming sadness when she realised the one person she wanted to tell wasn't there. She would've loved to have talked to Philip right now. He would join in her celebration and give her lots of encouragement. It felt like a bitter sweet victory. Sweet, in that she'd finally left her job, but bitter, because she didn't have the one she loved to share it with. There, she'd admitted it, she still loved him. Now she had all the time in the world, she would write a letter to Philip and try and explain everything to him. She owed him that at least.

Jane was going to keep the news about what had happened at work to herself for the time being.

She would tell Neil later because if she started talking about it, she would get angry all over again and she wanted to be calm for the family meal.

The driving instructor was dropping Lara off at home and Greg was coming to collect her after tea. Jane had made a chilli and was just helping herself to a glass of wine when Neil and Lara walked in together. Neil went over to kiss Jane. It was always on the lips now, not on the cheek as it had been before.

She served out the dinner and poured Neil a large glass of wine. Lara looked uncomfortable and Jane was dying to know her news.

'You're not going to like what I've got to say but please hear me out 'cause it's something I've thought a lot about,' Lara started. 'I've changed my mind about VSO and I don't want to go to university.'

Neil was just about to interrupt when he thought better of it.

'I've decided to get a job. I've seen the career advisor at college and have been researching things that interest me. I want to do something in finance like you dad, either banking or in accounts for the council or health authority. It's a good career and there are good prospects.' She paused and waited for the response.

It was Neil who spoke first. 'If you're sure that's what you really want, then it's already decided.' Jane was keeping quiet but was disappointed because she believed university gave you much more than just an education. However it was her daughter's life and she must do with it as she saw fit.

If only Jane had taken her own advice.

'There's more,' added Lara. 'Greg and I are getting engaged on my eighteenth birthday and we're going to get a flat together. I know he's the one and I want to spend my life with him.' She hardly paused for breath.

This time both of the parents were speechless, but they couldn't preach to Lara because they'd been the same age when they first met. And they'd had to get married because of the pregnancy. Not great role models, Jane thought.

Lara looked at Jane. 'Say something mum.'

'Sorry sweetheart, it's just a bit of a shock. I'd guessed you had changed your mind about VSO but I thought you were just a bit late filling in your UCAS form. You don't really want my opinion about you and Greg, you just want me to be happy for you. So I will be,' Jane answered diplomatically.

Lara thought there would be fireworks so she was a bit shocked at her parents' reaction.

Jane felt she needed to explain herself a little further. 'I know there's no point in trying to change your mind. Who knows what's the best thing to do? But I believe you should go your own way in the world and make your own mistakes. Not that I'm saying what you're doing is a mistake.'

Neil thought they were too young to get engaged and said so, but not in an argumentative way. Lara respected their opinions and the rest of the meal was taken up by plans for her eighteenth birthday/engagement party, which she wanted to be at the local village pub.

Jane was tired of always being rational and level-headed and wanted to shout as she had earlier. Since her outburst in Richmond, in front of Philip, Jane had tried to keep her temper in check. But it was starting to show its ugly head, as it had done this afternoon; although she'd felt justified in her anger, Mr Brown had borne the brunt of it. She felt it wasn't just about the job that she was venting her anger. 'Life happens - between the plans' was a phrase that came to mind at this moment and seemed very relevant to her life.

Chapter 37

It was the beginning of May, and Sally's pregnancy was really starting to show. Wearing baggy clothes was only just hiding her bump. She knew it was time to talk to Neil. She waited until the day of the staff meeting when all but the partners left at four-thirty. She spent longer than usual in the toilet, waiting until all her colleagues had gone, then went downstairs to Neil's office. She looked through the blinds and saw he was on his own.

She knocked on his door. Neil had thought everyone had gone home.

'Come in,' he shouted and looked up.

Sally opened the door and walked in. Neil was surprised.

'Hello,' he said in a tone of voice that showed he was obviously pleased to see her. 'To what do I owe this unexpected pleasure?' he asked, with a smile on his face.

'We need to talk and I need to show you something.'

He looked intrigued. 'Come and have a seat.'

'Before I sit down…' She lifted up her top and her bulge was suddenly obvious to the world.

'Shit,' was all Neil could find to say.

'I'm glad you're being grown up about this!' Sally retorted.

'Sorry, but surely I'm allowed to be surprised. I'd actually noticed you'd put a bit of weight on, especially round your tits, but never thought anything of it. How far are you?' he asked.

'I'm twelve weeks. I thought I could get away without telling anyone for at least four months but, because I'm so thin, it's started to show earlier.' She was trying not to show any emotion.

'Without stating the obvious, how did it happen? I thought you were on the pill,' Neil asked.

'I was. It must have been the day you left. I just forgot to take it, and before you get defensive I don't expect anything from you. I'm just letting you know.' Sally felt like crying and felt her bottom lip quiver.

Neil got up from behind the desk and took her in his arms. Touching her felt wonderful and all his old emotions came flooding back.

'I'm sorry you've had to go through this on your own.' He bent down to kiss her.

Against her better judgement, she kissed him back. She hadn't expected this, but she'd wanted it to. Every night since he'd left she'd secretly hoped Neil would come to his senses and realise he wanted her. All the while she'd been pretending she was unaffected by his departure, but it had been pure bravado. She'd almost had herself convinced.

Neil had fantasised about her bigger breasts for weeks and put his hand inside her bra and fondled her engorged nipple. He pulled her top over her head and undid her bra. Then he pulled down her elasticated trousers so he could see her naked flesh. She still looked gorgeous.

'Can I make love to you?' he asked.

This was more than Sally had hoped for. She nodded, so he undid his trousers and let them slip to the floor. His erection was enormous and she couldn't wait for him to be inside her. As he entered her he was gentler than usual because of the baby, but he was so turned on he came in no time at all. Sally sat astride him, kissing him all over until he became hard again. She'd so missed their lovemaking and the one lover she'd had since she split up with Neil couldn't hold a candle to him.

They both lay on the floor exhausted. The blinds weren't closed but Neil didn't care, he'd wanted her and nothing was going to stop him.

He continued fondling her breasts and even as they were having a conversation he had a hand between her legs feeling how moist she was. He was so horny when he was with her.

'What do you want from me?' Neil asked.

'Whatever you decide to give me.' Sally replied. This was going far better than she'd expected.

'Of course I'll more than adequately provide for the baby, but have you told anyone it's mine?' The cogs in his head were working overtime.

'No-one, apart from my mum and she doesn't live around here,' Sally replied.

'How about you tell everyone it's someone else's? And we keep our affair a secret until I find a way to tell Jane. If it comes out at work then one of us will have to leave. I'm afraid it would be you. I love you Sally. I never stopped, but it's complicated at the moment.'

That's all she'd wanted to hear and would agree to anything now he'd said those words.

'Can we still see each other?' she asked, hoping he could still make time for her.

'Of course we can. I could arrange it that you come and work for me again and we could carry on as before. I can visit you at the flat after work and I'll find excuses at the weekend to see you. It'll be just like before, but even better.' Neil was getting turned on just thinking about it.

Sally knew just what to do to drive him mad and she put her own hand between her legs, he instantly got hard and entered her again for the third time.

Neil was very late home from work that night and blamed the staff meeting for going on too long. He now had to face reality, his mistress was pregnant. What a mess. Just when he thought that his life was getting simpler this had to happen. He was now supporting Jane as well, since she'd walked out of her job. This baby was going to be a big drain on his resources but he knew he couldn't leave Sally. He was addicted to the sex. What would happen when the baby was born was anyone's guess. Could she still screw right up to giving birth? That was all that Neil could think about.

Every day Jane had been working on her letter to Philip. She would write a few sentences at a time and then screw the paper up. She didn't know what to say, or how to explain it so that it would make sense. At least Neil was off her back, he still wanted to make love but at least it wasn't twice a day any more. She welcomed the break. She'd asked Daisy and Sarah for their advice but they told her to follow her heart. How could she follow her heart when it didn't know what it wanted either?

She still spoke to Sarah regularly and Oliver was doing so well that he could now come home at weekends. She wanted to arrange another visit because she missed them so much and didn't feel she had anyone to talk to up here. Zoe had had her baby, a cute little girl, Maria, weighing 7lb1oz. She'd seen her for coffee on a couple of occasions but Zoe had little time for anyone else other than the baby, which was understandable. Jane had never made much time for friends because she'd been too busy working and now she was beginning to regret it.

Neil's job was much busier than usual and, as a result, he was spending more time in the office and less time at home. Without Toby she really would be lonely. She must finish the letter to Philip so she could concentrate on finding a new career to relieve the boredom.

Chapter 38

Philip was just about to set off to work on a beautiful sunny day in June when he received the letter. He opened it and was shocked to discover who it was from. He hadn't heard a peep out of Jane since he'd left for Cornwall earlier in the year. He knew she still asked after him. Sarah had told him but he'd given up any hope of direct contact a long time ago.

He knew he didn't have time to read it now otherwise he'd be late for work. He placed it delicately on the coffee table and decided that to give it the time and respect it deserved he would leave it until he returned home. She had taken months to write the letter so surely he owed her more than a quick five minutes in the staff room over a hurried cup of black coffee?

Philip loved every day in his job but today he couldn't give it one hundred percent, he kept thinking about Jane's letter waiting on the table. After a day's work he declined the offer of a pint with his colleagues and made the short trip home in record time. He reached for a cool can of Stella Artois out of the fridge, picked up the letter and went to sit in his garden in the warmth of the summer sun. His heart was pounding as he started to read.

'My dearest Philip,

I'm sorry it's taken me so long to write to you but believe me I've been wanting to write this letter since March. Do you remember when we last met I said I had something to tell you but I wasn't ready. Well now I am. Here goes. Please read what I have to say with an open mind and trust that I'm not insane.

It was about last July when I started having a dream. It kept recurring, maybe weekly to start with and then it would happen about twice a week until by September it was happening nearly every night. It was always the same. I won't go into too much detail, suffice it to say it was about a girl in the Second World War who received a letter telling her of the death of her fiancé. He was a fighter pilot and had been gunned down over Germany. The most interesting thing was who the letter was from, a Mr and Mrs St.Claire.

I'm now imagining your face. You're probably thinking 'Sarah is called St.Claire' and, yes, as it turns out, it's the same family. The young man who was killed in my dream was called Daniel St.Claire, and after quite a lot of research I managed to track down his sister, Sarah. When I went to Cornwall last year it was to meet her. This is where I have to apologise for the first time. I should have told you the truth from the beginning, but it was all so alien to me. I kept it to myself for fear of ridicule. If it's any consolation I didn't tell anyone else either.

Sarah's mother had kept the very letter I saw in my dream and I read it. How amazing is that? The

- 354 -

letter had been sent to his fiancée Nora, who lived in Catterick village. My next task was to find her because, although I had met Sarah, I still didn't know why I was dreaming about them.

I'm sorry for the second time because I got you to go to Catterick under false pretences. I said I was tracing an old aunt. That was a lie. I was looking for Nora. I'm not sorry we went to Richmond for the weekend, as we had the most perfect time.

Do you remember the old woman, Barbara? You said you reminded her of someone. Hold that thought, all will be revealed. Nora had long since died but she did have a daughter. For weeks I drew a blank in finding her because I didn't know her last name. When you went to Cornwall for your interview I decided to go up to Richmond again to see if I could shed any light on who this Daisy was.

Imagine my surprise when I saw a poster advertising a demonstration of mediumship by a lady called Daisy Ledbury and a man called Steven Holford. I didn't know if she was the right person but it was worth a try, especially seeing it was on the same night as I was there.

I got tickets for me, my mum and George and we went along. Now this is where you really have to keep an open mind. Daisy was indeed the daughter of Nora and Daniel but what she told me, and still believes, is that I'm the reincarnation of Nora. I was born on the very day Nora died, the 15th November 1971. Ring any bells? And at exactly the same time. She also believes Daniel reincarnated at the same moment. Do you know anyone who was born on that day in close proximity to me, i.e. in the same hospital? Is the penny starting to drop? Because it didn't for me.

It wasn't until I overheard Sarah and Daisy talking about how much you looked like Daniel, after they had seen his photograph, and how they believed you had been Daniel in a past life that it all started to make sense. A relative term I know, because it makes no sense in our rational universe.

In hindsight I think that's why we fell in love so quickly and why we had such a deep connection from the outset. I didn't believe it at first but I do now. What really convinced me was the way we have managed to save Oliver's life. If I hadn't have had this dream Daisy would never have met Sarah and her family, and Oliver wouldn't have found a bone marrow donor.

Whether that was the main reason for it all I'm not sure, but it's good enough for me. I hope, while you're reading this, you have a cold can of lager in your hand to help yourself to keep calm. I don't know what possessed me to keep it all from you. I even got Sarah to lie to you about where we first met, and I know she didn't like being party to the deceit.

I hope you can forgive me and that we can still be friends. I think about you constantly, living your dream in your idyllic hideaway. Sarah told me that where you are is wonderful. I've also left my job. It was just too much pressure and I'm taking a career break.

Other news, Lara is engaged and is living with her boyfriend, Greg. He's the one that put his head *through our plate glass window. An unusual way to meet, don't you think?*

And Simon is gay, with a long-term boyfriend.

I'm glad that you still see Sarah. You must be a great comfort to her, as every time she looks at you she'll see the brother that she never met. I keep in touch with Daisy and we are due to meet up again soon.

This is now officially the longest letter I've ever written but I feel so close to you when I write. I wished I'd have done it sooner. I hope you'll reply.

Your soulmate

Jane xx

Ps. If you're finding it hard to believe, look up 'Synchronicity' by Carl Jung, and there are also some good books about reincarnation on Amazon.

Whatever reaction Jane had tried to elicit by writing the letter she couldn't have imagined the floods of tears Philip shed as he read it. They were tears of confusion, regret, sadness and, finally, relief. If only they could have been honest with one another at the outset they might still be together. He hadn't told anyone about his hallucinations for the same reason as Jane hadn't told him about her dream. People would think him insane.

Jane's revelation actually explained everything; his love of flying, his affinity to Cornwall and, more importantly to him, his love for Jane. The hallucination was actually a flashback to the moment of his death and he assumed the intense leg pains were the same thing. She'd had a dream, he'd had his flashbacks, and it was absolutely fascinating how it had now all fallen into place and made perfect sense.

The traumas they'd both suffered had all been clues from the universe to help them discover the truth of who they really were. He surprised himself by his reaction because a few months ago he would have laughed in anyone's face if they'd suggested he'd lived before, but now he was accepting it, as if it were an everyday occurrence.

He couldn't leave it at that. He was now more convinced than ever that they should be together. The Universe didn't go to all this trouble to rearrange itself for them to ignore it and think they knew better.

He had to come up with a plan. The more he thought about it the more he believed it would work. He needed Daisy's number.

Chapter 39

Jane was on tenterhooks every time the postman arrived. Philip must have had the letter for over a week now and she'd still had no reply. Surely he couldn't be so annoyed with her that he could ignore everything that had happened between them? Because of the anxiety she felt over Philip she couldn't concentrate on anything, so she'd put finding her new career on hold. The house had never been so clean and tidy and Toby was enjoying his three walks a day. Today she fancied doing something indulgent so she was going to treat herself to some retail therapy at Meadowhall, a large shopping complex on the outskirts of Sheffield.

She liked to shop on her own because she could please herself how many times she went back to try on the same clothes. She was meeting Madge and George for tea later in the day so she would have at least four hours to shop. She didn't have to be back to get Neil's tea. He was at a conference all day and wouldn't be back until late.

She only lived twenty minutes away from the shopping centre and pulled into the car park at just after eleven. Her aim was to buy some new summer clothes; skirts, shorts and matching tops and sandals, which she desperately needed. Maybe buying clothes would spur her on to book a holiday.

The only negative side to going abroad was she would've to put Toby in kennels as she couldn't expect Lara to come home for a week now that she had started her new job. She'd heard of dog sitters who would come to your house and look after your dog. Maybe that would be a better option for Toby. She'd been searching on the internet for holidays but when she found something of interest to her Neil wasn't enthusiastic. He'd tended to find fault with either the resort or the accommodation.

She already had one holiday booked. She was going to stay with Sarah for a few days in July. She was taking Toby and they would enjoy taking long walks on the beach together. She was looking forward to it already. She'd hoped that Philip would be speaking to her by then and they could perhaps meet for lunch or something, but that was never going to happen if he didn't reply to the letter.

Daisy had phoned her last night asking if she wanted to go and stay for the weekend. She realised it was short notice but she was giving another demonstration of mediumship in Thirsk and thought Jane might be interested, seeing as she'd enjoyed the last one so much. Jane had mentioned it to Neil over dinner last night and he'd said that she might as well go, as he would be at work most of the weekend finishing a large set of Corporation accounts before the deadline on Monday. She told Daisy that she would love to visit as she hadn't seen her for a couple of months and she'd like to catch up. Toby would also love wandering round the large grounds.

Simon was due home in a couple of weeks for the summer holidays. He was bringing Michael for the first two weeks and then they were going off to Michael's uncle in the South of France, to pick fruit, for the remainder of the summer.

Simon had seemed much happier since being with Michael. He'd done well in his first year exams and was predicted to get a first or an upper second class honour's degree. They were going to share a flat with another gay couple for the second year. He'd followed his bliss and it was working out for him. Jane was very proud of him.

Lara was also sorted. She'd secured a position in the most unlikely of professions for her, the police. She wasn't going to be an officer but a civilian working at the Head Quarters in Wakefield. She was a trainee human resource officer and had started as soon as her exams had finished. Greg had changed companies and was now a trainee manager for a chain of restaurants. He'd bought a beautiful solitaire diamond ring as a birthday present for her, and they seemed ecstatically happy. They were even saving up to buy their first house. How time moved on, Jane thought. It was just her that needed sorting out.

Her favourite shop in Meadowhall was House of Fraser, so she headed there first. She loved it when she was in the zone and everything she tried on fitted and looked great. She'd nearly spent up after only one shop but they didn't have any sandals she liked, so it was off to find a good shoe shop. It was relatively quiet today, which she preferred. She couldn't stand it on a Saturday when you couldn't see a hand in front of your face for the crowds.

She was looking in Clarks' shop window when she caught a reflection of someone she thought she recognised. Wasn't that Sally? She could just see the back of her but she would recognise that distinctive colour and style of hair anywhere. Even though there was no animosity between the two women she didn't feel inclined to go and talk to her.

She watched from a distance and saw she was going into Mothercare. Jane nearly dropped her bags of shopping as Sally turned round. She must be at least five months pregnant. After a quick mental calculation she realised the baby must have been conceived in January or February. Jane suddenly felt very nauseous and dizzy. She flopped down on the nearest bench before she passed out. She came around after a few seconds. She hadn't had much breakfast, so that could explain the faintness. Or it could be the shock of looking at the potential child of her husband.

She definitely didn't want Sally to see her now so she kept her head down, as if trying to find something in her shopping bags. Eventually she looked up and saw Sally apparently talking to someone who was hidden from view by a large pillar. Suddenly this person grabbed her hand and pulled her toward them. That's when Jane saw who it was. Neil. He was taking Sally in his arms and giving her a kiss. A long, lingering kiss. Not one between friends who had just bumped into each other by coincidence.

The bastard, she thought. She'd give him conference! All those late nights at the office and meetings in the evenings had been bollocks. He'd gone and done it again, and she'd genuinely believed he'd changed. She went through a gamut of emotions from anger to sadness, but the most prevalent was regret. Regret for letting Philip go so she could save her family, which in reality had never needed saving at all. She suddenly felt so stupid and gullible. She'd given up the one man she truly loved because she'd thought it was the right thing to do.

She couldn't bear to be in their presence a moment longer. The sandals could wait. She picked up her bags and ran in the opposite direction. She didn't want Neil and Sally to know that she'd seen them. It would give the game away, and now she was going to play the game as well.

She broke every speed limit going home. She could hardly see through the tears as she let herself into the house. Toby came to greet her with a big lick and she bent to stroke his soft fur. She buried her head in his neck and sobbed. Not about Neil and Sally, they were welcome to each other, but for what she'd lost. She'd been given a second chance with Philip, they'd travelled through time to be together and she'd blown it.

She had to work quickly before Neil suspected anything. She retrieved the divorce papers, which she'd kept, just in case. She signed them and put them in an envelope addressed to her solicitor. She then rang the bank. They'd been with the same one since they got married and everyone in the branch knew them. She asked to make a transfer of funds between accounts. The cashier gulped when she told them how much, but it was possible. She'd requested twenty thousand pounds to be transferred from three different accounts to the current account. It would be available to draw on within the hour but she would have to come in person. No cash machine would let her have that sort of money.

Even though she'd left estate agency she still had a lot of contacts and called in a favour from an ex-colleague at a rival firm. 'How soon could my house be put up for sale?' she asked.

'How soon do you want?' Paul replied.

'How about yesterday? We want a quick sale. If I e-mail you all the dimensions and photographs can you get it on the internet today. We had an HIP done last year when we were thinking of moving and it's still valid. You e-mail the contracts to me and I'll get them signed and drop them off, addressed to you. Send the details to everyone who wants a house like ours. And... a bit of discretion would be appreciated. Thanks, you're a gem.' Jane put the phone down.

She'd forged Neil's signature in the past, with his consent, so what was the difference? It wasn't as if she was doing him out of any money, she was just taking what was rightfully hers.

She retrieved two cases from the loft and started packing her clothes. Toby wondered what was going on but she stroked his ears and told him he was going with her. She sent two texts to her children. She'd had enough of being 'Mrs Nice Guy' and defending Neil. They read. 'Your dad's a lying cheating bastard. Sally pregnant and I'm leaving him. I'm going away. Will be in touch. Love you mum xx' She pressed send.

She found all the house's dimensions on the estate agent's particulars from when they'd purchased it. She faxed the whole document to Paul.

Her next stop was the bank. She collected her passport and driving licence for proof of identity and filled out a withdrawal slip for twenty thousand pounds. That should be sufficient funds until the house sells, she thought. She posted her envelope and left the contract at the estate agent's.

With all the upset she'd completely forgotten she was supposed to be having tea with Madge and George. She knew they'd understand. She sent her mum a similar text. With the cases in the boot and Toby strapped in the back she set off down to Cornwall. If Sarah couldn't put her up she didn't know what she'd do. She hadn't thought that far ahead.

The only clue that she'd left was scrawled in lipstick on Neil's best shirt.

'I KNOW' was all she'd put. She'd left it next to the kettle.

Chapter 40

It was all arranged, Daisy had invited Jane for the weekend on the pretext of going to one of her demonstrations. She'd suggested that Jane travelled on Friday morning to miss the rush hour traffic. Philip had withdrawn some of his redundancy money and chartered one of the planes from *Island Flights*. Terry Trevellan had been more than happy to accommodate him as Philip had proved to be a real asset to the company and was a very popular pilot. Terry had charged him the minimum for the weekend, Philip would only have to provide the fuel.

Philip had got Daisy's number from directory enquiries and had telephoned her immediately after reading Jane's letter.

'Hello, is that Daisy Ledbury?'

'It is.'

'You don't actually know me, I'm Philip Sinclair.' He paused, not knowing what to say next.

'Philip, lovely to hear from you at last. I've heard so much about you.' Daisy was so excited to be actually talking to her own father, albeit in another body. A minor detail, she thought.

'I know it's a bit cheeky but I need to ask you a favour. I've just received a letter from Jane, did you know about it?'

'I didn't know she'd actually written it but I knew she was going to.'

'I won't bore you with the contents apart from to tell you that I need her back in my life. We should never have broken up, but we did and now I need to repair it.'

'How does it involve me?'

'I want to fly up to see her. Do you think you could invite her for the weekend on the pretext of... oh, I don't know. Could you think of something?'

'I know just the thing,' Daisy laughed.

Throughout the conversation it never occurred to him that he was speaking to his own daughter!

The plan was for Philip to arrive at Daisy's house on Friday night and surprise Jane. He'd found a small airfield close to Daisy. She would make up an excuse to leave the house to go and collect him. Philip and Jane would talk, she'd see the error of her ways and then they'd live happily ever after. Slightly naïve, he thought, but wishful thinking never hurt anyone. It had worked for Cinderella. He'd only got one more sleep before he would see the love of his life again. He remembered saying a similar thing to his mother before holidays and Christmas. He counted down in sleeps.

Daisy had been a very willing participant in the plan and thought it was a lovely, thoughtful idea. Philip asked her to keep it to herself and not tell anyone, not even Sarah or Ben just in case they inadvertently let it slip to Jane. There was only one problem with his big idea, unbeknownst to Philip, Jane wasn't going to Daisy's. She was on her way to Cornwall to see him.

Jane hadn't let Daisy know her change of plans. She would telephone her tomorrow, once she was settled. After all it had only been a casual arrangement and they could always catch up another weekend. Jane was in no rush to get to Cornwall so she took plenty of breaks to walk Toby, and twice to get a bite to eat.

Her mind couldn't stop re-hashing the Neil and Sally situation, and she wondered if he'd actually meant any of the things he'd said to her since he'd been back in the family home. On the face of it he'd seemed happy being with her, since moving back in February, but he couldn't have stopped seeing Sally at all. Zoe had told her they were finished. Maybe Sally had lied to her as well. All she could think was that he was a damned good actor. He'd certainly had her fooled.

She'd received replies to her texts from all three people concerned, all supporting her. Lara was particularly shocked and was really annoyed at her dad. She said she'd never forgive him this time.

Neil had thought it was a good idea of Sally's to spend the day together. There was a conference he could have attended, it's just that he wouldn't be going. He enjoyed having an affair with Sally much more than he'd enjoyed living with her. He'd got the best of both worlds and, as far as he was aware, Jane didn't suspect a thing. He was still attentive towards her and he felt he was even a little bit more relaxed.

The sex was still fantastic with Sally. The pregnancy had seemed to make her want it more than ever and they were getting more adventurous in the locations they chose. They hardly ever made love in the house anymore and had found a few places at work to sneak a quickie during the day.

Sally loved being pregnant and she loved Neil. Everything was going so well.

He'd picked her up at nine and they'd called for breakfast at a motorway service station. Sally needed to buy some things for the baby so they decided to go to Meadowhall. Neil quite liked shopping and thought he could buy a few things for himself, although he would have to leave them at Sally's so Jane wouldn't become suspicious.

Because of the distance from home they walked round the concourse holding hands. Sally loved the intimate gesture and it felt as if they were a real couple. She couldn't walk for long because of her pregnancy so they kept stopping for a coffee. She'd tried on a number of occasions to raise the topic of what would happen when the baby was born but Neil had said there was, 'plenty of time to discuss that.' She was convinced that Neil would leave Jane and move back in with her. She knew he loved her.

When they'd bought a few essentials for the baby Neil said it was his turn to shop.

'Let's go in here,' he said, leading her into an upmarket man's outfitters. He picked up a couple of pairs of trousers and asked if he could try them on.

'Certainly, sir, please follow me,' the assistant said, leading him to the changing rooms.

'Can my wife come in with me please? I like to get her opinion.' Neil asked.

'Of course. If you need any help just give me a shout'. The assistant left them to it.

'I won't need help in what I'm going to do,' he sniggered and started to feel Sally's swollen breasts. True to form it didn't take him long to get an erection and he soon had her bent over the chair. They both kept very quiet and resisted the urge to snigger. He didn't even try the trousers on and they both left the shop as quickly as they could.

They had lunch in the food court and, because she was pregnant and couldn't drink, Sally offered to drive home so that Neil could have a couple of glasses of wine. He actually had three large ones. They took their time over a beautiful spaghetti carbonara and tiramisu. It was four o'clock when they finally left Meadowhall and arrived back at Sally's flat, three-quarters of an hour later. Sally wanted him to come in and spend a bit longer with her but he'd had enough of baby talk and thought he should be getting home. He'd enjoyed his day with Sally, but still wanted his own space.

He climbed into his Range Rover and set off for home completely forgetting that he'd had three large glasses of wine at lunch. As he pulled away at the traffic lights he turned the corner and clipped the curb which caused the car to swerve, right in front of a police car. That was it. The blue light was illuminated and they signalled Neil to pull over.

'Shit' he said out loud.

The police officer walked over and asked Neil to step out of his car.

'A bit of careless driving there sir. Where are you going?' the young officer asked.

'I'm on my way home from work. My hand must have slipped off the wheel. Sorry about it.' Neil tried to be as contrite as possible.

'Have you been drinking sir?' The officer moved closer to Neil's face. He could smell alcohol on Neil's breath.

'I just had one glass at lunchtime, a few hours ago,' he answered.

'Well, just as a precaution I'd like you to blow into this.' He handed Neil a breathalyser.

He hoped and prayed it would be negative and that the food had soaked up some of the alcohol but, no, it wasn't to be.

'I'm sorry sir, it looks like it's positive. Can you get into the car please? I need to take some details.' The officer led him to the police car.

The whole incident was incredibly humiliating for Neil. He had to go down to the station with the police officers and a garage was called to collect his car. The police wouldn't let him drive home. He phoned Jane to see if she would pick him up. He knew he'd have a lot of explaining to do but he'd come up with something, however she hadn't answered and her mobile was turned off.

He ordered a taxi from the police station to take him home, which cost him thirty pounds. When he arrived home it was in pitch darkness. He let himself in and shouted to make sure no-one was in. He turned the kitchen light on and that was when he spotted the shirt with just the two words written on it.

Neil slumped down onto a kitchen chair with his head in his hands. Could his life get any worse? He doubted it.

Chapter 41

Jane pulled up outside Sarah's house in the early evening. She'd been stuck in rush hour traffic coming out of Falmouth. The house was in total darkness. She'd rung Sarah at the last service station but she hadn't answered. Sarah didn't have a mobile phone. She described herself as a dinosaur when it came to technology. Jane had continued on, hoping she'd just gone shopping or popped out to see a friend.

She should have thought her plan through but, because she'd been so eager to get away, she'd just left things to chance. She had Ben's number in her mobile phone and she dialled it.

A young boy answered in a very grown up voice. 'Hello can I help you?' He'd obviously been practising.

'Could I speak to your mummy or daddy please?' Jane asked.

'Yes, I'll just get him. Daddy, the phone,' he bellowed. Jane was momentarily deafened.

'Hello,' Ben said, taking the receiver from his son.

'Hello Ben, its Jane. I'm looking for your mum.'

'You're out of luck I'm afraid. She's gone to stay with my sister and won't be back until tomorrow morning.'

'Bother, now what am I going to do?'

'Where are you?'

'I'm outside her front door. I just came down on the off chance, silly really but it's too late now.' Jane could have kicked herself.

'You must come here,' he offered. 'The boys can share a bedroom and you can have Stuart's room.'

'I don't want to put you to any trouble, and I've got my dog Toby.'

'Even better, the boys love dogs and now Oliver is well he can be around them. So please come, we'd love to have you,' Ben pleaded.

'Well if you're sure, that would be lovely.' Jane thought it would be nice to be around children when she was feeling down, they had a knack of cheering you up.

He only lived fifteen minutes away, towards Falmouth, and she found it easily even though she'd only been to the house once before. Both Anna and Ben greeted her with a hug. They hadn't forgotten for a second what she'd arranged for their son.

'I've just spoken to mum and she's so sorry she's not here but she'll set off early tomorrow and would love you to stay,' Ben said, inviting Jane inside.

After the boys had gone to bed, and Jane had read them both a story, the grownups ate the meal Anna had prepared earlier. They opened a bottle of wine and Jane confided in them as to why she'd come down at such notice. They were shocked and very sorry. Ben knew a bit about the story of how his mother and Jane had met but Sarah hadn't gone into great detail. He'd meant to ask his mother on more than one occasion but, when Oliver had become so ill, everything else had just gone out of the window.

He asked Jane to fill them both in so she told them the whole story, right from the first time she'd had the dream. They just sat there, open-mouthed. Jane no longer felt embarrassed about the recent events and had gone beyond caring if people didn't believe her. But funnily enough they did. Everyone she'd told was absolutely fascinated by the story and listened with baited breath.

They opened another bottle of wine and Jane realised how much better she felt talking about things rather than keeping them bottled up. Ben and Anna asked her lots of questions about past lives and receiving messages and she suddenly felt very knowledgeable. It's amazing how things change and move on, she thought.

This time last year, for example, she'd known nothing about any esoteric subject and here she was talking about them as if it were the most natural thing in the world. When they eventually retired to bed she slept in the older boy's room. She lay there looking at the posters of Disney-Pixar films. His favourite was obviously *Cars*. She smiled as she dropped off to sleep, anticipating seeing Philip tomorrow. She had the dream for the first time in months and woke up with a start at three o'clock. Just like old times, she thought.

She woke up wondering where she was, before she realised she was a guest in Ben's house. Only a few miles away the love of her life was getting ready to fly up to Richmond to see her, only she wouldn't be there, and neither would she be going. Things were a bit hectic in the house this morning. Two boys had to be gotten ready for school. Oliver still went to the hospital school because he wasn't quite strong enough yet to mix with other children in a normal educational environment.

Ben had set off to his job early and Anna would go to work when she'd dropped off the boys. Breakfast was a hurried affair and Anna was making packed lunches at the same time. Jane remembered those days well and was really appreciative that her own children had grown up.

At this time in her life Jane didn't want to rush about anymore. She'd spent too much time living in the fast lane and now she was determined to slow her life right down. She still hadn't decided what work she was going to pursue but the money she had would tide her over for a while.

Jane and Toby were ready to leave at the same time as Anna was taking the boys to school. They all exchanged hugs and Stuart didn't want to let Toby go.

'Please mum, can I have a dog like Toby?' Stuart begged. He'd loved spending time with the spaniel and Toby had slept in the boy's bedroom the previous night.

'It wouldn't be fair to have a dog when we're out at work all day.' Anna tried to reason with him, but was failing miserably.

'Please tell her, auntie Jane, that he'd be no trouble.' Stuart had his arms round Toby.

'I wish I could Stuart, but Toby needs quite a lot of looking after. He needs plenty of exercise to keep him from getting bored.' Jane tried to be as diplomatic as possible. 'A smaller dog might be better if your mum and dad finally give in.'

'Come on you two, let auntie Jane go and see grandma. We'll have to have a family meeting later.' Anna needed them to get into the car, otherwise she would really be behind schedule. Oliver had joined in hugging Toby. Luckily he was an even-tempered dog and accepted the two boy's hugs with good grace.

'Thank-you for having me at such short notice,' Jane said to Anna, 'and thank-you Stuart for letting me have your bed.'

'Are you going straight to Sarah's?' Anna asked.

'No, I thought I'd take Toby for a walk on the beach. It's my favourite pastime.'

'Please, can I go mum? Please?' Stuart begged.

'You know you've got school. Get in the car now.' Anna used her stern voice and, despite violent protestations, Stuart and Oliver did as they were told.

Jane thought she would try somewhere new to walk with Toby. She opened her map book of *Dog Friendly Walks*. She wanted somewhere with sand or shingle and, even though it was the opposite direction to Helford where Sarah lived, she opted for Porthcurnick.

It was only accessible by foot so she parked at the top of the hill, put Toby on a lead and walked down the path. The beach was sheltered from the cool wind by steep cliffs and there was only one other dog walker at the far side of the cove. By the sea was Jane's favourite place. She'd always had an affinity for the coast but she'd never lived there. Maybe it was time to rectify that.

Jane looked up at the sheer size of the cliffs and felt totally insignificant in the great scheme of things. These structures had been here for millions of years and would continue to exist for the next million or so. It put her minor troubles into perspective. Whilst Jane was marvelling at the wonders of nature, Toby had decided to take off. He was running full pelt to the far side of the beach.

'Toby! Come back boy.' Jane hadn't brought her whistle and he was too far away to hear her pitiful cry. There was nothing else for it, she'd have to run to try and catch him up. Jane had never enjoyed strenuous exercise and was soon bent over double, panting and catching her breath. Luckily Toby had stopped and was digging in the sand, with not a care in the world.

'Bad dog,' she said sternly, not that Toby seemed to care. Jane looked around her and gained another perspective of the beach and cliffs. She looked up and saw a large double-fronted detached house set back a short way from the cliff. The majority of the house was painted white, with deep blue shutters at the windows. It had the most spectacular views imaginable. Jane recognised the house, she'd been there before. She hadn't just seen a picture, she'd actually been inside. She could visualise the interior layout and she knew that she'd slept in a bedroom at the front of the house.

She wanted to examine it closer and walked towards the steps that would take her back to the top of the cliff. Toby bounded up them, pulling Jane along in his wake. The steps brought her out directly in front of the house. She stood and stared and found that tears were rolling down her face. She suddenly felt an overwhelming sadness and knew that what she was feeling was Nora's emotion. This house must have figured in Nora's past and Jane could only assume that it was Daniel's childhood home.

Did she have the nerve to knock on the door and ask? Why not? They could only turn her away.

Jane opened the gate and put Toby's lead over the gate post. She walked up the path and rang the doorbell. An elderly gentleman came to the door.

'Sorry to disturb you. I know it's a strange question, but do you know who lived in this house before you?' Jane asked, smiling at the elderly occupant.

'We've been here over thirty years but I seem to remember the couple were called Ann and Robert. I can't think of their surname. It was a funny one.' The man's brain was working overtime.

'St.Claire?' Jane prompted.

'That's it. Why do you ask?'

'Because I'm a friend of their daughter's and she described the house to me. As I'm in the area I thought I'd come and see it for myself.' Only a slight exaggeration, Jane thought.

'Do you want to have a look round?' the man offered.

'I'd like to take a look at the garden at the back if you wouldn't mind.' Jane didn't know why she'd made such a strange request.

'Certainly. There's a gate at the side, just help yourself. You can bring your dog if you'd like.'

'Thank-you, that's so kind.' Jane went to fetch Toby then the old man led them into the back garden.

It was laid mainly to lawn, with trees and shrubs around the perimeter. Jane walked along the path until she came to a very old, spreading, beech tree. There was a wrought iron bench underneath its branches. Jane sat down. She knew this was a significant place and for the second time she was moved to tears. Her memory was working overtime because it wasn't just Jane's memories she was recalling, they were Nora's as well.

She remembered being happy here and glanced down at her left hand. That's it! It was here in this very spot in 1941 where Daniel had asked Nora to marry him. The memory was hazy but it was still a memory. The current owner was watching her from the kitchen window and waved as she looked up. She couldn't sit here for much longer; she was stretching his hospitality to the limit already.

She waved back and the memory slowly vanished. What a morning! She would make her way back to Sarah's house and check out her findings, but she knew without a shadow of a doubt that what she'd just seen in her mind's eye had happened in this garden all those years ago.

Philip was up early. He'd only packed a small bag because he hoped he could persuade Jane to fly down to Cornwall with him and spend a few days there. She'd told him in her letter that she wasn't working and didn't have to look after Lara anymore because she was living with her boyfriend.

He'd looked at the weather forecast and noticed it had forecast storms in the North of England later this evening, so he would set off mid-morning and hang around up there, rather than risk getting caught in any adverse weather.

Philip had become good friends with his landlords and always had a quick chat as he was leaving for work. Nev was usually outside having a quick fag, because he wasn't allowed to smoke inside. Philip had told him of his plans and he'd shouted, 'Good luck' as Philip got into his car.

Neil had woken up with a rotten headache when his alarm had gone off at six. He'd opened a bottle of wine when he'd arrived home last night and thought of the old expression 'You might as well be hung for a sheep as for a lamb'. He wasn't enjoying being a sheep this morning! He'd ordered a taxi to take him to work and then went upstairs to pack a few things. He was going to check into a hotel in the centre of Leeds, which would work out a damn sight cheaper than taxi fare there and back to Woolley each day. He hadn't been able to contact Jane and didn't know where she was. Lara had put the phone down on him and Simon's battery must be flat.

He would see Sally at work and explain everything. He could always suggest staying with her. The taxi dropped him off at work just after eight. He saw the cars of the managing partner and one of the board members in the car park. He wondered what they were doing here. He hadn't forgotten a board meeting on top of everything else, had he?

He went into his office and found them sitting in front of his desk waiting for him.

'Good morning gentlemen, to what do I owe the pleasure?' he said, trying to keep it light-hearted.

'Good morning Neil, we need to talk,' said Bill Doyle, his boss, gravely. Neil went to sit behind his desk and looked at the two men. 'We've got a problem,' Bill continued.

Surely they can't have heard about the drink driving already? Neil thought.

'It's been brought to our attention by someone here in the office who, let me say, is only concerned about you, that your behaviour with another member of staff has, how shall I put it? Not been professional. You've been seen coming out of the store cupboard and you weren't collecting supplies. Also you've been heard in the mens' toilets.' He paused, waiting for Neil's reaction.

Neil didn't know what to say. His life was in such a mess already and now this. He did something that he'd never thought he'd do in a million years, he started to cry. He felt so ashamed of himself and had turned into someone that he didn't even recognise himself.

Bill was visibly shocked at Neil's outburst. 'Steady on there Neil, don't get upset. I'm sure we can work something out. We know you've been under a lot of pressure at home but we're here to talk about how we can move forward. We don't want to get rid of you because, until this incident, your behaviour has been exemplary and you're a valuable asset to the firm.'

It took a few minutes before Neil could pull himself together to speak.

'I'm sorry about that. To make matters worse I got done for drink driving last night. And my wife has left me again. I take it you've noticed Sally is pregnant? Well, yes, before you ask, it's mine. I know I have a serious problem and I promise I'll get help. But please, don't fire Sally. She needs this job and it was all my suggestion. The sex was the only thing that helped and I know it's embarrassing hearing about it, just as it is talking about it, but I'll get the name of a counsellor after we've finished here. If that's what you meant by moving forward?' Neil waited for their reaction.

It was Malcolm, the company board member who spoke next.

'We thank you for your candour. It can't have been easy admitting that you have a problem. Do you need to take some time off? If so, we can arrange some leave of absence, if it'll help.'

Neil thought about it for a moment and said 'That would be good, thanks. My wife seems to have disappeared and won't speak to me. Neither will my children. I need to find somewhere to live closer to work as I won't be driving for at least a year. I also need to find someone to help me.' By saying it out loud Neil felt a weight had lifted off his shoulders and he started to feel the best he'd felt in ages. He'd got some of it off his chest and finally admitted he'd got a problem.

Bill and Malcolm had expected much more of a confrontation, a lot of denial and defensiveness, so were pleasantly surprised at Neil's reaction.

Malcolm in particular felt very sorry for him and thought, 'There but for the grace of God, go I'. He'd had an affair with his secretary a couple of years ago but luckily he'd seen sense and ended it before it all came out into the open.

'If you take your leave of absence immediately we'll say to anyone who asks that you're having a family emergency. We're going to have to speak to Sally, but we won't fire her. Have you decided what you're going to do about her situation, or is it early days? You can tell me to mind my own business, if you'd rather,' Bill said.

'I do love her and if she'll have the new me I'll stay with her, but I need to sort myself out first. She doesn't even know about the drink driving yet. I was too ashamed last night to tell her,' Neil admitted.

'If we have a word with her when she comes in, you can then both go and have a long talk at home afterwards. She can take a few days off as well, if it will help,' Bill offered.

Neil felt choked up again. 'I can't begin to tell you how grateful I am that you've been so understanding. I promise you'll have the old, ultra-efficient Neil back in no time at all.' He got up and went round the desk to shake both mens' hands.

'We'll talk to Sally, she should be in by now. You go tidy yourself up and have a coffee. Then you can both disappear,' Bill said.

Neil sat in the staff room on tenterhooks, waiting for them to finish with Sally. She looked slightly pale when she walked into the room. She went over to Neil and put her arms round him without saying a word. They stood and held each other for the longest time.

'Let's go,' was all Sally said. She took hold of his hand for everyone to see and they walked out of the office.

Chapter 42

Philip had chartered a Cessna Skyhawk, one of the four-seater planes from *Island Flights*. He'd opted for it because he could fly all the way to Richmond without stopping to refuel. He set off later than he'd intended because all the paying customers had to be airborne first. It was just after eleven when he asked for clearance to take off, then he taxied down the runway and pulled back on the control column taking him into the air and, hopefully, to a new life.

At approximately the same time Jane was arriving at Sarah's. She was a bit early and went to sit in the garden to read a book. Toby went to have a good sniff round the plants and trees. She didn't have to wait long before she heard car wheels on the gravel drive. Toby began to bark.

Jane went to greet Sarah with a hug.

'I'm sorry I wasn't here when you arrived,' Sarah said, apologetically.

'No, it's my fault. I should have telephoned first, but it didn't matter. Ben and Anna were very kind and we all had a lovely evening. I filled them in about Nora and Daniel.'

'Were they OK? I didn't go into too much detail as you never know how people will react. Ben has always seen things in black and white and has been very sceptical in the past.'

'I think maybe the situation with Oliver changed their opinions and gave them a new perspective on life. They both seemed very interested.'

'I think you're right.' Sarah smiled. She preferred to think of her son as understanding.

'Anyway, what brings you down here all of a sudden?' Sara asked, wondering what had changed in Jane's life.

'How long have you got?' Jane laughed.

Sarah made them both a drink. Then they sat in the sun while Jane explained everything, from seeing Neil and Sally in Meadowhall to writing on his best shirt in lipstick. Sarah was both amused and sorry. She wasn't at all surprised however, as both she and Daisy didn't think Neil and Jane were well suited. She could now hold out some hope that Jane and Philip would get together. Now, they would make a perfect couple!

Jane told Sarah that she wanted to surprise Philip after work that day. Sarah gave her clear directions to his house in Chenyl and was so excited that Jane wanted to talk to him. Jane told her about the long letter she'd written to Philip and that, as yet, he hadn't replied. Sarah knew how Philip still felt about Jane but it was up to him to tell her himself.

'Do you want some lunch before you set off?' Sarah offered.

'That'd be lovely. I'm starving. We had such a long walk on the beach this morning, we went to Porthcurnick.' Jane waited to see if the name rang any bells with Sarah.

'What made you go there? Did you know that's where my mum and dad lived and where I spent my youth?' Sarah remembered fondly.

'I didn't, but I do now. It was ever so strange, although you'd have thought I'd have learned my lesson by now and accepted that there's no such thing as strange. I looked in my map book as I was leaving Ben's and felt drawn to go there. While we were walking Toby decided to run off to the other end of the beach. I don't know what possessed me to look up but I did and I recognised the house. I walked up to have a closer inspection and, you know how cheeky I am, I knocked on the door. I asked the man who answered if he had any idea who had lived there before him. He remembered they were called Ann and Robert.'

'It must be about thirty years ago when my parents sold that house. It was just too big for them so they downsized to a bungalow.'

'Anyway, I asked if I could look around the garden.'

'You didn't? Why on earth did you want to see the garden?' Sarah couldn't believe Jane's nerve.

'I felt it had meant something to Nora, and I was right. While I was sitting on a bench I had a memory of Daniel asking Nora to marry him. I felt ever so emotional and began to cry. Just when I think I'm getting used to all of this, something else happens. I assume I'll start to get even more memories in time.'

'Does it feel strange when you remember being Nora? I can't imagine what it's like.'

'No, it just feels like I'm remembering further back in time. I can't explain it really.'

'I think you're very lucky, although I can barely remember what's happened in my lifetime never mind having to remember another one.' She laughed. 'Will a sandwich be OK for lunch?'

'Yes, it'll be lovely, thanks.'

After lunch Jane set off to Land's End. She didn't know that area of Cornwall as when she'd been little the family used to stay in either Padstow or Newquay. She had to keep stopping to look at the map. She really must invest in a Sat Nav. As she drove along Jane contemplated the situation with regards to Neil. She knew she would have to speak to him sooner or later but felt she couldn't face him just at the moment. She'd ceased being annoyed and realised that it was never going to work between them. They'd changed too much over the years and, despite getting on better in recent months, still didn't have enough in common to make their marriage work.

She knew she was still in love with Philip and hoped she hadn't left it too late. She was worried that, in the time they'd been apart, he might have found another woman to love. She postulated that it could be the reason he hadn't replied. She was feeling incredibly apprehensive as she followed Sarah's directions towards his house.

Sarah thought he finished slightly earlier on a Friday, so Jane wanted to be there when he got home.

The lanes in that part of the world were very narrow and she didn't even know if she was on the right one. The village of Chenyl was only tiny and she nearly missed the turn into Philip's drive. She assumed she'd got the right place, it was just as Sarah had described. Toby started barking as two huge Irish wolfhounds bounded out of the front door of the large house.

A man followed them out and made his way over to Jane's car,

'Hello, can I help you?' the man said, hoping she was a potential paying guest.

'I'm looking for Philip Sinclair, have I got the right address?' Jane asked hopefully.

'You certainly have, but he's not here, you've just missed him. He's away for the weekend.' Neville looked carefully at Jane and wondered if he should tell her where he'd gone. She looked so disappointed, his heart went out to her.

'Was he expecting you?' Neville enquired, hoping he could salvage the situation.

'No. I haven't spoken to him for a while. I'm an old friend and I thought I'd surprise him.' Jane couldn't hide her feelings and looked as if she was about to burst into tears.

'It's probably not my place to say, but he's gone flying up North,' Neville said tentatively, 'to see a girl.'

'Oh no! I'm too late. Did he say who she was?' Jane asked with panic in her voice.

Neville made sure he'd remembered correctly. 'I think he said her name was Jane.'

Jane started to laugh. Both of them had come up with the same idea, to surprise each other, but it had backfired horribly. She was at one end of the country and he was at the other. It all started to make sense now; why Daisy had been so adamant about her coming up this weekend, because she was in on the plot. Sarah had obviously not been party to it because she wouldn't have let her carry on with the wild goose chase. Neville looked confused.

'I'm sorry; let me explain. I think I'm the girl he's gone to see. We both had the same idea at the same time but we're evidently not psychic enough,' she joked.

'What a bugger!' Neville joined in the laughter. 'What are you going to do now?' he asked, enjoying the drama.

'I'm going to ring my friend Daisy and give her a piece of my mind. Fancy tricking me into visiting her like that, but I'm also going to have some fun.'

'Do you want a drink of something while you're scheming?'

'A cup of tea would be lovely. Would it be OK to let my dog out?' Jane looked over at the two dogs sunning themselves at their master's feet.

'Don't mind those two, they're as soft as brushes. They like other dogs but can't eat a whole one. Only joking.' Neville laughed.

Toby looked about nervously as he jumped out of the car in to yet more strange surroundings. The Irish wolfhounds and Toby all had a good sniff at each other, then settled down to sleep.

'He's made himself at home already!' Neville said as he walked off to make the tea.

What a lovely man, Jane thought, and also what a wonderful place to live. She looked about and saw there was another cottage in the extensive grounds as well as Philip's converted pigsty. It looked empty at the moment and was probably for holiday lets. She might see if they had any vacancies, although she doubted it in such an idyllic place.

Jane got out her mobile phone and rang Daisy's number. She put on her best sore throat and started coughing! Daisy picked up and said, 'Hello'.

Jane continued the fake cough and said in her most pathetic voice, 'Hello, it's Jane. I'm sorry I won't be able to make it today, as you can hear I've come down with this awful cold'. She coughed again for effect.

Daisy went quiet and Jane imagined her brain going into overdrive. She had to say something.

'Oh, I'm so sorry to hear that, but are you sure you won't feel better for our fresh air?' Daisy was obviously thinking on her feet.

'I'm in bed and am going to stay here all day. I feel too weak to drive.' Jane was laying it on thick. She could tell Daisy was starting to get desperate.

'I could always come and get you, that way you'd be pampered as well.' Daisy sounded pleased with the idea she'd quickly thought of.

'If it's all the same to you I'll leave it, there'll be other times.' Neville had returned with the tea and was listening in to the conversation.

'You minx,' he mouthed to Jane.

She decided to put Daisy out of her misery because she was starting to feel guilty. Her friend was struggling and only trying to help. Jane returned to her normal voice.

'I'm sorry Daisy. I just couldn't resist teasing you.' Jane laughed.

'What do you mean? Where are you?' Daisy was confused.

'I'm outside Philip's in Cornwall. I came down to surprise him.'

'Shit! Pardon my French. I suppose you already know that Philip is on his way up here to surprise you?'

'So I understand, his neighbour has just told me. What are we going to do? Is Philip there yet?'

'I don't think so. He was going to ring me when he landed. We've arranged that I pick him up from the airfield. I don't know what time that'll be.'

'At first, when Neville mentioned Philip was flying I took it to be a figure of speech. I've got an idea. If I can find the number of the company he works for maybe they could radio in and tell him to turn round.' Jane she was full of good ideas today.

Neville interrupted. 'I've got a directory. The company is *Island Flights*. Philip wears it on his tee shirt every day.'

'Great, you go and find the number and I'll ring.' She then addressed Daisy again. 'If you hear from him in the meantime ring me back, but hopefully he's still mid-flight. Also, give Sarah a ring. She thinks Philip is still here and that I've come to see him. Speak to you soon, 'bye.' Jane switched the phone off and waited for Neville to come back with the number.

She rang *Island Flights*. A woman answered 'Island Flights, how may I help you?'

'This is a very strange request. I'm trying to locate Mr Philip Sinclair as a matter of urgency. I understand he's chartered a plane from you for the weekend. Is there any chance you could radio him and ask him to return home?'

'Who am I speaking to?' the woman asked.

'My name is Jane Barclay. I don't know if he told you where he was going this weekend but he is flying up to Richmond to see me. There's been a bit of a misunderstanding and I'm standing outside his house.' Then she added, pushing her luck, 'I wondered if you could also be discreet as I'm trying to surprise him.'

'Ah, so you're the girl he's gone up to see are you? He told us all about you. It's such a lovely story. I thought he'd gone to surprise you'. The woman was obviously enjoying the situation.

'Yes I am, and yes he was. It's a long story and one I would love to tell you later but I'm in a hurry.'

'He set off a while ago so he'll probably be there by now, but I can try for you. Stay on the line and I'll get back to you shortly.' Jane was put on hold and soon tired of listening to the inane music.

If everything had gone to plan Philip would've landed a while ago but he was having a problem with the fuel gauge. It had suddenly dipped to nearly empty after he'd only been flying half-an-hour. He couldn't risk it only being a fault of the indicator, so knew hc had to land to check it out. He'd been flying over the Bristol Channel and knew of an airfield in northern Somerset that his boss's friend owned. He'd radioed in to tell Terry about the problem, who then contacted his friend. It was arranged that Philip would land at the airfield and one of the technicians would check it out.

That had been three hours ago. It turned out the fuel gauge had stuck but he was now ready to go again. He'd just been cleared for takeoff when he heard the radio.

'Golf-alpha-delta-foxtrot, are you reading me?' a voice sounded in his ear.

'Golf-alpha-delta-foxtrot receiving, is there a problem?' Philip asked, surprised to hear Cherry, the receptionist.

'Terry requests that you please return to base, he'll explain when you get here. Over and out.'

'Roger that, over and out.' Philip wondered what had happened but assumed it must be something to do with the faulty gauge.

He took off in the same timeslot but flew back towards Cornwall. If he changed planes and set off straight away he could still get there before Jane.

Jane had been holding on for what seemed like forever but Cherry came back on the line. 'All sorted. He'll be back in just over half-an-hour. He only got as far as Somerset.'

'Thank you so much for doing that for me. What did you tell him?' Jane asked.

'I said that Terry, our boss, needed him to come back,' Cherry answered.

'I'm going to set off now. I'll see you soon.' Neville gave her directions.

'Hopefully if all goes to plan I'll see you back here in a bit. Thank-you for all your help,' she said to him.

'Don't mention it. I love a little adventure, not much happens down here.'

'By the way, is that cottage a holiday let?'

'Yes it is. It should be occupied as we speak but I had a cancellation today. I was spitting feathers, letting me down at such short notice. I'll never be able to rent it out for this week now. Do you want to leave Toby here with me, he looks settled?' Neville asked.

'If that's OK, he seems to have made some friends.' Jane went to say goodbye to him and told him she wouldn't be long.

Her little surprise had turned out to be not so little and she felt guilty that she'd put so many people to so much trouble, but the course of true love never did run smooth, she thought.

Chapter 43

Sally drove Neil back to her flat and made them each a cup of double espresso coffee. They were still in shock after their respective meetings. Sally had received a slap on the wrist and was told that she should've known better. Didn't she realise how close she'd come to losing her bright career? She felt suitably admonished and was grateful that they'd seen fit to give her a second chance.

On the way home in her car Neil had confessed to being caught drink driving and told Sally that Jane knew about them and had left him. They still had a lot of talking to do and things to sort out. Once inside Sally's flat Neil went on the internet to try and find some counsellors that dealt in sex addiction. Sally said they ought to have counselling for couples as well if they intended to stay together and bring up a baby.

Neil was going to stay with Sally but had decided that he should sleep in the spare room and pay rent until their relationship was sorted out. Also he knew he had to speak to Jane. Sally had been given two days off work and they'd managed to find a psychologist who could give them a preliminary appointment the following day. Sally had agreed to drive Neil over to Woolley to pick up some more things. He kept ringing the house to warn Jane but no-one answered. She must have gone away, he thought.

On the face of it Sally should've been upset but she just couldn't be. She was going to get him after all, the man she loved. It had taken some time and a horrible set of circumstances to get there but it had finally happened and he was prepared to change for her. He wanted to be with her and it seemed he wanted the baby. She'd never guessed that Neil had a sex addiction, she just thought he was horny and fancied her a lot, although recently when he kept suggesting doing it at work twice in a day alarm bells should have rung.

If they were going to make the relationship work they couldn't slip back into the same routine as before. She would have to take some responsibility and start acting more like an adult. She was glad that Jane had found out because, being honest, she was getting tired of being the other woman. A decision had been made, whether it was his or not, and Sally doubted Jane would have him back this time.

Despite all the awful things that had happened to Neil in the past twenty-four hours he seemed more relaxed than she'd seen him for a long time. Maybe the pressure had been building up over time and all this had brought it to a head? While she'd been in the shower he prepared her a lovely meal to say thank-you for being so understanding. Hopefully it was the start of good things to come.

Daisy rang Sarah and they had a good laugh about the bizarre set of circumstances of the day. Sarah brought her up to date about Jane and Neil and told her about the long letter Jane had written to Philip, though she already knew as Philip had told her.

They both agreed that if only the two of them could have talked to each other from the outset this silly mistake wouldn't have happened. Funnily enough Daisy hadn't had any messages from the Spirit world about Jane or Philip and was just as much in the dark as everyone else. But she preferred it that way.

Back home in Leeds, George had turned up at Madge's house with a ring. He'd no idea whether she would accept his proposal as they hadn't really talked about marriage before. He'd been given a message at a service, which Madge hadn't attended, that he should make an honest woman of her. He never thought he could love again after he lost his beloved wife. But he had fallen in love. Madge wasn't a replacement for his wife, she was so different. But they both deserved to be happy again and living together without getting married didn't sit comfortably with him.

Madge was expecting him. They were intending to go to the cinema and then for a meal. He was going to ask her to marry him in the restaurant, or not if he lost his nerve. He was feeling very anxious. What if she laughed at him? No, Madge wasn't like that. But she was an independent woman and might not want to be saddled with another husband at her time of life. He'd discussed it with his own daughter, who was very pleased for them, and he'd intended to mention it to Jane yesterday if he could've caught her on her own. But Jane had cancelled, saying she was going to Cornwall on some errand or other.

He knew that Madge was worried about Jane and that she'd hated the fact that Jane had taken Neil back. She'd known all along that it wasn't what Jane had really wanted and was elated when she'd texted her yesterday to say she was going to find Philip. Hopefully this had put Madge in a good mood and on the side of true love again. He would soon find out. He knocked on the door and walked in.

Jane had hidden her car round the back of the *Island Flights* building so Philip wouldn't spot it. Terry was now in on the surprise. Cherry felt it was only fair to tell him because she'd told Philip that it was the boss that wanted him to return to base. All three of them were standing on the runway looking for a sight of Philip's plane, but they heard it before they saw it. Jane ran inside the building, leaving Terry and Cherry to greet him.

Philip negotiated the runway and performed a perfect landing. He turned off the engine and got out.

'What's the problem Terry? Is it the fuel gauge? Because I thought it was mended,' Philip asked impatiently.

'No, nothing like that. One of your old customers wanted you particularly, to fly them up North. I said you were already on your way but he offered to pay us extra to come back for him. He's in the office.' Terry even managed to keep a straight face.

'You mean you had me turn round on my day off to get you some extra money?' Philip wasn't impressed as he stormed off to meet his new passenger.

Jane opened the door and stood looking at Philip. All the old emotions came flooding back and she ran into his arms. 'Surprise!' Philip couldn't believe his eyes. He'd thought she was in Richmond but, no, she was standing here, right in front of him. He held her face in his hands and looked deep into her eyes.

'Welcome home my darling,' he whispered and then kissed her. Gently at first, then with longing. He'd thought about her constantly since she'd left his flat on that awful day in February. They hadn't spoken since. The only contact they'd had was the letter she'd written. When they finally broke apart Terry and Cherry started clapping.

'Well, it looks like I'm not the only one into subterfuge,' Philip laughed. He couldn't be mad and went over to shake Terry by the hand.

Philip and Jane walked hand in hand to their respective cars. She told him she'd come to stay for a while. He was overjoyed. She followed him back to Chenyl. Neville was looking out of his kitchen window and dashed outside as soon as he spotted them. Toby followed and was so giddy when he saw Jane and Philip.

Jane gave Neville a potted history of what had happened and once his curiosity was satisfied he disappeared back inside, leaving them alone. Jane felt exhausted and went into Philip's cottage to collapse in a large comfortable armchair. It certainly didn't look like a pigsty. It was tastefully decorated with cottage-style furniture. It wasn't to her taste but Philip was there so anywhere would be wonderful.

They had so much to catch up on.

'I can't believe you're finally here. I've dreamed about you sitting in that armchair chatting about your day ever since I've been here. In fact, I know you'll think I'm stupid, but there've been times when I've actually talked to you. The sad thing is, you never replied.'

Philip had gone beyond caring whether Jane thought he was mad. He knew from now on he needed to be honest and if that meant making himself look stupid, so be it.

'I know what you mean. I used to tell you all about my day when I was in bed. I'd replay a conversation in my mind and I'd even ask your advice.' Jane had already taken the first step in honesty when she'd written him the letter.

'There's something I need to tell you.' Philip sat opposite Jane on the other armchair. 'You had your dreams and I had my flashbacks.'

'Flashbacks, what do you mean?' Jane said, puzzled.

'Daniel was trying to reach out to me, just as Nora was doing to you, but instead of it being through a dream, I had…incidents. The first one was that pain in my legs. It had been getting progressively worse until I went to Spain. You know I ended up in hospital after blacking out, well I never told anyone the whole story. It was while I was in the air. Everything suddenly went black and I found myself behind the controls of a Second World War Spitfire. It was as if I was actually there. I remember feeling sheer terror as I realised that the wing of my plane was on fire and I was going down. It only lasted for a split second and then I came back to normal, flying the Cessna.

'I didn't tell the doctor because it would have meant a whole new barrage of tests and I just wanted to go home. Everything seemed to return to normal so I tried to put it out of my mind.' Philip felt as though he was being unburdened as he spoke about it for the first time.

'Why didn't you tell me?' Jane asked.

'For the same reason you didn't tell me. Our relationship was relatively new and I didn't want anything to jeopardise it. With hindsight it was the worst decision I could have made.'

'I know what you mean. If only we'd been honest from the start we wouldn't have had to go through this torture.' Hindsight is a wonderful thing, Jane thought.

'I believed that was the end of it, but do you remember when my nephew Jimi came to stay and I took him to Eden Camp? It happened again there but this time it was even more vivid. I actually remember seeing the German plane that shot me down. I felt the searing pain in my legs as my plane was blown apart and, luckily for me, I was knocked unconscious just before I died.' It was the first time that Philip had recounted that story.

'My poor baby.' Jane went to sit at his feet. Then she reached up to stroke his face. 'We both went through so much and the worst thing was we didn't have each other.' She reached up again and kissed him.

'The silly thing is, when I read your letter it made sense of everything. I never told you this either, but when we were in Catterick I got a strong feeling of déjà vu when I was looking at, what I now know to be, Nora's first home. I just knew I'd been there before.'

'But I didn't get that feeling at all. The only thing I was ever shown was my dream.' Jane sounded frustrated. 'Recently I had a memory of Daniel asking Nora to marry him. It would have made my search easier if I'd have had flashbacks as well.'

'Maybe it was never meant to be easy. Maybe we've both had to go on a journey to find out who we were, and this journey has taken us down very different routes. It explains everything to me, my obsession with flying from being a small boy and my total lack of commitment to anyone but you. When I got your letter I did some research of my own. I'd heard of reincarnation but it had just been a theoretical concept. I'd had no direct experience of it. But apparently there are dozens of examples of people who remember their past lives.' He felt totally at ease talking about it with Jane.

'So I understand. Daisy told me about an American woman who remembered living in Ireland. They even made a film about her. So does that mean we're not that unusual after all?' Jane asked.

'I don't mind being unusual if I've got you by my side.' Philip bent forward to kiss her.

Jane's mobile phone was going mad, first with Daisy and then Sarah, both ringing to find out how the meeting had gone. Neil had left loads of messages asking her to please ring him. Both Lara and Simon had rung to check she was OK.

She would reply but first she'd something more important to do. She took Philip's hand and led him to the bedroom. They slowly undressed each other, treating it as if it were their very first time. They stood and looked at each other. Philip admired her body, Jane still regarded him as the most beautiful man she'd ever seen. He pulled back the bed clothes and gently laid Jane down. Then they made love. It was slow and deliberate yet with all the longing and passion of true lovers. They'd all the time in the world and they were going to make the most of it.

Afterwards Philip looked at his true love. 'My life is finally complete. I couldn't have you in 1941 but I can now, and I'll never let you go again. The sun set on our love once but every day from now on it will rise on our life together. I love you more than I can ever express.' To Jane it seemed as if Philip was looking directly into her soul.

He kissed her. Then she said, 'I left my only daughter back in 1971, when it must have broken my heart because I needed to be with you. They say everything happens for a reason and if the reason is that we can be together, forever, I'll be eternally grateful. I love you and I'm so sorry it took me this long to realise it.' This time she kissed him.

It was dark when they finally surfaced. They'd made love for hours. Philip hadn't had sex since the last time with Jane and he was insatiable. That suited

Jane fine. She would give herself to him as many times as he wanted.

'Do you want to go out for a meal?' Philip asked when they were finally up and dressed.

'That would be lovely, where shall we go?' Jane would have agreed to anything she was so ecstatically happy.

'There's a lovely country pub up the road where they do beautiful food. I eat there a lot, but always alone. Tonight I can show you off,' Philip said proudly.

'You get ready. I'm just going to make some phone calls.' Jane said. She had to return all the texts and calls from her family and friends.

They both spoke to Daisy and Sarah. It was obvious from the tone of their voices that both were really happy for them. Jane phoned Simon next and told him all about Philip. He was over the moon for his mother. He'd secretly hoped it wouldn't work out with his dad because his parents had turned into very different people. And his mother had done so much for everyone over the years she really deserved some happiness.

Lara was just pleased she was OK, but Jane didn't go into as much detail with her daughter. It was better talking with her face to face. She sent Neil a message saying she would ring him the following day for a long chat. She received a message back and could almost feel the relief in his text.

As Jane got ready Philip admired her every move. They'd been apart for so long. They weren't letting each other out of their sights for even a second. Jane's phone beeped. It was a cryptic message from her mother.

'Hope all OK. Got some news. Let me know when you're home. Mum x'

Typical of her mother, she thought lovingly. There's always something happening in her life.

Jane would go home in time but only to collect some personal things and sort the house out. She didn't want anything from her old life, it was over and she was starting anew. She'd learned the hard way that possessions don't make for happiness. 'if you could do without it - you didn't need it" was her new motto.

She'd decided that if the larger cottage in the grounds was still available she'd make the suggestion to Neville of having it on a long term let and suggest that they could let the pigsty out to holidaymakers. Neville might not go for it, but it was worth a try.

As she was drying her hair, she thought about Nora. If Daniel had survived he would probably have lived in Cornwall with her, near his mother and father. She was sure they would've been ecstatically happy, just as her and Philip were going to be. She'd never felt like Nora was a part of her before today, but as she looked at Philip all she could see was Daniel. She smiled the biggest smile in the world. Then she thought back to her Tarot reading. Rosa had been correct. She'd fallen in love with someone she'd known before and she'd been given a second chance. There was no way was she going to blow it this time.

Chapter 44

Jane stayed with Philip and they enjoyed sharing every minute together. Neville had been happy to go along with her idea so she and Philip had moved into the larger cottage and the pigsty had become the new holiday let. She'd discussed her career with Philip and he was supportive of her doing whatever made her happy. Money wasn't the biggest motivator anymore. Peace of mind was far more important.

The idea that she'd had about being a Feng Shui consultant was starting to take shape. She'd done a lot of research on the internet and was halfway through an online course. She'd learnt all about energy and realised there was a lot more to it that moving a bit of furniture around. The idea was for the whole house to be in harmony with nature and that would then facilitate the flow of energy through the rooms. It had really opened her eyes and she was beginning to realise there was so much more to this world than she could see or feel.

Their lives were idyllic. Philip still loved flying and couldn't believe he got paid very well for doing something he loved. Jane spent her days studying and taking Toby out for long walks on the beach or along the cliffs. It was such a wonderful part of the world to live in and neither of them tired of the magnificent view from Land's End. They ate out in various restaurants or took turns to make each other a beautiful meal.

They'd become very good friends with Neville and his partner, Roy. They shared many a good bottle of red wine or two at each others' houses. Jane had put together a flyer and delivered them around the local area, offering her Consultancy Services and, slowly but surely, through word of mouth, work was starting to come her way. The free monthly ticket to the Minack theatre had proved very popular and she and Philip both looked forward to the productions. Jane had even started helping out, selling tickets and helping Neville in whatever ways she could.

Philip had invited Jimi to spend some time with them over the summer holidays and he'd started to develop an interest in flying too. Philip even let him accompany him on a few flights. His interest in the war had paid off as he'd got an A-star in his GCSE and was going to study History at Advanced level.

Simon and Michael went down to stay with them in Cornwall before heading off to the South of France. The weather had been fantastic. They'd spent their time sunbathing or learning to surf, and they both sported a brilliant tan before they left. Simon looked so happy and Michael was a really nice young man.

Jane had helped Lara negotiate the deal on her first house, a small two bedroom terrace in a leafy suburb of Wakefield, within walking distance of her place of work. They were in the process of decorating it. Lara loved playing house. Jane hadn't seen it apart from having a virtual tour over the internet but it looked lovely and cosy.

It seemed a shame to leave such a beautiful place to go on holiday but Philip had promised his mum and dad that he'd bring Jane to meet them.

'You are honoured, I usually only get my dad picking me up. Mum waits at home.' Philip waved at both his parents who were standing in the arrivals' lounge.

'They're here to check me out and if they don't approve they'll put me on the next plane home.' Jane joked. She was actually looking forward to meeting Philip's parents, who'd seemed so lovely over the phone.

'Hi Mum, what are you doing here?'

'That's no way to greet your mother. I've come to welcome our guest. You must be Jane. It's lovely to finally meet you. I'm Beryl.' She gave Jane a welcoming hug.

'And I'm Michael.' Philip's dad introduced himself. He was standing next to Philip and for a split second they were the double of Daniel and his father in the photograph that Sarah had kept. Both were tall with dark brown hair and brown eyes but, as in the photograph, his dad was broader and stronger. Jane was taken aback and realised she was staring with a gormless expression on her face.

'Sorry. You looked so familiar for a second. I'm very pleased to meet you.' As he hugged Jane, Michael looked more self conscious than his wife.

The villa only had two bedrooms and the second one was much smaller than Philip and Jane were used to.

'It'll be cosy in bed tonight. We'll have to cuddle up.' There was a small double-bed in the room, whereas they were used to a king size.

'What a shame.' Jane wrapped her arms round him and kissed him lovingly.

'Do you want to go for a swim?' Philip asked, unpacking his swim shorts.

'Absolutely. Lead the way.' Philip showed her to the communal pool. Jane looked longingly at the deep blue water, and then dived in.

'It's freezing! Come on then, coward.'

Philip jumped in, splashing her.

They spent an idyllic two weeks sunbathing and swimming every day. One of their favourite pastimes was taking long walks on the beach,

'Whatever happened to that shell collection?'

'What shell collection are you talking about?' Jane said, totally lost.

'You remember! The shell collection you made when you were younger. Don't you recall telling me?' Philip didn't know why he'd asked the question in the first place.

'I think you might have lost the plot. I know it's been a hard day,' Jane laughed.

'Sorry, forget I mentioned it. I must have my wires crossed.' Philip was feeling embarrassed at having made a fool of himself.

'I did like shells and I often brought the big ones back to show my mum and dad,' Jane said. 'But I don't remember ever telling you. I might have done though.' She could feel Philip's discomfort.

'I bet that's a memory from Daniel's past. One day we may even get shared memories because, even though I can't remember the shells, I do get the feeling we've walked hand in hand along a beach in the past, and I don't mean recently.'

Jane kept getting a really strong feeling of déjà vu. She wondered if these memories would become more prevalent now she'd accepted who she was. She was looking forward to more memories like the ones she'd started to have and felt quite excited at discovering more about the life she and Philip had lived before.

Beryl and Michael Sinclair were really pleased that Jane and Philip were a couple again. They hinted to Philip on more than one occasion that, 'he should marry this one.' It turned out to be a very different holiday to the one Philip had experienced earlier in the year. They both felt even more relaxed when they returned home two weeks later.

It was the end of July before Jane felt like going home. She owed it to her eighteen-year marriage to hear what Neil had to say for himself. She'd phoned him the day after she arrived in Cornwall, to tell him where she was and to say that the house was up for sale. They still had a lot to discuss.

Philip had used up all his holiday entitlement so she had to go to Yorkshire by herself. She even left her precious Toby behind. He loved his new house so much she didn't want to disturb him. Besides, Philip was just as besotted with him as she was.

Her old house no longer felt like home. It was empty of furniture, Lara and Greg had taken a lot of it and Neil and Sally had the rest. It seemed like an empty shell with all their belongings missing. It proved that a home was not the bricks and mortar but the personal possessions. There had been a few viewings on the house and a couple had put an offer in to buy it. She intended to discuss the offer with Neil and hopefully they would be rid of it soon, thus freeing up the money for her to invest in a property with Philip.

As she locked the door for the last time she felt choked. She'd loved her house and she would miss the good times she'd had in it with her family. She took one last stroll round the garden and looked out across the undulating fields. You could see for miles on a gloriously sunny day like today.

She'd arranged to meet Neil on neutral ground in the cafe at the Yorkshire Sculpture Park. Neil had aged in the last couple of months and didn't seem as confident or as full of himself as he once had. He stood up when she arrived and went to kiss her cheek.

There was an awkward silence before he spoke. 'Thank-you, for agreeing to meet me today. I really appreciate how hard it must be for you.'

'Not anymore. I'm fine, honestly. I'm so happy with Philip. We both love living in Cornwall. It really was the best thing to do. How's Sally?' she enquired.

'Getting bigger. She's due the first week in October so just over two months to go.'

'Are you excited?' Jane found she was genuinely interested in what Neil had to say.

'I am now, but I suppose I'd better fill you in on what's been happening to me, unless Simon has already told you.'

'No, he's not mentioned anything.' Jane was intrigued.

'I've been having counselling for my problems. It all came to a head when two members of the Board hauled me into their office. I'd been seen having sex with Sally in the store cupboard.' Neil could actually laugh about it now and Jane joined in the giggling.

'It's not funny, I know, but my counsellor has helped me come to terms with it all. I go to a group, like Alcoholics Anonymous, only it's for sex addicts. Apparently it was my way of coping with all the stress and the discontent I'd been feeling. I found sex a release for all my pent up anxiety. I'm sorry if I ever put you in a compromising position or made you feel uncomfortable. I know you didn't really enjoy the time at Newmillerdam but I was addicted to the thrill and at the time didn't care about your emotions.' Neil looked genuinely apologetic.

'I'm sorry I never realised it was a problem for you. We both had stuff going on that each of us was oblivious to. But it seems to have worked out for the best; you look relaxed now.' Jane smiled at her, soon to be, ex-husband.

'I am thank-you. It's really great with Sally. She brings out the best in me. I always thought that what you and I had was the best, so I hope you don't mind me saying this. We should have split up years ago. It's not that I didn't love you, I did. We made the best of the hand we'd been dealt. If you hadn't have got pregnant then we may have just drifted apart. Then we stayed together for the children and time marched on. Neither of us questioned what we had, we took it at face value.' Neil paused and Jane took it as a sign to interject.

'Why don't couples talk? I never knew you felt like this. I thought it was just me that felt discontented with my lot. Do you feel as if you've wasted your life?'

'Absolutely not. We had some fabulous times and even up to the end I loved being with you. We always had a great friendship and we were a good team. Is Philip the one for you? You seem happy when you talk about him.' Neil was pleased they were having this opportunity to clear the air.

'He is. I now firmly believe that we've lived before, and we've come back this time to be together. It might sound farfetched to some but it all makes sense to us. I don't understand how it can happen. I'm just glad it did.' Jane could feel the conversation was coming to a natural conclusion.

'Did Simon mention I've been banned from driving for a year? I was breathalysed on the day you saw us at Meadowhall.' Neil looked at his watch. 'I'm going to have to go soon. I told my driver I'd only be half-an-hour.' Neil seemed more embarrassed about confessing that than he had done about his addiction counselling.

'Have you any more shocking news? Let's get it all out in the open.' Jane couldn't believe her usually unassuming husband had been through so much.

'No, I think that about sums it up,' he laughed.

'Before we go hadn't we better discuss the house?' Jane suggested. 'It is the main reason for meeting. Do you want to accept the offer? I think it's fair and they've got nothing to sell.'

'Whatever you think, you're the estate agent.'

'OK I'll ring Paul and tell him to go ahead. In two weeks the decree absolute should be through. Have you plans to marry Sally?'

'I am going to ask her, but whether she'll have a sex addicted drunk remains to be seen!'

'Don't be too hard on yourself, she could do much worse.' Jane smiled at him. Nearly all the loose ends had been tied up. She wished him every happiness in his new life with Sally and the baby.

'Do you fancy one last shag for old times' sake?' Neil quickly followed it with, 'only joking!' They both laughed. They shared one last hug and kiss, because after today they would never need to see each other again. They'd probably bump into each other at births, weddings and christenings, but Jane felt that another chapter in her life had come to an end.

Epilogue

Madge did say yes to George's marriage proposal. Everyone was there, ready to celebrate the marriage of the happy couple. It was the 21st December and the families of Nora and Jane, and Philip and Daniel, had hired a castle on the edge of a loch in Scotland.

They'd chosen Scotland because it was neutral ground. Everyone had to travel, but some further than others. Philip had flown up the Cornwall contingent, which now included Daisy. Toby had stayed back in Cornwall with Neville and had become the father of the most unlikely combination of Springer spaniel and Irish wolfhound. No-one knew how he'd managed it! The puppies were so cute, albeit a little odd. Stuart had finally persuaded his mum and dad to get a dog and they were having one of Toby's puppies as soon as they were ready to leave their mother.

When Jane had moved down to Cornwall permanently, to be with Philip, Daisy had felt cut off in Richmond. She'd already made her mind up that the house was too big for her so she'd decided to put it on the market. The sale had finally gone through in October. She was staying with Sarah until she found out where she wanted to live but there was no hurry as they both had a lifetime of catching up to do. She was still working with Steven and they intended to continue touring twice a year, to different locations around the country.

She'd raised a lot of money from the sale of her house and because she'd no children she decided to give some money to Jane and Philip. Then she gave a large sum to Sarah, so she could provide for her children and grandchildren. She also donated a substantial amount to charities, such as the Anthony Nolan Trust, so that more children could get the much needed bone marrow that had saved Oliver's life.

Daisy was enjoying being around family and saw Ben, Anna and the children every Sunday, for dinner at Sarah's. She was also a regular visitor to the cottage at Chenyl to see Jane and Philip. The more time she and Jane spent together the more she could see of her mother, Nora, in Jane. They had the same turn of phrase and shared many of the same mannerisms. She felt that after thirty-eight years she was finishing the relationship that she'd had with her mother before she'd so prematurely passed on.

Jane's house in Woolley had finally sold. After the mortgage had been paid off the profits were shared between Jane and Neil. Jane had put her money in a bank and was looking around Cornwall trying to find a property for her and Philip. She was hoping to find a large barn conversion with outbuildings that they could rent out for holidays.

Her future aim was to run courses on 'Feng Shui with Interior design'. She'd already started earning quite a decent living offering her services to wealthy people in the area. Philip had started teaching flying lessons again, with a view to offering week-long courses with accommodation. They'd seen a couple of old barns and were in the process of having architects and builders look into the feasibility of adapting them.

Simon and Lara now had a half-brother because Neil and Sally were now the proud parents of a baby boy called Alex, born in October, and weighing 7lb 2oz. Jane thought he was absolutely gorgeous. Lara had forgiven her dad and she was a regular visitor to their new house in Chapel Allerton, a lovely and quiet suburb of Leeds. She loved spending time with Alex, and Jane believed it wouldn't be long before she had one of her own.

Neil and Sally had got married. Both Simon and Lara went to the wedding. It had been a low key affair. Neil had invited his mother, who actually approved of Sally. They'd met on a number of occasions and Mrs Barclay was besotted with her new grandson. Sally didn't invite her own parents to their wedding; they would have only spoiled her special day. Neil, Sally and Alex went to Scarborough a few days later to take her family for a posh, slap-up meal which went someway to placating them.

Sally was going to return to work part-time and hire a nanny to look after Alex. She'd spent so long studying for her Accountancy exams she wanted to get the chance to use her new found skills. Neil had hired a private chauffeur to drive him to work and to his clients, until he could apply for his licence again.

He'd been discharged from his therapist after completing his course of counselling sessions and was feeling much better. He'd learnt a lot about himself over the past few months and vowed he would never let a situation get out of hand again. He was very happy with Sally now that they had a much more balanced relationship.

Simon travelled to Scotland with Michael. They were both in their second year now and were well integrated into the gay community in Liverpool. Lara had driven up with Greg in their new BMW. They'd both been promoted at work and were living life to the full.

George's daughter felt slightly overwhelmed with the number of relatives and friends Madge had invited. There was only her, her husband and eight year old daughter Sam. But Sam went off to play with Oliver and Stuart and they all became good friends. Everyone was so kind to her; she soon felt part of the family.

Oliver was nearly back to the fit and healthy little boy he'd been before his illness. He still had to go to the hospital for checkups but now they were only every three months. He'd also returned to his old school at the start of the term, in September. Ben and Anna had felt very honoured to be invited to the wedding and not a day went by when they didn't count their blessings.

Madge looked around at all the people from both her real and adopted families. She was very proud. They'd all supported her on this, her special day. She'd been in total shock when George proposed to her in Frankie and Benny's. George had intended it to be in beautiful surroundings but Madge had fancied one of their burgers so that was where they ended up.

He didn't actually get down on bended knee but he did get the ring out and slipped it on her finger. The whole restaurant applauded and he was very embarrassed. Bless him, she thought. She did love him and secretly thanked her husband for giving this union his blessing.

The minister from their Spiritualist Church had travelled up with them and was going to perform the marriage ceremony. Madge had bought a pale blue suit with a long flowing skirt for her big day and had chosen to carry white lilies. The strong, heady aroma of them had already started to permeate the room.

She'd chosen not to be given away but Jane was going to be at her side for the whole service. Jane's dress was a contrasting blue. It had a tightly fitted bodice and a voluminous skirt. She loved it and had put it on first thing in the morning. She loved the way it moved whenever she did.

The castle's large hall had been laid out to resemble their church. They'd had a makeshift platform built and Madge had asked if Daisy would say a few words of philosophy after the service. There were so many flowers festooned around the room the fragrance was divine.

Madge looked around the curtain as people took their seats. There were fifty guests, including friends who'd made the journey. Everyone looked so smart and had made such an effort for her. She felt incredibly grateful.

George was already in his seat. Philip, his best man, was sitting next to him. Madge walked in, with Jane. to Unchained Melody by the Righteous Brothers. The service was beautiful and had something for everyone. There were a few handkerchiefs taken out as Madge and George said 'I do'. Jane looked at her mother and smiled.

Daisy was sobbing as it reminded her of her own mother, who she still missed very much. Jane went up and put her arms around her, drawing her close. 'Don't worry I'm here,' she whispered, and Daisy could feel the truth of that statement.

The wedding breakfast had been prepared by outside caterers and was delicious. Four courses of local Scottish food had everyone slackening their belts or opening the top button of their skirts. Then it was time for the speeches. George only said a few words, just thanking everyone for coming to celebrate this perfect day. He acknowledged his first wife and Madge's first husband, which was a thoughtful gesture. He then thanked Madge for making him the happiest man alive.

Philip stood up next and spoke. 'It's been a funny old year and as it comes to a close let's take a minute to reflect. At the start of the year many of us didn't even know each other, and now look at us. We've found family and connections we didn't know existed and we're all bound together with love. Let us now all share in the love Madge and George have found together and carry it with us as we go about our lives. Here's to you both. Please be upstanding and raise your glasses to the bride and groom. Cheers!'

Everyone stood up and toasted the happy couple's health.

'I don't want to steal anyone's thunder,' Philip continued 'and I have got the blessing of Madge and

George, but most of you know the history of me and Jane by now. For those of you who don't, find someone to tell you the story. It's fascinating. Nora was the last person to receive the St.Claire ring. It was given to her by Daniel on their engagement in 1941. When Daniel was killed in action and Nora found herself pregnant she felt she couldn't hold onto it, for reasons known only to her. So it went back to Daniel's parents and then to the only St.Claire left at the time, Sarah, who has given it to me...' he held it up for everyone to see. There were gasps when the guests saw how beautiful it was, '... to give to my special lady, who single-handedly has been responsible for the happiness of so many people in this room. With her dogged determination she researched her dream and wouldn't give up until she had all the answers, and I thank God she did. Jane, would you come up here please?' Philip paused as she went up to join him.

'I know I'm not a pure St.Claire, the name has been altered over the years, but I am in spirit. Jane, would you do me the honour of becoming my wife?' He placed the ring, the same one that Daniel had given to Nora, on Jane's finger.

'Nothing would give me more pleasure,' Jane said. Philip kissed her and everyone cheered.

Sarah and Daisy winked at each other. Only they and the two lovers standing kissing knew the true meaning of what had just happened. Nora and Daniel back together after fifty-nine years, or in just the blink of an eye. Another little soul wriggled inside Jane and in a few months would make the Sinclair family complete.

Coming soon, the new novel from Lindsay Harper,

'Memory Letters'

Every family has skeletons in the cupboard.

Emma and Leah have never met, yet they share an emotional bond. Emma is married and is a GP living in Yorkshire. Leah is divorced and runs her own soft furnishing company in Warwickshire.

Why had Emma's mother kept secret letters, dating back to 1960, hidden in her attic?

Who was the stranger at the craft fair who posed for his portrait painting for Leah's birthday?

The answer to these and other questions would become clear as Emma and Leah discover startling revelations about their past and, in a series of synchronistic events, are led to find each other. But living happily ever after is far from simple in this tale of intrigue, betrayal and infidelity from the author of 'A Second Chance.'